Princess Maritza

Percy Brebner

Contents

PRINCESS MARITZA

BY

Percy Brebner

CHAPTER I.
PLAYING TRUANT

A breezy morning after a night of rain. Fleecy clouds, some in massive folds and fantastic shape, some in small half-transparent wisps like sunlit ghosts, were driven rapidly across the blue. Hurrying shadows flecked the swelling bosom of the downs, and where the grass was long it rippled like a green sea, making rustling music. Overhead the larks fluttering upward, ever-diminishing specks to the empyrean, carolled their joyous song, and a thousand perfumes filled the air. It was a morning to live in, to enjoy, to take into one's lungs in deep, intoxicating draughts, until the sorrows of life and its cares were forgotten; a morning that lent strong wings to ambition, filling the future with hope and the promise of realized desires.

Something of the aspect of the morning was reflected in the face of the man who stoutly climbed the downs against the wind. He was above the average height, but did not give the impression of being tall. His frame was well knit and muscular; strength and power of endurance above the common were evident in every movement; and there was a quiet determination in his face which proclaimed him one of those who would be likely to succeed in anything he undertook, no matter what dangers and difficulties might stand in his path, one who would march straight forward to his object even as he breasted the downs this morning. Most men would have pronounced him handsome, judging, as men ever do, by build and muscle; women might have hesitated to give an opinion in spite of the well-cut, clean-shaven face, and the dark blue eyes which never looked away from a person with whom their possessor talked. Perhaps there was a want of sympathy in the face, a certain lack of that gentle deference which so appeals to women in a man, that silent recognition of the woman's power which is so pleasant to her.

Desmond Ellerey had had little to do with women. He did not pretend to understand them, and it had never occurred to him that there was any reason why he should strive to do so. He had experienced pleasant moments in their company, but one woman was pretty much the same as another to him, and it is quite certain that no such thing as a faded flower, or a glove, or love token of any kind held a place among his treasures. No woman in the past had given him a single heart throb which love lent a sense of pain to, and it seemed unlikely that any woman would wish to do so now. For Desmond Ellerey was a man under a cloud, a very black cloud, the gloom of which even this breezy morning could not entirely dispel from his face. He had set himself to bear his burden bravely, but the task was a heavy one. Surely those straightforward blue eyes gave the lie to much that was said against him?

There were few hours in the day in which he did not brood over his trouble, over the loss of his career which it involved, and as he approached the top of the downs his eyes were bent upon the ground in deep thought, while in his heart was fierce rebellion against the world and his fellow men.

He was suddenly startled by a sharp and shrill "Hallo!" and at the same moment was aware of a straw hat racing past him a little to his left. A run of a few yards enabled him to intercept it, and he grasped it in his strong fingers, regardless of the flowers and ribbons upon it. Then he turned to discover the owner.

She was standing on the summit of the downs, her loose hair streaming in the breeze. She did not come to meet him, but waited for him to go to her.

"I am afraid it is not improved," he said, handing her the hat.

"I hardly expected it would be when I saw the way you dived for it," she answered with a smile; "but thanks all the same. Had it got past you, it would have been good-bye to it altogether. Isn't this a morning?"

"Very pleasant after the rain," he said.

"Pleasant!" she cried. "Is that the best you can say for it? Pleasant! Why it makes me feel that there is nothing in the world which is beyond my power; no difficulty I could not fight and overcome; no danger I could not despise and laugh at. My blood is full of the very fire I of life, and I pant to do something-something unexpected, outrageous, desperate. Don't you ever feel like that?"

"Sometimes."

"It is good to be a man," she went on. "He has the world before him, with its high places waiting to be won. There is nothing out of his reach, if he strive sufficiently, no honor he may not win to. Oh, I wish I were a man!"

There was a half-whimsical smile upon Ellerey's face, at her enthusiasm, and in his eyes a look of admiration, which he could not conceal, at her beauty. Her loose hair streaming in the wind was the color of burnished copper, rich as a golden autumn tint in the glow of an evening sun. Her eyes were dark, yet of a changeful color, as full of secrets as a deep pool in the hollow of a wood, quiet, silent secrets which presently, when the time came, a lover might seek to understand, yet promising angry and tempestuous moods should storms happen. Her lips, parted often as though she were waiting for someone with eager expectation, revealed an even row of pearly teeth, and the pink flush of health and beauty was in her cheeks. She was tall: with her hair done up, would have passed for a woman already, Desmond thought; with it down, and her frock to her boot-tops, she was still a girl, a beautiful girl, a very pleasant picture to contemplate.

"Being a man is not always such a grand thing as you suppose," Ellerey said after a pause.

"He has a freedom which a woman never has," the girl answered quickly. "Oh, yes, women try, especially in this country, I know, but it is never the same. She cannot be a statesman, she cannot be a soldier. She cannot take her life by the throat, as it were, and win place and power by the sheer force of a good right arm as a man can."

"But she often succeeds in ruling the man after he has won place and power," Ellerey answered.

"That sort of conquest does not appeal to me."

"Ah, but it will some day," he returned quickly, and then he half regretted his words, remembering she was but a girl.

She looked at him curiously for a moment, a smile upon her lips, yet a little anger lurking in her eyes.

"You think I am very young," she said.

"Are you not?"

"And very innocent, or ignorant, or whatever word you would use to explain me."

"You can hardly have probed life very deeply yet," said Ellerey.

"Much deeper than you would imagine," she answered. "You are not so very wise and old yourself, are you?"

"Indeed, no; I fancy I am more of a fool than anything else," he laughed.

"You should not let yourself think that," she said gravely. "To think highly of one's powers is half-way to success. That sounds as if I had stolen something from a copy-book, doesn't it? But no, I am speaking from experience. Why do you laugh? Some of us have to touch life's hardships early."

"You do not show the marks of such experience," said Ellerey, hardly knowing whether to treat her seriously or not.

"No, but I might, were I conscious of what is before me. I am not as other girls. There is a destiny I have to struggle towards, an end I must win. It was born into, handed down in my blood through generations of men of action. The ambition of those generations of men beats to-day in the heart of a woman. It is a pity, but I shall win, or die fighting."

"At least the spirit in you deserves success."

"Come a little this way," she said, touching his arm, and then she pointed down into the valley below them. "Do you see that building yonder, white among the trees, with a point of conical roof at the end of it?"

"Yes."

"Do you know what it is?"

"No."

"By this time they are hunting for me all over that place down there. I heard the bell ring half an hour ago. That's a school, a big, expensive, fashionable school, where they teach young ladies how to behave properly, how to grow up to rule those fighting men we were speaking of, how to fit themselves to be their wives, and in due time the mothers of their children--in short, how to fulfil their destiny, woman's destiny. They are trying to teach me."

"You? Then--"

"Yes, I'm one of the girls there, and I've played truant, and--yes, I think I shall go back presently, when I have taken my fill of freedom and this glorious morning."

"And will get punished, I am afraid," said Ellerey.

"Perhaps; but it will not be very heavy punishment. It is strange, but they rather like me there, in spite of everything."

"I do not think that is strange at all."

"No, you wouldn't; you're a man," she answered quickly, "and men are weak where attractive women are concerned, all the world over."

Such a declaration coming from a truant schoolgirl somewhat startled Ellerey, and yet, as he looked at her, he was more conscious of the woman than the girl.

"Oh, yes, I know I am attractive," she went on, and there was no deepening of the color in her face as she said it. "I am glad that it is so. My looks will help me when the work of my life begins in earnest, when I have played the truant from school for the last time, and do not go back."

"Then you intend to run away eventually?"

"Yes, unless another way should seem better. That shocks you. I often shock them down at the white house yonder, and they excuse me because I am a foreigner. You English are so polite. You do not seem to expect foreigners to know how to behave, and you make excuses for them. It is very funny. It makes me laugh," and she laughed so merrily that her former gravity seemed more unnatural.

"You speak English perfectly. I should not have taken you for a foreigner," said Ellerey.

"And French, and German, and my own tongue, I speak them all perfectly. I have lived in all these countries. It was necessary."

"And you do not like England nor Englishmen?"

"I have not said so," she answered; "but here in England I am being taken care of, kept out of mischief, and sometimes I feel like a prisoner. It is only that which makes me dislike England. Of Englishmen I know little, but I have read about them, and they have done some good, brave deeds. They are, perhaps, just a little conceited with themselves, don't you think? There is no one quite like an Englishman it would seem."

"There are all sorts, good and bad," said Ellerey carelessly. "At the best he wants a lot of beating; at the worst, well, he wants a lot of beating that way, too. How is it you feel like a prisoner?"

The girl drew herself up to her full height. There was something haughty in her demeanor, occasioned, perhaps, by the careless way in which he asked the question. She felt that he was treating her rather like a spoilt child, while she felt herself a determined woman.

"In my own country I am a princess," she said.

"Indeed?"

"You do not believe me?"

"Why not? You look every inch a princess," he answered.

"It is so like a man to say what he thinks will please," she returned with a flash in her eyes. "You do not believe me, but you are afraid to say so. Go down there and ask them."

"I do not disbelieve you," said Ellerey quietly.

The girl relented in a moment.

"We should be very good friends, you and I, if we knew each other. You have ambition. I can see it in your face."

"I had, Princess."

"Hush, no one calls me that here. Why do you say you had ambition?"

"You would not understand."

"Try me and see," she said, standing close beside him as though to measure her strength against his for a moment. "You may trust me. I would trust you anywhere, in peace or war."

Ellerey looked at her curiously for an instant, with a sudden desire to take her into his confidence. Then he shook his head slowly. It was pleasant to hear such faith expressed in him, and he was unwilling to destroy the faith of this fair woman. Altogether a woman she seemed to him just then.

"You will not. Never mind, perhaps one day you will. Only never speak of ambition as something past. That is weak and unmanly."

"Upon my honor, you do me good," Ellerey exclaimed.

"And you me," she answered eagerly. "To look at you makes me feel strong. It is good when a man makes a woman feel like that. I am a woman, although I am still at school. There is southern blood in me, and we become women earlier than English girls do. Listen! There are England, and France, and Germany, and Austria, and Russia all interested in me, and nothing would please them all so much as my death. As it is, I am a difficulty in all their politics. They would like me to forget who, and what, I am. They would marry me to some nobleman of no importance, if they could, just to keep me quiet."

"And you will not be quiet."

"No. Why should I be? Would you? In my country a usurper is upon the throne, kept there, held there, like a child who would fall but for its nurse's arms, by all the Powers of Europe. It is I who should be there. It is I who will be there one day. Shall I tell you? There are hundreds, thousands, of men who are ready to strike in my cause when the time is ripe. Even now there is a statesman working to set these countries at cross purposes with one another, and when they quarrel, then is my opportunity. You shall see. That is why I said I would be a man if I could. It would be so much easier for a man, but as it is, a woman shall do it."

"I hope you may. You deserve to."

"But you doubt it?" she said.

"There seem to be heavy odds against you."

"That helps me. It stirs up the best that is in me. It is good to have something to struggle for, something to win, and if I may not win, I hope to fall in the press of the fight, and, to the loud funeral music of clashing steel, find the death of a soldier. What is your name?"

"Desmond Ellerey."

"It is an easy name to remember. Well, Desmond Ellerey, if your ambition finds no outlet in England, come to my country, to the city of Sturatzberg, and claim friendship with Princess Maritza. She shall find you work for your good right arm."

She walked away from him as though she had bestowed a great favor, never looking back. She went in the opposite direction to the school, her truant spirit not yet satisfied, and Ellerey watched her until he lost sight of the tall, graceful figure in a fold of the downs. Then he turned and went slowly back the way he had come.

Desmond Ellerey had declared that she had done him good. It was true. Although he walked slowly, his spirit was stirred within him, and his blood ran with something of its old vigor. Faced by a thousand difficulties, this girl had the courage to look upon them bravely, and to believe in her power to overcome them. That was her secret, the belief in her own power. He had faced his difficulties bravely enough, but he had not had the courage to hope; therein lay his weakness, and this girl, this princess, had shown it to him. He had allowed himself to drift into a backwater; it was time he pulled out into the stream again, and fought his way back to his rightful place, inch by inch, against whatever tide might run.

For some little time he had been staying with Sir Charles and Lady Martin, two people who had looked into his eyes when he had denied the charges brought against him, and had believed him.

As he crossed the lawn toward the house he met his host.

"I have had an adventure, Charles; I have met a princess."

"There are some pretty rustic maidens in the village. I have been struck with their beauty myself."

"I mean a real Princess; at least, she said so," Desmond answered. "She was playing truant from school, a large white house, on the other side of the downs."

"Do you mean a tall, red-headed girl?" asked Sir Charles.

"Have you seen her?" Desmond asked.

"No, but I know all about her."

"Ah, I thought you couldn't have seen her, or you wouldn't describe her as a tall, red-headed girl. She's the most beautiful woman I ever saw. She spoke the truth, then; she is a Princess?"

"Oh, yes, but the sooner she forgets the fact the better for her and for--for everybody. She is the descendant of a line of rulers chiefly remarkable for their inability to rule, and her chance of ascending the throne of her fathers is absolutely *nil*, fortunately for Europe. You are not a student of contemporary history, Desmond, or you would know something about Wallaria and its exiled Princess."

"I am not a diplomat, but a soldier--at least, I was," Desmond answered. "Still, I should like to improve my knowledge."

"That is easily managed," said Sir Charles. "If you come into the library I can find you a heap of literature concerning this little wasps' nest of a state, and when you have mastered the position, thank your natal stars that you were not born to take a hand in ruling it. It is a menace to Europe, Desmond, that's the truth of the matter. Wallaria may at any time be the cause of a European war. If this Princess of yours had her way, that time would not be long in coming."

For the remainder of the day Desmond Ellerey filled a corner of the library with tobacco smoke, and his head with a thousand details concerning Wallaria. When he went to dress for dinner he felt that he had been reading an absorbing romance, and blessed the good fortune which had brought about the meeting on the downs.

"Helen and I have been talking about you, Desmond," said Sir Charles after dinner.

"Not revising your opinion of me, I hope."

"No," said Lady Martin, "but thinking of your future. Why not travel for a little while, Desmond; for a year or so? It will give time for the truth to leak out. It will leak out, you know, even as a lie does."

"I have made up my mind to go abroad," said Desmond quietly. "I shall clear out of England before the month is over. It has been awfully good of you both to have me here at a time when most of my friends found it convenient to forget me. I shall not come back until the men who were so ready to accuse me have eaten their words and the country so ready to dispense with my services asks for them again."

"That will come in time," said Lady Martin.

"I am glad to hear your determination," said Sir Charles. "Where are you going?"

"To Wallaria."

"Wallaria!"

"Why not? It seems there is room for a soldier there."

Sir Charles looked grave.

"But, Desmond, supposing--"

"I know what you would say," returned Ellerey quickly. "Supposing Englishmen should have to fight against Wallaria, and I should have to carry arms against my country; well, with whom does the fault lie, with England or with me? England has dispensed with my services, believing a lie; she drives me from her, and makes me a renegade. What allegiance do I owe to England? I will offer my sword to Wallaria, and if she will have it, by Heaven, she shall."

Lady Martin put her hand upon his shoulder, pressed it in kindly sympathy for a moment, and then left the room.

"Sleep on it, Desmond, you will think better of it in the morning," said Sir Charles.

"You have been very good to me, both of you," said Ellerey, turning round suddenly when Lady Martin had gone. "I can never thank you enough. It seems poor gratitude to pain you now. Such a contingency as we imagine will probably never arise, but I have decided to go."

"The Princess has bewitched you."

"Nonsense. Am I not offering my sword to the usurper, her enemy? My ambitions have been nipped like a tree in the budding here, and I see a new outlet for my energies yonder, that is all. My own country despises me. I hope for better things from the country of my adoption."

CHAPTER II.
MONSIEUR DE FROILETTE

At a turn of the road which had been deserted for some two hours past, a man suddenly reined in his horse to a walking pace. He had ridden far, for his dress was dusty, and the animal showed signs of fatigue. The evening was stormy-looking, and there was a bite in the wind blowing from the higher lands to the plain.

The road ran, with many a twist and turn, between dense woods on one side, and rugged waste ground, with tangled patches of undergrowth, on the other. Here and there a clearing had been made in the woods, and a rough dwelling erected, but they were apparently deserted; there were no signs of life about them this evening. The man rode easily, yet with constant watchfulness. The times were unsettled and dangerous, and the slightest unfamiliar sound instantly attracted his attention. He was accustomed to be on the alert, and whatever thoughts held sway behind his gloomy looks, they were not sufficiently absorbing to render him careless for a moment.

Suddenly he pulled his horse to a standstill, turning sharply in his saddle to look back upon the way he had come. Then he examined his holster, and, moving his horse to a position which gave him a better command of the road, sat quietly waiting.

The sound which had attracted his attention grew rapidly nearer, and presently three riders came round the bend at a gallop, one some paces in advance of his companions. He pulled up short, seeing the motionless horseman by the roadside, scenting danger and ready for it; but the next moment he raised his hat with pronounced courtesy, and bowed low in his saddle.

"Pardon, monsieur," he said, "but one sees a possible enemy in so unexpected an encounter."

"Unexpected, monsieur?"

"I said so. May I add fortunate, too?"

"Such enemies as you suggest seldom stand singly," was the rather ungracious answer.

"And in these times wise men seldom ride alone, monsieur," came the quick retort. "I travel with an escort myself, you see, Captain Ellerey. I do not make a mistake, I think; you are Captain Ellerey of his Majesty's Regiment of Chasseurs?"

"That is my name."

"And you are returning to Sturatzberg? Good! We can proceed together," and without waiting for an assent to this arrangement, he ordered his servants to go forward, and watched them until they had disappeared. "Now, monsieur, we may go forward at our leisure."

"I have not the honor of--"

"My name. Ah, it is of small consequence. Jules de Froilette, at your service. It is unknown to you?"

"I think so, but your face seems familiar," said Ellerey, as they went on together.

"Ah, yes. I go to Court sometimes."

"And I but seldom, monsieur."

"Then you may have seen me in the streets of Sturatzberg. I know the city well, and have nothing to hide. I have interests in this country, let us say, in timber; it is the answer I give when I am questioned, for no one respects a lazy man. A voluntary exile from my country, I have no quarrel with France, nor she with me. In these days men are become cosmopolitan, is it not so?"

"It looks like it in Sturatzberg," Ellerey replied.

"Monsieur is also an exile, and has no quarrel with his motherland?"

"At least I do not speak of it, Monsieur De Froilette."

"Pardon me, I am not inquisitive. You crave for excitement, so come to Sturatzberg. The promise of adventure will ever attract men of spirit and--"

"And the failures at home," suggested Ellerey.

"I was going to say men of courage," De Froilette answered, "but the failures come, too, and succeed--sometimes."

"You are as doubtful of the reward as I am," said Ellerey, laughing.

De Froilette did not join in his merriment.

"A Captain of Horse is not to be despised," he said slowly, glancing furtively at his companion.

"True, but he remains a Captain of Horse. I expected rapid events in this country, and quick promotion for those who came out of the struggle with their lives. Instead, we have an expedition against some brigands' fastness, which is deserted when we arrive, or a troop to quell a petty riot which has fizzled out when we get there, and that is all."

"And monsieur thirsts for more; the desperate encounter and the bloody sword; for high place and Court favor."

"Is it too great an ambition?" Ellerey demanded. "Do we not all from the bottom rung of the ladder look eagerly toward the top--the student to the masters of his profession, the apprentice to the seat of his employer? Why should not a soldier look for high favor at Court?"

"Such favor must be won, Captain Ellerey."

"I am willing to win it."

"Patience. You shall not always find those fastnesses deserted, those riots quelled when you arrive. This is the waiting time, the preparing time, and there are difficulties in the way of promotion. Let me ask you, are you loved in your regiment?"

"Neither loved nor hated."

"And in the city?"

"I have few friends. A Captain of Horse does not command them."

"That is not the reason. It is because you are a foreigner," De Froilette answered. "You are welcome to fight this country's battles, welcome to get killed in them, but you must not participate in any rewards. If Sturatzberg could do without us, how many foreigners would wake tomorrow in the city, think you?"

"All Europe has talked of such a rebellion, but it does not come," said Ellerey.

"It will," was the answer, "and if you are strong enough you may take the reward."

"You speak in riddles."

"Is it wise to speak plainly?" and De Froilette swept out his arm as though the prospect before them gave the answer. They had left the woods and the rough country behind them, and were approaching houses, for Sturatzberg had grown and spread itself beyond its walls. In the distance the lights of the city blinked under the dome of growing darkness, while to the right a long line of light marked the citadel and the palace of the King.

"There are ever-watchful eyes, ever-waking ears about us, looking and listening for treachery," De Froilette went on. "Every man suspects his neighbor, and has fingers ready for the knife handle. Yonder in the citadel, amid the laughter and the music, a dozen plots will creep forward a space before the dawn. Does monsieur, the Captain, long to play a part in the intrigues there?"

"Yes, so that it is honest."

"Monsieur must decide. We part here, it is better so. Come to me to-night, at the Altstrasse, 12, at ten o'clock. We can talk further. Until then, *au revoir*" and De Froilette put his horse into a canter, leaving Ellerey to pursue his way alone.

Entering the city by the eastern gate, Ellerey crossed the Konigplatz at walking pace on his way to his lodging by the Western Gate. They were a pleasure-loving people in Sturatzberg, working as little as possible, and spending without a thought of the morrow. The cafes were full to-night, the laughter sounded genuine enough, and there was little indication of the coming storm of revolution so confidently predicted by De Froilette. Ellerey's mind was busy with the events of the afternoon. For two years he had been in Sturatzberg, ready to seize the opportunity of distinguishing himself whenever it arose. It had not come yet. His life had been passed on a dead level of inactivity, and the stirring times he had hoped for seemed as far away as ever. Many a time had his thoughts gone back to that breezy morning on the downs, and he devoutly wished that Princess Maritza would come to Sturatzberg, so that he might go to her, claim friendship with her, and ask for that work for his good right arm which she had promised to give. Who was this De Froilette, and why should he take an interest in him or wish to help him? For such favors there was always a price to be paid in some form or other. Would it be wise to go to the Altstrasse? And another question came to him, a question that set his pulse beating faster for a moment. Was this De Froilette an emissary of the Princess Maritza? Might she not be in Sturatzberg now? Might he not see her to-night? "I would risk anything for that," he said, as he swung himself from the saddle, "and whatever the adventure is, so that it has a spice of danger in it, it is welcome. I shall know how to take care of myself if the price asked be too heavy."

A big, bearded man came forward to take the horse, and the manner in which he drew the back of his hand across his mouth suggested that he had left the tankard hastily.

"Has anyone inquired for me, Stefan?"

"No, Captain, I have been undisturbed until now," the man answered in a deep voice well suited to his frame, as he led the horse away. Knowing his soldier-servant's weakness and his capacity for indulging in it with impunity, Ellerey wondered how long a time he would require undisturbed before signs of his potations showed themselves. Drink heavily he certainly did, but since he never exhibited any ill effects from it, at night or morning, it would have been unjust to call him a drunkard.

The Altstrasse was of the old town, a narrow thoroughfare of gaunt houses which now sheltered a dozen families in rooms where the wealthy had once lived, and in which Ministers and Ambassadors had entertained the wit, beauty, and bravery of nations. These glories had departed to the palatial buildings which had grown up round the citadel, leaving the Altstrasse as misfortune may leave a gentleman, the marks of breeding evident though he be clad in rusty garments. Over the doorways, through which tatterdemalions, men, women, and children, flocked in and out, were handsome carvings, deep-cut crests and coats-of-arms; ragged garments were hung to dry over handsome balustrades and wrought-iron railings; while in the rough and broken roadway garbage, cast there days since, lay rotting where it had fallen. Poverty had seized upon the place, flaunting poverty, seeking no concealment. Ellerey had passed through the Altstrasse before to-night, but the surroundings had had no particular interest for him then. Now they arrested his attention. What plots might not have birth and grow to dangerous maturity in such surroundings, among such people as these? The rabble had overrun these deserted mansions; might it not one day hammer at the doors of the palaces by the citadel yonder with demands not to be gainsaid? What manner of man was this De Froilette, what ends had he in view, that he should live in such a place?

Number 12 looked as faded as its neighbors, showed even fewer lights in its windows, and, except that no small crowd hung about the closed door, was no whit more attractive than ever. Ellerey's summons was answered immediately, however, and he entered a large bare stone hall, the dim light which hung in the centre disclosing many fast-closed doors on either side.

"Monsieur is expected," said the man deferentially, leading the way down a stone passage and up a flight of stairs to a landing corresponding with the hall below. But how different! Here was luxury. A deep carpet deadened the footfall, rich curtains hung over windows and doorways, and ancient arms were upon the walls. Ellerey had little time to appreciate more than the general effect, for the man, drawing back a heavy curtain, opened a door, and without making any announcement stood aside for him to enter.

"Welcome, mon ami, welcome," said De Froilette, coming forward to meet him. "Confidences are easier here than on the highway."

The room was perfect, the abode of a man of taste with the means to gratify it to the full. It was costly and unique, a collector's room, discriminately arranged, and the owner, motioning his guest to a chair, was worthy of his surroundings. In the afternoon he had been muffled in a cloak, and Ellerey had noticed little of his appearance beyond the fact that his eyes were dark and restless. Now he saw a man courtly and distinguished in a manner, with a clever, earnest face, at once attractive and inviting confidence. His hair, cut short, and his beard trimmed to a fine point, were black with a few streaks of white in them, but his face was young looking, the lines few and faint. His fifty years sat lightly upon him. One would have judged him a student, or a traveller, rather than a politician, or a man fighting life strenuously.

"My surroundings surprise you?" he said, with a smile.

"Such things are hardly looked for in the Altstrasse," Ellerey answered.

"They are a part of myself, Captain Ellerey, but I wish to remain in privacy. Your elect of the city do not naturally visit in the Altstrasse, and I have rooms below bare enough to impress uninteresting people with the fact that I am a poor sort of fellow, and likely to be an unprofitable acquaintance. For my friends--well, you see, I have other apartments."

"I thank you for the preference shown me," said Ellerey, with a bow.

"And since we parted have been speculating on the reason, is it not so?"

"Naturally."

"I think I can help you; I believe you can assist me. There is the position in a nutshell. I am honest. I make no pretence of liking unprofitable friends myself. But we will talk afterward, monsieur," he added, as a servant announced supper, and De Froilette led the way into an adjoining room. The meal was faultlessly served at a round table lighted by candles in quaint silver candlesticks. Although not exactly an epicure, De Froilette understood a supper of this description as perhaps only a Frenchman can, and his taste in wines was excellent. He led the conversation into general topics, talked of Paris and London with equal ease and knowledge, and of Berlin, Vienna, and St. Petersburg only a little less intimately.

"I have said I am cosmopolitan," he explained. "After all, it is the greatest nationality to which a man can belong. Coffee in the library, Francois."

De Froilette ushered his guest into another room, which from floor to ceiling was lined with books--books on all subjects and in many languages. A huge writing-table, littered with letters and foreign newspapers, occupied the centre of the apartment, which was evidently a working room, though luxurious in all its appointments. De Froilette did not speak until the servant had placed the coffee on a side table and had left the room, when he turned suddenly toward Ellerey.

"I followed you to-day, monsieur; it was not a chance meeting."

"I am not surprised," said Ellery. "Twice before you overtook me I heard the sound of galloping horses, and was prepared for an enemy."

"And instead, behold a friend," De Froilette laughed, pushing a silver box of cigarettes across the table. "You must bear with me if I am prosy for a time. I can promise you that the end of the story is better than the beginning."

Ellerey settled himself to listen attentively.

"The history of this country, monsieur, is composed, as it were, of the rough ends and edges of the histories of other countries. Every crisis in Europe causes trouble of some kind here, and first one family and then another have become paramount in Sturatzberg. All the Powers have recognized one fact, however, that Wallaria must be kept inviolate; so it is that this is an independent kingdom to-day. The position is unique, and gives the King, within his own realm, a power more autocratic than the Czar's should he care to use it, since he has only to play off one great Power against another to preserve himself from attack. You follow me?"

Ellerey murmured an assent, wondering what this recital was to lead to.

"It is clear that his Majesty does not use this power," De Froilette went on. "He may be timid, he may lack ambition, we will speak no treachery; but in times past there have been ambitious monarchs, and still little has happened. Why? Because, monsieur, recognizing that this country is one of the chief factors in preserving the peace of Europe, the nations have sent the ablest men they possess as their Ambassadors to Sturatzberg. Your British Minister is a case in point. The result is that to the present time no monarch has risen with courage enough, allied to sufficient political acumen, to take his own course, carry it to success. Have you ever realized, monsieur, that Sturatzberg might play with the nations of Europe as a gambler plays his hand of cards?"

"I am no diplomatist," Ellerey answered.

De Froilette shrugged his shoulders as though the point were immaterial to him, and went on:

"To all appearance, the facts are to-day as they have always been, with one great and important exception--the people. The people are awaking to the sensation that they are ruled and oppressed, for so they consider it, by foreigners. They have had secretly preached to them, and they understand, what possibilities there are; and a wave of national enthusiasm is silently stealing through the length and breadth of the land. The bolder spirits have already declared against law and order, as it exists, by flying to the hills and associating themselves with the brigands there. The forces under the outlaw Vasilici, I am told, increase daily. You have heard of him, Captain Ellerey?"

"And have tried to find him," Ellerey answered, with a smile. "But his fastness in the mountains was always deserted when we got there."

"Some day it will not be. A leader worthy of the cause will be found. The people will remember that there are others with an equal, or better, right to the throne than his Majesty, and then you will have the revolution."

"I presume, monsieur, the leader is found, and only awaits the opportunity?" said Ellerey.

"You are right, Captain, she is found," De Froilette answered slowly.

"A woman!" Ellerey exclaimed, and he felt the color flush to his face as he spoke. He forgot for a moment that his sword was pledged to the King. His thoughts went back to that breezy morning on the downs, and the tall, straight girl with her bright hair streaming in the wind.

De Froilette laughed.

"A woman, Captain Ellerey, who destines you for high service. Let her plead for herself," and as he spoke he opened the door, and stood aside with bowed head.

A woman entered. Tall she was, and of imperial mien. Diamonds glistened in the coils of her raven hair. Her face was beautiful, her smiling lips and deep, soft eyes, full of sympathy and tenderness, seemed incapable of any stern expression of anger. A woman born to rule, born to lead, but not the woman Ellerey had expected to see.

It was the Queen, and Ellerey bowed low before her.

"You have not been unnoticed by us, Captain Ellerey," she said in a low voice, "and we would have you more constantly at Court."

"I shall obey your Majesty," Ellerey answered.

"There are stirring times at hand," she went on; "times in which men may strive and win. His majesty, the King, is fettered, politically bound, by conflicting interests, watched, carefully nursed by this Power and by that. He is unable to move as his people would have him. It is for me to act for him in this matter, secretly until the appointed hour strikes. Remember, Captain Ellerey, I am Queen as his Majesty is King, with equal rights, not as consort merely. Your sword is pledged to me as to the King. Therefore I can demand your service. I prefer to ask it."

"Your Majesty is gracious."

"It will be secret service, for the present secret even from the King. I may require it to-morrow, a week hence, or it may be in a month's time. I cannot tell. It is perilous service, but that will not deter Captain Desmond Ellerey. May I claim your full and perfect allegiance?"

"I hold myself entirely at your Majesty's disposal."

"You shall not find me ungrateful," she said, giving him her hand. "Choose you a dozen stout men on whom you can rely. Good pay you may promise them. Have them in readiness to set out at an hour's notice. Then wait and watch. We shall call you into private audience on some occasion, either personally or by Monsieur De Froilette, and now that we have found the man, may the time be quick in coming."

There was delicate flattery in her words and manner, yet withal perfect consciousness of her own power, the power that beauty gives. Ellerey felt the magic of her influence, and his eyes looked unflinchingly into hers for a moment; the woman in her understood what manner of man he was in whom she trusted. "If I read you aright, Captain Ellerey," she said, with a radiant smile, "it is not your nature to be frivolous, to catch pleasure as it flies and play with it while the bubble lasts; yet must you school yourself to do so. The light-hearted cavalier and careless lover will not be suspected of any deep design, and it would be well that that should seem your character at Court. More easily will you keep the nearer to our person, for love of pleasure and the gratification of the moment is thought to be our end and aim also. Even his Majesty is deceived in this, and knows not that under the surface we are working night and day in his cause. Monsieur De Froilette shall see to it that you have ample opportunity to be merry, and I promise you active, hazardous service, work after your own heart, in the near future."

"In the one as in the other, I shall hope to win your Majesty's approval," Ellerey answered.

The Queen turned, and retired as quickly as she had come. De Froilette bowed low as she passed out, but exchanged no word with her, nor did he attempt to follow her. Her coming and her going had evidently been prearranged for Ellerey's benefit.

"I surprise you for the second time to-night," said De Froilette, as he closed the door.

"Yes, I expected another woman--Princess Maritza."

De Froilette started at the name, and looked keenly at his companion. For an instant he showed surprise, perhaps annoyance, but he was quickly himself again, and asked quietly:

"What do you know of the Princess Maritza?"

"I have studied something of the history of this country in my leisure, monsieur, that is all; and I fancied you might be interested yourself in the fortunes of the exile. You spoke of others with an equal or better right than his Majesty."

"I was thinking of the Queen. The Princess is impossible. Her fathers sat upon the throne, it is true, and by their misplaced ambition and folly not only lost the support of every foreign Power, but alienated the love of the people besides. Her father barely escaped assassination. The Princess is known to me, as her father was. At present she is in England."

"Does she make no claim for herself?"

"She might were the throne vacant, but she could not succeed. The people would never accept her. In two days will you do me the honor of accompanying me to Court, as her Majesty desires?"

"The honor will be mine. I thank you for bringing me into notice," Ellerey answered.

"I will come for you at your lodging," said De Froilette, and then a servant entered, apparently without being summoned, and in silence conducted Ellerey to the bare hall again. All the doors were fast closed as before, but the air seemed to vibrate with life and the silence to be ready to break into a hoarse roar of voices at a moment's notice. Yet only in a window here and there was there a dim light when Ellerey looked up at the gloomy house as he stood alone in the Altstrasse.

CHAPTER III.
THE WOMAN IN THE SILK MASK

Once alone, there were many questions which Ellerey regretted he had not put to his host, and some misgivings arose in his mind whether he had not been led to promise service which might be contrary to the oath which he had taken to the King. The scheme to enlist his help had evidently been carefully considered and prepared, with the result that he had pledged himself to some hazardous task of the nature of which he was entirely ignorant. Not a clue had been given him, and were he desirous of turning traitor, he realized that it was not within his power to do so. Not a word of information could he speak, and who would believe that alone, and apparently unattended, the Queen had visited the Altstrasse at midnight? That she had done so for the purpose of speaking to him proved to Ellerey that her need for him was urgent; that she had explained nothing pointed to the fact that she was not inclined to trust him fully at present.

"I judge there is work for my sword," he said, as he drew his cloak closer round him. "It would seem there is employment for my wits also. At least, I have my wish: a part to play which holds possibilities. A Queen, a designing Frenchman, and an ambitious Captain of Horse, who may be a fool. Well, the drama may prove exciting. We shall see!"

Desmond Ellerey was, after all, an adventurer, of the better sort, perhaps; driven to the life by force of circumstances--yet still an adventurer. His position proclaimed him one. He looked for reward from the country which had purchased his sword, and had no inclination to fritter away his chances of espousing any cause but the winning one. At the same time he was an Englishman: a birth privilege carrying with it weighty responsibilities, which he could not away with as easily as he had cast aside his country. There were few ties to bind him to England. He had become that unenviable member of a family--the black sheep. He had run deeply into debt; a fact that had grievously told against him when he had to face the accusations which had ruined his career. In withdrawing from England he had probably left only two friends, Sir Charles and Lady Martin, who would ever trouble to send a kindly thought after him. His going had aroused the keenest satisfaction in the breast of his brother, Sir Ralph Ellerey, tenth baronet of the name, who was quite ready to believe the very worst that was said of Desmond, remarking that it was little more than he expected. Sir Ralph's cast of mind was perhaps narrow and ungenerous, but, since the sympathy so usually shown to the open-handed spendthrift was not forthcoming in this case, it must be assumed that popular opinion condemned Desmond Ellerey, and sympathized with Sir Ralph. It had been easy, therefore, for Desmond to become a stranger to his native land; it was impossible for him to forget that he was an Englishman: that a peculiar code of honor was demanded of him by the fact.

The Altstrasse was deserted as he passed through it; the lights were out in most of the houses, and silence was over the whole city. The sky was black with clouds, giving promise of heavy rain before morning if the wind dropped. Ellerey walked quickly, his ears alert, and his eyes keenly searching every shadow on either side of him. Attacks in the street for the purpose of plunder were of too general occurrence to make a lonely walk in Sturatzberg safe or desirable at night, and in this quarter of the city help would be slow in coming.

As he turned out of the Altstrasse, a woman, coming hastily in the opposite direction, ran against him, and, with a faint cry, started back in fear. A cloak was gathered tightly round her, showing nothing of her dress and little of her figure, and the hood of it was pulled so low down that little of her face was visible.

"Help, monsieur!" she cried, striving for breath, which came in spasmodic pants after her running. "Help, monsieur, if you be a man!"

"How can I serve you?"

"Ah, a soldier!" she cried, seeing the cloak he wore. "Quick! There is no time to delay. While we speak, murder is being done."

"Where?"

"Come. It is a house yonder. Are you armed? Ah, but they are cowards, and only attack defenceless women!" And she plucked him by the arm to compel him to follow her. She did not appeal in vain.

"Show me," Ellerey said, and taking her hand, that he might help her pace, he ran with her, their footsteps resounding along the silent street.

As they ran, he tried to get a better view of her face, but in vain. He noticed that her cloak, which flapped outward with every step she took, revealed a rich white skirt beneath, and there was the rustle of silk. She kept up bravely with him, seeming to gain new courage in his company. She led him round two corners, across a dark square, and to the open door of a house in a small street beyond. "Quick! They are within. Straight up the stairs to the first floor."

Ellerey released his hold of the girl; indeed, she pulled her hand away that she might not detain him from dashing to the rescue, and, as he touched the stairs, he heard the door close with a loud reverberating slam behind him.

"Quickly!" she cried after him.

The house was dark and quiet, doubly quiet it seemed now that the door had closed. Not a sound came from the rooms above, as Ellerey went up the stairs. If murder were here to-night, he had surely come too late.

He had reached the top of the stairs, had stretched out his hand to feel his way by the wall, and had paused to listen for a sound or to discern a glimmer of light to guide him, when suddenly the air about him seemed to break into life, and before he had time to turn and throw his back against the wall, strong arms were about his shoulders and legs. In an instant Ellerey had grasped one man in the darkness, and kicked himself free from a second, who went rolling down the stairs, uttering curses as he struck the balustrade heavily, making it crack to breaking point. Another received his heel squarely in the face, and dropped with a thud upon the floor, a thud that almost had the sound of finality in it. Meanwhile the man he had seized wrenched himself free, and another pair of arms were flung round Ellerey's waist, obviously to prevent his getting at any weapon he might carry. Ellerey strained every nerve to free himself from this assailant and to get his back to the wall, striking out right and left, now hitting a man's neck or shoulder, now landing a heavy blow between eyes he could not see, anon beating the air only. How many his adversaries were he could not determine. The air was full of panting breaths and growling imprecations, of swaying bodies, and heavy blows, which were, for the most part, wide of the mark. Every moment Ellerey expected to be his last; expected to feel the sharp thrust of a blade, or to fall into sudden oblivion before the sound of the revolver shot had time to reach his ears. Yet he still lived; fighting, struggling, being slowly spent by the odds against him. Why did these murderers not end it? Were they fearful of injuring a comrade in the darkness, or were they desirous of not injuring him too severely? Indeed, it seemed so. Had he fallen into a trap, baited with the frightened woman who had petitioned him for help? The thought that he could have been such a fool, that so transparent a device should have deceived him, maddened him, and he redoubled his exertions to free himself, trying to drag his assailants with him to the head of the stairs, so that he might fling himself and them down, and chance regaining his liberty in the shock of the fall. But the men appeared to perceive his motive, and redoubled their efforts, too, straining every nerve to end the struggle. The man who held him round the waist was dragged this way and that, yet never for a moment relaxed his hold. Other hands were upon his legs now, and Ellerey suddenly felt his feet drawn together with a snap. The next instant he was thrown backward, knees were pressed upon his chest, his arms were twisted and caught with a rope, his ankles bound together, and he was helpless.

"I'd like to bury this knife in your cursed carcass," whispered a voice in his ear.

"I've been expecting you to do so," said Ellerey, panting for breath. "Why don't you?"

"I don't know. By Heaven, I don't know why not."

"Well, I'm sure I don't," panted Ellerey.

"Is he secure?" said another voice.

"Yes," at least half a dozen voices answered. "Then drag him in. Perhaps we'll have leave to despatch him presently."

A door was opened, and, with scant ceremony, Ellerey was dragged by his feet across the floor into a room. The door was shut again, and someone produced a lantern.

Ellerey found himself lying in a bare room with seven or eight men standing in a circle round him, regarding him with sullen and angry looks, yet with curiosity and some respect; and on more than one face there were marks of the struggle, savage flushes that would blacken to-morrow, and blood on lips. He looked from one to the other, but saw no face he recognized, yet they were not such a murderous set of scoundrels as he had expected to see, and although more than one of them, perhaps, would have taken the keenest pleasure in burying a knife-blade in him to revenge the hurt he had received, it appeared evident that some consideration held them back. Whatever they contemplated doing, murder was not their intention.

"It takes a lot to knock the sense out of you," said one man, and Ellerey thought he recognized the voice which had ordered him to be dragged into the room: "and there are one or two of us who have something to settle. That must wait for a more convenient season."

"If I am to make a fight for it, it certainly must," said Ellerey, with a smile. "I suppose it's no use asking you to loosen my wrist a little. The cord is very tight."

"Not a bit of use."

"May I know why you have trapped me in this way? I should like to see the little hussy who deceived me."

The men laughed.

"She's a safe bait, is a woman, all the world over," said the spokesman, "and this one's finished her part of the business well enough. Now our parts have got to be done. Some time to-night you received a token. We want it."

"You are welcome to any token I received," Ellerey answered.

"Give it me, then."

"Because I received none," Ellerey added.

"That's a lie," said one man.

"It is well for you that I am bound hand and foot," said Ellerey quietly. "If I remember your face, I may ask you to repeat that some day."

"I ask you again to give me the token you received to-night. Once it is in my hands, you are free to depart," said the spokesman.

"And I repeat that I received no token to-night," answered Ellerey.

"Search him!" cried several voices, and at a gesture from their leader, they fell on their knees beside him.

It was rough handling Ellerey received for the next few minutes. His coat was torn open; rough hands were thrust into his pockets, and even his under-garments were rent apart lest by any means he should have secured the token next his skin.

"There is nothing," they said, rising to their feet one by one. The last man knelt a moment longer, and turned an evil eye toward his chief.

"May it not happen by an accident?" he said. "An accident would be forgiven, and it would be so much safer."

The dim light shone on the keen blade the man had ripped eagerly from his girdle, and Ellerey doubted whether the chief's word would have power to save him; whether, indeed, it would be spoken. His salvation came from quite an unexpected quarter.

"Why that knife, Nicolai?" said a voice which caused the man to spring to his feet, and made Ellerey turn his head. "You would dare to disobey my commands, Nicolai? Stand aside. I have no faith in you."

The ruffian slunk back into the shadows of the room without a word. Ellerey was astonished that so mild a reprimand should have so great an effect. He looked at the dim figure, which the mean light of the lantern revealed; a woman's figure, closely cloaked from head to foot, while an ample scarf was wound round her head, and her face hidden by a silken mask. She had entered by a door somewhat behind him, and he and the man who was so desirous of killing him were the last to become aware of her presence.

"Have you found it?" she demanded, after a pause.

"No; he declares no token was given. At any rate, it is not upon him," answered the man who was in charge of the ruffians.

The woman took the lantern from the man who carried it, and, as she held it up, saw more distinctly the faces of the men about her.

"He has given you trouble, it seems. You bear marks of the conflict. Eight of you."

"And two on the stairs who have not yet recovered," said one.

"He should be a good man, then, for a hazardous enterprise," and the woman bent down, holding the lantern low to look into Ellerey's face.

Ellerey could see the eyes through the holes in the silk mask, but they told him nothing. He had hardly noticed the eyes of the woman who had stopped him at the corner of the Altstrasse; he did not know whether they were the same. This woman seemed taller; yet there was a familiar ring in her voice. She gazed at him for some moments in silence, and then, standing erect, handed the lantern to one of the men. Behind the mask she smiled. "Your cut-throats, madam, have made a mistake. I have no token," said Ellerey.

"Do any of you know this man?" she asked, turning to her followers.

"A foreigner," growled one. "A soldier," said another.

"A King's man," said a third, "and better put out of the way, if I may advise."

"You would be as Nicolai yonder, under my displeasure," she answered sharply. "Have a care. I shall know how to deal with the first man who disobeys me."

Was this the Queen? Ellerey thought she must be, half-believing he recognized something familiar in her manner. Was this her method of proving his daring before she fully trusted him?

"You have no token?" she said, addressing Ellerey.

"No, madam."

"Yet you went on a secret mission to the Altstrasse to-night?"

"I went openly."

"Openly! To visit whom?"

"Surely, one who lives in the Altstrasse," Ellerey answered.

"And were graciously entertained?"

"I ate and drank, madam, and both food and drink seemed to me of excellent quality."

"And afterward?"

"We talked."

"Monsieur De Froilette, you, and--"

"Yes, madam, we talked, and smoked, but the matter of the token surprises me. I heard no word of such a thing mentioned."

"I am inclined to believe you," she answered. "You have not yet been sufficiently proved."

"I would bow my thanks for your compliment, were I able. I make but a sorry picture at the moment, I fear, but my ragged and hardly respectable appearance you will excuse. May I know to whom I am indebted for this adventure?"

"Not yet. I may have need of you again."

"An invitation less hastily devised would please me better," said Ellery. "I am not rich enough to adventure such good garments as these often."

"A bullet would certainly have made less havoc with them, Captain Ellerey," she returned.

The mention of his name startled him.

"A word of warning," she went on. "Beware of Monsieur De Froilette, and of any enterprise he may handle. There will be specious promises, but small fulfilment. Beware of the lady who visited the Altstrasse to-night. Hesitate to do her bidding. Unless I mistake not, you will thank me for the warning one day," and then, turning to the men about her, she said, "Unloose him."

They hesitated, and did not move.

"Unloose him, I say," and she stamped her foot sharply.

Two or three fell on their knees beside Ellerey and unfastened the cords, and, stretching his limbs to take some of the ache out of them, he rose to his feet.

"You are free," she said; "but for the safety of these men, you must consent to be blindfolded, and led to the place you came from."

"By the same lady who brought me here?" Ellerey inquired.

"That might hardly be to her liking," was the answer.

At a sign from her, Ellerey's eyes were bound with a scarf, and in a few minutes he was being guided along the streets.

"One moment, monsieur," said one of his guides, presently. "There are footsteps, surely!"

Ellerey stood still and waited, listening. He heard no footsteps, and presently did not perceive the breathing of the man beside him. Then he understood the ruse, and tore the bandage from his eyes. He was alone at the corner of the Altstrasse, and the rain was beating slantwise into his face.

CHAPTER IV.
THE COURT OF STURATZBERG

Ellerey's servant had fallen asleep on a settle, partly induced, perhaps, by the liquor the empty tankard beside him had held, but he started, wide awake on the instant, as his master entered. Ellery expected him to remark upon his sorry condition, as he threw off his cloak, but the man did not do so.

"There has been some rough handling in my neighborhood to-night, Stefan."

"That's plain enough, Captain," was the answer. "They were good clothes, too."

"And interest you more than the man inside them," said Ellerey, grimly.

"For the moment, yes. The man is unhurt, while the clothes are only fit for the rag-shop or to be given to me."

"And, for choice, you would sooner have a corpse to deal with, so that the clothes were untorn?"

Stefan shrugged his shoulders.

"I could spare most of my acquaintances to be made corpses of, for acquaintances are easier come by than good clothes. It was a street attack, Captain, I suppose?"

"They are common enough in Sturatzberg," Ellerey answered lightly.

"The tale will serve as well as another," Stefan returned. "If I tell it, I am not compelled to believe it, and if I chance to be lying, it is no sin of mine."

"Why, rascal, what else should it be?"

"It might be a friend turned enemy, or the pursuit of a woman, or the touching of one of the many intrigues in Sturatzberg; but let it be a street attack. Was any man left sobbing out his life in the corner of the wall? It is well to have the story complete."

"No; it was an encounter of blows and bruises only."

"In such a plight as yours most men would have had some boast to make, pointing to their own condition to prove their statements. I have heard of half a dozen men lying dead, or dying, at a street corner, victims to a single sword, yet was there never a corpse to be found in the morning. Your easy boaster is ever a ready liar."

"Patch up the clothes and wear them, Stefan, if you can persuade your bulk into them," laughed Ellerey. "Some day, perhaps, when I am certain of your affection, I may tell you more of the adventure, and ask your help."

The man took up the tankard, looked into its emptiness, and put it down again. Then he turned round suddenly: "Some time since I was offered higher pay to serve another master, Captain."

"Why didn't you go?"

"I'm beginning to think I was a fool, since you trust me so little," Stefan answered; "but I may yet prove a better comrade in a tight place than many. Good-night."

A soldier, one of his own troop of Horse, Stefan had drifted into Ellerey's service, perhaps because he was a lonely man like his master. He appeared to have no ties whatever, nor wanted any, and declared that the first man he met in the street who was old enough might be his father, for anything he knew to the contrary. His mother, he knew, had died bringing him into the world; a wasted sacrifice, he called it, since the world could have done very well without him and he without it. Being in it, he took all the good he could find, and if he held his own life cheaply, he was even less interested in the lives of others. Women he hated, and his good opinion could be purchased by a man for a brimming tankard, and lasted, as a rule, so long as any liquor remained.

It was hardly wonderful that Ellerey should not trust such a man with any secret of his. Yet the soldier's parting words, and the look on his face as he spoke, made him thoughtful.

"I shall want at least one stout companion on whom I can rely," he mused. "I might choose a worse man than Stefan."

He spoke of his adventure to no one else. He did not even attempt to locate the house into which he had been decoyed. To show too much interest in the affair would only be to attract attention to himself and his movements, which was undesirable, whether it were her Majesty who had taken occasion to test his courage, or others who, knowing the Queen's schemes, sought to defeat them. One thing appeared certain. Some token was to come into his possession, and was to bring peril with it.

On the second evening, Ellerey accompanied Monsieur De Froilette to Court.

"You are prepared to be frivolous, monsieur, as her Majesty wishes?" said De Froilette, as they went. "You will find it tolerably easy, but, pardon the advice, make few friends; they are a danger to one with a secret mission."

"Do you speak of men, monsieur, or women?" Ellerey asked.

"I spoke generally, but perhaps I was thinking of women," was the answer. "Of one man, however, beware. There is a little, ferret-eyed devil at Court who can spy out secrets almost before they are conceived--the English Ambassador, Lord Cloverton. He is a great man, and I hate him."

Ellerey had no time to ask questions, for the carriage stopped, and the next moment he was following De Froilette up the wide staircase which many people, men and women, were ascending. His companion spoke to no one as he went up, nor did anyone address him. To the casual observer, he might have passed for an unimportant personage in that gay throng, but Ellerey, who had every reason to be interested in the Frenchman, noticed that many people turned to look after him, whispering together when he had passed. Ellerey himself attracted some little attention, due, he imagined, to the fact that he was in De Froilette's company, until he chanced to be left alone for a few moments at the head of the grand staircase. Some half-dozen paces from him four men were engaged in earnest conversation. From their position they could scrutinize every one who ascended the stairs or crossed the vestibule, and it seemed to Ellerey they were there of set purpose; more, that his arrival had been expected and waited for. One of the four was a man of about his own age, richly dressed, and of distinguished bearing. He appeared chief among his companions, who addressed him with a certain deference, and followed his movements, so that when he turned to look at the newcomer, Ellerey found himself the focus of four pairs of eyes. He met their searching looks with equal inquiry, but experienced a certain attraction toward the man who led the scrutiny. He might be an enemy, but he looked as though he would prove an honest and open one, incapable of anything mean or underhand. Presently he made some remark to his companions, who nodded acquiescence, and then they separated, and were lost in the crowd crossing the vestibule, just as De Froilette returned.

"Pardon me for leaving you, monsieur; shall we seek her Majesty?"

Ellerey passed with the Frenchman into a magnificent room, brilliantly lighted from a domed roof, one of a suite of rooms which were all of splendid proportions. From the distance came soft, dreamy music, hushed in the murmur of voices. There were a great many people present, and dancing had commenced in the ball-room. It was a brave assembly, men wearing brilliant uniforms and the decorations of every nation in Europe, and women beautiful in themselves, glorious in sheen of satin, rustle of silk, and flash of jewels. Women's light laughter answered men's jests--on every side were gayety and careless acceptance of the pleasures of the passing hour. It was difficult to believe that under it all lay deceit and treachery. Ellerey was inclined to doubt it, as he followed his companion.

In one of the rooms, surrounded by a group of men and women, with whom she turned to speak and laugh between the welcome she extended to each new arrival, sat her Majesty. She was even more beautiful to-night than when she had come to the Altstrasse, and, surrounded as she was by beautiful women, seemed to hold by right the central position of the group. Jewels glistened at her throat and in her hair, and across her breast she wore the scarlet ribbon of the Golden Lion of Sturatzberg.

"Ah, Monsieur De Froilette, you are welcome," she said. "I was just saying that your countrywomen are the most accomplished, the most fascinating, in Europe, and Count von Heinnen laughs at my opinion."

"Your Majesty will not understand," said Von Heinnen, in guttural tones which ill agreed with a compliment; "I loved the women of France until I arrived in Sturatzberg."

"I would narrow the Count's limit, and say the palace of Sturatzberg," said De Froilette, bending over the Queen's hand.

"No word for the women of their own country," laughed the Queen. "Are we so unpatriotic, Baron Petrescu?" and she turned to a man who was standing close behind her.

"I fear so, your Majesty. I have been in England, and, for my part, I think the English women are the most beautiful in the world."

Baron Petrescu was the man who had looked so searchingly at Ellerey in the vestibule. He looked at him now, as though his answer had some reference to him; and the Queen, who did not seem too pleased with the frankly spoken answer, following the direction of the Baron's glance, let her eyes rest on Ellerey for the first time.

"Captain Ellerey, you, too, are welcome," she said. "You come but seldom to Court. As an Englishman, you will doubtless support the Baron's opinion."

"I find something to contemplate in all women, your Majesty, but, as yet, I have placed none above all others."

"That confession should fire feminine ambition in Sturatzberg," laughed the Queen. "Spread the report of it, Monsieur De Froilette, and we shall witness excellent comedy, or tragedy--I hardly know which love may be. Oh, you are doubly welcome, Captain Ellerey, for the sport you shall give us, and we will ask for a repetition of that confession constantly. The first time you look down before our questioning eyes, and stammer in your answer, we shall know that love has laid siege to the citadel of indifference, and captured it." Ellerey smiled, as he moved aside to make room for others. He would have approached Baron Petrescu had he been able to do so, but he was prevented; first, because someone who knew him slightly spoke to him, and, secondly, by a general movement in the room occasioned by the King's entrance.

When the history of Ferdinand IV. comes to be written, the King will probably have as many characters as he has biographers. The character given him will so entirely depend upon the point of view. As he walked slowly across the room, his manner was not without dignity, but had little graciousness in it. There were a few who feared him; many who despised him; some who hated him; and from east to west of his kingdom it is doubtful whether a dozen loved or admired him. In appearance he was cadaverous-looking, tall and thin, with a stoop in his shoulders. His skin was parchment-colored, and his eyes heavy and slow of movement.

Europe's plaything, a witty Frenchman had once called him; but those about him found it hard work often to make him dance to their piping. Perhaps no one understood him better, or had greater influence with him, than the man who now walked a pace or two behind him, and was so small that, beside the King, he looked almost ridiculous. His mincing gait, and his apparently nervous deference to everyone about him, would have amused those who did not know the man, or until they had made a more careful study of his face. Nature seemed to have tried her hand at a caricature, and had placed upon this diminutive body a leonine head. The face was a network of lines, as though wind, rain, and sunshine had worked their will upon it for years. The hair was white as driven snow, and thick, shaggy, and long, while, set deeply under heavy brows, his small eyes were never still. For a fraction of time they seemed to rest on everyone in turn, and to note something about them which would be stored up in the memory.

"A ferret-eyed devil, monsieur, is it not so?" whispered De Froilette in Ellerey's ear after the Ambassador had passed. "He has already noted your presence, and will know all about you before he sleeps--if he ever does sleep. We must be very frivolous to escape detection."

To be frivolous at the Court of Sturatzberg was no difficult matter. Whether it was the report of what he had said to the Queen had made him especially interesting to women, or whether those steady blue eyes of his were the attraction, Ellerey found it easy to make friends. He studied to catch the trick of pleasing with a light compliment or pleasant jest, and before many days had gone had earned a reputation as an irresponsible cavalier; one whom it would be dangerous to take too seriously or believe in too thoroughly. Such a man was, for the most part, after the heart of the feminine portion of the Sturatzberg Court, and that he played the part well the Queen's smile constantly assured him. In one point, however, Ellerey was peculiarly unsuccessful. He had been attracted to Baron Petrescu, and went to some trouble to become acquainted with him, but to no purpose. Either the Baron avoided him intentionally, or a train of adverse circumstances intervened. Not a single word passed between them.

On several occasions the Queen made Ellerey repeat his confession, and he did so with a smile upon his lips.

"I expected downcast eyes and a stammering tongue to-night," she said one evening, and as Ellerey looked at her, she glanced swiftly across the room toward a small group, of which a woman was the centre--a beautiful woman, with a silvery laugh which had the spirit and joy of youth in it. By common consent, her beauty had no rival in the Court of Sturatzberg. Men whose tastes on all else were as wide asunder as the poles were at one in praise of her, and even women were content to let her reign supreme. Her dark eyes, fringed with long lashes, were, perhaps, the most perfect feature of a perfect face. They could persuade, they could reprove, and it was dangerous to look into them too constantly if one would not be a slave. Her hair, which had a wave in it, and was rich nut-brown in color, was gathered in loose coils about her head, a veritable crown to her, and her voice was low, as if compelling you to listen to some sweet secret it had to tell, a secret that was only for you.

"I can still make my confession, your Majesty," said Ellerey, wondering whether his words were quite true, for he had looked into this woman's eyes many times. Then he went toward the group, quick to observe that Baron Petrescu left it at his coming. Ellerey understood that the Queen must have watched him carefully. To this woman he had certainly paid more attention than to any other. She was in close attendance upon the Queen, was treated by her with marked favor, and many envious and angry glances had been cast upon Ellerey, because she seemed to find pleasure in being with him. Ellerey could not deny that the time spent in her company sped faster than all other hours, but he had another reason for seeking her so persistently. He had seen little of the face of the woman who had cried to him for help that night at the corner of the Altstrasse, being more concerned with what was required of him than with her who petitioned, but somehow this woman always reminded him of that night. Whenever she walked beside him, he recalled that other woman who had run hand-in-hand with him through the deserted streets. Was she the woman, or, at least, was she aware of what had occurred that night? Why had she so easily given him her friendship? Why should she so obviously prefer his company to that of others? There was some reason, and yet she had made no confession, had stepped into none of his carefully prepared traps. Did she know Maritza? Were those Maritza's eyes which had looked through the silken mask?

"You will dance with me, Countess?"

She placed her hand upon his arm at once.

"You are ever generous to me," he said, as they went toward the ball-room. "I wonder why?"

She looked up at him. He might have been laughed at for not understanding such a look.

"A Captain of Horse is a small person in Sturatzberg," he said carelessly.

"Even if he is honored with her Majesty's friendship?" she asked.

"Is he?"

"Well, are you not? I can judge by what I see, and you seem welcome always."

"I have noticed that, Countess, and have thought sometimes that you might tell me the reason."

"Of her Majesty's welcome, do you mean?"

"Of her welcome, and of your own kindness to me," Ellerey answered.

The woman laughed.

"I think Englishmen are slow of comprehension," she said.

"But a Captain of Horse, Countess?"

"Who may be of much higher rank to-morrow, and in his own country may be--Ah! you know, so many come to Sturatzberg."

"Many vagabonds, Countess."

"Oh, yes, and others," and then she made a gesture that they should dance, and they floated gracefully out among the couples gliding over the floor of the ballroom to the strains of a sensuous German waltz. Ellerey danced well. He had earned the reputation in many a London ball-room, and the Countess Frina danced as few English women can, with the soul of the music in her feet.

"Those others are sometimes difficult to distinguish," Ellerey said presently.

"Not to a woman," was the answer. "She has an intuition which is denied to most men. Indeed, I only know one man who has it in the fullest sense, in greater measure even than most women, and he is an Englishman, curiously enough. Yonder!"

With a touch she directed Ellerey's attention to one side of the room, where Lord Cloverton was standing talking to two men. He seemed to be interested in the conversation, but at the same time took notice of every couple which glided by him. Ellerey thought the Ambassador's eyes rested upon him for a moment, although he did not go near him.

"He, too, has noted you," the Countess whispered, "and if you have aught to conceal, Captain Ellerey, take care that the secret be well buried, or those small eyes will spy it out."

"You do not like the Ambassador?" said Ellerey, as he guided his partner to a deserted seat in an alcove.

"I admire him. It is not the same thing, but admiration I cannot help. There would have been desperate work for you soldiers long since had it not been for Lord Cloverton.”

“And that would have pleased you?”

“It would have given my friends a chance of distinction,” she answered. “And turned some friends into enemies, Countess. Surely you must know that. There are such conflicting interests in Sturatzberg.”

“I have taken great care in choosing my friends,” she answered.

“Ah, then, you have a very definite idea to which interest you are attached.”

“Of course.”

“And which is it?” he asked in a whisper, leaning toward her.

“The same as monsieur’s,” she said.

Ellerey was baffled. He had expected to surprise her into a confession. He did not suppose he had subjugated this woman so completely that she would make her interests identical with his own, and he could only explain her answer by presuming that she was sufficiently in the Queen’s confidence to know something of the mission to which he stood pledged.

“You seem very certain of me, Countess.”

“Have I not said that I take great care in choosing my friends?”

“I cannot conceive any reason for your faith in me, unless---”

“Well, you may question me.”

“I had lately a strange adventure, Countess, in which a woman was concerned. She found me after midnight at the corner of the Altstrasse, and---”

“Monsieur! monsieur!” she exclaimed, holding up her hand. “Do you imagine I should visit the Altstrasse for my politics, and after midnight, too?”

“I confess that was in my mind.”

“It pleases you to jest, Captain Ellerey, and I am in no mood for such jesting.”

She rose, and he was forced to take her from the ballroom. He had succeeded in making her angry, and had gained nothing. He had been ill-advised to question her.

“You must pardon me,” he said.

“You must earn your pardon, monsieur,” was her answer, as she turned away with another partner who had approached, leaving Ellerey perplexed.

“A love quarrel, monsieur? I have noted several; they are frequent here.”

At the slight touch on his arm Ellerey turned to face Lord Cloverton.

"Hardly a quarrel, my lord; certainly not a love one," he said.

"I was mistaken then, or you think so, Captain Ellerey. Love is a curious disease at all times, and in all places, difficult to diagnose sometimes. In the Court of Sturatzberg one has ample opportunity of studying it. I may be right after all, Captain Ellerey. I have more knowledge of this Court than you have; I have spent a longer time in it."

Lord Cloverton moved forward smiling, evidently expecting Ellerey to walk beside him across the room.

"I endeavor to fit myself to my surroundings," Ellerey said, as he walked slowly by the Ambassador's side, striving in vain to accommodate his step to the mincing gait of his companion.

"Quite so, but it is hardly the best atmosphere for a young man to develop himself in."

"Perhaps not."

"You interest me, Captain Ellerey."

"Since when, my lord?"

The small, deep-set eyes were turned upon him for a moment, as though to gauge the full meaning of the question, and they looked into steady blue eyes, which, perhaps, made Lord Cloverton more interested than ever, although he did not say so. "You are thinking that I might have taken notice of a countryman before this," he replied. "Well, perhaps there is something in the thought. Still, you were not brought to my notice at the Embassy. I heard no mention of Desmond Ellerey as a friend of anyone connected with the Embassy, nor, indeed, any remark that an English officer was serving his Majesty the King of Wallaria."

"No, my lord, my friendships are few, and, in truth, I have no great desire to increase the number."

"I might, indeed, repeat your question--since when?" laughed Lord Cloverton, "for lately surely you have made many new acquaintances, and move in the sunshine of Royal favor."

"I am afraid I have not been conscious of the fact," Ellerey returned. "I must be more careful to study his Majesty."

"I was speaking of the Queen."

Ellerey looked at Lord Cloverton in astonishment.

"Indeed, I think you are mistaken. Her Majesty is very gracious to all. I do not think she has been especially so to me."

"Another mistake of mine," said the Ambassador, with a smile. "I am full of them to-night. They began immediately after dinner. I dropped two lumps of sugar into my coffee, instead of one. It made it abominable, and I had to leave it. But there is another reason why I have become interested in you lately. I heard that you were the brother of Sir Ralph Ellerey. I know Sir Ralph."

"We are certainly sons of the same father; our relationship has got no further than that. If you know my brother well enough to accept his opinion about me, you have, doubtless, accorded me a very low place in your estimation."

"I am supposed never to accept another man's opinion about anything," the Ambassador replied; "certainly, I seldom do in judging men I come in contact with. Sir Ralph, however, gives some prominence to the name of Ellerey, and his brother can hardly hope to pass through the world unnoticed."

"I am succeeding beyond my expectations," said Ellerey.

"Are you?"

"Believe me, my lord, I am."

They were standing apart in a corner of one of the rooms. There was no one near enough to overhear their conversation. Lord Cloverton glanced over his shoulder to make sure of this before he went on quietly:

"I have heard that Desmond Ellerey was obliged to leave a crack cavalry regiment on account of his cheating at cards and for other dishonorable practices. I took you to be this same Desmond Ellerey."

"Yet another mistake to-night, my lord," Ellerey answered, looking the Ambassador unflinchingly in the eye. "The Desmond Ellerey you speak of was an unfortunate English gentleman and honorable soldier, whose services his King and country had no further need of. He was foully murdered by a lie. The Desmond Ellerey who has the honor to speak to you is a Captain of Horse in the service of his Majesty Ferdinand IV. of Wallaria, and looks for favor and reward only from the King and country he serves."

He turned on his heel as he spoke, and the Ambassador stood looking after him until his figure was lost in the moving crowd.

CHAPTER V.
TWO VISITORS

L ord Cloverton sat in his private room at the Embassy, a knitted brow and tightly-closed lips showing that he was deeply occupied in a problem which either baffled him altogether, or which, having been solved, gave him considerable anxiety. He had pushed his chair back from the table, and his attention was concentrated on the papers he held in his hand. They had come during the past few days, and although he had read each one carefully on its arrival, he had put them aside until he could study them together. They were all before him now, and he had spent the greater part of the morning reading them, and in piecing together the information they contained into one complete and intelligible story. It was not an easy task, and the result he arrived at gave him little satisfaction.

"This pestilential fellow will make trouble for us," he said to himself, and then he went systematically through the letters again.

"Absolutely no doubt of his guilt," he read slowly from one of them. "He denied everything, of course, but the evidence was exceedingly strong against him. That he accepted the verdict and disappeared in the manner he did, would seem to confirm the truth. That is what I cannot understand," said the Ambassador, arguing the point to the empty room. "Why did he accept it and disappear? Why didn't he stand and face the frowning world and beat it? That is what I should have expected from such a man, and with such eyes, too."

He took up another paper.

"The question can hardly be reopened, my lord, and since it was closed nothing has transpired to suggest that there was any error of justice in the matter. Of course he might bring an action for slander in the civil courts, and for this purpose be persuaded to return to England."

The Ambassador shook his head; he had not much faith in persuasion in this case. Then he turned to another letter and read one paragraph in it more than once. It impressed him.

"'I feel convinced that Desmond Ellerey is an innocent man. One has such convictions without being able to explain them. That he accepted the inevitable I think I can understand, considering the weight of evidence against him; and although I endeavored to persuade him against his determination to offer his sword to another country, I can appreciate his point of view since his career had been ruined in his own. If you think any good will come of my writing to him, making on my own account the suggestion contained in your letter, I will certainly do so, and shall, of course, not mention that I have heard from you, or that we are known to each other.'" The Ambassador looked at the signature--"'Charles Martin.' An excellent man to have for a friend, and I believe he is right."

He turned over another paper signed Ralph Ellerey.

"He does not count," said the Ambassador with a gesture of contempt, and threw the letter aside without troubling to read it again. Then he rang a bell upon his table, and a man entered.

"Ask Captain Ward to come to me."

The Ambassador was pacing the room with little short steps when the Captain entered. "Do you know a Desmond Ellerey, who lodges by the Western Gate, Ward?"

"I know there is such a man, but I know nothing about him."

"He is likely to be dangerous. I want you to keep an eye upon his movements. He is friendly with Monsieur De Froilette, and is in her Majesty's favor. I do not want you to make Ellerey's acquaintance. I don't want him to know who you are, for the present at any rate."

"I understand."

"I should be glad to see him turn his back upon Wallaria; failing that, I am uncharitable enough to hope he may meet with an accident," said Lord Cloverton.

"That might be arranged," was the answer.

"Sturatzberg is having a bad effect upon your moral sense. At least we will try persuasion first," and it was difficult to tell from the Ambassador's smiling face whether a sinister thought had entered his head or not. After a moment's pause he added: "Will you also have a telegram sent to Sir Charles Martin? Just say, 'Please write, Cloverton.' He will understand."

The extent of the Ambassador's interest in him would have surprised Ellerey considerably had he known of it. After his interview with Lord Cloverton he had half-expected that he would seek to question him further, or, if he had any reason to suppose he was in his way, might bring pressure to bear upon the King to dismiss him from the army. He certainly did not do the one, and Ellerey had no reason to think he had attempted to do the other. At Court the Ambassador had bowed slightly as he passed him, and the flicker of a smile had been on his face for a moment when he saw him crossing the room with Countess Mavrodin, almost as though he wished him to remember what he had said about a lovers' quarrel. Ellerey had made his peace with the Countess as speedily as possible. He was likely to make so many enemies that he could not afford to lose a friend, and he felt that this woman was a friend. He had duly humbled himself and had been forgiven, and even when she questioned him about his adventure in the Altstrasse, he refused to speak of it lest he should again offend. He succeeded, as he hoped to do, in raising her curiosity.

"But if this woman so resembled me, surely it would be a satisfaction to me to know something more about her," she said.

"It was dark, Countess, but she seemed to be pretty. That misled me perhaps. I was foolish to imagine for a moment that it could have been you."

Ellerey knew that such an explanation would not content her. Would it satisfy any woman? He had only to wait and she would ply him with further questions, and, if she were not the woman, would not rest until she had discovered who the other woman was. She would probably help him to some explanation of his adventure in the long run, her curiosity leading her to play the part of a useful ally.

The days passed and no message came from the Queen, neither did he see nor hear anything of De Froilette. The Frenchman was not at Court, and Ellerey did not meet him in the streets of Sturatzberg. He did not go to visit him in the Altstrasse; it had been agreed that he should not do so.

After consideration Ellerey had taken Stefan into his confidence. He believed the rough soldier had some affection for him, so had told him something of his adventure in the Altstrasse, and of the mysterious mission he might be called upon at any moment to perform. Such men as Ellerey wished to enlist in the enterprise were not easy to find. There were plenty of adventurous spirits ready for any service so they were well paid, but such men were quite likely to desert him at the critical moment if they saw any benefit to themselves in doing so.

"Now, Stefan, can we find the men we want?" Ellerey asked.

"A dozen of them?" queried the soldier, thoughtfully. "Twelve trusty comrades? It's a large order in a world where it's safest to trust nobody."

"There is adventure, there is good pay, two attractions to the soldier of fortune."

"Yes, Captain; but the soldier of fortune in Sturatzberg is a scurvy sort of rascal. He's not over fond of his trade when there's any danger in it. But I'll sound one or two I know of, and you can see what you think of them. And mark this, Captain, don't pay them too much until they've earned it. A few coins to oil their courage is enough to begin with."

The choosing of the men became Stefan's work, but only half a dozen had been determined on when Ellerey received an unexpected letter from Sir Charles Martin.

It was a pleasant letter of friendship, such a letter as brings forcibly to the senses of the mind the sunlight and shadow dappling an English lane, and the familiar sounds and refreshing fragrances which linger about an English home. Toward the end Sir Charles turned to a painful subject, but wrote hopefully. "Let me urge you," he said, "to return home. I am convinced that the time has come for you to begin to slowly prove that you are innocent. While the affair was fresh in people's minds you were at a disadvantage, but that time is past. One thing I may tell you. A person very highly placed has expressed his complete belief in you. Come home, Desmond."

Ellerey was musing over this letter and the remembrance it brought with it, when Stefan entered. "A gentleman to see you, Captain."

Ellerey rose hastily. The one or two brother officers who visited him stood on no such ceremony as this. He bowed in silence as Lord Cloverton came in. Neither of them spoke until Stefan had closed the door.

"You will pardon the intrusion, Captain Ellerey."

"I am honored, my lord," said Ellerey as he placed a chair for his visitor.

"I am still interested in you, you see," said the Ambassador, "but have not considered it wise to draw attention to ourselves at Court. A man in my position labors under a disadvantage of never being supposed to speak a word that has not weighty matter behind it. Some people will find a mystery in my simple utterance of 'Good-evening.' You and I are both Englishmen, and to be seen often in intimate conversation would start a small army of rumors on the march."

Ellerey bowed. He intended to let the Ambassador lead the conversation.

"Do you mind looking at me, Captain Ellerey?"

Ellerey did so, and for the space of thirty seconds the two men gazed into each other's eyes.

"No, I do not believe it."

"To what do you refer?" Ellerey asked.

"To that card scandal of yours. I believe you are an innocent man. Why don't you prove it?"

Ellerey took up the letter which he had thrown on the table when Lord Cloverton entered.

"Do you know Sir Charles Martin?" he asked, holding the letter out to him.

"I have heard of him. Who that is interested in English politics has not? I may live to see him Prime Minister. What, do you wish me to read this?"

"If you please." Lord Cloverton read the letter through.

"Evidently an intimate friend of yours. You could not have a better sponsor for your character. I think he gives you excellent advice."

"You would give me the same, Lord Cloverton?"

"Certainly."

"Why?"

"Because you are an innocent man. It is your duty to fight for your character to the last ditch."

"Why should you suppose I am not fighting for my character?" Ellery asked.

"Here in Sturatzberg?"

"Why not? Words will never mend a broken reputation; deeds may."

"Deeds done here will not count in England."

"And in England, or for England, I am debarred from doing anything. A sorry position, is it not, my lord?"

"I am advising you to alter it."

"But you have not told me why," said Ellerey. "Shall I tell you the reason, Lord Cloverton? You wish me to leave Sturatzberg."

"Why should I?"

"That you must tell me."

"There is a candor about you, Captain Ellerey, that compels straightforward treatment in return, and you shall have it. I have a misgiving that your presence here will tend to hamper my work, and by my work I mean England's interests. I do not pretend to know exactly in what direction you will hinder me, but I can guess, and you are too good a man to be crushed while striving against your own country. Go back to England. I thoroughly believe in you, and you shall have my hearty support in your endeavor to establish your innocency."

"You are very good, my lord, and I thank you; but I regret that I cannot comply with your wishes. I shall not leave Sturatzberg."

"You prefer to be crushed?"

"Yes, in the service of my adopted country. We fight with different weapons, Lord Cloverton."

"Then it is to be war between us?"

"You seem to say so. I cannot leave Sturatzberg."

"Is it not possible that some sense of honor may exist here, that officers here may not care to associate with one who has been convicted of cheating, even though he be a foreigner?"

"I am not afraid that Lord Cloverton will spread such a report of me."

"My country stands first with me, Captain Ellerey."

"But not to make you dishonorable. You are attempting to do yourself an injustice. Besides if I were driven to use such weapons in self-defence, is it not possible that Lord Cloverton has some enemies in Sturatzberg?"

"Many, no doubt."

"I might suggest, for instance, that he had secretly sought to alienate the loyalty of one of his Majesty's officers."

"Enough, Captain Ellerey," said Lord Cloverton rising. "I see that we must unfortunately be enemies. It is a pity. You will be crushed under the Juggernaut of international politics."

"It may be so, it may not," said Ellerey. "Believe me, I am not unmindful of your kindness; but as I have said, we fight with different weapons. You wield the power of the politician; I have only my sword. We cannot therefore meet in hand-to-hand encounter. I should hesitate to use my sword against my countrymen, but until British soldiers hold the heights above Sturatzberg there is no need to consider that question; and your work, I presume, lies in preventing any chance of such a contingency. If you could forget that I am an Englishman, and remember only that I am a Captain of Horse, subject to the commands of my superior officer, you would understand my position better."

"You are a difficult man to deal with, but I rather like you," said the Ambassador, holding out his hand. "I regret that Fate makes us enemies, and if at the last moment I can save you from being entirely crushed, I will."

"Thank you. I, too, may find an opportunity of rendering you a service, my lord."

As Lord Cloverton went quickly away, a man who had been sitting at a small table in a cafe opposite, who had sipped two glasses of absinthe and smoked innumerable cigarettes, rose hastily and crossed the street. His dress was travel-stained, and he had evidently ridden through dirty weather, for his boots were thickly cased with mud. Ellerey was almost as surprised to see De Froilette as he had been to see the Ambassador.

"You have been away from Sturatzberg," he said.

"I have only just returned," De Froilette answered, throwing out his arms to draw attention to his clothes, "and before going to the Altstrasse came to prepare you. I have been waiting at the cafe opposite until Lord Cloverton came out."

"And wondering why he visited me?" asked Ellerey, smiling.

"Wondering, rather, how far you would be successful in deceiving him."

"He was disposed to be friendly," said Ellerey, carelessly taking up Sir Charles Martin's letter from the table and putting it in his pocket. "Friendly! A trick of his, monsieur, a trick."

"Exactly. We have agreed to be enemies."

"Ah, but that was foolish," said De Froilette quickly. "You should have played with him even as I do. He believes that I am very friendly, while I hate him."

"That is your method; it is not mine. I am not an adept at crawling, even to the

British Ambassador."

"What does he suspect?" asked De Froilette after a pause, during which he had seemed inclined to resent Ellerey's words.

"Naturally, he did not say, and I am unable to guess, which is hardly remarkable, seeing that I am entirely in the dark myself."

"But why did he come?"

"He used his knowledge of some friends of mine in England as an excuse for visiting me, but he had probably taken upon himself for the time being the office of spy. As I had no information to give, he has returned little wiser than he came. When am I to be fully trusted, monsieur?"

"You are fully trusted now, Captain Ellerey, but the time for striking has not arrived. It approaches, however. Until the man in Sturatzberg was ready we could not proceed. Look at me; I have come from a journey. I have been doing my part, and I come to you and say, Be ready. At any moment her Majesty may send for you."

"I am waiting," said Ellerey.

"Not to-night, perhaps, nor to-morrow, but soon."

Knowing the Frenchman's secretive method, Ellerey was convinced that the time was at hand. Were it not, De Froilette would hardly have risked seeking him at his lodging; he had been so careful to avoid all appearance of intimacy with him. Ellerey was not inclined to place implicit trust in De Froilette. He did not pretend to a keen insight into other men's characters, but he conceived that De Froilette would not be likely to lose sight of his own interests, no matter whom he served, nor how humbly such service might be tendered. Ellerey was not even convinced that the Frenchman's support of the Queen's schemes was whole-hearted, and believed him quite capable of giving just so much help as would presently enable him to thwart her and reap benefit for himself. Whatever the mission was which he was about to undertake, Ellerey intended to do his utmost to carry it to success; and if De Froilette by chance stood in his way, it was not likely to be merely a question of words between them.

More subtle, more given to abstract reasoning, a successful student of character, it must be said for Monsieur De Froilette that he fully trusted Captain Ellerey, in so far that he believed he would do whatever task was set him better, probably, than most men would. That he would be a match for such men as Lord Cloverton, with the weapons Lord Cloverton would use, he did not expect, and that the Ambassador had visited Ellerey troubled him not a little. That Lord Cloverton could possibly suspect the true state of things he did not for a moment believe; but every hour's delay now would be in the Ambassador's favor, and the sooner the blow was struck the better--the more hope of success was there. Everything was ready, and it was now that De Froilette's anxiety was greatest. He was too complete a schemer not to realize how often it was the small insignificant thing which served to ruin great enterprises built up with so much care and elaboration. Over and over again he had tested every point in his plans, and had not succeeded in finding any weak spot. There seemed to be no contingency he was not prepared to meet, for which he was not ready; and yet a sense of misgiving, almost amounting to a feeling of insecurity, oppressed him as he walked along the Altstrasse. The people hanging about the door saluted him, for the Frenchman had been liberal to his poor neighbors, and had an excellent name for charity. He had made many friends of this kind in Sturatzberg, and since he had confessed to disliking unprofitable friends, it must be assumed that he looked to reap some reward from them in the future. He was not the man to pay merely for respect and smiles.

He went to his room, the room in which he and Ellerey had sat talking after dinner, the room to which the Queen had come. A pile of unopened letters was upon the desk, for Monsieur De Froilette employed no secretary, and he turned over these letters without opening them before ringing for Francois.

"Well, Francois?" he said as the man entered. He always asked the question in the same manner when he had been absent for any time, and listened to the servant's answer without interrupting him. The answer was usually a long one, full details of the happenings during the master's absence, not of those in the house only, but of those in the city as well. To-day, however, there was no long answer. Francois seemed fully aware of the essential point.

"Monsieur, the Princess, she has left England!"

"My good Francois, you are uninteresting. That happened weeks ago. The Princess is cruising to the British Colonies. It is known, indeed was arranged, by the British Government."

"It was, monsieur, that is right--it was; but the Princess found a substitute for that voyage. She did not go. She slipped away quietly, and no one knew." De Froilette's face was suddenly pale. He did not speak, but Francois read the question in his eyes.

"It is so, monsieur," he said. "The Princess Maritza is in Sturatzberg."

CHAPTER VI.
FRINA MAVRODIN'S GUEST

For some time Monsieur De Froilette remained silent. The return of the Princess was a contingency he had not provided for.

"Where is she?" he asked suddenly.

"Alas, monsieur, I do not know," Francois answered. "She has powerful friends in Sturatzberg, and they conceal her well. I saw her for one moment in Konigsplatz. She was alone, and entered a shop there. I followed her, but she was gone. I called myself her servant, and inquired about her, making the sign that has so long been used by her partisans to secure an answer. It had no effect. I was told that I was mistaken, that no such lady as I had described had entered. Do you not understand, monsieur, the sign must have been changed?"

De Froilette understood only too well. At his very door were enemies, the more dangerous because they had been partially admitted into his plans. He had himself given them reason for watching him, and the opportunity of doing so. That was past and beyond reparation, but this arch schemer was not the man to stand idly regretting a mistake. Even mistakes might be used to advantage.

"I will dress, Francois," he said presently. "I had not intended to go to Court to-night, but this news compels me."

"And how shall we find the Princess, monsieur?"

"We will not trouble. We will set others to do that. Matters will be for our benefit in the end, Francois. Quickly, I must dress."

De Froilette dined alone and dismissed the man who waited upon him as soon as possible. A portrait of Queen Elena stood on a side table, and he got up and placed it beside him, contemplating it thoughtfully as he sipped his wine.

"If we succeed," he mused, "there is high place and distinction to be won. This

Englishman may win it for me. In a revolution a King's life is as other men's, dependent on the hazard of a die. If I read her smile aright I shall have my reward. And if we fail?"--he paused to consider the course of events in such a case--"who knows? My reward might come the easier. There would be few shelters open to her. Only in defeat through Princess Maritza's influence is there danger to me. Success or failure otherwise, what does it matter? I shall win. The paths to mountain peaks are ever rugged, but men reach the summits. Why should I fail? The road to power may be closed against me, but the road to love--" And he gazed into the eyes of the portrait, finding an answer in them. This man of action was a dreamer too.

When he entered the palace that evening, De Froilette inquired whether Lord Cloverton had arrived, and being answered in the negative, remained at the head of the stairs, speaking a few words to this acquaintance and to that, bowing a well-turned compliment to one fair lady, or meeting another's pleasantry with an answering jest. He was in excellent good humor.

Presently Lord Cloverton came mincing up the steps, pausing half a dozen times to greet acquaintances. He, too, was in excellent humor; but then he seldom allowed people to see him otherwise.

"How I hate the man," De Froilette said to himself, going toward the Ambassador as he reached the vestibule. "May I have a word with you, my lord?"

"A thousand, my dear Monsieur De Froilette. Ah, a private word is it?" he added as the Frenchman led him aside.

"My lord, you have my greatest esteem, as you are aware."

Lord Cloverton bowed.

"If, as a loyal Frenchman, I would see France predominant in the affairs of this country, that is natural, is it not so?"

"Most natural indeed, and, monsieur, I say frankly, France is playing a very worthy part."

"No doubt, my lord," De Froilette answered. "I am but a looker-on, with certain business interests which politics might affect, and therefore I take some notice of politics. Perhaps I see more clearly than some, my lord--the lookers-on often do; and I am convinced that British policy is at the present moment the safeguard of Wallaria."

"I rejoice to hear it, monsieur."

"And if you will allow me, my lord, I will add that your presence in Sturatzberg is the great security."

"You flatter me," Lord Cloverton returned. "You will be pleased to learn that I have received no notification that I am likely to be removed from Sturatzberg."

"That would indeed be a disaster," said De Froilette. "So, my lord, any small help, any little information I can give you, I shall give gladly. Regard for yourself and my business interests will prompt me. We have all a vein of selfishness in us."

"I am honored by your confidence, and you will be welcome at the Embassy."

"I will give you the information now," said De Froilette. And he lowered his voice as he leaned toward the Ambassador: "The Princess Maritza!"

"Is in Australia at present, I believe."

"Exactly," said the Frenchman. "Making a tour of the English Colonies. A delicate attention to an honored guest and unfortunate exile, designed to keep her out of the way while the present unsettled feeling in Wallaria lasts; is it not so?"

"Your political acumen is not at fault."

"No, my lord, but yours is. The lady at present in Australia, or wherever she may be, is not the Princess, but a substitute. It needs very powerful friends to carry through such a deception as that."

Lord Cloverton turned sharply toward him, and, as Francois had done, De Froilette answered the unasked question.

"Yes, my lord; Princess Maritza is in Sturatzberg."

"Hiding where?"

"That I do not know. You will doubtless take means to find out. Command me if I can help you in any way."

"I thank you for the information. If you are not mistaken, the wayward child has been very ill advised. I gather, monsieur, that your business affairs would suffer were such a thing as a rising in the Princess Maritza's favor to take place?"

"Have I not said that there is a selfish vein in all of us?"

Lord Cloverton smiled, and together they crossed the vestibule.

Their short colloquy had not been overheard, nor had their presence been particularly noticed there except by one person--the Countess Mavrodin. She had reached the head of the stairs as De Froilette had leaned confidentially forward toward the Ambassador, and she hastily greeted a friend, keeping her standing at the top of the stairs while they talked. She had good reason to be curious regarding such a confidence between two such men, and while she laughed and talked she watched them. She did not move until they had crossed the vestibule, and when they separated she followed Lord Cloverton.

Desmond Ellerey met her and found her in a gracious mood.

"Have I quite pardoned you for mistaking me for another woman that night in the Altstrasse?" she said gayly.

"I hope so; indeed, I thought so."

"I am sorry. I ought to have reserved some of my displeasure."

"Why?"

"So that I might demand a favor."

"You have but to demand, Countess."

"Then stay with me and keep me near Lord Cloverton," she said.

"What! Has he incurred your displeasure, too?"

"Must I give reasons for my demand?"

"No."

"Then you trust me?"

"As I would trust any woman."

For a moment she seemed satisfied, and then she turned toward him.

"Is there a meaning underneath that? Do you trust no woman?"

"I have learnt my lessons in a hard school, Countess. I trust few, either men or women, and I have more knowledge of men than women." They followed Lord Cloverton across the rooms, and she noticed every one to whom he spoke. Presently he stood to watch the dancing for a moment, but he seemed to avoid any person who might detain him in conversation for any length of time.

"I think the Ambassador will leave early to-night," the Countess said. "May I beg another favor, Captain Ellerey? Will you see that my carriage is ready waiting for me?"

Ellerey went to do her bidding, wondering why she was watching the Ambassador so keenly. It took him some time to find her servants, and as he returned he met Lord Cloverton. With the slightest of recognitions the Ambassador got into his carriage.

"The Embassy, quickly," he said.

Countess Mavrodin came down the stairs as Lord Cloverton drove away.

"I thank you," she said. "I have a habit of remembering favors."

"I shall remember that you have said so," Ellerey answered. "Indeed, I can even now ask one. Only this afternoon Lord Cloverton was pleased to tell me that he looked upon me as an enemy. Should you discover anything which might affect me, will you tell me?"

"He said you were an enemy; then I am not suspicious in vain. Yes, I will tell you if I can. One word, monsieur. You neither trust women nor men, so perchance the warning is unnecessary; but of all men at least distrust one--Jules De Froilette."

"Did her Majesty bid you give me that message?" Ellerey asked.

"No, monsieur; it is an original idea. I have ideas of my own sometimes. I have one now. If you are leaving the palace, I will drive you to the Western Gate." She was pretty, and Ellerey was only human. Strictly speaking, his duty was to remain, lest the Queen should send for him; but he helped the Countess into her carriage and seated himself beside her. She refused to be serious as they drove through the city, and when Ellerey entered his lodging he was left to wonder at what point the incidents of the evening touched his mission. Why should the Countess become suddenly interested in the movements of Lord Cloverton? and since she was closely attached to the Queen, why should she warn him against De Froilette, who was also deep in her Majesty's confidence? The problem was beyond his power to solve.

Frina Mavrodin was a far more important person in Sturatzberg than Ellerey imagined. It was not only at Court that she was popular; she was besides the Lady Bountiful to the poor. She was immensely wealthy, and her beautiful home by the river, in the southwest of the city, had been called the beggars' paradise, for those who asked charity were seldom sent away empty. The general criticism of her was that she was a pretty woman, very adorable, a little frivolous perhaps, and possessed of much more heart than head. She seemed to take delight in such criticism, and to be at some pains to fully merit it. But there was another side to her character which few persons ever got even a glimpse of. Her profound knowledge of current politics would have startled Lord Cloverton, and her capacity for intrigue and scheming would have astonished even Monsieur De Froilette into admiration. There were few clubs and societies in Sturatzberg, where discontent was fostered and secret plans discussed, which were not known to Frina Mavrodin. She was conversant with their secret signs, their aims, and their means, and knew by sight most of their influential members. A single word from her would have sent many a man to prison who walked the streets freely. Perhaps, in all Sturatzberg, there was only one person who gave her credit for such knowledge, and who was content to be guided in some measure by her advice.

This person, at present, occupied a suite of rooms in Frina Mavrodin's house, and this evening she reclined at full length among the cushions of a low couch, and watched a door at one end of the room expectantly. Her hand was stretched out to a bowl of flowers on a table by her side, and she plucked a petal at intervals which she crushed and let fall. Something of the girl's character seemed to be in the action. She was not weary, not worn out with the day's work or pleasure, whichever it might have been, but was waiting anxiously, irritably even, for news, or for someone's coming. Her hair had loosened by contact with the cushions, and fell about her shoulders in luxuriant copper-colored tresses. Presently the door opened, and an elderly woman entered--an English woman, plain in feature and resolute in manner.

"You have been spoiling your flowers," she said, seeing the scattered petals on the carpet.

"Never mind them. Has Dumitru come, Hannah?"

"Just come."

"Then bring him in, bring him in. Why do you wait?" exclaimed the girl, half-rising from her reclining position. "I cannot afford to have fools about me in such times as these."

"You haven't," the woman answered bluntly, evidently quite used to the petulant moods of her mistress. "I was one when I came out of Devon to a heathen place like this; but that time is past." And she went to the door and beckoned to a man to come in. As he entered she went out, closing the door behind her. When she had gone the man dropped swiftly on one knee by the couch.

"Well, Dumitru?"

"He returned to-day," said the man, rising and standing erect. "He went straight to the lodging of this English Captain."

"And then?"

"To Court, Princess."

"And his mission, Dumitru--was it in my interests, think you?"

The man made a fierce clicking sound with his tongue.

"Ah, no, no, no; and again a hundred times, no. He is for the Queen a little, and for himself very much. Have you still a doubt, even now? A sudden death should be his reward."

"Patience, Dumitru."

"The English Captain had another visitor to-day--the British Minister."

"This English Captain is in great requisition, it would seem," she said.

"Aye, he is a man, I grant you that--strong, resolute, and rides as though horse and rider were one piece."

"And honest, Dumitru. I have looked into his face and thought him so."

"Can one judge so easily?" asked the man. "Besides, honest or not, he is for our enemies."

"Our enemies must be swept aside," she said imperiously, as though not only the will, but the power to do so were hers.

"Thus, Princess," and the man's dark eyes gleamed as he just showed the keen, thin blade of a dagger which he carried in his cloak.

"Not without my command, Dumitru," she said hastily. The man bowed low, disappointed perhaps that the same spirit was not in her as was in him.

"We may use this English Captain for our ends," she went on. "I have a way and you shall help me, Dumitru, when the time comes. That Lord Cloverton has visited him shows that some new pressure is to be brought to bear upon him. We shall see how he stands in this, whether firm or not, and may learn how to act ourselves."

"He is ready to act when the token is given him," said Dumitru. "He has a few desperate men who are pledged to his service."

"You are sure of this?"

"Quite sure."

"Who will follow for love of him?" she asked.

"They are of the kind who follow more readily for money," answered the man.

The girl remained thoughtful for a few moments. Something in the man's information had set her thoughts running in a new channel, and while she mused

Frina Mavrodin entered the room hurriedly.

Dumitru bowed low before her.

"You are early," said the Princess.

Frina turned to Dumitru.

"Captain Ellerey has returned early to his lodging, too; it would be well to watch. I do not think it will happen to-night, but should any messenger seek him we must know at once."

"Go, Dumitru," said the Princess, and when he had gone she turned to her companion: "What has brought you home so early?"

"You, Maritza. I wondered whether you had remained safely here, or whether you had again jeopardized your cause by going so openly into the streets. It is known that you are in Sturatzberg."

"By whom?"

"That lynx-eyed servant of De Froilette's saw you, as you know. You thought he would believe himself mistaken, but I knew better. His master returned to-day, and to-night I found Monsieur De Froilette and Lord Cloverton in confidential conversation. When two men who hate each other as they do, agree, it is time to prepare for the storm. You must remain an absolute prisoner here for a while."

"I am tired of inactivity."

"You will not have to wait long," Frina answered. "Within an hour, I warrant you, there will be spies out in every quarter of the city to try and find your hiding-place. You are safe so long as you remain here. What an advantage it is to have such a reputation for empty-headedness as I have. No doubt De Froilette played a trump card in telling Lord Cloverton of your presence in Sturatzberg. The task of finding you will occupy the Minister's attention for a little while, and if De Froilette is ready, he will seize the opportunity to strike his blow. That is why I offered to drive Captain Ellerey to his lodging. If the token is to be given to-night he will not be there to receive it."

"It may be sent to him," said the Princess.

"That is why Dumitru watches by the Western Gate."

"The moment the token is given I must know," said Maritza. "I have a plan. I have had plenty of lonely hours in which to mature plans. I am longing to put them into action. We are too cautious, Frina."

"Your want of caution in going openly into the city has nearly ruined us, Maritza."

"I have many friends in the city."

"True, and many enemies; and it is the enemies who happen to be in power. Do not be impatient."

"Over-caution may be as fatal as impatience," Maritza answered. "We should advance a step each day, each night; do we advance?"

"So fast that we shall have to run quickly to keep abreast of affairs shortly. A few weeks ago had you any real hope of being in Sturatzberg? Yet you are here. Had you even a suspicion that Jules De Froilette had been working in his own interests for these two years past, and not in yours?"

"True, Frina, we have advanced. Heaven help De Froilette when I touch power. Who knows what injury he may not have done to my cause in these two years? And he has succeeded in drawing this English Captain into his schemes."

"Captain Ellerey does not like De Froilette," said Frina. "Tell me your plan, Maritza."

The Princess drew a flower carefully from the bowl and held it to her face, as though she were absorbed for a moment in its beauty and fragrance.

"Captain Ellerey left the Court with you, to-night," she said. "That was wisely thought of. Did he come willingly?"

Frina laughed, such a joy in the laugh that the Princess looked at her in astonishment.

"Yes, he came willingly, most willingly, I think."

"You hope to win him to my cause?"

"He is a man, I am a woman; I shall try."

"And then?"

"Then, Maritza--ah, we run on too fast. Tell me your plan."

"It is strange," said the Princess slowly; "but in England, as I told you, I once met Captain Ellerey. I told him who I was, and promised him work for his sword should he ever come to Wallaria."

"You told him that! Why?"

"I am a woman, and he is a man," the Princess answered.

For a moment the two women looked into each other's eyes. Then Frina, looked down and straightened a fold of her dress, while Maritza bent to inhale the perfume of the flowers in the vase. The Princess did not tell her plan, and Frina Mavrodin forgot to question her.

CHAPTER VII.
THE TIME ARRIVES

Within a short time of Lord Cloverton's return to the Embassy, spies and secret-service agents were abroad in the city endeavoring to discover the whereabouts of Princess Maritza. The Ambassador at once telegraphed to the Foreign Office in London, and received the answer that the report of her return to Wallaria was absurd, that she was certainly on her way to Australia. This confident answer, however, did not satisfy Lord Cloverton, in spite of the fact that no news of the Princess was forth coming. That she could have returned to Sturatzberg without his knowledge, more, without the knowledge of any of those who were so eager to keep her out of the country, seemed impossible; but then in diplomacy it was often the impossible things which happened. He was too astute a man to underrate the undoubted ability of De Froilette. There were few men who probed more accurately the likely trend of future events, or who were quicker to recognize opportunities and seize them than the Frenchman, and Lord Cloverton argued that he was far too clever a man to tell such an unlikely story merely to serve his own ends. He would know that the very improbability of the tale would have the effect of drawing attention to himself and his actions. No, whether the report were true or not, De Froilette believed it, and evidently saw danger to himself in the presence of Princess Maritza. At the same time he might perceive a favorable opportunity in the state of affairs to exploit his own plans, and Lord Cloverton took the precaution to have the Frenchman under careful observation.

The unexpected information had also caused the Ambassador to reconsider Captain Ellerey's position in Sturatzberg. It was quite possible that he knew more about the Princess than any one else. He was the kind of man who would have nerve and determination enough to attempt a desperate venture, and having little to lose and all to win, might go far toward success. He and De Froilette apparently held little communication with each other; the characteristics of the two men were antagonistic; and the Englishman might be quite as capable of playing a deep game as the Frenchman was.

It was a sleepless night for the Ambassador. This was just such a complication as might embroil the nations of Europe in strife, an excuse which might serve to snap diplomatic relations and spread the lurid clouds of war from the Ural range to the shores of the Atlantic. One thing seemed certain, De Froilette had not repeated his information broadcast. No intimation reached Lord Cloverton that the report had even been whispered in any of the other Embassies, and there was some consolation in this.

No news came during the following day. Wherever the Princess was, her secret was well kept, probably because only a few persons had been admitted into it, and it seemed evident that no special movement had taken place in her favor, or had even been arranged for. Some bold *coup d'etat* might be in contemplation, and although the many and diverse interests in the country were probably sufficient to render any attempt abortive in itself, yet such an attempt might be the one thing needed to fan the smouldering ashes into flame, starting a conflagration which would burn throughout Europe. Such fires never die out--they are always smouldering.

Any person who had watched Lord Cloverton closely when he went to the palace that night, would have been struck by his particular alertness. He was observant of the composition of the different groups in the rooms, of those who were chiefly about her Majesty, and of those who danced together. The slightest confidential whisper near him attracted his attention, and more than once he caused a blush to mount to a pretty woman's cheeks by suddenly surprising a murmured love passage meant for no other ears but her own. To those to whom he spoke he succeeded in giving the impression that he had only a few moments to spare them, that he was purposely keeping himself free, but he managed to suggest that it was not business, but some pleasure he anticipated.

He glanced round all the rooms in search of Captain Ellerey, who either had not yet arrived, or had already retired into some quiet corner, probably with the Countess Mavrodin. The last conjecture was wrong, however, for standing in a position which commanded the entrance to the suite of state rooms, the Ambassador presently saw Frina Mavrodin on the arm of an *attache* of the Austrian Embassy, an offshoot of a princely house who, rumor said, had already been twice refused by the fair lady, and was only awaiting an opportunity to adventure his case for a third time. He was evidently persuading her to dance with him, and she was laughingly protesting, perhaps promising to do so later in the evening. She was, however, not averse to his company, for she palpably kept him by her side, and they remained talking and laughing together, the man extremely happy, the woman watchful and rather preoccupied, the Ambassador thought.

For half an hour or more she remained there, evidently using the Austrian's presence to keep herself free from other companions. Several spoke to her, but since the *attache* did not move away, the new arrivals were obliged to leave her after exchanging a few words. At last Lord Cloverton noticed that the expression of her face suddenly changed. She looked at him, or rather beyond him, and turning to discover the cause, he saw Desmond Ellerey crossing the room toward her. He also became aware that Baron Petrescu was standing close to him and that he was watching Ellerey, too.

Frina Mavrodin spoke quickly to her cavalier, telling him perhaps where he would find her for the promised dance, but at any rate she dismissed him. For a few moments Ellerey stood beside her, her smiling face raised to his, and then they went slowly toward the ball-room.

"The little comedy interests you, my lord."

"Well, Baron, my white hair gives me credit for greater age than does the feeling of youth which is still in me. I am young enough, even now, to recognize love, and to take an interest in it--in others, of course."

Baron Petrescu shrugged his shoulders rather contemptuously.

"The moth ever flits to the candle, and usually gets burnt," he said.

"Would not the lodestone be the more apposite simile?" asked Lord Cloverton. "In that case the attraction brings no hurt, Baron."

"Time will show which is the best simile," was the answer. "He interests me, this Captain Ellerey."

"He interests the lady too, it seems," replied the Ambassador. "Indeed, Captain Ellerey interests many people."

"I trust his courage is equal to his ambition," said the Baron with a smile. "There are others striving for the same prize, my lord, who do not easily accept defeat, and are content to pin their honor to the sword's point."

"Jealous," said Lord Cloverton to himself as the Baron turned away, still with a smile upon his face, but with a movement of his shoulders which suggested an angry bird ruffling its feathers. "He means mischief. Ellerey may find his hands fuller than he expects, if the Baron's weapon is as ready as his tongue. Sentiment compels me to wish my countryman victory, but politically--ah! a cunning thrust which would lay him aside for a few weeks would be very convenient to me, and perhaps not the worst thing which could happen for him." And Lord Cloverton went toward the ball-room.

The Countess and her cavalier had disappeared.

"Are you still watching the Ambassador?" Ellerey had asked, as she placed her hand upon his arm.

"No."

"Then let us get out of the crowd. Few people seem to know of the alcove off the ball-room."

"And why such a desire for solitude, Captain Ellerey?" she said, seating herself in a corner and making room for him beside her.

"Not solitude, Countess, but restful companionship. I am not desirous of living perpetually under the eye of Lord Cloverton, and, after what he said, I imagine he watches me pretty closely."

"And is as closely watched," she replied.

"Have you found out anything which affects me?" Ellerey asked after a pause.

She hesitated.

"Not directly."

"Indirectly, then?"

"Perhaps, a little. It is a small matter, but it interested me. It has nothing to do with Sturatzberg, but with England."

Ellerey was silent. Could Lord Cloverton have repeated his story?

"May I know the nature of the--crime is it?--which is imputed to me?"

"It is no crime, Captain Ellerey--rather a romance. I should have repudiated the idea of a crime in connection with you."

"Countess, that is the kindest thing you have ever said to me."

She looked into his face, and the color came into her own.

"Are we not friends?" she said, "and is it not the elemental part of friendship to believe nothing ill? I would hardly believe a confession of crime, though your own lips spoke it. No, this information was about a woman."

"Unknown women are a dangerous subject between us, Countess," said Ellerey, with a smile. "I am barely forgiven yet for the mysterious lady of the Altstrasse."

"This is not an unknown woman, but a very famous one--none other than Princess Maritza of Wallaria. You have heard of her?"

"I have not only heard of her, but seen her and spoken to her."

"And admired her?" she asked.

"Yes, her beauty and her indomitable courage."

"That is what I heard, that you admired her."

"It is a very strange thing for you to hear. I only saw her once, for ten minutes, perhaps. She was a schoolgirl, and playing truant. We met upon the downs one breezy morning, a hat blown away by the wind served for introduction, and I have never seen her since."

"It was not for her sake, then, that you came to Wallaria?"

"Ah! is that what Lord Cloverton thinks!" exclaimed Ellerey. "Now I understand his attitude more clearly."

"You do not answer my question," she said.

"Her story of the state of affairs in Wallaria certainly gave me the idea of seeking fortune in this country."

"And love?" she said.

Ellerey looked at her quickly and wondered. He was not one of those who believe that they have the power of charming any woman, and his companion's sudden question and attitude startled him. More than one answer sprang to his lips ready to trip lightly and pleasantly to her ears, but they were not spoken. Instead he laughed gayly and said:

"A Princess and a poor Captain of Horse, Countess? Such a flight of fancy after ten minutes' conversation! Oh, you jest and laugh at me."

There was a further question in her glance and attitude, but it was not asked, for a man appeared at the entrance of the alcove.

"I have been seeking you, Captain Ellerey," he said. "Her Majesty commands your attendance. Will you come with me?"

Ellerey rose at once.

"You will pardon me, Countess. I must make another opportunity of quarrelling with you for laughing at me. Shall I take you back to the ball-room?"

"No, thank you. I am tired, and will stay here." And with a low bow Ellerey left her.

The fact that he had been sent for and the probable meaning of that interview, did not take first place in Frina Mavrodin's thoughts for a time. She was considering Ellerey's answer to her question, trying to understand it when viewed in the light of the Princess's declaration. Maritza could only have intended her to understand one thing, and to-night she had endeavored to surprise the truth from Captain Ellerey. Had she succeeded in learning anything? Surely in such a casual meeting no lasting impression could have been formed, and yet love works in sudden and inexplicable fashion sometimes. The Princess seemed to have treasured the memory of that meeting; Ellerey admitted that it was the cause of his coming to Sturatzberg. Frina Mavrodin remembered, as though they had been noted down in one continuous story, everything Captain Ellerey had ever said to her, and the manner in which he had said it. She had allowed herself to indulge in a dream, which had had naught but pleasure in it until the Princess had looked into her eyes in so strange a fashion; and now that she had sought the truth from Ellerey himself, she was still left in doubt, in a half-waking uncertainty, which had a sense of pain in it.

It was some time before the thought that Ellerey was with the Queen came uppermost in her mind, urging her to be on the alert. She was in the act of rising when a shadow fell upon her, and Lord Cloverton stood in the entrance.

"Alone, Countess!" he exclaimed. "What great event has happened in Sturatzberg?"

"None that I am aware of, my lord."

"And yet you are alone. It is so rare a circumstance that you must pardon my astonishment."

"Even such a frivolous person as I am welcomes solitude sometimes," she answered.

"I would not allow my dearest friend to so malign you, Countess," said the Ambassador, seating himself beside her. "I expected to find Captain Ellerey with you."

"You wish to speak with him?"

"Yes, but it can wait," answered Lord Cloverton carelessly. "Success is the result of skilfully seizing opportunities, and in finding you alone an opportunity comes to me. Will you spare me a moment?"

She bowed a smiling acquiescence as though the question were unnecessary.

"Like me, Countess, I am sure you take little interest in uninteresting people, therefore you must have found this Captain Ellerey interesting. So have I--so interesting, indeed, that I have wondered why he came to Wallaria."

"He has not given me so much of his confidence as you appear to imagine, my lord."

"He has not told you! Ah, then I will, in confidence, Countess, in confidence."

"I understand, and I shall respect it," she answered, eager to learn what explanation the Ambassador would give.

"He had enemies in England who made certain charges against him which were absolutely without foundation; but so skilfully had they been manipulated that Captain Ellerey was unable to prove them false. His nature is an impatient one, and in anger he turned his back upon England and came to Sturatzberg. In Wallaria there were possibilities. I can understand his action, Countess; it was a natural one in a man of his independent character, but it was foolish. It gave credence to the tales which had been circulated. Now, Countess, influential friends have taken up his case, and he ought to go back to England."

"But why tell this to me, my lord?"

"A woman's persuasion, Countess, is all-powerful."

She looked at him quickly.

"But you have told me this in confidence. How can I approach the subject and yet keep confidence?"

"You flatter me most delicately by asking my advice on such a matter. Is it not true that a woman can frame her questions so that a man is compelled to answer?"

"Some men, perhaps."

"Captain Ellerey, I think," said the Ambassador.

"Under certain conditions."

"Exactly," he answered.

"When the questions are asked by one particular woman," she said.

"You have caught my meaning exactly, Countess."

"But as it happens, Lord Cloverton, I am not the one particular woman."

The Ambassador turned a smiling countenance toward her.

"My dear lady, you do yourself a gross injustice."

The look he expected to find in her face he did not see there. He had believed himself possessed of one secret. He suddenly perceived that he had possibly discovered another--one that might be even more certainly used to his own advantage, and he made haste to turn it to account.

"If I am mistaken," he said slowly, "Captain Ellerey sinks in my estimation as a stone in water. If I am wrong your displeasure should urge his return to England, for he is no fit cavalier for Countess Mavrodin. He would be a mere adventurer to whom every woman is a pleasant plaything--one whose honor is for barter to the highest bidder. Such men may well be advised to return to their native land."

"As I am not the one particular woman so am I not a plaything, my lord. Has your philosophy no position which a woman may occupy between the two?"

"In this case I think not."

"Such a small position as friendship, for instance," she said, rising. "Captain Ellerey and I are fast friends."

"I hardly know whether I can congratulate you," said Lord Cloverton, rising, too, and showing no sign of annoyance or recognition of defeat.

"You will pardon me, but I fear I may have been missed," and then as they passed into the ball-room he went on, "I will respect your confidence, but may I suggest that your knowledge of Captain Ellerey's affairs may be useful to him? Why not advise him yourself? At present he is with the Queen; when I see him again I will tell him that you wish to speak to him."

"I have already given him my advice, Countess. I thought to do him a service by sending him a more powerful advocate." And the Ambassador left her and went quickly toward the vestibule. As she turned, Monsieur De Froilette bowed low to her; he too was hastening toward the vestibule.

When Desmond Ellerey had followed the messenger across the ball-room, his guide suddenly paused and said in a low tone:

"Her Majesty is in her private apartment, and I am instructed to take you there.

Will you come with me this way?"

He turned from the ballroom and led Ellerey along a corridor and through a door, which he locked after him. They passed up one corridor and down another for a little distance, and then ushering him into an ante-room, his guide left him there while he went to inform the Queen of his arrival. In a few moments he returned, and, holding open a door, bid him enter.

The Queen was alone, seated by a table at which she had been writing. Ellerey approached her and bent over her hand.

"The time has come, Captain Ellerey," she said. "You are ready?"

"I am only waiting your Majesty's commands."

"You have been sent once or twice, Captain Ellerey, to dislodge a certain brig-and called Vasilici from his fastnesses in the mountains, and have experienced dis-appointment perhaps in not finding him."

"That is so, your Majesty."

"It was never intended that you should find him," she answered. "For months past loyal subjects have been gathering in the mountains with Vasilici, waiting for our word to revolt against the thraldom this country is under to foreign nations. In the future it is for us to dictate, not to obey. His Majesty, watched as he is, cannot act freely, so the duty devolves on me. It is for you to proclaim that we in Sturatz-berg are ready, by carrying a token to Vasilici, which I will give you, and which you must guard with your life, Captain Ellerey. The mission with which you are intrusted is a hazardous one. Faction is rife in the country, and spies lurk in every corner of it. Even now there may be some setting out upon the road to bar your way to Vasilici. But for the trusted bearer of this token await high honor and great reward."

"Even for a foreigner?" asked Ellerey.

"You are no more one, Captain Ellerey. This is the land of your adoption, and by this service are you not proving yourself a worthy son?"

"Your Majesty commands. I am content to trust to your Majesty for my reward; but one thing troubles me."

"What is that?"

"The revolution--for such it must be--will heat men's blood against the for-eigner. May I ask consideration for Lord Cloverton and his staff at the British Embassy?"

"You have our word that no harm shall come to them. We are not fighting Embassies, but the riff-raff which has come into our land--the adventurers who bear themselves as though they were our masters. We have been under an iron flail from the palace to the hovel. It is against this subjection that we rebel. You are prepared to fight and win with us."

"I am waiting for the token, your Majesty."

"I love a man of few words," she said; "and as surely as success will come, I pledge my word that the ribbon of the Golden Lion of Sturatzberg shall be yours, Captain Ellerey, and with it revenue sufficient to bear it fittingly. This is the token," she went on, baring her arm, on which, just above the elbow, was a bracelet of iron, a chain joining together four medallions. "It is an ancient treasure of Wallaria, worn, it is said, by savage kings in this country before ever the Romans had trampled it with their all-conquering legions. I will seal it in this box, which you must guard with your life and bear to Vasilici. Seeing it, he will welcome you as he would ourself. With him return triumphantly to Sturatzberg, and if a rabble of rebellious soldiery, led away by traitors who are among us, stand in your way, I can trust Captain Ellerey's sword to cut a path through it. Will you unclasp the bracelet for me? the fastening is difficult."

As she held out her arm the door opened, and the servant who had fetched Ellerey entered.

"Monsieur De Froilette, your Majesty, has just informed me that his Majesty is on his way here."

For one moment the Queen stood undecided.

"Do not unfasten it, Captain Ellerey," she said, laying a detaining hand upon his. "To-morrow, some time before midnight, it shall be sent to you. Not to your lodging, that might be dangerous. Wait for it at the Toison d'Or. It is an inn of no repute in the Bergenstrasse, which runs toward the Southern Gate. This same messenger who came to you to-night shall bring it, sealed as I have said. Then make all speed to Vasilici, who lies in the neighborhood of the Drekner Pass. Now go. Quickly. He will show you the way."

It was by a different way they returned.

"The Toison d'Or about midnight," said his guide as he stood to open a door, "and monsieur would do well to leave his lodging by the Western Gate as soon as he has prepared for the journey. This passage will take monsieur to the vestibule."

As he went toward the staircase, determined to leave the palace at once, Ellerey saw Baron Petrescu leaning against the marble balustrade talking to one of his companions. There were certain men at Court who appeared to follow the Baron like his shadow. He was watching all those who left the palace as carefully as on a former occasion he had scrutinized all those who entered it, and again Ellerey's appearance seemed to release him from his labors. With a whispered word to his companion he moved hastily among the people who were crossing to the stairs, and contriving to jostle Ellerey, came to a standstill directly in front of him.

"I am waiting, monsieur," he said.

"For what?"

"Your apology."

"You jest with me. I have none to make."

"Monsieur is slow to appreciate," said the Baron, with a curl of his lip. "He forgets that he has stared most insufferably at me on many occasions, and that now he attempts to bar my progress."

"I appreciate that you wish to quarrel with me," Ellerey answered bluntly, "but I am in no mood for quarrelling. Will monsieur oblige by standing out of my way, or must I be at the trouble of throwing him down the stairs?"

The answer came quickly and was to the point. With a sudden sweep of his arm Baron Petrescu struck Ellerey sharply across the face with his glove.

Perhaps there was something in Ellerey's expression which made the Baron's companion step hastily to his side. Experience may have taught him that Englishmen have a strange habit of punishing such insults on the spot with a total disregard of all formalities. Perhaps it was his action which prevented Ellerey carrying out his intention. He drew himself up to his full height, the air whistling through his clenched teeth as he caught his breath, and then he bowed slightly to the Baron, who turned away, leaving his companion to settle the matter.

"Monsieur will give me the name of a friend, so that we may arrange for this affair to-morrow."

"Why not to-night? I never sleep upon my quarrels."

"Impossible, monsieur."

"Is not the choice with me?"

"Certainly, but--"

"Then I say to-night," Ellerey answered. "There was a moon when I entered the palace."

The man shrugged his shoulders, disgusted at the utter barbarity of these English-men.

"The name of your friend, then, monsieur?"

Ellerey was in a difficulty. He could think of no one to whom he was desirous of intrusting an affair of this kind. Before he could reply, however, he felt a touch upon his arm.

"Can I be of service?" The speaker was an Englishman and a stranger to him.

"You will be doing me a great favor, monsieur, and I thank you."

The stranger at once went aside with the Baron's friend, In a few minutes he returned.

"Come, Captain Ellerey. It is in half an hour's time." And with an assenting inclination of his head Ellerey went slowly down the stairs with his companion.

As he did so a woman came from a corner, and leaning over the balustrade, watched the descending figures. Her face was pale, and her lips trembled.

"I have sought you for my promised dance," said a voice behind her. "What is interesting the Countess so much?"

"I was thinking that the moon will be setting shortly," she answered absent-mindedly. "In an hour it will be dark or very nearly."

"Well, Countess, what can that matter?" said the Austrian *attache*.

She looked at him vaguely for a moment, thinking of the man who had just descended the stairs. Then she said with manifest effort and a faint smile as she laid her hand upon the *attache's* arm:

"No, indeed; what can it matter--to me?"

CHAPTER VIII.
THE IRON BRACELET

When Lord Cloverton left Frina Mavrodin he hurried to the vestibule and sent a message to the King, asking for an immediate and private audience, and De Froilette saw the Ambassador go to the King's private apartment soon afterward. De Froilette knew that this sudden audience could only relate to one of two matters--either Lord Cloverton had made some discovery respecting the Princess Maritza, or else he was aware that Ellerey was with the Queen and was about to make some move which would defeat any conspiracy which might be in progress. That the Ambassador had any idea of the real state of affairs, De Froilette did not believe. He did not go at once to warn the Queen. It was only as the King and the Minister were leaving the private apartments that he realized the danger.

Lord Cloverton was troubled. The various pieces of the puzzle which he had fitted into places to his satisfaction suddenly seemed inadequate to fill the places he had assigned to them. To-night he had discovered a depth in Frina Mavrodin the existence of which he had never suspected. She had fenced him with his own weapons in a manner he was little accustomed to, and he had signally failed to make use of her in the way he desired. True, she had told him that Ellerey was with the Queen, but she had mentioned it as a circumstance of small importance. Was it? Was the casual information meant to mislead him? This frivolous woman was beginning to take a new position in the Ambassador's calculations, and he began, almost unconsciously, to look for some large space in the intricate puzzle which she might possibly fill. He had imagined that love linked her to Desmond Ellerey, and he was apparently mistaken; it was only friendship, and such friendship might mean anything.

He spoke to Captain Ward, telling him to be particularly observant of Ellerey, and then went to the King. It was unusual with him, but for once he had not determined what course of action to take even when he entered the King's room.

"What important twist have affairs taken, my lord?" asked the King.

"It is to prevent any twist that I ventured to ask for this audience, your Majesty. I am forced to refer again to a subject which, on a former occasion, gave you some displeasure. You must pardon my importunity, since I believe the danger is imminent."

"I am all attention," the King answered, conscious of the slight embarrassment there was in Lord Cloverton's manner.

"As you are aware," the Ambassador went on slowly, "I have always considered many of the plots which from time to time become apparent in Sturatzberg of small importance. I have, on the other hand, consistently warned your Majesty of the danger which might at any time manifest itself in a sudden development of the tactics of the brigands in the mountains. Their chief, Vasilici, may be a chief only in name, and it is certain that during the past few months many have joined him who are not brigands in any sense of the word, and who, I conceive, are merely using this outlaw as a convenient cloak to their wider and more sinister intentions."

"Certainly you have always been an alarmist in this matter," said the King, with a smile. "Whatever their intentions may be, the fact remains that they have always fled at the approach of a handful of troops."

"Which is rather unnatural, it seems to me," Lord Cloverton answered quickly. "Whatever else he may lack, your brigand is not deficient in courage, and it must be remembered that the troops sent against these men have never succeeded in finding a trace of their spoils."

"Do you suggest that they have been warned of the expeditions sent against them?"

"I think it probable."

"By whom, my lord?"

"We might laugh at the danger, your Majesty, could I answer that question," replied the Ambassador. "It must be remembered that there are many in Sturatzberg who, while personally loyal to you, are not satisfied with your foreign policy; who believe that Wallaria is too much under the direction of the greater European

Powers, and would help you to emancipation in spite of yourself."

"A judgment which is the outcome of ignorance, Lord Cloverton."

"I think so, but it is not reasonable to suppose that they do," returned the Ambassador. "Such a feeling is prevalent in all grades of society in Sturatzberg, from her Majesty Queen Elena, down to the beggars in the Altstrasse."

"The Queen, my lord!" exclaimed the King sharply.

"I do not speak hastily, your Majesty, Queen Elena has all those attributes which go to make a great ruler. She has courage, diplomacy, tact, and deep in her heart lies a living, beating interest in her country's welfare."

"Such praise seems merely the mask for an accusation, my lord. I must request you to be more explicit."

"To be so, your Majesty, was my reason for asking for this interview. I humbly protest, however, that I make no accusation in the ordinary sense of the word. Her Majesty's conception of her country's welfare is, I venture to think, an erroneous one, although I imagine her desire is only to help forward a policy which she believes is near to your heart."

"Enough, Lord Cloverton, let us get to the root of the matter quickly. Our absence will be remarked and occasion comment."

The King spoke irritably, and the Ambassador felt the delicacy and difficulty of the position. He was not quite sure of his ground. He was rather in the position of one who draws a bow at a venture, and yet he had a shrewd suspicion in which direction the mark lay. Of one thing he was certain--the danger; and he felt justified in taking any risk for the purpose of preventing trouble.

"To-night the Queen has given a special audience to a countryman of mine, a Captain Desmond Ellerey in your Majesty's service," said the Ambassador, speaking quietly and concisely. "This Captain Ellerey is a man of courage and resource, in a way an adventurer, prepared for any hazardous enterprise if he is once convinced that it is in the service of his adopted country. I believe the Queen intends to send him upon some secret mission which, although she may be ignorant of the fact, will militate against your Majesty, and against your peaceful policy."

"An accusation of treason!" exclaimed the King. "You go too far, my lord."

"I make no such accusation; I only fear an act which may lead to treason in others, and seek to prevent it."

"Why not question Captain Ellerey?"

"I have done so, but to no purpose."

"I will question him," said the King. "Why not question her Majesty?" Lord Cloverton suggested. "Captain Ellerey is with her at this moment."

"You shall go with me, Lord Cloverton," said the King. "Since you have such suspicions it is no time for secret questionings. Her Majesty shall hear your accusation and shall answer it."

The Ambassador bowed. The King's decision pleased him. If he had not succeeded in raising the King's suspicion, he had raised his anger, which would serve the same purpose, and Lord Cloverton still held the trump card in his hand.

The moment Ellerey had left her, the Queen glanced hastily around the room. She slipped the box she had shown him underneath some papers in her drawer, and then with a smile reseated herself, and, drawing paper toward her, she rapidly began to write a note to Frina Mavrodin.

She rose quickly with a little gesture of surprise when the King and the English Ambassador were announced. The King strode into the room, anger still in his face, but Lord Cloverton came to a halt near the door.

"Your Majesty is welcome," said the Queen, "but you look troubled. I fear I spend too little time helping to share your Majesty's difficulties."

"To defeat intrigues is my hourly occupation, Elena, but there are some intrigues, or whispers of them, which call for special treatment; they are not to be met by counterplot, but by open speech and outspoken denial."

"Am I accused?" the Queen asked.

"Lord Cloverton has seen fit to warn me."

"Of what?" she asked innocently, looking toward the Ambassador.

The King hesitated for a moment, almost as though he wished Lord Cloverton would speak. "To-night you have received Captain Ellerey in private audience," he said after a moment's pause.

"I have."

"May I know for what purpose?"

The Queen looked first at her husband, then at the Ambassador, her glance lingering on the latter for a moment.

"I cannot tell you why," she answered slowly. "It was a matter of no great importance, but it was essentially private. I would be unfair to Captain Ellerey to speak of it."

It may have been the flicker of triumph upon the Ambassador's face which urged the King on.

"We expected to find Captain Ellerey still with you."

"The audience was a short one," was the answer.

"I am afraid I must demand to know its purport," said the King. "I do so in your own interests."

"You wish me to deny some accusation Lord Cloverton has made against me. I tremble lest I may be unable to do so. Of what frivolity do I stand accused?" and she smiled at the Ambassador with an innocent expression on her face pleading for lenient judgment.

"Of no frivolity," said the King. "Lord Cloverton has suggested that you have despatched this Captain Ellerey upon some secret mission to the enemies of our country, seeking to do us a service, but in truth jeopardizing our policy of peace, perchance our throne. In substance, my lord, that is your accusation, I think?"

"That is so," returned the Ambassador.

"To what enemies?" asked the Queen, after a pause.

"Is there any need to particularize?" said the King irritably. "The accusation is either true or false."

"It is false."

The denial was quietly spoken, but an angry flush glowed in her cheeks. "By your Majesty's leave, such an accusation should be definite, and again I ask, what enemies?"

"I will be definite," said Lord Cloverton. "Doubtless you have not considered well--"

"Be direct, too, my lord; what enemies?"

"I will. I mean those enemies who are in communication with the traitors who have joined the brigand Vasilici in the mountains."

"You accuse me of holding communication with these men?"

"Your Majesty must pardon my bluntness, I do."

"You are pardoned, and thanked also," she said lightly. "Such bluntness comes more directly at the heart of the matter than much diplomacy, and is more easily answered. I deny the charge." And then, turning to the King, she went on: "For my own protection I am constrained to tell you the purpose of Captain Ellerey's visit to me. He has quickly received the favor of one of the ladies of our Court, a favor for which I am in some measure responsible. When Captain Ellerey first came among us, he furnished us with subject for jesting by declaring that no woman had ever played a serious part in his life. I expressed a belief that such a statement would rouse feminine enthusiasm in Sturatzberg, and I have since often questioned him whether he could truthfully repeat the declaration. It was a jest, but seriousness has come of it. Captain Ellerey's ambition has flown high, even to the Countess Mavrodin. Such an ambition must bring him bitter enemies, in numbers like leaves in autumn; and if to-night I have persuaded him against soaring so high, if I have made Frina Mavrodin's position in Sturatzberg plainer to him and endeavored privately to warn him against such an ambition, have I done aught to pander to my country's enemies or to jeopardize your Majesty's throne?" The question was asked in such a manner as to make the King laugh.

"No, but by my faith, your interference may have jeopardized the lady's happiness. Is she to have no voice in the matter?"

"I fear she is somewhat fascinated by Captain Ellerey," said the Queen with a smile, "but such a thing as marriage is not to be thought of. Think of it. Frina Mavrodin and a Captain of Horse! You English place no limits to your ambition," she added, turning to Lord Cloverton.

"Love leaps over all obstacles," said the King.

But her Majesty was ready with arguments to prove that the affair was no laughing matter. She even suggested that such a marriage might have a political significance, might lead to complications which would have serious consequences, even to some revolution such as Lord Cloverton had accused her of fostering. It was no laughing matter as his Majesty would make it, and her interference was not unnecessary, but intended to serve the State. Even were Captain Ellerey to rise to great distinction, she argued, such an alliance would still be fraught with danger. The Countess Mavrodin with her wealth, with her prestige, and her close connection with the noblest houses in Sturatzberg, was not for a soldier of fortune, as, at the best, Captain Ellerey was. She became eloquent upon the subject, and the King watched the Ambassador, a smile upon his lips, in anticipation of his discomfiture.

"I had already begun a letter to the Countess," said the Queen, taking up the paper on which she had written a few lines. "I want to show her plainly the impossibility of such a thing. Are you satisfied, Lord Cloverton?"

The Ambassador had remained standing by the door and had not taken his eyes from the Queen as she talked rapidly. There was no tell-tale expression on his face to indicate his thoughts. Now he advanced.

"Your Majesty thinks then that this folly, so far as the Countess Mavrodin is concerned, is a serious matter?"

"I want to find out."

"If I am any judge, it is," said Lord Cloverton, "more serious with the lady than with the man. Her words went far to confirm my ideas respecting Captain Ellerey, her manner betrayed her own secret."

"You have spoken to her!"

"Yes, only to-night. Your Majesty exaggerates the political significance of such a marriage, I feel sure; it would make enemies for Captain Ellerey, no doubt, but he is the kind of man who is very capable of defending himself. A greatly daring Englishmen is an awkward man to encounter, and there seems to be a general desire to enlist the sympathy of Desmond Ellerey. That has made me suspicious, and using some knowledge which I possess concerning him, I have endeavored to make him apply for leave to return to England."

"To save him from the Countess?" said the Queen.

"No, your Majesty; to prevent his being drawn into a plot which seeks to overthrow the present government of this country."

"Is there such a plot?" she asked innocently.

"A dozen have existed ever since I came to the throne," said the King. The Ambassador's persistency made him angry.

"Hiding themselves in holes like hunted vermin," Lord Cloverton returned sharply, "afraid to strike, afraid to be seen, with no plan of action ready, and altogether futile. I do not speak of such plots as these, but of one particular plot, whose ramifications spread and grow from end to end of Wallaria, penetrating to the very heart of the nation as surely as tree roots push their way to water. The head of it looks up watchfully from the hidden intrenchments on the mountains at intervals, waiting for the moment to strike. Anxiously is it waiting now."

"For what?" cried the King. "In heaven's name, for what, Lord Cloverton?"

"For the token her Majesty delivered to Captain Ellerey to-night."

A profound silence followed this deliberate accusation. So unflinchingly was it made, so evident was it that the Ambassador had some knowledge which he had not divulged, that the King found no words to utter. He looked helplessly at the Queen like a man who has received a blow which has dazed him for the time being. The Ambassador's knowledge startled the Queen, too, but she did not shrink before his steady scrutiny. She was the first to break the silence.

"I gave no such token," she said.

Lord Cloverton started slightly at being given the lie so directly. What subterfuge was a woman not capable of?

"You have your answer, my lord," said the King, moving toward his wife.

The Ambassador bowed. He could hardly pursue the matter further unless the King assisted him, and he turned to leave the room.

"You are not satisfied?" said the King sternly.

"No, your Majesty."

"What proof can you have? What was the token?"

Lord Cloverton turned quickly. It was the very question he had hoped for.

"A sacred treasure of Sturatzberg, the iron bracelet her Majesty is accustomed to wear upon her arm." Again there was silence, and, set as his face was, the mask was insufficient to hide the Ambassador's excitement. The Queen stood for a moment quite conscious of the dramatic effect of the silent pause, and then she made three rapid strides toward the Ambassador. With a sudden sweep of her right hand she ripped open the left sleeve of her gown from wrist to shoulder and thrust out her arm to him.

"I demand your apology, Lord Cloverton."

She stood imperiously before him, looking down at him. Fire was in her eyes, an angry flush upon her cheeks, triumph in look and gesture. It would have gone hard with any subject who had dared to accuse her. The Ambassador was obliged to murmur his apology, for, tightly clasped upon the gleaming white and rounded arm, was the bracelet of iron.

CHAPTER IX.
THE DUEL

The aspect of the night had changed when Ellerey and his companion left the palace. Fleecy clouds raced across the sky, veiling the face of the moon at intervals, and making her light fitful and uncertain. The air struck cold after the warmth within, but beyond drawing his cloak a little closer round him, Desmond Ellerey seemed indifferent to the night and to the business he had in hand.

He asked no questions, and with his eyes bent on the ground followed his companion mechanically. The cause of the quarrel interested him more than the issue of it. Why had Baron Petrescu drawn him into this duel? It had obviously been carefully planned, and the insult deliberately given at a moment when Ellerey was least desirous of placing his life in jeopardy. He could only assume that her Majesty's schemes were, to some extent at least, known to the Baron, and that having other interests to serve, he was bent on incapacitating him from performing the mission he had undertaken. That the Baron had any personal quarrel with him he did not believe.

Ellerey's companion, on the other hand, was interested in the night. Each time the moonlight grew pale, or died out altogether for a moment, he looked at the sky and glanced quickly at Ellerey. He was the more excited of the two.

"This is a treacherous light for our work," he said, presently. "We should have been wiser to have waited until morning."

"I have other work for the morning," Ellerey answered.

"Are you a skilful swordsman? The Baron is."

"Is he?" said Ellerey, indifferently. "I have some reputation in my regiment, but doubtless I shall be a better judge of my skill presently. Where do we go?"

"To tell the truth, I hardly like the rendezvous," was the answer. "It is a stretch of sward behind an obscure tavern in this part of the town. Did I not know the Baron to be an honorable man, I should have refused the meeting in such a place. Your decision to fight to-night made our choice limited."

Ellerey stopped and looked about him. They had turned from a side street into a narrow thoroughfare with tall, dark houses on either side. The neighborhood looked particularly uninviting.

"Where are we?" he asked suddenly, remembering that he knew nothing of his companion, and that by accepting the service he had so readily offered he might be quietly stepping into a trap. Such a thing would agree very well with the rest of Baron Petrescu's behavior.

"Beyond knowing that we are in the purlieus of a lower part of the town and on the outskirts of the city, I am as puzzled as you are."

"You seem very credulous of the Baron's honesty, monsieur, to agree so such a place as this. Which way now?"

"To the bottom of this street, where we are to wait. The Baron's friend will meet us there."

"We will keep the appointment so far," said Ellerey shortly. "I came to meet Baron Petrescu, but I am not minded to step blindly into a nest of cut-throats." He strode on as alert now as he had been indifferent before, and it was not until they had nearly reached the end of the street that his companion spoke.

"One moment," he said. "By that light yonder we are to wait. You do not trust me, Captain Ellerey?"

"I have not said so."

"That admits my statement," was the answer. "Until a moment ago that aspect of the case had not presented itself to me, but on reflection I can hardly wonder at your distrust. The circumstances tell against me, but had I been in any conspiracy against you, I should hardly have called your attention to the strangeness of the rendezvous. I have, however, a better guarantee of my honesty: I am a countryman of yours, an Englishman. I like this affair as little as you do; but if you are minded to see it through, I have a sword and the will to fight beside you should there be any attempt at treachery. There's my hand upon it."

It was not the words, but the manner in which they were spoken that convinced Ellerey, and he took the hand held out to him.

"Forgive my momentary suspicion," he said. "We meet by the light yonder, you say."

The light came from a dim lamp in an upper window. It might have been placed there as a signal, or some poor seamstress, in the struggle for a livelihood, might be ruining her health and sight by it. It must, at any rate, have been very constantly there, or it would not so readily have been mentioned to mark a place of meeting. As they went toward it, the figures of two men became dimly visible standing in the shadow of the wall. One advanced to meet them, and addressed himself to Ellerey's companion.

"I much regret this unusual mode of procedure, but it is unavoidable under the circumstances and in view of your friend's decision to fight to-night. May I request that you will follow us in silence?"

The other man moved from the shadow. It was Baron Petrescu; and going to the house which was next to that in which the lamp shone, he knocked twice at the door in a peculiar manner which was evidently a known summons to those within. Some considerable time elapsed before the summons was answered, but the Baron showed no impatience, and this manifest knowledge of the ways of the establishment did not inspire Ellerey with confidence. Once within, murder and concealment of the crime might be easy. Who was there in all Sturatzberg to know that he had ever entered this house? And how many were there in the wide world to care whether he ever left it?

Presently the door opened a little space, and a shaggy head was thrust out in a truculent manner. Whether the Baron spoke to him, or whether the man recognized his visitor, Ellerey could not determine, but the door was opened wide, and they were admitted into a small, ill-lighted lobby. The entrance was a private one, not a usual *cafe* entrance, but the smell of stale liquor and smoke and the reek of highly spiced dishes proved that the *cafe* was under the same roof, and proclaimed it as a resort of that lower stratum of society which loves its food pungent and highly flavored. That there was such silence in the house was surprising.

"A private visit, Theodor," said the Baron. "We do not join the assembly to-night. Reassure them, and let us have a word with you."

Theodor opened one of the folding-doors in the lobby, and in a stentorian voice shouted some word, which Ellerey did not catch. Its effect was magical. Immediately there arose a loud hum of voices, the clinking and clatter of innumerable glasses and plates, and the rattle of dice and dominoes. Then Theodor let the door swing to again, muffling the sounds of this living hive, and led the way into a small bare room at the side.

The Baron's companion now became the spokesman.

"We have a little matter to settle, Theodor, a private quarrel which does concern the good fellows yonder, and of which they must know nothing. The grass alley in the garden will serve our purpose. Let us out quietly, and have a care that no one wanders that way to cool an aching head until we have departed."

Theodor looked from the speaker to his companions, each in turn, and Ellerey keenly watched the man's eyes to note if any look of understanding were exchanged. He could detect none.

"Of course, of course, it is a good spot for such matter, but if one is killed?"

"Well, Theodor, there is earth enough in the garden for burial."

Theodor shrugged his shoulders.

"And you will call none to help you with that work?"

"No. Have I not said that the matter is private?"

"And there is no surgeon."

"I have sufficient skill for that," was the answer. "Come, Theodor, time presses, and the moon will not serve us long."

"Is it in the cause?"

"No," said Baron Petrescu, sharply, as though he were afraid some different answer would be given, but Ellerey could not help believing that the cause, whatever it might be, was at the bottom of the whole affair, that the Baron had designedly insulted him that evening because of it, and that his speedy removal was considered necessary to the well-being of it. Theodor did not seem to believe the Baron's statement either, but it was apparent that either he had not the power or the desire to oppose the Baron, for he answered quickly:

"I see. Will an hour be enough?"

"More than enough."

"Good. Then in one hour I will walk through the garden, and shall find it empty. I shall know that anyone with an aching head is free to cool it there, and if there be a grave to trample on, what matter? No one will know."

Without further words he led the way down a narrow passage, at the end of which he quietly unbarred a door.

"Three steps down," he said by way of caution, as he stood aside to let them pass. He watched them until their figures were lost in the shadows of the garden, and then he closed and barred the door again.

It was a garden of some extent, and little heaps of chairs and small three-legged tables showed that on warm nights the frequenters of the cafe drank their wine and threw their dice there instead of within. The lights in the house--the cafe seemed to occupy only the back of it--shone through the shrubberies, and the murmur and clatter were plainly audible as the four men crossed the lawn and went toward the end of the garden along tortuous paths which made the really short distance seem a long one.

At last they came out on to a level piece of turf surrounded on all sides by high hedges, through which were many openings leading to other parts of the garden, and through one of which they had come. There were trees here and there, the long shadows thrown across the turf, and without absolutely obscuring the moonlight, they made it extremely difficult to fight a duel by. Baron Petrescu walked to one end of the lawn, and Ellerey to the other, leaving the two seconds together to make final arrangements. Once convinced that his adversary contemplated no treachery, Ellerey sank again into his indifferent state, paying no attention to the choosing of the ground, taking no note of the light, nor considering how he might best use his position to the full advantage. The Baron, on the other hand, was quick to observe exactly how the shadows fell, and to calculate every chance which might help him.

"We are ready, Captain Ellerey."

Without a word Ellerey threw off his cloak and coat, and taking his sword, weighed it in his hand, testing its poise and balance.

"In case of accident is there anything you wish me to do?" asked his companion; "anything to take charge of, any message to send? The affair has been so hurried that there has been no time to make these small arrangements."

"Thank you, there is nothing," Ellerey answered. "Under the circumstances I am fortunate in not possessing a friend in the world who cares a snap of his fingers whether I am living or dead."

"Nor a woman?"

Ellerey hesitated for a moment.

"The Countess Mavrodin might be interested to learn that I was dead. Yes, if anything should happen, please tell her."

"But in England?"

"There is no one," Ellerey answered.

A cloud passed over the moon as the combatants faced each other, and not until it had passed was the signal given. Then steel rang on steel with a music which sounded weirdly in the night. No other sound was there save a rustling in the leaves now and again as though they trembled in sympathy to some swift lunge or quickly parried thrust. The moon shone clearly for a space, touching the swords into two streaks of flashing light, and painting the men's set faces with a cold hue, ghostly, and deathlike. The Baron had a reputation as a swordsman, had stood face to face with an antagonist many times before, and more than once had seen his adversary turn sightless eyes to the morning sky. It was therefore, perhaps, only natural that he should have contemplated his encounter with the Englishman with equanimity. At the same time Ellerey's determination to settle the quarrel at once and by moonlight may have had the effect of making him more cautious than usual. Certainly his second, who had often seen him fight before, marvelled at his deliberation to-night. The well-known brilliancy of his attacks was wanting, and he could only suppose that the Englishman was a more worthy swordsman than he had imagined. Whatever deliberation the Baron used, he at first pressed the fight far more than Ellerey, whose whole attention seemed occupied in defending himself. He was less attractive to watch than the Baron, slower, it seemed, in his movements, and with less invention and resource, yet Petrescu appeared to gain no advantage. Every thrust he made was parried, if rather late sometimes, still parried, and he found that his adversary's wrist, if less flexible than his own, was of iron. He changed his tactics, he pressed the fight less and less, hoping to make the Englishman careless, and tempt him to attack more vigorously. In a measure the device succeeded. Ellerey's point began to flash toward him with a persistency he had not expected, but there was no less caution. Twice, thrice, the Baron used a feint and thrust which had seldom missed their intention, and had proved the undoing of many an adversary; but now they were met in the only manner it seemed that they could be met successfully. At the third failure the Baron's computation of the Englishman's skill underwent a rapid change. He had met his match, a foeman worthy of his steel, as consummate a swordsman as himself; and if for a moment there was a sense of disappointment, it was quickly followed by one of keen satisfaction not unmingled with a feeling of friendship for his antagonist. There was that in Baron Petrescu which he had received no credit for, even from his friends. What contempt he had had for Ellerey disappeared, and a desire to win for the mere sake of winning took possession of him. All the thoughts which had prompted him to this duel were forgotten; he was no longer intent on killing his adversary. Now to verify his superiority and to prove it to this worthy foeman was his ambition, and it was in this spirit he pressed the contest with increased energy. The night became full of eyes for him, eager eyes, watchful of his skill, and hushed in the silence a thousand voices seemed ready to proclaim his victory.

There was no such complication of thoughts in Ellerey's mind. The Baron had grossly insulted him, had forced this quarrel upon him, and he meant to punish him if he could. Whether he killed him or not was of small consequence so long as he thoroughly taught him a lesson.

Yet to him also the night had eyes, and the air a feeling of movement in it, stealthy movement that walked on tiptoe and held its breath. The steel sang, now high, now low, distinct sounds and continuous. The breeze rustled the leaves then and again, but something else was stirring in the night, now behind him, now to his right, just where the high hedges enclosed the lawn. Once he heard it like the rustle of some startled animal among the dried and fallen leaves, and again he heard it, less distinct perhaps but more pervading, as when a crowd waits spellbound.

The Baron's attack grew fiercer again; twice he nearly broke through Ellerey's defence just when the sounds were audible in his ears. The Baron's most dangerous thrusts, and the coming of the sounds seemed to synchronise, as though there were a connection between them, as though they were parts of some whole. Ellerey almost expected to read a solution of the mystery in his opponent's eyes, which glittered in his pale, moonlit face. But the solution was not in the Baron's eyes--it was behind him. For one instant Ellerey glanced over the Baron's shoulder to the thick-set hedge beyond, and in an alley there the moonlight fell for a moment upon a pale face thrust forward a little too eagerly. The night was alive with eyes.

"It is treachery, then, after all!" Ellerey burst out suddenly, and as he spoke he used the Baron's own particular feint and thrust, and his sword point ran swiftly and smoothly into soft flesh.

With a low cry his adversary staggered back and fell, and in that moment the night was full of voices, too. Men rushed with angry cries and gesticulations from every alley of the garden, some to this side, some to that, to surround the little party. In an instant the seconds had drawn their swords and were beside Ellerey.

"Back, you fools!" came faintly from the wounded man, but the eager crowd did not heed, even if they heard, him as they rushed to the attack in overwhelming numbers.

"On my oath, Captain Ellerey, this is no work of mine," said the Baron, attempting to stagger to his feet, but falling to the ground again.

His second, too, shouted to the crowd, using the Baron's name to enforce his words, but he might as well have shrieked forbiddance to the incoming tide. The mad crowd rushed upon the three men from all sides, and although the flashing swords kept them back for a few moments, and harsh cries told that one blade or another had done its work, it was certain that only in flight was their safety against such odds.

As one ruffian staggered back with a yell of pain from the point of Ellerey's sword, the Baron's second whispered in his ear:

"Make for the alley just in front of you, to the left, to the right and then to the right again. There is a door in the high wall of the garden. You are safe if you can reach it. It is you they want, they will not harm the Baron. Rush for it. I will keep them off as long as I can."

Ellerey whispered the same instructions to his second, and then, waiting until the crowd had fallen back for a moment, he suddenly rushed forward, using his sword and his clenched fist to force himself a passage. The crowd was taken by surprise, and a cloud hiding the moon at that moment was in Ellerey's favor. Before they understood his intention he had reached the alley.

"To the right, then left, then right!" he shouted to his companion, who was running swiftly at his heels.

"To the door!" rose the shout behind him, and the whole garden was full of rushing feet.

Ellerey gave a cry of triumph as he caught the latch of the door and pulled it open, half turning to his companion as he did so. Had he been an instant later that exultant cry would have been his last, for at that moment a dagger flashed down upon him, and only by a quick spring aside did he avoid the blow. The man who had followed him so closely was not his second.

Before his adversary could recover himself, he struck him full in the face with the hilt of his sword and sent him reeling back into the arms of the foremost of his companions. The next instant Ellerey had slammed the door behind him, and was in a narrow lane on the other side of the wall.

CHAPTER X.
THE FOLLY OF A SOLDIER

It was not until he had run some distance along the lane that Ellerey stopped to listen, and fully to realize that his companion was not beside him. There were no sounds of hurrying feet in pursuit. He could not have out-distanced his enemies so completely in so short a time; either they had come no farther than the door in the wall, or had turned in the opposite direction, perhaps following his companion.

With his sword still in his hand, held ready for deadly work at a moment's notice, he retraced his steps, his senses sharp set to detect the slightest sound or movement near him. Heavy clouds had engulfed the moon now, the darkness was extreme, and the silence of the night unbroken. He went forward carefully; the darkness might hold a legion of foes, and the silence be a trap to catch him. Ellerey found the door with difficulty, indeed by chance, for it was cunningly hidden. Whatever the danger, he must enter the garden again in search for his comrade. The door was shut, and as he felt along it from top to bottom, touching no latch nor handle, nor keyhole even, he realized that entrance that way was barred. The door only opened from within. He had stepped back to consider how, and at what point, he could best scale the wall, when a slight movement close beside him caused him to stand on the defensive in a moment.

"Is that you, Ellerey?"

"You got out, then? Thank heaven!"

"Yes; I didn't speak because I thought you were one of them, and just now I'm no match for a babe in arms."

He was leaning against the wall a few feet from the gate. Ellerey had supposed him farther off by the faintness of his voice.

"Are you hurt?"

"Nothing serious, I think, but I've had a good deal of blood let out of me. I should have occupied that grave in the garden for a certainty had it not been for the Baron's second, who stood over me when I fell, and, when the blackguards retreated from the door, put me outside. This wasn't the Baron's doing."

"Perhaps not," Ellerey answered. "Can you manage to walk?"

"Yes, if you'll let me hang on to you, and we don't have to go far. When I was put outside something was said about going to the left."

"We'll go to the left, then; but I haven't an idea where we are."

The wounded man was weaker than he imagined. Before they had gone fifty yards he began to reel, and even as he suggested that Ellerey should go on and get help, he fainted. Ellerey took him in his arms and carried him. His one idea was to get as far away from the scene of the night's adventure as possible, but his progress was slow. His comrade revived presently, but although he tried to walk again, the task was beyond him. So Ellerey carried him, resting at intervals, all through the night. As long as darkness lasted and they were on the outskirts of the city they were unlikely to be stopped and questioned, but with dawn it would be different. Ellerey was without his coat and cloak, there had been no time to seize them as he rushed from the garden, and he carried a grievously hurt man in his arms. The first peasant, trudging to his early toil, who caught sight of them would run and tell the news as he went. Such publicity was to be avoided at all costs, or there would be small chance of his being at the Toison d'Or, in the Bergenstrasse, to keep his appointment. Already a long, thin streak of gray showed low down in the east, and Ellerey pressed forward as quickly as possible to find an asylum. He passed the first scattered dwellings he came to, having no desire to knock up some sleepy peasant and have to combat his inquisitiveness, as well as his annoyance, at being so unceremoniously disturbed. Presently where two cross-roads met he espied a small habitation, from which a thin wreath of smoke was rising into the morning air, and decided to try his fortune here. He had set his burden down by the gate when an old woman came from the house with a pail going to a well in the garden for water.

"Good mother," Ellerey called out, "I would claim your hospitality."

The woman turned to look at him, then set down the pail and came to the gate.

"What is it? Defend us, there's blood on him!" she exclaimed, pointing at the prostrate man. "An attack in the night by some ruffians who would have murdered us, good mother. My comrade is wounded, you see. Will you give him rest here while I go into the city for help?"

"It is ill work assisting strangers," answered the woman.

"Look at me; is there not honesty in my face?"

"Aye, I quarrel not with your face, but there is that on your tongue which does not greatly please me."

"The accent of a foreigner?" asked Ellerey. "Shall I tell you a secret? The time is coming when you shall have little enough of such an accent through the length and breadth of the land."

"For such a prophecy you are welcome," she answered, opening the gate. "You may come in."

Ellerey carried his companion up the garden path, and with the help of the woman and her grandson, who stared in wonder at their coming, soon had him comfortably placed on a pallet in the little room.

"Send Dr. Goldberg to me," said his companion; "he lives close to the palace, and is a friend and discreet."

The mention of the name caused Ellerey to look closely at the man's face for a moment. He had been a true comrade, and Ellerey had given little thought to his identity; now he wondered, and a smile wrinkled the corners of his mouth.

His companion in safe keeping, Ellerey began actively to consider his own affairs. He knew Dr. Goldberg by reputation, but he had no desire to visit him just now. To invent a tale to satisfy the doctor would be difficult, and might well be left to the wounded man. He took up his companion's cloak--he could hardly go into the city as he was--and then left the room, beckoning the woman to follow him.

"I will send the doctor at once, good mother," he said, "and there is something to help my poor thanks. Can you give me a piece of paper and lend me a pencil?"

The golden coins clinking in her hand would have purchased a far greater service. The pencil and paper were brought, and Ellerey wrote rapidly for a few moments; then tore the paper in half. He folded each portion carefully, placing one in his pocket, the other he kept in his hand.

"If the lad would earn something, send him after me quickly," he said, and then he went up the garden path and took the road to the city.

In a few moments the boy overtook him.

"Do you know the palace, my lad?"

"Yes."

"To the right of it there is a large square."

"I know it," answered the boy; "the foreigners who hate us live there."

"I would curb that young tongue of yours, or you'll be using it squealing for mercy under the whip. Ask there for Dr. Goldberg's house, and give him this paper. Do you understand?"

The lad nodded.

"Run quickly then, and afterward come to me in the Grande Place. You know the statue of King Ferdinand there? I shall be beside it. Away with you. The quicker you do your errand, the greater your reward."

The lad needed no second bidding. He started off at a brisk trot, and Ellerey pursued his way to the city. The gates were open, and there were few abroad in the streets as yet; but the thought of the many hands which had sought to despatch him in the garden last night made Ellerey proceed with greater caution than he had ever exercised. Only a few in the dim light could have seen his face sufficiently to recognize him, but he drew the cloak up to his chin and concealed his face as much as possible. He avoided the larger thoroughfares, being undesirous of meeting any acquaintances; and in the smaller streets which he traversed he might at any moment come face to face with one of that crowd he had so recently escaped from. He went warily, therefore, looking for the slightest glance of recognition in the face of every man he met.

In the neighborhood of the Grande Place he lingered in a side street until he saw the lad approaching the statue, when he went to meet him.

"You delivered the letter?"

"Yes. I was asked who gave it me, and I said a man I did not know."

"That was true enough," Ellerey returned. "Here's for your trouble. Would you earn more?"

The boy's eyes glistened as his fingers closed on the silver. It was easy to buy faithful service in Sturatzberg so long as no one was near to offer a higher price for unfaithfulness. Ellerey judged that such a messenger as this lad would pass unchallenged and unnoticed.

"Take this to the Western Gate and ask for the lodging of a Captain called Ellerey. He has a servant named Stefan--give him the paper."

"He shall have it."

"There is double payment, then. Run, I shall know if your errand is quickly done, and woe-betide you if you loiter." And having watched the lad disappear, Ellerey went quickly down a side street, and by many turnings and doublings on his track, sought to escape any spy who might chance to be watching him.

At dawn Stefan stretched out his huge limbs upon the settle, and awoke with a heavy grunt. No matter how deep his potations on the previous evening, he always awoke early; not fresh, perhaps, that were too much to expect, but with his wits clear. Sitting up, he glanced round the room for signs of his master's return, and, seeing none, grunted again in wonder. A tankard was on the floor beside him, and he drank the flat remains from last night's measure with a wry face. Then he pushed open the door of his master's room and looked in.

"Empty!" he said, satisfied that his master had not entered without being heard. "Here's another street quarrel, maybe, and more torn clothes to sell to the rag-man."

Then Stefan made his morning toilet. It was a simple process. His ablutions were taken at irregular intervals, sometimes at long intervals, and this was not the time for them. He ran his fingers through his hair to take some of the tangle out of it, shook his great frame to force his clothes into comfortable position, tightened his loosened belt, and took off his boots. For a few moments he sat on the settle, his legs stretched out wide apart, then he drew his boots on again, and stamping himself firmly into them, was ready for whatever the day might bring forth.

The street was still silent and deserted as Stefan went to the door and looked to right and left. The neighborhood was one of the last in the city to stir itself. If Stefan felt any anxiety regarding his master, there was no expression in his face to mark it. He was stolid and imperturbable; would have remained so probably had Ellerey been carried up the street dead on a shutter. He grunted now and then, walked half a dozen paces from the door and back to circulate his blood, and then leaned with his shoulders against the wall as though he were a fixture there until desperate necessity moved him.

The boy, who turned quickly into the street, and then came along slowly, looking to this side and that, hardly appeared the kind of visitor necessary to move the soldier. Stefan looked at him because there was no one else in the street to look at; but he was little interested. As the lad came nearer, however, the soldier became aware that the sleepy street was beginning to rouse itself. The blind in a window of the house opposite was drawn aside for a moment, and a face looked out. The aspect of the morning seemed speedily to satisfy, for the blind quickly fell back into its place again. Without actually looking up, Stefan had seen those peering eyes, and curiously enough they had him interested in the lad, who suddenly stopped in front of him.

"Can you tell me where a Captain Ellerey lodges?"

"Were you told to go into a street and bawl for information like that until you found him?" asked the soldier gruffly.

"I spoke no louder than I always do," answered the boy.

"Then it's a hale pair of lungs you've got concealed in that body of yours. I'm nigh deaf with your shouting. Come within the doorway, my lad, and whisper. Perhaps I'll catch the meaning of your question when it does not drum through me like the cry of a drunken crowd of rioters."

Somewhat abashed, the boy did as he was told, and repeated his question in a lower tone.

"By a strange chance he lives in this selfsame house, but he's not abroad yet," said Stefan. "We do sometimes sleep, and our day doesn't begin at cock-crow."

"I don't want him," said the lad, "I want his servant, Stefan."

"By another strange chance he lives here, too. What do you want with him?"

"Is he abroad yet?"

"Aye, he never sleeps at all."

"I live too nigh the city for fairy-tales," said the boy. "Will you bring me to this same Stefan? I have a message for him."

"Don't bawl it, lad, whisper. He's of a delicate constitution, this Stefan--I know, for I am he."

The boy looked doubtful for a moment.

"Is that truth?"

"I like your caution," Stefan returned. "You'll succeed, whether you deal with men or women, though the women will bring out all your mettle, I warrant. Yes, truth, I am Stefan."

"I was to give this paper to you."

The soldier opened it and read it, not without some difficulty, it seemed.

"Who gave you this?"

"A man, I know no more of him."

"Good. Which way lies your home?"

"On the road toward Breslen."

"Good again. Get you home quickly, and look you, my lad, should any ask what errand you have been on this morning, be a fool and forget. If your memory's too good, it's like enough some friend of mine will be spoiling those fine lungs of yours. Hast ever heard a man try to shout with a sword thrust through him?"

"No, sir."

"I have," Stefan answered. "It's a fearsome sound, like a whisper bubbling up through water. I'd be sorry to hear it from you. Off with you."

Stefan watched the boy out of the street, then he went in, and striking a match, burnt the paper, scattering the charred fragments on the hearth.

"Here's news that's an excuse for wine," he said, pouring out a liberal draught into the tankard. "A man gets rusty as an old lock with waiting. This will grease the action somewhat."

"It's early hours for such refreshment," said a voice at the door.

Stefan winked one eye over the rim of the tankard at the intruder, but did not pause in his drinking until three parts of the liquid was gone. Then he drew the back of his hand across his beard and mustache and sighed with satisfaction. "Never too early to drink thanks for good tidings, Monsieur Francois."

The Frenchman, with a quick glance round the room, stepped in, a smile upon his lips. He had told his master more than once that this servant of Captain Ellerey's was a drunkard and a fool, and that little was to be got out of him because nothing was ever trusted to him.

"And what are the good tidings," he asked.

"You'll be laughing at me, because you don't understand my disease, Monsieur Francois. I hate women."

"Hate them! *Ma foi*! Then is your disease very lamentable."

"Well, there it is--I hate them," said Stefan, "but there was one woman who would not hate me, do what I would. She was a bonny wench, so far as I am a judge, of bigger girth than most you meet, and with an arm of muscle to appeal to a soldier like me. At the street corner she'd wait awhile to see me pass, and she'd remark on the cut of my features and the stalwart looks of these legs of mine. I took no notice, but her love was proof against a trifle of that kind. She'd 'make a husband of me some day,' she said, and those that heard her told me the saying. There's a vein of superstition in my composition, and for months past I've been expecting her to keep her word. When a woman's set upon a matter, where's the hole a man may find safety in? Tell me that, Monsieur Francois."

The Frenchman shrugged his shoulders, thinking what a fool his companion was.

"This morning there comes a lad looking up and down the street to find me, and he says to me, 'Where lives Stefan, he who is servant to that Captain Ellerey we hear so much about?' And I answers cunningly, knowing the value of caution in such times as these. At last I admit that I am, and he says, 'There's a fat woman'--that's what he called her, Monsieur Francois--'There's a fat woman you're afraid of because she's going to marry you.' I sweated from every hole in my skin, thinking the time had come. Then says he: 'You needn't be afraid any more. She was married yesterday to a timber-cutter from Breslen way, and he'll tame her fast enough like you might a hungry sparrow in winter time.' Good tidings, Monsieur Francois, believe me, though I doubt the taming and pity the woodcutter. Why, the muscles in her arm wouldn't blush to be seen by the side of mine, and a woodcutter would have to cut deep into the forest before muscles stood out like these." And with a great laugh Stefan bared his brawny arms for the Frenchman's inspection.

"Very beautiful," said Francois.

"I believe you. Too good to waste in fondling a woman. Ugh! What brings you so early to the Western Gate?"

"I have a message for the Captain."

"Ah, from Monsieur De Froilette?"

"I only carry messages for my master."

"I'll deliver it. Tell me quickly, and you shall taste a drop of real Burgundy, to keep the morning air out of your return journey."

"I was to tell it to the Captain personally."

"What!" thundered Stefan, "am I not to be trusted, then?"

"You know the value of caution in these times," said Francois, "you spoke of it just now. Monsieur De Froilette is over-cautious, Stefan; that is the truth."

"It is a weakness of all masters," the soldier replied, "and so they overreach themselves. Give me a little confidence, and I am content, but distrust me, and my ears are ever on the stretch to catch news which I may use to my advantage. But I have no quarrel with you. The Captain is out, you must await his return, and while you wait you shall taste his Burgundy."

"Out! So early!"

"Oh, he's in love, I think, for he walks under the stars often, and on his return sighs like a gathering storm. I hear things, Monsieur Francois. I know."

The wily Frenchman nodded sympathetically.

"Perhaps I might find a market for what you know."

"That's been in my mind these many days," Stefan answered. "It's the first word that sticks in my throat. I've never let out secrets before, maybe because no man has told me any. Come, the wine may loosen my tongue."

He took two tankards and a key from the shelf, and led the way along a passage. The Frenchman followed eagerly, laughing at his companion's simplicity. It would be strange if Stefan could not tell him some news which would be useful to Monsieur De Froilette.

"You have your wine in safe keeping," he said, as Stefan went down into a cellar, bidding Francois to wait until he had struck a light.

"Would you have us keep it in the doorway for every thirsty throat in Sturatzberg? Come down now. Sit you on that empty barrel there. Here's wine should make you dream to your heart's content. The Captain will think that it has leaked somewhat. Scurvy treatment, Monsieur Francois, to have such wine in hiding and never ask a soldier comrade to pass an opinion. So we help ourselves."

"To his wine and to his secrets, eh?"

Stefan drowned his loud laughter in a copious draught, while Francois sipped with the air of a connoisseur.

"Fit for a king's palate," he murmured.

"Say rather for the gods. Nectar, monsieur, nectar! My secrets bubble to my tongue as the wine bubbles to the surface."

"Turn them into good money, Stefan. After all, what is this English Captain to you?"

The soldier set down his tankard and lowered his voice into a confidential whisper.

"There are some who take me for a fool," he said, coming nearer to his companion. "The Captain did not return last night, and there have been watchers in the street."

"Watchers? Go on, Stefan, what else?" said the Frenchman, eagerly.

"Aye, I saw one draw back a blind in the house opposite not an hour ago. What do you make of that, Monsieur Francois?"

The answer was a smothered gurgle, for a cloth had been suddenly tied across the Frenchman's mouth. It was in vain that he tried to free himself. He was no match against the muscles Stefan had shown him a little while ago; and before he had fully realized what had happened, he was bound, gagged, and lying on his back on the floor.

"You'll have ample time to find out how much of a fool I am, Monsieur Francois," said Stefan, "for unless a miracle should happen you'll be sharp set for a meal before you leave here. Never look so solemn, man; you won't die. I'll send and release you as soon as it is safe to do so; and if it will save your character I'll let your master in the Altstrasse know that you did your best to carry out his instructions and make a fool of me. Should you be able to drag yourself about presently you have my full permission to hold your mouth under any tap there in the cellar, and we'll never ask for payment of the score." And drinking the wine which remained in his own tankard and also in the Frenchman's he left the cellar, locking the door after him.

A few minutes later he walked down the street with a self-satisfied smile, a strapped-up bundle under his arm, and was soon lost to view in the lower purlieus of the city. That night seven horsemen left Sturatzberg, riding singly, and not all by the same gate. But, by whichever gate they left, they halted when they had ridden out of sight, and turned aside to reach the Breslen road. The last to go was Stefan. He went by the Southern Gate, and once free of the city, urged his horse forward toward the forest which lies between Breslen and Sturatzberg.

CHAPTER XI
IN THE BOIS

The Bois lay without the Northern Gate. The work of planting gardens and cutting carriage roads through the nearer stretches of the forest which touched the city on this side was due to Ferdinand I, whose statue stood in the Grande Place, the only useful action of which he had ever been guilty, it was said.

Early in the morning men riding in the Bois had inquired of one another whether the story concerning Baron Petrescu were true. One had heard this, another that. It was whispered that the Baron had been killed in a duel by a member of the British Embassy, who had also been seriously wounded; and again, that he had wounded his adversary and had then been nearly killed by his adversary's partisans. Then one man inquired the name of the woman and another where the duel had been fought, for there was a law against duelling, although it was seldom enforced. The true story did not become public property, but it was presently known that the Baron's wound was a slight affair after all, and that the duel had not been fought with a member of the Embassy. Captain Ward had certainly been injured, but that was the result of an accident; they had Dr. Goldberg's word for it. It was then that the younger wiseacres smiled. Baron Petrescu was an easy lover, and had been punished for some indiscretion. Some townsman, perhaps, with the luck on his side, had got the better of the master of fence. No wonder the Baron wished to keep the matter quiet. Lord Cloverton knew the true story. Captain Ward had sent to him directly Dr. Goldberg had got him home, and the Ambassador shut himself in his room to consider his course of action. After his failure to entrap Queen Elena last night, and the King's anger consequent upon his accusation, his position was an extremely difficult one. The Queen had outwitted him, but the fact remained that

Captain Ellerey was not to be found at his lodging this morning. He had ascertained this fact. There was no doubt that Ellerey had some understanding with her Majesty, and might have already left the city on his mission. The token might have been changed at the last moment. He had failed to arouse the King's suspicion through the Queen, but the interests at stake demanded instant action, and another method must be used. So Lord Cloverton went to the King and again apologized for the mistake his zeal had led him into. Her Majesty had, of course, proved how innocent her audience with Captain Ellerey had been, but the fact remained that Ellerey was the moving spirit in a rebellion. The sooner means were taken to obtain possession of his person the better. In this manner the Ambassador quickly made his peace, and messengers galloped hastily through the city from the palace.

The night had been a sleepless one for Frina Mavrodin. From the moment she had seen those figures descending the stairs, her thoughts had been fixed in one channel. She knew the Baron's reputation as a swordsman, and her heart went with the man who had met his insult with so swift a demand for retribution. The cause to which she was attached, for which she was prepared to squander her wealth, to give her life even were that necessary, had compelled her companionship with this adventurous Englishman. She had met him in a spirit of raillery, measuring her woman's wit and beauty against his brusqueness, and his resourcefulness and calm determination had won her admiration. The cause was altogether forgotten sometimes in the mere pleasure she had in being with him. He was not as other men, quick with a compliment, ever ready to please. Not a word of love had he spoken to her, yet his eyes had always sought her first in the throng, whether it were in the Bois or at Court, and, having found her, he looked no further. If she indulged in dreams sometimes, they were shadowy visions, pleasant enough, but taking no distinct shape, demanding no definite consideration.

The awakening had come when Princess Maritza had spoken of him. She had said little, but Frina had read the deeper meaning underneath her words. As a Princess, Maritza had watched the man's career, believing that one day he might prove useful to her cause; but as a woman she had also remembered the circumstances of their meeting, and had treasured them in her heart. Only with this discovery had Frina Mavrodin become fully conscious of all Captain Ellerey's companionship meant to her. The flood-gates were suddenly opened, and the rushing torrent of her emotions threatened to sweep away all thought of the cause she had worked for, and loved, and believed in. Almost had she told him her secret to-night by her eager questions, and the blood mounted to her cheeks as she remembered. How would he have answered her had he not been summoned to audience with the Queen? Leaning at the open window, looking at the heavy clouds which presently obscured the moon, she passed a night of restless anxiety. Somewhere, perhaps very near her, the man she loved had faced death to-night, calmly, fearlessly; even now he might be lying with sightless eyes toward the coming day, the new day which was so long in coming.

It came at last, and with her eyes bathed to remove all traces of the night's vigil, she went as usual to breakfast with the Princess, who was always an early riser. Since the night they had spoken of Captain Ellerey there had arisen a subtle difference in their relations toward each other. It hardly amounted to restraint, but the Countess was more reserved, and the Princess talked little of her hopes and plans. She made more show of taking her companion into her confidence, but told her less. For this difference, perhaps, Frina was chiefly responsible. Maritza felt that she had grown lukewarm, not to her personally, but toward the cause which took so few and such trifling steps toward its end. She did not wonder at it. No day passed in which she herself had not a period of despair, a passionate longing to drive things to a speedy conclusion, though the end brought failure. To her, her cause was paramount, and she would not allow herself to think of Desmond Ellerey apart from it; yet when Frina had in a manner claimed him, she remembered that morning on the downs, every hue of land and sky, every sound that had sung in her ears, every perfume the air held, and the centre of all was this man, who seemed then to be her possession. He had come to her country, not at her bidding, perhaps, but at her suggestion surely, and she had a right to his allegiance. It was a woman's argument, and a weak one, yet her heart seemed to excuse her.

They were still at breakfast when Dumitru was ushered in.

"Pardon, Princess, but I have news--important news. It could not wait."

"You are welcome, good Dumitru. Does the news mean action? Such is the only news I long for now."

"Yes," was the answer. "This English Captain is about to move. Whether he has the token or not I do not know, but Baron Petrescu believes he has. Last night he picked a quarrel with him, and they fought, and--" "Fool that he is!" exclaimed the Princess, starting from her seat. "Does not the Baron know that I had work for this Englishman? and now he has killed or maimed him in a useless quarrel."

"But it was not so, Princess; it was the Baron who fell."

Frina Mavrodin had also risen from the table, her hands clasped firmly together in her excitement, and a little sigh of relief echoed Dumitru's words.

"A new experience for Baron Petrescu," she said calmly.

"Ah, Countess, this Englishman is a devil," the man went on rapidly. "I had it from one who watched the fight. There was little moon, and the light was dancing and treacherous. The Baron used all the art which before has brought death when he willed, but this English Captain cared not. He knew all the Baron's art, and besides something which the Baron knew not. The Baron would have been killed had not those who were watching saved him."

"They interfered?" said the Princess.

"Yes, to save the Baron."

"They did not stop at that?" said the Countess eagerly. "Tell me what happened."

"Have I not said he is a devil?" answered Dumitru. "They rushed upon him and he fought them all. A sword thrust here, a blow with his fist there, a savage breaking through them, and he escaped--unhurt."

"Splendid!" exclaimed Frina, her face aglow.

"Splendid, Frina? Is not the Baron our friend?" Yet there was a glow in Maritza's eyes, too.

"And is not Captain Ellerey the man you have work for? You should rejoice."

The Princess looked at her for a moment, and then she smiled. "Yes, it was splendid, as you say. What more, Dumitru?"

"The friend of the Englishman was killed, I think. He was of the Embassy. There will be much questioning over the affair."

"The Baron's folly is likely to ruin us," said the Princess.

"There is still Captain Ellerey," said Frina.

Dumitru looked at the Princess, the slightest flicker in his eyes attracting her attention.

"I am not sure the other man is dead," he said. "Might I suggest that the Count-

ess should drive as usual, and hear what is said in the Bois? Then to-night we can
plan and arrange. The time has surely come."

"Will you, Frina?"

"I will, and you may rest assured that I will have the whole story by to-night."

When she had left the room Princess Maritza turned hastily.

"What more, Dumitru?"

"Much more, Princess; but it is only for your ears."

Frina Mavrodin had sped along the corridor so swiftly that she did not hear
the door locked after her to prevent her sudden return or the intrusion of others.
For a while she had no thought but a half-barbaric satisfaction that Baron Petrescu
had justly suffered for his unprovoked insult; but this was succeeded by fears for
Ellerey's safety. He had escaped last night, but he had other enemies besides those
who had attempted to assassinate him in the garden-more dangerous enemies, perhaps. She determined to know nothing, to school her face to indifference, while she
eagerly learned all she could.

She lunched with a friend, the wife of a member of the Austrian Embassy
who had often quite unconsciously given her valuable information, but she could
add nothing to her knowledge to-day. She knew Baron Petrescu had fought a duel
and had been wounded, but she did not know who his opponent was. Later, in the
Bois, Frina heard many versions of the story, but not in one of them was Captain
Ellerey's name mentioned. She did not understand it. There was some undercur-
rent of intrigue going on of which she was ignorant. Her carriage was drawn up to
the side of the road, where she was holding a small court of pedestrians, when she
caught sight of Lord Cloverton. It was seldom that he walked in the Bois, but that
he should be there in confidential colloquy with Monsieur De Froilette was nothing
short of marvellous.

Lord Cloverton saw the Countess, and stopped a little distance away. He wanted to speak to her, but had no desire that De Froilette should be a third at the interview.

"I am exceedingly obliged to you, monsieur," he said to his companion. "Any
information respecting Captain Ellerey's whereabouts just now will be of immense
advantage to me--that is, to the country. He is one of those reckless young men
who, while winning our admiration, do not blind us to the fact that they are dan-

gerous."

"Ah, I have admired him and seen the danger for a long time," De Froilette answered. "The commercial interests I have in this country force me to keep pace with its politics. I am not an expert, and it is sometimes very difficult."

"I can quite believe it," said the Ambassador, looking, however, wonderfully incredulous. "I do not fancy I have ever heard in which direction your commercial interests lie."

"Timber, my lord."

"A profitable business."

"I hope so in the future. At present there is too much unrest. With the Princess Maritza in Sturatzberg--"

"In that I think you are mistaken, monsieur."

"No, my lord. Mine was trusted information. Through the same channel I shall learn where Captain Ellerey is."

"A spy, monsieur?"

"He would be hurt to hear himself called so. He is a servant of mine, interested in my business, and a valuable fellow. He has known Captain Ellerey's movements for months past, and even now, I warrant, is at his heels. You shall hear from me, my lord, the moment he returns."

"A thousand thanks, monsieur; you will place me under an obligation. And the value of the news will depend on the state of the timber trade," he added to himself as he turned away. "Something has frightened Monsieur De Froilette; I wonder what it is."

Joining the little crowd round the Countess Mavrodin, he entered into the conversation with the heartiness of a man who hasn't a care in the world; and one by one the others withdrew, it was so evident that the Ambassador intended to remain. Frina Mavrodin desired nothing better. Lord Cloverton could doubtless tell her the truth, and although she did not for one moment expect him to do so, she thought she could probably draw it from him with the help of the knowledge she already possessed.

"My horses are getting rather restive, they have been standing so long. Will you drive with me, Lord Cloverton?"

He thanked her and got in beside her.

"One seldom sees you in the Bois," she said.

"No. I will be honest. I sometimes sleep in the afternoon, Countess."

"And to-day?" she queried, with a laugh. "To-day business brought me. I hoped to see you."

"Surely you flatter me. Since when have you considered me capable of being business-like?"

"I am all seriousness, Countess. Politics in Sturatzberg are as dried wood stacked ready for burning, and a torch is already in the midst of it. Until now the torch has been moved hither and thither, giving the wood no time to catch; but now I fear the flame is held steadily. I seem to hear the first sounds of the crackling."

"I seem to have heard the beginning often," she answered, "but a swift hand has always saved the situation."

"The danger has never been so imminent as it is now, Countess."

"Are you not still in Sturatzberg to cope with the danger?" she asked, turning to him with a radiant smile. "I stand alone, Countess; what can one man do? I wonder whether you can credit me with disinterestedness, whether you can believe that I have the welfare of this country at heart while carrying out the policy of my own?"

"Is not that the position of every Ambassador?"

"Nominally, perhaps. I was asking you to believe something more definite in my case," he returned. "Do I ask too much? In a measure, you and I are drawn together in this crisis. We should be allies."

"Are my poor wits of service either way?"

"A woman is always a valuable ally, and the Countess Mavrodin knows her power. No, I am beyond turning pretty speeches to-day," he went on quickly; "the times are too serious for them. You know, Countess, what occurred last night?"

"I left the palace somewhat early," she said; "but there was an air of constraint about. What caused it, Lord Cloverton?"

"I was referring to Baron Petrescu's affair. No one has talked of anything else to-day."

"And you can tell me the truth of it," she exclaimed. "I am glad. I have heard many stories since I entered the Bois."

"I was expecting to hear the real truth from you," said the Ambassador, fixing his eyes upon her.

"From me! Am I the wife of some *bourgeois* in the city to inflame the Baron's susceptibilities into indiscretion? It is some such tale I have heard."

"But which you knew to be untrue, Countess."

"I have thought more highly of Baron Petrescu than that, I admit."

"Naturally, seeing that Captain Ellerey is not a *bourgeois* of the city, and has no wife as far as I know. My young countryman is no boaster beyond his worth, it would seem. The Baron has found his match."

"Is that the truth of it?" she asked innocently.

"I congratulate you upon your champion," returned the Ambassador. "You look surprised, Countess; but in the inner circle of such a Court as we have here in Sturatzberg such secrets will find a tongue."

"You have changed your serious mood, my lord, it appears, and I am at a loss to understand the pleasantry."

"Believe me, Countess, I was never more serious. Something of the Baron's political leanings are known to his Majesty, and the affair has assumed a political significance in his eyes. The law has lain dormant, it is true, but duelling is an offence against the crown, and the King has seen fit to set the law in motion. Captain Ellerey is sought for in Sturatzberg. I would do my countryman, and you, a service if I could."

"How am I concerned? I may thank you for your courtesy if you will tell me that."

"Is it not true that you were the cause of this quarrel?"

"It is absolutely false."

"Stay, Countess, it may be that you are unaware of the fact, but I have the best reason for knowing that such is the case."

"Captain Ellerey had no cause to draw sword on my behalf, Lord Cloverton; neither of his own wish, nor at my bidding, did he do it."

"Strange," mused the Ambassador. "It is evident that he thought of only one person last night. He left instructions with his second that you were to be immediately informed if any harm befell him. He left no other message or remembrance to anyone."

She was not sufficient mistress of herself to prevent the Ambassador noting that the information was pleasant to her.

"It may have been presumption on his part," he went on slowly; "still such thought can hardly be without some interest for you. No doubt you would render him a service if you could."

"My friendship would prompt me to do so."

"Then urge him, Countess, to withdraw from Sturatzberg. The torch now put to the dried wood is in his hand. What is he to me? Nothing; but I would save him if I could. What he is to you, I do not know. I am not skilled with women; but for your country's sake urge his departure. It must be done promptly, for I warn you the fire has already caught hold, and not all, even now, shall escape the burning."

"Your appeal to my patriotism might stir me, Lord Cloverton, did I know where to find Captain Ellerey."

"In that, Countess, I cannot help you. I had hoped you would know. Have I your permission to stop the carriage?" She inclined her head. They had returned close to the spot from which they had started. There were fewer carriages in the Bois, and hardly any pedestrians now. Lord Cloverton had, however, seen a man standing close to the roadway, and he beckoned him to the carriage.

"What news?" he asked sharply.

"Every gate is closely watched, my lord. By the King's orders Captain Ellerey is to be stopped if he attempts to leave the city."

"I fear we are too late to render any service," said the Ambassador, turning to the Countess. "It is a pity. The hand that holds the torch can hardly escape."

"It is not thought that the Captain has already left, but all efforts to find him have failed," said the man, and then at a sign from Lord Cloverton he withdrew.

"I believe we are allies at heart, Countess; it is a pity we have no power to act."

"Perhaps you exaggerate the danger."

"I fear not," he answered, as he stepped from the carriage. "I foresee evil days for Sturatzberg. Good-day, Countess; if I can save the situation, it must be by the sacrifice of my countryman, I fear. It is a pity."

He stood bareheaded until the carriage had driven away, and then went quickly toward the Embassy. If Frina Mavrodin knew where Captain Ellerey was, as Lord Cloverton was convinced she did, she would warn him. Whatever interests Ellerey had at heart, he would not chance disaster by attempting to leave the city until the watch upon the gates was relaxed to some extent. There must, therefore, be delay in whatever plot was in hand, and a few days now were of priceless value.

Politics had little place in Frina Mavrodin's thoughts as she drove homeward through the city. She had denied that Desmond Ellerey had drawn sword in her cause, and yet might he not have done so after all? What she had seen might only have been the end of a quarrel. Baron Petrescu may have spoken some light word concerning her which Ellerey had resented. If Lord Cloverton had spoken the truth, Ellerey's last thought had been of her. She was quite content that her fair fame should rest in his keeping. Now he was in danger. Whatever Lord Cloverton's aims might be, one thing was certain--the city gates were closed against Ellerey's departure. Without warning he would almost certainly be taken. How could she help him?

There was confusion at her door when the carriage stopped. Servants were in the hall expectantly awaiting her.

"What is it?" she asked.

"In your absence, Countess, we were powerless," answered her major-domo, pale even now with indignation. "The order was imperative."

"What order?"

"The order to search the house."

The Countess started, but was self-possessed again in a moment. Not all her servants knew of the identity of the Princess.

"For whom were they looking?"

"For an English Captain named Ellerey," was the answer. "I said that no such person visited here at any time, but they would not believe me, and searched the whole house."

"And found--"

"No one, Countess."

The man was wise; he said no more before the other servants.

"I will complain to his Majesty," Frina answered, and then she went quickly to the apartments occupied by the Princess Maritza. Hannah met her on the threshold. "Has she not returned, my lady?"

"Where is she? How did she have warning?" asked Frina.

"She had gone long before. She went without a word to me. When they came asking for some Englishman, I had just wit enough to answer that I was your lady-ship's servant, and knew no Englishman; but it was hard work not to ask them what had become of my Princess."

"And Dumitru?"

"Gone, gone. I always took him for a cut-throat with that naked knife hidden in his shirt. I believe he has made away with her."

"Peace, woman. Say nothing. A word may ruin her. You can go."

"But, my lady--"

"You can go, I say."

There was a tone in the command that brooked no disobedience. The woman left the room hastily, leaving the Countess alone.

Alone. A wild rush of thoughts overwhelmed her. The hope and joy that had budded in her heart were suddenly blighted. The world seemed to slip away from her, leaving her alone indeed.

CHAPTER XII
GRIGOSIE

The Toison d'Or was an ancient inn standing back from the Bergenstrasse and reached by a narrow court. It did not advertise itself, was not easily found, and its frequenters were few. Those who used it seemed to use it often, for the landlord welcomed them like old friends. They were of the poorer sort, and the want of comfort in the place did not disturb them; perhaps the quality of the liquor made amends.

It presented a narrow front to the court, the great walls on either side appeared to have squeezed it. The two little windows above, the signboard flat against the wall, and the single door rather suggested a face; and the door, out of the perpendicular, looked strangely like a mouth awry uttering a cry of pain. The building was deep, however, and there was a long, narrow, low-pitched room at the rear, of which all the frequenters of the place were not aware. This room, even in broad daylight, was dim, and it grew dark there early. It was still light in the wider streets of the city, but in this room a candle was burning on the corner of a table, beside which a man sat. He had pushed back the remains of a meal, and his fingers played reflectively with the tankard which the landlord had replenished a few moments before.

The landlord had asked no questions, had attempted no conversation. When Desmond Ellerey had entered and called for liquor, he had made a sign to the landlord as he had been instructed, and which was perfectly understood. Two men were drinking in the doorway at the time, and when they had gone the landlord led Ellerey to the long room.

"There will be inquiries for me, landlord. Whoever gives the sign bring him in at once, but no one else, mind."

The landlord nodded.

"Let me have food and drink. I care not what so there is plenty of it. I have not broken fast since yesterday."

Throwing aside one cloak which he carried over his arm, and loosening the one he wore, Ellerey disclosed the fact that he was well armed, and booted and spurred for a journey. Earlier in the day Stefan had met him at a tavern in the city, bringing these clothes with him as directed in the note which the boy had delivered. The remains of the Court uniform which he had worn last night had been hidden away, and there was nothing now in Ellerey's dress to mark him as a King's officer.

He had already waited three hours, or more, and began to grow impatient. The men who had been chosen for this desperate service were already on their way to the place of rendezvous, and men of this description were wont to fret at delay and inactivity. He wanted to be away himself, and until he had the Queen's token safely in his possession he could not put aside his fears that it would not come, that something had happened to prevent her sending it. The King's sudden interruption last night might have forced her to change her plans, might possibly have caused her to sacrifice him to save herself. At the best, delay must be dangerous, and he chafed at his enforced idleness, which made the minutes drag.

At last the door opened and a man entered. It was the same man who had come to summon him to the audience last night. "You are welcome," Ellerey said. "I began to think some circumstance had intervened."

"We have only just escaped such a calamity," was the answer. "By some means Lord Cloverton had received information of our plans. In the presence of the King, immediately after your departure, he accused her Majesty of trafficking with the brigands in the hills, and challenged her to show the bracelet. It was fortunate that the Queen could do so, and indignantly demand apology. The first move is much in our favor, for the accusation made the King extremely angry, and the British Ambassador is in ill favor to-day. His hands are tied for a little while, at any rate."

"That I would believe if I saw the knotted cords about his wrists, but not otherwise," Ellerey answered. "My worthy countryman is not so easily beaten."

"It is true her Majesty bid me warn you, but without the King what can he do?"

"He is capable of anything, and has the English vice, or virtue--it depends on the point of view--of never knowing when he has got the worst of it."

"Her Majesty is fortunate in also having an Englishman for her messenger."

"Thank you, monsieur. I think there is something of the same spirit in me."

"There is the token, Captain Ellerey," and the man handed him a small sealed box. "The streets are yet full, so it would be wise to delay your departure for a while. Her Majesty also bid me give you this, an earnest of what shall fall to the share of her successful messenger."

In Ellerey's palm lay a ring, the jewel in it catching light even from the feeble ray of the candle. For one moment Ellerey was disposed to refuse the gift until he had earned it, the independence of the Englishman rising in him; but a brief hesitation gave the spirit of the adventurer opportunity to rise uppermost. He might fail, and for his life be compelled to leave Sturatzberg. It would be some consolation not to go altogether empty-handed.

"I thank her Majesty," he said. "I shall keep it as a key to win her further favor should I deserve it."

"Then I will leave you, Captain Ellerey. Fortune smile on you and on the cause."

As the door closed upon his visitor, Ellerey secured the sealed box and the ring about his person in such a fashion that the treasure lay close to the skin. While life was in him no one should rob him of it. Then he sat down to possess his soul in patience until the streets should grow dark enough and empty enough for his departure.

It was market day, and he had elected to go by the Southern Gate at the hour when many would be leaving the city on their homeward journey. He had no desire to be recognized, and he hoped to pass unnoticed in the crowd. Stefan had arranged to have his horse waiting for him at a forester's cottage off the Breslen road, a mile from the city. By making the meeting-place in the forest toward Breslen, precaution was taken that should riders be seen going in this direction their real destination would never be suspected. The brigands lay in the mountains near the Drekner pass, in exactly the opposite direction to Breslen, and a wide detour round Sturatzberg would have to be accomplished when the united band set out in earnest upon its expedition. The token was at last in his possession, his comrades awaited him, and Ellerey was anxious to be gone. But he was not the man to fail by being too precipitate. None knew better the value of deliberate caution, and with Lord Cloverton fully alive to the danger, there might be many obstacles to face which had not entered into his calculations. So Ellerey sat there waiting, while the candle burnt lower, casting, as the room darkened, a sharper outline of his figure upon the wall.

"Time, surely, now!" he exclaimed at last, starting to his feet. "Landlord."

The door opened so suddenly that the handle must have been turned even as Ellerey shouted. But it was not the landlord who entered. Two figures came in swiftly and closed the door.

"Pardon, Captain Ellerey."

"Well, sirs, what would you with me? I have little time to waste. I have already called the landlord to pay my reckoning," and as he spoke Ellerey raised the candle above his head to see what manner of men his visitors were.

"Friends, Captain," said the foremost of the two, making the same sign which had gained admittance for the bearer of the token.

He was a man of set features with a pair of keen eyes deeply sunken. His figure was lithe and sinewy, his movements quick and not ungraceful. His dress was of the better peasant class, a short knife was sheathed in his girdle, and one hand rested lightly on the hilt of it as he stood motionless under the Captain's scrutiny. He might have been a forester. His companion stood silently in the shadows behind him.

"By that sign you should know the business I have in hand, and that I have no time to waste in words."

"True, Captain. We are from her Majesty, and know that the token has been delivered into your keeping here to-night. You have comrades waiting for you, but too few, such is the Queen's opinion, and she bid us join your company."

"I do not like the arrangement," Ellerey answered. "My comrades are picked men that I know the muscles of. I know nothing of you."

"It's a poor welcome, Captain, but it must serve. I have other news for you which may increase our value."

"You run on too fast, my friend," said Ellerey. "Your coming at this eleventh hour ill fits with my precaution."

"We have horses without the city, Captain; we are not ill conditioned for the enterprise."

"You may pass muster for a man. What is your name?"

"Anton."

"You have muscle enough to strike a good blow on occasion, but I know naught of your courage. And your companion there, what of him? Step into the light and let me look at you. How are you called?"

"Grigosie, if it please you, Captain."

He stepped out of the shadow as he spoke, and with his arms folded across his breast, threw back his head defiantly, as though such inspection were little to his taste. He was a lad in figure and in voice. His face was innocent of even the down of dawning manhood. His limbs were clean cut and supple, but they looked too young for stern endurance. His dress was similar to his companion's save that it was green in color, and he wore a cap of green drawn down to his brows.

"You're a good-looking boy enough," laughed Ellerey, "but Heaven forgive her Majesty. Does she think I am bent on some summer picnic that she sends a child to bear me company?"

"We are wont to go together, Captain. Grigosie is a good scout, and I warrant is likely to prove useful," said Anton.

"For cooking and bedmaking maybe. We shall have little opportunity for either one or the other,"

"Nor should I do either of them except of my own will," said the lad.

"A stroke or two of the whip would make you tell a different tale," said Ellerey; "and you may thank your lucky fortune that I will not take you, for the whip would certainly follow."

"I have heard of Captain Ellerey," said the boy, "but never that he was a bully."

Ellerey looked at him quizzically.

"Well, lad, I did not mean to hurt your feelings. You do not lack courage, and you'll grow into a stout man for rough work some day. In this expedition I cannot use you."

"I can use a sword and am a master of fence, and the sword is not the only weapon which victory hangs upon."

"Peace, Grigosie; I will give the Captain an excellent reason for taking you."

"Peace, yourself, Anton. Am I to be taken out of charity? Set me to prove my worth, Captain."

"I have no time, lad," said Ellerey, picking up his cloak. "Anton may come since we are few, but---"

"There is a fly on the wall, Captain."

"Well, what of it? You are a strange lad."

"It is gone, I warrant; but in case I have missed--darkness."

Two revolver shots cracked in quick succession as he spoke, and the room was in darkness. Then the landlord rushed in.

"The candle is out; light it again, landlord," said the boy, and then when it had burnt up he pointed with the revolver to the spot where the fly had been and where now there was a hole. "I do not think I missed."

"Leave us, landlord," said Ellerey. "It was the deciding of a foolish boast."

The lad slipped the revolver into his pocket again and refolded his arms.

"That was a foolish jest, youngster," Ellerey said. "Do you think such boastfulness fits you for such work as ours?"

"There are few who could have done it," was the answer.

"True."

"Such precision might serve you were your enemies three to one."

"True again."

"Then ask me to go with you," was the prompt reply.

"May I not even take you out of charity?"

The lad shook his head with a smile, and there was something very winning in his smile.

"Very well. Will you come with me?" asked Ellerey.

"To the death."

"Your hand on that bargain."

"I'll earn the grip of comradeship before I take it, Captain. Until then it is for you to order, be it to cooking or to bedmaking."

"You'll serve for sport and as a relief to monotony, if for nothing else," said Ellerey. "Orders, then. We must be starting."

"You have not heard my further news," said Anton. "It is not time to start yet."

Ellerey turned upon him angrily. Was his authority so soon to be questioned?

"Every gate is closed against Captain Ellerey by the King's orders," said Anton. "It has been so since noon to-day."

"Is the scent so hot already?"

"We shall leave the city, but not yet. The lad here will show us the way," Anton answered. "You see I am to be of some service quickly, Captain," said Grigosie. "Trust me. My way is clear enough, and no King's order has power to bar it. We must wait a little. I have some money in my pouch; may I pay for liquor?"

"You're doing me good, youngster," laughed Ellerey. "Order your drinks, and tell me who they were who fathered and mothered you that you have such wit. You are not fashioned after the usual breed in Wallaria."

"I am of the pure breed which is being forgotten in the bastard race. I am of the old stock reared without the city walls. Anton can answer for me."

"That I can."

The drinks were brought, but the lad drank sparingly. Ellerey liked him none the worse for that. If wine were found upon the journey, one sober comrade, though he were a lad, might be more profitable than half a dozen boasters. The boy talked brightly, and his air of boastfulness fell from him. There was a tone of deference to the Captain in his manner which sat gracefully on his young shoulders.

"Were it not that they brought your favor, I should regret the fly and the candle," he said presently. "I crave your pardon."

"Say no more of it. We'll give you better marks before long, maybe."

"You carry two cloaks, Captain. How is that?"

"One my own, one I borrowed this morning. I am going to leave it with the landlord to be returned."

"Wear it until we are free of the city. It may conceal you from some prying eyes. I warrant you are well looked for to-night."

"Have we far to travel to this exit of yours?"

"Some distance, and by narrow ways. If there should be prying eyes we must close them quickly. We want no shouts to raise a rabble. Is it not time, Anton?"

"Yes, the gates have been closed for half an hour."

"Come, then," said the lad. "Must we go through the court?"

"There is no other way," Anton answered.

"Then Captain, will you permit that Anton and I go first?" said Grigosie. "Follow close upon our heels; but should we stop, do not you; overtake us and push us roughly aside, and we will overtake you again in a moment. Your pardon that I seem to lead in this matter, but I know the road we must take."

Ellerey returned a gruff assent to the arrangement. He had looked into the boy's eyes and seen honesty there, but he was not going to walk carelessly, for all that.

The inn was empty, so was the court, and there were few people abroad in the Bergenstrasse. Grigosie and Anton, leading the way by scarce a dozen paces, turned almost directly from the main thoroughfare into a side street, and had soon turned to left and right so often that Ellerey would hardly have found his way back to the Toison d'Or. Not once did they stop, and if they looked back to see that their companion was following them, Ellerey was not aware of the fact. He kept close upon their heels, ready to stand on the defensive at the first sign of treachery, but he took little notice of where they led him.

Suddenly a street corner struck him as familiar, and the next moment the truth flashed upon him. It was the street he had traversed last night. At the bottom there they had met Baron Petrescu. Even now the light was dimly burning in the upper window as it had been then. Grigosie and Anton stopped, but when Ellerey reached them he did not push them aside; he stopped, too. "And now which way?" he asked.

"Toward the light yonder," Grigosie answered.

"My lad, there is a point beyond which I trust no one," said Ellerey. "I know that light."

"It marks our point of safety."

"Yours, perhaps; not mine."

"I do not understand, Captain."

"If you are innocent, how should you? If you are false, why should you? Last night I had an appointment beneath that dim lamp. With difficulty I escaped with my life."

"But you did escape; you know how. To-night there will be no duel. We shall go direct to that door in the wall."

Who was this youngster that he knew so much?

"It seems to me a desperate chance even if you are honest in advising it," said Ellerey. "Look you, lad, I give you warning. My life I am prepared to give, but if by treachery it is taken, I'll see that you bear me company on that journey, even as you have sworn to follow me to the death on the other."

"I am content," was the short answer. "Muffle your cloak about your face and leave me to speak."

They went together toward the light, and Grigosie knocked at the door as Baron Petrescu had done. There was the same delay, the self-same shaggy head was thrust out to the intruders. Silence reigned again until the stentorian voice had shouted, and then the clattering and the voices started instantly.

The man led them aside into the same room.

"Pass us out through the garden and ask no questions," said Grigosie.

"Who have we here?" asked the man, pointing to Ellerey. "Neither ask questions nor answer any," Grigosie returned.

"That's too pert a tongue to satisfy me," growled the man. "Signs and passwords are easily stolen. I'd sooner let some one bear witness with me after last night."

In an instant the lad was beside him. What he said was in so low a tone that Ellerey could not catch a word, but the effect was magical. The surly brute became alert and obsequious. He led them quickly down the passage, and opened the door leading into the garden. Perhaps Grigosie did not altogether trust him, for he caught him by the arm, saying that he should see them safely through the garden, and Ellerey noticed that Anton was particular to keep close to the man.

At the door in the wall the boy stopped.

"Your cloak, monsieur," he said, turning to Ellerey "You wish it returned, do you not?"

Ellerey gave it to him and nodded, but did not speak

Grigosie gave the cloak to the man.

"Theodor, see that this is returned to Captain Ward at the British Embassy. Send it by a trusted messenger, and let him say that he had it from Captain Desmond Ellerey to-night, an hour before midnight--mark the time--when he met him in the Konigplatz. Good-night."

The man bowed low as he opened the door for them. When it had closed upon them Grigosie turned to Ellerey.

"Are you satisfied, Captain?"

The boy's knowledge astonished Ellerey.

"You have reproved me twice to-night, youngster; first for being a bully, now for doubting you."

"My anger is forgotten," laughed the lad. "The cloak was a good thought. They will know that you were in the city to-night, and they will search Sturatzberg for you all day to-morrow. So we gain time. Our horses await us on the Breslen road; and yours, Captain?"

"Also on the Breslen road."

"Then, Captain, will you order the march? My brief command is over."

CHAPTER XIII
THE CASTLE IN THE HILLS

The first light of a new day awoke a chorus of blended voices within the depths of the forest. The early matin praise of the birds rose high and clear above the low-hummed hymn of the insects. The trees shook out their rustling garments, glorious autumn robes of color, scattering the dewy tears of night before the smiling day. Among the fallen leaves were hasty rushes to and fro, while rabbits flashed across the narrow open tracts.

There was stirring, too, in a dry hollow securely hidden by dense undergrowth from any traveller who chanced to pass that way. The whinnying of a horse sounded on the morning air, the rough rubbing of leather trappings, and the sharp click of steel. There were gruff laughter and gruffer oaths, man's salutation to the new day, and some low spoken words of discontent.

The addition to their number was not pleasing to them. The more they were, the less would each man receive as reward, they argued. Last night they were half-asleep, and had barely roused at Ellerey's coming. The men who had come with him, they supposed, were soldiers of fortune like themselves, men they knew, and even they were not welcome; but with morning discontent broke out. The new arrivals were not soldiers, were strangers to them, and one at least was a mere lad. What good was he in their company?

Stefan did not complain. He noted Anton from head to foot, and did not like him. He looked at Grigosie and he laughed aloud. He turned to find Ellerey close beside him.

"This is the first day of the festival, then, Captain?"

"Festival?"

"Surely since we have such company. Some of these fellows might have brought their sweethearts with them had they known the kind of expedition they were engaged for. You bid me choose carefully, picked men who held life and death in such easy balance that they would take whichever happened without a murmur; and now you bring us a lean forester who is good for naught but felling trees, and a lad whose mother might still whip him without offence."

"The lad is well enough, Stefan, and served me well last night."

"Thank him, then, and send him home again. I have a message to send into the city. It will be employment for him to take it."

"No, he goes with us."

"There'll be much grumbling, Captain. These fellows like comrades they know the stomach of."

"I'll answer for the boy."

"You'd best do it quickly, then, or there'll be one or two riding back into Sturatzberg as yesterday they rode out."

"If that is their spirit I'd sooner have lads like yonder beside me in a tight place," Ellerey answered angrily. Then he went to the men who were looking to their saddle girths preparatory to mounting. "Comrades, we have a journey before us which may run smoothly, but which may bring us hard knocks. The reward is generous to those who win through. Are we prepared to take our chances one and all?" He paused, but only a grunt of tardy consent answered him.

"Last night I brought two others to join in our enterprise."

"What need of them?" growled one man, "and one of them a boy."

"They go with me whoever else stays behind," said Ellerey, turning quickly to the man who had spoken. "Haven't you faith enough in me to trust my discretion?"

There was no reply.

"It must be tacit obedience, swift action to my command from every man who bears me company. Mount."

In a moment every one was in his saddle excepting Ellerey himself, who stood with his horse's bridle over his arm.

"Yonder lies the Breslen road, an easy morning's canter into Sturatzberg. Who likes may ride that way and free himself from my authority."

No man spoke or moved.

"Then are we comrades, and do not growl among ourselves," said Ellerey, springing into his saddle. "Forward! You must find some other carrier for your message, Stefan."

"And soon, or I'll have murder on my soul," was the answer, as the troop rode singly out of the hollow and picked its way along a forest track.

It was high noon before they chanced upon a woodcutter and his boy.

"Give me leave, Captain," said Stefan, bringing his horse to a standstill. "Here's one may take my message. Aye there, how far is it to Sturatzberg by the shortest road?"

"Five miles by foot, but riding you'll scarce do it in ten," answered the woodcutter. "Will you or the lad carry a message there?"

"To-morrow I would. I go with a team there, taking timber."

"To-morrow," mused Stefan. "Why not? He'll last until then. Well, then, to-morrow. Here's a key. Take it to the Altstrasse. Do you know the Altstrasse?"

"Surely. I have a brother living there."

"To the Altstrasse--thirteen--to the house of Monsieur De Froilette."

"I have heard of him."

"Then you will do him this service," said Stefan.

"Give him the key, and say that if he has lost his servant, this key fits a certain cellar door in a certain lodging by the Western Gate. He will guess which lodging. His servant, loving wine too much, lies behind that cellar door, howling for his liberty."

"I'll take the message."

"Here's for refreshment by the way," said Stefan, tossing him the key and a coin. "Monsieur De Froilette will reward you liberally, I warrant."

"And who shall I say gave me the key?"

"Say a woman you met by the road, if your conscience will sanction the lie; if not, say a man, and word my picture as you please so that you make it handsome enough. But do not fail to deliver the message, for the man behind that door is slowly dying, and, if you do not go to his rescue, will surely curse you from his grave."

"What does this mean, Stefan?" Ellerey asked, as the troop rode on, laughing at their companion.

"Francois was watching us, and saw the boy who carried your message to me yesterday. He came to question me, thinking me a fool, and went with me to the cellar to hear my story and to drink your wine. He got no story, and little wine for that matter, unless the ropes have slipped from his wrists and ankles. I tied him securely before I made him free of all the cellar contained. He'll be wanting food badly by to-morrow, when his master finds him."

"It was well done, Stefan. We want no spies about us; but why should Monsieur De Froilette spy upon me?"

"For the same reason that a hawk watches its prey; it's his nature. You may snatch chestnuts out of the fire for monsieur, but it's only the charred husks will be your portion if the dividing is left to him."

All that day they kept to the forest, making a wide detour round Sturatzberg. Progress was slow along the narrow tracks, and they went singly for the most part, careful of their horses' steps. That night they lay within a circle of trees, deep hidden in the woods and far from the road. For two days they were able to hold to the forest, and had no expectation of being surprised. They met no one save an occasional woodcutter or charcoal-burner, and once they disturbed some robbers who were perhaps near the place of their hidden booty. On the third day they were on the edge of the forest, and much open country lay between them and the mountains. The utmost caution was necessary now.

Ellerey called Grigosie to him.

"Anton said that you would be useful at scouting work."

"Yes, Captain."

"You will go forward with Stefan. Use your eyes and ears well."

The lad saluted, and presently rode out with Stefan. Anton asked to go with them, but this Ellerey would not allow. He was glad of the opportunity of separating Grigosie from his companion for a little while. He had no reason to suspect them, but keeping them apart was a precaution. Ellerey had instructed Stefan to use the lad well, and with a grim smile upon his face the soldier rode with his youthful companion, keeping silence for a time.

"You're a slip of a lad for such work as we have on hand," he said presently. "How came your mother to part with you so early?"

"Rest her soul, she's dead."

"Your father, then?"

"Dead also," answered Grigosie.

"Well, you knew them, and understand whether their loss was a big one or not," said Stefan. "Parents haven't counted for much in my case, so I'm not qualified to speak of their usefulness. You've managed to grow into a likely sort of lad. Who's had the training of you?"

"I'm my own manufacture for the most part," answered Grigosie, "but I'm not too proud to learn from an old campaigner like you, Stefan."

The soldier drew himself up in his saddle, and looked knowingly at his young comrade.

"There's sense in you. Maybe I can teach you a few things. My experience has been wide and peculiar, and if you listen to my advice and model your fighting on mine, you'll make a soldier, not of my girth, perhaps, for that's a gift of nature and not to be had for the asking."

"No; I shall always be of the lean sort, I fear," said Grigosie.

"Don't you be discouraged, lad. There's often good stuff in the lean ones. It's deep potations that give a man breadth sometimes, and his habit of growling strange oaths that gets him credit for valor."

Grigosie plied him with questions, and heard many a strange tale of fighting in which Stefan had done marvellous things.

"Is there no reward for bravery in Wallaria?" said Grigosie at last. "How is it that no great distinction has come to you?" Stefan turned toward him and shut one eye.

"Dodge the distinctions, lad, as you would the devil. They lead to Court and the society of women, two things to be avoided."

"Why so, Stefan?"

"Court fetters a man as a chain does a dog, and is unnatural, while a woman is the keenest weapon in all the devil's armory."

"I have heard some well spoken of," said Grigosie.

"And they are the most dangerous," said Stefan. "Why do you suppose women were made pretty and fashioned to wear pretty clothes?"

"Indeed I cannot tell."

"To conceal their natural defects, lad. Whenever you see a pretty woman, look at the next harridan you meet, and remember that the difference between them is only on the surface."

"You are too hard, Stefan," said Grigosie, laughing heartily.

"Wisdom, youngster--the ripe wisdom of experience."

"I wonder whether the Captain is of your way of thinking, Stefan."

"I have seen him pause in the midst of his drink sometimes, which has made me anxious."

"The fetters of the Court, perhaps," said Grigosie.

"Seemed to me it was more like a woman," was the answer.

That night they encamped between two spurs of the lower hills. Two hours before sunset they had begun to ascend from the plain. It was among the hills they would be looked for as soon as the object of their mission were known; and having chosen a camping-ground which could easily be defended against odds, Ellerey placed sentinels to prevent any surprise. The camp-fire was pleasant to draw close to, for the night was cold. Ellerey lay in a half-reclining position, his feet stretched toward the blaze; and at some little distance on the opposite side the men were sitting in a circle playing cards, Grigosie and Anton standing beside them, looking on.

"There, boy, what did I tell you?" he heard Stefan say as he turned to Grigosie. "A woman again plays me false, and it's the queen of hearts, too."

The boy laughed. Evidently he and Stefan had become fast friends during their day's ride together. It was a merry laugh, pleasant, Ellerey thought, after the gruffer tones of the soldiers.

Presently the boy left Anton's side and threw himself down by the fire near Ellerey.

"Are you tired, Grigosie?"

"A little. Lately I have not been used to so many hours in the saddle. What point do we make for to-morrow?"

"The Drekner pass. Do you know it?"

"I was quite a youngster when I last crossed it," was the answer. "There used to be a castle there, perched on the hill-side like an eagle's eyrie."

"So many years cannot have passed since then that the castle should have crumbled away," said Ellerey, with a smile. "I expect it is still there."

"You do not know the pass, then?"

"No."

Grigosie lapsed into silence, and then after a while he said suddenly: "Some day I hope to be an honored soldier like you are, Captain."

"Wish better things for yourself, Grigosie."

"Are you not honored, then?"

"Enough to be given a dangerous post."

"And to receive good reward if you succeed. The Queen will load you with gifts--and, perhaps, greater happiness still, some other woman will smile on you."

"You begin to think of such things over early," Ellerey answered. "You'll have your troubles soon enough that way, no doubt."

"Already, Captain."

"So soon?"

"This is a southern country, and we begin early. Are you a woman-hater, as Stefan is? In the back of my mind there is a reverence for women."

"Keep it, lad, if you can; it may bring you to much good. For my part, I hardly know my position in the matter."

"Would telling the tale to me help your judgment?" inquired the lad.

"A man does not speak of such things often, Grigosie."

"Ah, your love tale has advanced some way, then. It was not a glance and a passing word, and a thorn left in the heart to hurt terribly at times. That was my case."

"There is a woman I deeply respect and honor," said Ellerey. "To love her would be much to my advantage."

"Why not, then?" asked the boy.

"Because of a memory, the memory of another woman. With her it was a passing word and a look; but they came to me when life was at its darkness, and I have never forgotten them. It was an early morning in England, a morning that has no equal in the whole world, full of sunshine and breeze and perfume; and she came into it suddenly and unexpectedly. She would not choose to remember me if she thought such a memory lingered in my heart. She was out of my reach even then, and in those days I was something more than a Captain of Horse."

"But after this enterprise you will be something more."

"I cannot become a Prince, Grigosie, and my lady of the breezy morning was a

Princess."

"Really, or is that your fanciful name for her?"

"Really a Princess," Ellerey answered. "I wonder why I should be telling this story to you?"

"Is there not sympathy between all who love?" Grigosie answered. "It is the one common bond there is in the world, knowing no difference of creed or nationality."

For two days the little band journeyed in the mountains, keeping to the lower track on account of the horses. Progress was slow, for the going was rough, and the horses often had to be led. The track lay between the lower hills and the main mountain range, and they had lost sight of the open country, which lay below them. It was late in the afternoon of the second day that they crossed a spur which jutted out toward the plain, and from its vantage ground Grigosie was the first to point out the head of the pass, a precipitous opening in the mountains to their left. At the same time Stefan, looking across the open country, pointed out a cloud of dust on the horizon.

"That means a moving body of men," he said.

"In the pass lies our greatest security until we are prepared to meet the enemy," Ellerey answered. "If that castle of yours has not crumbled to dust, Grigosie, it will make excellent quarters for us."

The Drekner pass had long ago ceased to be used. Once, doubtless, it was the highway into Wallaria from the north, but that was long ago, not within the memory of the oldest man. Nature herself had closed the way by casting a great spur of the mountain into the deepest and narrowest part of the defile. It was still possible to climb this, but it had effectually closed the pass for all useful purposes; and the castle, which in old times had been used to guard the way, had fallen into decay. It stood gaunt against the hillside upon a natural plateau, the pathway to it, long and zig-zag, cut out in the hillside. Vegetation had taken root in the crevices of its broken walls, and some of the stonework, shivered by the lightning stroke perhaps, lay in the roadway at the foot of the hill. Silence reigned, and an eagle hovering on the heights above doubtless had his eyrie there. A thin stream of water trickled down the hillside, finding its way from the snow on the mountains, which reared white-hooded heads here and there above their humbler brethren.

"My castle in the hills!" cried Grigosie enthusiastically as a turn of the track brought it in view.

"Peace, Grigosie, and take that child's chatter of yours to the rear," said Ellerey. Then turning to Stefan, he directed him and another of the men to climb up carefully to the plateau. "Some outpost of Vasilici's may hold it," he remarked.

Leaving their horses, Stefan and his companion went up the zig-zag way and were lost to view. It seemed a long time before their figures stood on the edge of the plateau and waved to their comrades to ascend.

"My castle, Anton," whispered Grigosie. "It was I who told them that it stood here."

"They liked not your claiming it so."

"They will forgive much to my youth, even if I am put to cooking and bedmaking to-night as punishment," laughed the boy. "You shall be snug, Anton, and know that the gods are with us."

The incline of the zig-zag way had been carefully graduated so that it was possible to lead horses up, and they all dismounted and went singly. At the top of the path a stone gateway, broken and of small service now, shut in the plateau. This was the only means of reaching the castle, and in old times formed the first point of defence. "Empty, but an airy perch to spend the night," said Stefan, meeting them at the gateway. "Here's a trysting place for every wind that blows, and holes enough for them to whistle through."

This was evident. The walls were broken in every direction, and heaps of stonework lay scattered on all sides.

"The tower yonder seems to have held together," said Ellerey.

"Aye, there's fine sleeping room there, and you may see the stars through the roof."

But the tower had much to commend it. The door that closed it still hung upon its hinges, and in the lower chamber, at least, there were no rents in the wall save the window holes, narrow slits in the outside, but widening inward through the thickness of the walls. On one side stone steps, unprotected in any way, led to the floor above, which was entered through a trap door still in place and capable of being bolted down. Here the walls were broken in places, and part of the roof had fallen. More steps, which mounted to the roof, ended abruptly and were open to the sky. A turret had been displaced at some time and had crashed through, breaking part of the stairs away.

"We can make shift to stable the horses between some of the walls outside, and ourselves in the tower," said Ellerey. "It might be worse, Stefan, and with fortune our stay will be short."

"It must be if we're to live. There is no food for a siege," Stefan answered.

Meanwhile the men had unsaddled, and a fire was already crackling on the old hearth. There was promise of comfort for the night, and they were not disposed to grumble. While some looked to the horses, others made haste to prepare a meal. A kid caught earlier in the day suggested a feast. Others, finding a broken door, made shift to set it on four stones, improvising a table, on which they set out the wine flasks and the food they carried with them, while one man paced up and down the edge of the plateau watching the mountains opposite and the pass beneath.

Kid's flesh, even when roasted over a wood fire, may not be to the taste of all who can choose their viands, but it is honest food for all that, and no one round that improvised table uttered a word against it. More logs had been piled on the fire, and the blaze threw dancing shadows on the stone walls and lit up the rough faces of the men. They were silent for a while, their sharp set appetites fully occupying them, but a draught of wine set the tongues wagging again.

"A song, Stefan: I've heard you roar a good stave ere this."

"Not a love song, surely?" said Grigosie.

"No, of wine."

"In all the verse I ever heard love and wine strangely go together," said the boy.

"Proving that the joys of both are transitory, perhaps," said Ellerey, who sat beside him. He spoke only to Grigosie, but Stefan heard him.

"Love, Captain--a snap of the fingers for love; but wine's the very heart of life. There's wisdom and truth in wine, there's valor in it, and it's powerful enough to make even good sound men fall in love. There's a stave I've heard which you may have if you will." And with much sound but little music Stefan broke into song.

It was a tavern ditty, and not too nice in its sentiments, as, indeed, why should it be, to please its hearers? There was a lilt in its chorus which even Stefan's unmusical voice could not hide, and it set the men's heads nodding in time as they roared it out together, waking the echoes with the declaration that--"The eye of a maid may sparkle, And the fools may for love repine, But the wise man knows As his road he goes That the best of life's gifts is wine."

"That isn't true, is it, Captain?" whispered Grigosie. "We know better than that."

Ellerey laughed, but he was not displeased to keep the lad in low conversation. The song had let loose a flood of jest and anecdote which lost none of their ribaldry in the telling. They were ill suited for a boy to hear and batten on.

"Yes, lad; we know better, you and I," he said. "Let them talk, we need not listen."

"I suppose it is natural in youth to shudder at some things they talk of, and much I do not understand."

"Keeping such ignorance you will be the happier. And do not drink much wine to-night, Grigosie; you must take your turn at sentry duty. It is share and share alike in an enterprise like this."

"Grant, then, there be stars to-night. I never feel lonely under the stars," the lad answered. "It was good wine that was poured into my flask at starting; I have hardly tasted it until now. Is yours good?"

"It might be worse, and I was never a heavy drinker."

"Taste mine."

"No, lad; why should I rob you?"

"Indeed, it will be no robbery. If you do not take it I shall offer it to Stefan presently. It is too strong for me."

"I'll taste it before I sleep, if you will. The air is close here. Let us go and fill our lungs with mountain breezes."

The boy sprang to his feet at once, careful to take his wine flask with him, and followed Ellerey on to the plateau.

There were stars in the clear sky, and a crescent moon that seemed to be poised on a sharp edge of the higher mountains. The air was keen, tingling in throat and nostrils.

"...the wise man knows As his road he goes That the best of life's gifts is wine," came again the lilting chorus from the tower. It was the only sound that disturbed the silence--the silence of a world.

"A night for regrets, Captain, yet one to speed ambition," said Grigosie.

"Yours has been too short to accumulate regrets."

"They get heaped together very rapidly sometimes," was the reply. "How long shall we stay here?"

"Only until we have seen Vasilici and delivered our message."

"And then back to Sturatzberg with our demands backed by an army of patriots," said Grigosie. "And for the success of the scheme--how do you reckon the chances?"

"If I expected failure I should not be here."

"Your own ambition supplies the motive, then? There is no love for a cause behind?"

"Hush, lad; those are dangerous questions to ask a soldier. If I know that reward awaits success, it is as certain that failure means death. Those who employ my sword would not hesitate to sacrifice me to save the situation; so you see, Grigosie, you set out on a venture some enterprise when you joined my company."

"Yes, we may fail and die, and yet other nights will be just as full of stars as this is. I wonder how it is that such a beautiful world is cursed to go so awry."

"Chiefly, my lad, because most of us care nothing about the beauty, but think only of using it as a plaything. Let us go in again. You should sleep before you go on duty." Some of the men had already stretched themselves cut in sleep, and there was weariness in the slow speech of the others. Only Anton seemed really awake, and he did not speak as the two entered the tower.

"Here is the wine," Grigosie whispered, handing the flask to Ellerey. "Drink to success in it, to success in war--and love."

CHAPTER XIV
THE TOKEN IS DELIVERED

The logs burnt low upon the hearth, and only a feeble light was in the tower. Anton saw Ellerey drink the wine and then cast himself down not far from Grigosie; but it was too dim for him to see whether all his companions were asleep. Some certainly were, for they snored, and others were restless, for they shifted their positions at intervals and sighed heavily. Where Ellerey and Grigosie were there was deep shadow, growing deeper as the fire died down. One sleeper there was restless for a little while, and then his breathing proclaimed that his sleep was heavy. Once Anton thought there was a darker shadow within the shadow, which moved quite silently, but he did not speak; he only listened very eagerly and raised himself on his elbow a little. Presently Anton slept too.

Ellerey awoke with a start. Some shock in a dream seemed to wake him, and as he raised himself his hand went to his breast, as it constantly did on waking. The token lay there safely. Then he leaned over toward Grigosie and stretched out his arm. The lad's place was empty. He was startled for a moment, as men may be on awaking suddenly from a dream, but he quickly recovered himself, remembering that the lad was sentry part of the night.

He lay down again, being heavy-eyed, but could not sleep. The air was oppressive, and a dull pain was in his head as though a steel band were clasped tightly round his forehead. The dream was still surging unpleasantly through his brain, and at last his restlessness prompted him to go out on to the plateau.

The stars were still bright, but the crescent moon had gone. At the edge of the plateau, resting upon his gun, stood the motionless figure of the sentry. Ellerey did not wish to startle him, so coughed slightly to let him know of his presence.

The boy did not turn.

"Grigosie."

"Is that you, Captain? I was just coming to call you. Watch the mountain opposite, and tell me if my eyes are deceiving me. There is nothing for the moment, but wait, and look steadily."

The top of the opposite side of the pass stood out clearly against the sky, but below was darkness. Grigosie pointed to that part which lay rather below the level of the plateau on which they were standing.

"They must be good eyes to see anything there," said Ellerey.

"Wait," whispered the boy.

Even as he spoke there shone for a moment a wisp of light like a firefly in the darkness, and then another, moving a little below it. Several times this was repeated in different places in the darkness, the point of light gleaming for a moment only and then suddenly going out.

"They have followed us, Captain, and by morning will have climbed high enough to command this position."

"When did you first see the lights, Grigosie?"

"Not ten minutes ago."

"Get to the gate at the top of the zig-zag pass--quickly! I will call the others."

The boy ran to his post at once, and in a few moments the whole of the little company was upon the plateau watching the points of light which came and went on the mountain opposite. There was no more sleep that night, only a waiting for dawn; and as daylight crept slowly down them, the mountains looked innocent enough. The sunlight bursting suddenly over the eastern ridges glinted upon no points of steel betraying hidden men in the hollows of the hills. Ellerey and Stefan stood together looking for such a sign, or the thin curl of smoke from a camp-fire.

"There's no army from Sturatzberg yonder, Captain," said the soldier. "Whoever climbed there last night showed lights only to guide their fellows, either not expecting us to see them, or not knowing that we are here."

"The brigands, perhaps," said Ellerey.

"The same thought was in my mind," Stefan answered.

Sharp eyes watched from the plateau during the early hours of the morning. Weapons were looked to, and the horses saddled ready for any emergency; but no attempt was made to conceal their presence there. Sharp eyes doubtless had also watched their movements from the mountains opposite, for three men presently appeared in the pass below. By what path they came there the watchers on the plateau could not tell. No sign of them had they perceived until they suddenly stood in full view.

"To travel in such fashion those must be born mountaineers," said Stefan. "Shall I signal to them, Captain?"

"Yes. Let them come up the path; we will meet them at the top. Grigosie, you stand on the rising ground there, and if there be any sign of treachery see you repeat the marksmanship you boast of."

The three men came up the zig-zag path fearlessly. They did not pause when they saw the soldiers waiting for them at the ruined gateway, but came on until they halted some five paces in front of them.

"We are sent to know your mission in the hills," said one, stepping slightly in advance of his companions.

"From whom do you come?" inquired Ellerey.

"From a friend, if we make no mistake, one whom you are sent to seek near the Drekner pass. Are you from Queen Elena?"

"I am the bearer of a message to Vasilici."

"You are welcome, then. We will bring you to him."

"Is he far from here?"

The man turned and pointed up the pass: "An hour's journey."

"We will come. The message I carry will need prompt action, for across the plain there are troops watching the road to Sturatzberg."

"There are more ways than one to the capital, and many men in those troops perchance who will welcome the sight of us."

"I do not doubt it," Ellerey answered. "Is the way passable for horses? We shall not want to return here."

"Yes, to the entrance of the chief's resting-place. How many are you?"

"Ten in all."

"Your numbers guarantee a friendly message," was the smiling answer. "We will await you at the foot of the path."

As the men departed Grigosie lowered the rifle which he had held ready for use, his finger resting lightly on the trigger; but he did not move from his post until

Ellerey called him.

"Ready, lad; we march at once."

"You are satisfied with the embassy?"

"Quite. In an hour's time the first stage of our mission will be accomplished."

"And then?"

"The result lies on the knees of the gods," said Ellerey.

"Do we all go?" asked the boy. "Yes."

"And leave none to keep this refuge?"

"What should we want with a refuge? We have come too far for that. If success does not lie in the road before us, the only refuge we can hope for is in death."

"I have a strange liking for life, Captain, just now."

The men led their horses down the zig-zag path, Ellerey and Stefan bringing up the rear. Grigosie turned to look back at the ruined walls, and the tower standing gaunt against the mountain-side. He had enthusiastically called it his, and in the desertion of it there may have been some regret. From the castle the lad's eyes followed the shape and direction of the ridges which lay about it, as though to impress the picture on his mind, but he spoke no word, and studiously avoided Anton's eyes, which questioned him. He was in no mood to reduce the thoughts which surged through his brain to any order. They raged and beat against the unknown shores of the future as a wind-swept ocean will against a rocky coast, carrying with them his hopes and ambitions, which were driven to and fro like brave craft struggling against shipwreck. There was some reason why he should regret the comparatively quiet haven of that castle in the hills.

In silence he mounted with the others at the foot of the path, and the little band of horsemen proceeded at walking pace, so that the envoys from Vasilici, who were on foot, might keep up with them. Ellerey and Stefan rode side by side, and at a sign from the former fell a few paces farther in the rear.

"It is evident that we shall presently have to leave the horses, Stefan; you and Anton shall stay with them while the rest of us go forward to deliver the token. While you wait keep a keen lookout on the hillsides and on--"

"On Anton," Stefan suggested. "I need no bidding, Captain. I do not trust him. I should trust him still less had I not taken a liking to his companion, Grigosie."

"The boy is stanch, I think, but it is perhaps as well to have them separated," said Ellerey; "that is why I leave Anton to you."

"He'll be in strict company, Captain, have no fear."

"I see no reason to doubt success," said Ellerey, after a pause, almost as if he had misgivings and wanted to be laughed out of them.

"There are many who have looked upon success, and yet have not had arm long enough to grasp it," said Stefan. "It's as well not to smack the lips until the liquor is running in the throat."

Their way lay up the pass toward the narrow defile which nature had closed long ago. There was an upward incline, but it was quite easy for the horses. The pass gradually narrowed as they went, and the mountain-sides grew more precipitous, shutting them in like great walls on either side. Little foothold was there for a lurking enemy, and there were no deep gorges where an ambuscade might hide. To defend this part of the pass in the old days must have meant a hand-to-hand struggle in the narrow way. Ellerey noted this as he went. His life in Sturatzberg had made him observant.

Presently the leading horseman stopped.

"It is difficult work for horses from here," said one of the brigands. "They can be fetched afterward to the place the chief directs."

"You, Stefan and Anton, will stay with them," said Ellerey. "I will send Grigosie back with orders presently. Take orders from none but Grigosie."

Stefan saluted and gathered the bridles together, smiling to see that Anton was not pleased at being left behind He looked at his youthful comrade, who took no notice of him, and obeyed with an ill grace.

"Why should he leave us?" he asked, when the others had gone, climbing the slope in front of them.

"Why not?" asked Stefan laconically.

"It is the business of servants and lackeys to mind horses."

"But we have neither."

"At least we are given no honorable service."

"For my part, I do as I am told," said Stefan, "and you'll be wise to do the same. That young comrade of yours is capable of looking after himself."

Anton looked at the soldier curiously for a moment, but Stefan's thoughts were always difficult to read. His face never showed a sign of any meaning beyond the words he uttered.

Following the three brigands, the others climbed up the slope of the landslip which had filled up the pass. It was uneven ground, and they were soon hidden from their companions with the horses. Descending presently into a ravine, the brigands stopped.

"As a careful Captain, you will appreciate the caution of our chief," said the spokesman, turning to Ellerey. "We were ordered to bring you no farther than this. He will come to you here."

"We are only eight; let him come with no larger following," Ellerey answered. "There shall be precaution on both sides."

"I will give your message, but--"

"Unless he fulfils my terms I depart the way I have come, and make my terms in the shadow of the castle yonder."

"I will tell him so," said the man, and the brigands went quickly up the ravine and disappeared.

"This is their vantage ground," said Ellerey. "Stand apart, all of you, near enough to help each other, but not in each other's way should a rush come. Grigosie, stand there, carelessly as it were, but with ready fingers. We have no knowledge of the honor of these men."

They had not long to wait. From the bend in the ravine came three men, the central figure a man of great stature. He walked proudly, with long, swaggering strides and swinging arms. His long black hair, bearded chin, and beady eyes set under heavy eyebrows, gave a ferocity to his appearance which Ellerey did not find attractive. He looked like a man in whom the barbarian was still active, whose laws of right and wrong and honor were likely to be of his own fashioning--one in whom it would be dangerous to trust too implicitly. Yet he was a striking and a handsome figure, and his dress gave him distinction. A scarlet feather was in his hat, and he wore a scarlet cloak which the weather had stained. A heavy knife was stuck in his belt, and it was obvious that his companions treated him with marked respect.

"Is this bravado, or does he know that a hundred pairs of eyes are watching us?" said Ellerey.

Grigosie did not take his eyes from the three men. He stood in a careless attitude, one hand resting on his hip, the other thrust into his breast, and his fingers were upon a revolver. No gesture of the men escaped him, and long before they came to a standstill in front of Ellerey he had learned their features thoroughly.

The big man gave a short salute rather as acknowledging an inferior than answering an equal.

"You have a message for me, Captain."

"I can answer that question when I know who you are," said Ellerey.

The big man laughed, with a glance at his companions, who laughed too, pleased to humor him. "You are a stranger in these hills, or you would know me. I am Vasilici."

He did not call himself great, but his manner easily filled the omission. He glanced at Ellerey, and at the soldiers, to see the effect of his words.

"Then I have a message for you from Queen Elena."

"It has been so long in coming that I have almost grown tired of waiting," Vasilici answered. "I presume she would have done without my help if she could."

"I am only the bearer of one message," Ellerey said shortly. The fellow's insolent manner came near to raising Ellerey's temper. This was a dangerous ally the Queen had chosen. "Do you know the nature of the message I bring?"

"Aye, as I know the price to be paid for my help. The Queen has not dared to question my terms, has she?"

"I know nothing of the price. I might find it too high if I did."

"Nor were you sent to argue, Captain, but to deliver the token," said Vasilici, holding out his hand.

Ellerey swallowed his rages a best he could, with a determination to take the pride out of this boaster some day; and drawing out the sealed box containing the bracelet of medallions, handed it to the brigand.

"At last the great day dawns for me and for Wallaria!" Vasilici exclaimed. "The kingdom of the hills comes to power and honor."

"Did they tell you that an army lies in wait between here and Sturatzberg?" asked Ellerey.

"Fifty armies will not stop me and those I lead when I elect to strike," cried the brigand, snapping his fingers. "The puppets in Sturatzberg will either bow to me or squeal at their punishment when I enter the city."

"You'll find the gates shut and some good men to guard them," Ellerey answered. "I am in a position to know that."

"We may use you, Captain, and for good service there is something more than thanks."

Ellerey laughed loudly; it was the only way he could prevent himself from cursing this insolent scoundrel. He almost despised himself for being even in the same cause with this swaggerer. For a moment Grigosie glanced at him, understanding something of what was in his mind, but the next instant he had turned again to watch Vasilici. The man was a swaggerer through and through, although if the tales told of him were true he did not lack courage. He had for a long time impressed his followers with his bluster and attitudes, playing a carefully studied part before them, appealing to that vein of romance which life in the mountains had fostered in them; and he played the part now for the benefit of Ellerey and his comrades. Falling into a pose, he turned the box this way and that, as though the opening of it were a supreme thing which a little delay would materially add to. Then with a flourish he drew the knife from his belt and broke the seals, pausing again to carefully replace the knife.

"Freedom to this wretched land at last," he said, "and so I open the Queen's token."

The box fell to the ground with the packing it had contained, and then with an oath Vasilici drew himself to his full height, one hand upon the haft of his knife in a moment.

"Is this how her Majesty attempts to fool me!" he cried.

Ellerey took a step forward to look, and an oath burst from his lips, too. It was not the iron bracelet of medallions which Vasilici held up, but a cross of gold, curious in shape and workmanship, upon which the sun glinted as it swung by its little chain in the brigand's hand.

CHAPTER XV
THE RACE FOR LIFE

The action a man will take in a crisis is exceedingly difficult to gauge beforehand. As a rule, such moments happen from a chain of circumstances which the man has not foreseen, and therefore has made no preparation to meet, and his conduct is likely to be guided entirely by the attitude of those about him, without any question of right or wrong, without a thought of what has occurred in the past or what may happen in the future. This was Ellerey's position. He had expected to see the bracelet of medallions; instead he saw a golden cross. He knew that in some manner he had been deceived, and who but the Queen could have placed this unexpected token in his keeping? By his manner he knew that the golden cross held some meaning for the brigand, a meaning of which Ellerey was absolutely ignorant; and under other conditions he might have admitted his ignorance and entered into explanations. As it was, the whole bearing of Vasilici, his bluster and his swagger, had roused Ellerey's anger. He had felt that the man was a crafty enemy even at the moment of delivering what he supposed to be a friendly message, and the keen desire to show his contempt for him had made his tongue smart with unspoken words, and his hands tingle to be clenched and to strike. He had forced himself to decent speech and attitude, but now his anger asserted itself. No question of duty or expediency seemed to bind him; only a boastful enemy was before him to be answered in the same fashion as he questioned, and if that did not suffice, to be punished as he merited.

"That is the token as I received it," said Ellerey.

As the brigand had held up the token Grigosie had leant forward to see it, the color mounting into his cheeks. Now his enthusiasm appeared to get the better of his prudence, and he cried out:

"Long live our country! Down with all who dishonor her! The golden cross gleams in the light of God's good sun; it is a benediction on this day, a promise of brighter days to follow. Summon your legions, Vasilici, and on to Sturatzberg where the hornets are nesting ready for destruction."

The brigand glanced at the boy contemptuously.

"What bantam is this you have brought to crow for you?"

"The boy speaks well enough," said Ellerey. "There is the token, where is your answer?"

"Here, and here," was the quick answer, as he hurled the cross high into the air behind him, and at the same time blew a shrill whistle. "That is Vasilici's answer to liars, and this his swift punishment."

The man's movements were so lithe and quick, so utterly unexpected, that he had sprung upon Ellerey before the words had fully left his lips. The long blade of his knife caught the sunlight, even as the golden cross had caught it a moment ago, and Ellerey's upraised arm alone protected his breast from the downward thrust. But the swift stroke did not come. A revolver shot awoke the echoes of the hills, and with a howl the great brigand leapt backward, his knife falling harmlessly to the ground, and his arm useless to his side.

"The bantam's answer," cried Grigosie. "To me, Captain!" It was at once evident that Vasilici had not ventured to the interview without support. The hills in front of them were immediately alive with men scrambling downward to the very ground the little band occupied. Men were in the ravine behind them rushing up to cut off retreat that way. Cries and shouting were on every side, some calling for surrender, others shouting that the soldiers had been deceived by their Captain. In the sudden confusion Ellerey gave quick commands, as, with sword in hand, he sprang to the rising ground where Grigosie stood; but his orders were either not heard or came too late for obedience. Before the soldiers could come to him, the brigands were between them.

"It is madness to stay," whispered Grigosie. "The hill behind us is clear." The boy fired twice in quick succession at men who had raised their rifles ready to fire at them, and although in answer a dozen bullets sang past them, the aim was faulty in the excitement.

"Shoot them both!" was the shout.

"Shoot them!" thundered Vasilici.

"Come," whispered Grigosie.

They scrambled upward together, the unevenness of the hillside protecting them for a moment from the flying bullets.

"I marked our direction," said Grigosie. "We can keep to this kind path for a little way, and with luck cross the open presently toward the horses."

They ran on, crouching lest their heads should be seen and mark the direction they had taken. Grigosie refilled the empty chambers of his revolver as he went, and Ellerey put up his sword and took his revolver instead. Behind them the firing had ceased, but they could not doubt that they were being swiftly followed; and spread over the open which they must needs cross, a hundred men probably barred their way.

"Unless they were already there when we passed, they will hardly have time to intercept us," was Grigosie's answer to this fear.

"Probably they were there, lad," said Ellerey. "We've about an equal chance with the hare that is being coursed."

"He gets away sometimes," was the answer.

They ran swiftly, mounting higher and higher as they went. Once they caught sight of men running in the path below them, and presently of others climbing the hillside to reach the summit before them, but no shout told them that they themselves had been seen.

"Don't fire, Grigosie, unless it is absolutely necessary," said Ellerey. "It would betray our whereabouts, and we shall want all our cartridges to stop them across the open."

The boy nodded and ran on.

"The top at last!" he exclaimed. "That height yonder is our mark. If we can reach it we shall be in sight of the horses. How far behind have we left them?"

He stood for a moment to look back along the ridge under which they had come. Some distance away men were coming into view.

"Quick, Grigosie; it's speed now," said Ellerey.

The way before them was clear, and they ran side by side, careful of their steps lest a hole might mean a fall and a sprained ankle. Presently a bullet passed between them, and they began to run in zig-zag fashion to puzzle the marksmanship. Ellerey constantly turned to look back. There were many pursuers, some widely straggling, but a few of them were gaining rapidly. These did not pause to fire; they ran, judging their pace and distance to a nicety. Long before the point for which the fugitives were making could be reached these men would be upon them.

"We must stop them, Grigosie."

The lad looked back. He was beginning to pant heavily.

"Not yet," he said; "they are not close enough."

So they ran on. It was evident to Ellerey that the boy's pace was palpably slackening, and there was yet some distance to cover to the height, to say nothing of the final dash for the horses. The men behind were rapidly overtaking them. Ellerey could hear the dull, rhythmic pad of the running feet.

"Twelve paces, Grigosie," he murmured, "then turn sharply. Do not kill, lame them; their companions may stop to help them."

Ellerey counted the twelve paces aloud, and then they both turned. Four shots rang out sharply, and three of the foremost runners stumbled and fell. An answering bullet cut through Ellerey's coat sleeve, and there was the pain as of a hot skewer laid for a moment on his flesh as he and Grigosie ran on again.

"Every step lessens the distance, lad," he said encouragingly. "That will teach them to keep a little farther in the rear."

Still Ellerey turned constantly to watch their pursuers. One or two had stopped by their wounded companions, but the rest held on their way, undeterred by the fate of their comrades. Twice again did Ellerey count twelve paces, and he and Grigosie turned together and fired. The foremost runner on the last occasion was Grigosie's mark, and he missed him. The man had bounded forward to make his capture when Ellerey's revolver sounded again. It was not the moment to hazard a shot, to aim at the swiftly moving limbs. The man leapt into the air and fell sprawling on his face, and with one spasmodic kick lay still. Grigosie turned and ran on again without a word. They were close to the height now. It was to their left, and the boy pointed to a depression which lay between it and another elevation. The way was narrow, which was in their favor, and if only the brigands were not in force on the other side, and Grigosie had made no mistake in the direction, there was a chance of escape.

Ellerey let Grigosie enter the narrow way first, and then paused in the entrance. Only two men followed them, and seeing Ellerey stop, they fired. Ellerey fired twice in answer, and without waiting to see if the shots had taken effect dashed after Grigosie.

The boy had made no mistake. They had come out half-way down the rising ground which they had climbed directly after dismounting. Below them stood Stefan and Anton with the horses, and higher up the slope above them more of the brigands were hastily descending. Some of the men had gone this way to cut off their retreat, and the fugitives had not a moment to waste in their final dash for freedom.

Ellerey fired into the air to put Stefan on the alert, and seizing Grigosie's arm-- for the boy was nearly beaten--he dashed down the steep incline. Stefan saw them and spoke quickly to Anton, who for a moment seemed inclined to lose his head. The soldier's sharp command steadied him, and the moment Grigosie was beside him he lifted him bodily into the saddle and then sprang to his own.

"No others?" Stefan shouted, wheeling Ellerey's horse round toward him.

"No."

Without a word Stefan cast loose the reins of the other horses, and the next instant the four riders were galloping for dear life up the pass, Ellerey and Grigosie in the centre, Anton and Stefan on either side. Knee to knee they galloped, their bodies low upon their horses' necks. Several shots followed them, but went wide of the mark, and a bend in the pass soon covered them. Still they held on their way, speaking no word. There was only the sound of the rapidly beating hoofs and the rough purring of the leather as the legs rubbed the saddles.

Ellerey thought that along the pass any surprise or ambush was impossible. He had taken careful notice of the mountain walls which shut them in, but he was not so satisfied that they would find the castle open to them. Those who occupied it, if any were there, could hardly have heard of the failure of the meeting yet, and he therefore hoped that he might gain possession of it by stratagem. To ride out of the pass would be madness, with the armies from Sturatzberg guarding the plain. The castle was their only hope--their place of refuge, as Grigosie had prophetically called it.

Ellerey drew rein presently.

"We have distanced them," he said. "What do you think, Stefan--will the castle be empty?"

The soldier shrugged his shoulders.

"If any brigands still occupy the hills about it, they cannot know that our mission has failed."

"These fellows manage to signal very quickly to one another," Stefan answered.

"Then we must fight for its possession. It is our only chance."

"Our chance is a poor one if it comes to fighting," said Stefan.

"We will try strategy first," Ellerey said. "Let us ride easily."

"What happened?" queried Stefan.

"The box did not contain the right token, and they attacked us without a word of warning."

"What of the others?"

"Heaven knows. They hardly seemed to strike a blow after we were surrounded. It was Grigosie who thought of the way across the hills, and we've had to run for it like hunted rabbits, eh, lad?"

Grigosie smiled faintly, but did not speak. He was still panting after his tremendous exertion. Anton had stretched out a hand to support him in his saddle as they galloped.

"They are dead then, those others?" said Stefan.

"I fear so."

"And we've been deceived, sent into a trap like a lot of rats. There's a reckoning to be paid."

"Time enough to think of that, Stefan. Let us secure the castle first," said Ellerey.

"I'm fearing the reckoning must be left for others to pay," growled the soldier. "It's putting our trust in a woman that's been the curse of us."

No one contradicted him, and they rode on in silence until the castle came in view. It looked gaunt enough, as silent and deserted as when they had first seen it. There was no movement on the plateau, no sign that any living creature except themselves was near it.

"Look!" exclaimed Stefan suddenly.

He pointed to the hillside on which the lights had shone mysteriously last night. Here and there were moving figures descending the slopes. Whether they had caught sight of the riders and jumped to the conclusion that something was wrong, or whether they had learnt of the escape from signals across the hills, it was impossible to say. At any rate they were descending rapidly, and there was no time to lose.

"Once in the zig-zag path the odds will be more evenly balanced," said Ellerey. "Forward! Gallop!"

"It seems to me they are making for a point beyond the castle," said Stefan. "They are expecting us to ride out of the pass."

"So fortune favors us," said Ellerey. "Rein up altogether at the entrance to the path, dismount, and up to the plateau quickly."

Even as they stopped with exact precision, a loud challenge came from the opposite hill, and, no answer being given, several shots whistled across the pass and struck close to the entrance of the zig-zag way.

"Up with you quickly!" shouted Ellerey, who brought up the rear. "There is little harm in such firing, and they will think twice before they follow us."

"Careful in front, lad," Stefan called out to Grigosie, who led the way. "Keep sharp eyes, the plateau may be occupied."

The boy nodded, but he had been looking out keenly before the soldier's warning, leading his horse in such a manner as to cover himself as much as possible. The precaution proved unnecessary; the castle was empty. Stefan was right. The brigands had not expected the fugitives to make for their old resting place, and when they saw them go up the path they shouted as though victory were already won, nor did they attempt to follow them. Why should they? Their foes were caught surely as birds netted by the fowler.

"See to the horses, Grigosie," said Ellerey. "Put them as far back in the ruins as possible. Now, Stefan, Anton, we'll heap stones across this broken gateway at the head of the path. It shall be our first line of defence, and if it is taken we will see to it that it is dearly bought."

"It is not the fighting that frightens me, it's the empty condition of the larder," said Stefan.

"Truly we are pariahs on God's earth," Ellerey answered. "Every man's hand against us, but we'll snarl and bite awhile in our stronghold, and then make a dash out and die in the open."

They toiled with a will all through the afternoon, heaping fragments which had fallen from the ruins across the gateway, and driving in stakes, rudely fashioned from any planks they could find, behind the stonework to strengthen it. Grigosie, by Ellerey's orders, did not assist in this work, but stood sentinel upon the plateau. The boy had had as much as he could stand for one day.

It was growing dusk in the pass below when they had finished. Daylight was still upon the summit of the mountains, but twilight had gathered in the deep valleys and ravines. The brigands still hung about the pass, watching the castle, but keeping out of range. It did not appear that they had any intention of attacking it. As they stood together looking down upon their enemies, Ellerey told Stefan what had happened and the details of their escape.

"Surely those are our fellows, Captain." But there was no tone of pleasure at the escape of his comrades; no note of welcome in the soldier's voice.

"This looks like desertion," said Ellerey.

One of the soldiers below called out in a stentorian voice which carried clearly in the quiet air.

"Ho there, Stefan!"

"Well, comrade?"

"We're betrayed by that devilish Englishman. Is he there with you?"

"The Captain is here. What of him?"

"Throw him down to us along with the boy," was the answer shouted back. "He's tricked us all, and that imp of Satan has helped him. The token he carried was not from her Majesty. He's a conspirator against the King, and carried the golden cross. You know what that means. Throw him down."

"It were easier for you to show your courage and come and fetch him."

"Our good friends here will do that. We have other work in hand. We ride back to Sturatzberg to tell our story, and heaven help you if you are alive when we return. There'll be little mercy for the companions of that devilish Englishman. Will you come with us?"

"I'm too old to run away," shouted Stefan, "and the company of cowards is not to my liking. May they cut your throats on the plain yonder and ask for your story afterward."

The brigands yelled with rage, and the soldiers shouted back coarse oaths.

"It would do my soul good to have a shot at them," said Stefan.

"Let them go," said Ellerey. "We shall want every shot we have. We are not without friends in the capital who may hear of our need. Against their will these fellows may help us."

The soldiers below moved on. It was evident that here they were to part with the brigands.

"Hold them fast for punishment," cried the same stentorian voice. "We shall return with the true message. Down with all lovers of the golden cross! Death to them who serve Maritza! Down with Maritza!"

"What is that they shout?" said Ellerey.

The answer came loudly, borne upward on the air, as the soldiers put their horses into a canter and rode down the pass.

"Death to the Princess Maritza!"

"You hear, Captain. Some one has fooled us all."

"Princess Maritza!" Ellerey exclaimed. "What has she to do with us?"

"Sufficient to give us a violent ending," Stefan answered.

"The golden cross is the sign of her house, her token; and you, Captain, have been her messenger."

CHAPTER XVI
THE TRAITOR

Asmile wrinkled Stefan's face, not of amusement at the deception which had been practised upon them, but in expectation of disappointed rage from Ellerey. With diplomacy and the fine points of strategy Stefan the soldier had little to do. His business was fighting. It was his livelihood, and some day, near or far in the future as fate decreed, it would be his death. His respect for his fellows was measured by their power of withstanding him, and the man he had the greatest affection for, perhaps, was a soldier, now incapacitated, who had once in a melee succeeded in knocking him from his saddle. At the same time he believed in his own astuteness, not without some reason be it said, and in the back of his mind there was always a certain admiration for the man who could get the better of him. It is more than possible that if he ever married he would thoroughly respect his wife on account of her cleverness in having hoodwinked him into marrying her.

But the burst of anger did not come. Ellerey's eyes were fixed on the point in the pass round which the soldiers had disappeared, and for some minutes he did not speak.

"What is done must remain as it is," he said at last. "We have only ourselves to consider now. We must watch two and two, one on the plateau, one at the path. Anton and you, Stefan; Grigosie and I. It's short rations for us and careful use of cartridges. We must understand how our enemy is going to conduct this siege before we calculate our chances. What ammunition have we?"

It was little enough that the four of them could display. If every cartridge accounted for a man, small damage would be done to their foes.

"I flung a belt of cartridges in a corner of the tower before we left," said Grigosie.

They all turned to look at him.

"Did you fling some food into a corner, too?" asked Stefan.

"No, but I marked that birds used the plateau in the early morning," Grigosie answered.

"They'll be coming in larger numbers presently, and, maybe, get a good picking off the four of us," said Stefan. "You haven't happened upon a fountain of wine, have you?"

"That, too, is supplied, Stefan; you can hear it leaping down the mountain-side, and see it too," and the boy pointed to a corner of the plateau which was within reach of the narrow stream which, from the heights, fell with many a cascade into the pass beneath.

Stefan looked at him for a moment, and then said in disgust: "Water and birds; fairies' fodder."

"It might be worse," said Anton.

"Wait a day or two, comrade, and you'll be crying a different tale," said Stefan, "although, for that matter, the food will doubtless last our time. Had we, in our small circle here, half a dozen taverns filled from cellar floor to garret ceiling, those fellows yonder would give us little chance of visiting them. Keep watch here, Anton; I'll go to the gate."

"We'll rest, Grigosie," said Ellerey.

The boy turned and entered the tower, but Ellerey did not follow him at once. He paced in and out the ruined walls, his hands clasped behind him, deep in thought and troubled.

Who had deceived him? It could only be the Queen, or the man who had brought him the token, or perhaps De Froilette. Indeed, they might all be in a conspiracy to deceive him. Yet why should the Queen desire to deliver the token of Princess Maritza's house to the brigands? How could it serve her ends? De Froilette's position and political aims were less clear. Ellerey had never believed him heart whole in his devotion to her Majesty; yet surely he would have taken the precaution to find out how such a token would be received before sending it. He was not the man to risk the work of years without some real hope of success. Then Ellerey's thoughts turned to the woman who had craved his help in the Altstrasse, the manner in which he had been searched for the token, the masked woman who had come to look upon him, and the warning she had given him. Baron Petrescu, too, had probably forced the duel upon him because of the token, believing that it had been delivered to him that night by the Queen. At his interview with her Majesty, the token which had been decided upon was the bracelet of medallions; it was hardly likely that it would be suddenly changed. Somehow the bracelet had been filched from the sealed box, and the golden cross placed there instead. Ellerey decided that the power to effect this change lay only with the man who had brought him the token, and on this man he fixed the blame.

Whoever was responsible for it, the scheme had failed miserably, and it was difficult to see how success could ever have been hoped for. On the other hand it could hardly be supposed that all those who followed the fortunes of the golden cross were fools, acting upon sudden impulse, courting disaster. They must have had some reason for believing that the token would receive some consideration from the brigands and those who had gathered to their standard. Possibly they had themselves been deceived, even as they had attempted to deceive. Ellerey could not doubt that Princess Maritza had a considerable following in Sturatzberg, that the seeds of the rebellion were widely scattered. The soldiers now riding toward the capital would spread the news of failure, and the rebellion in self-defence might be forced to break into open conflict at once. Even then, would Maritza's followers give a thought to the remnant of the band who had carried the message? If Countess Mavrodin had a voice in their councils, as surely she must have, they might. The chance of rescue was a slender one, but a hope did exist.

Strange to say, anger at the trick which had been played upon him did not assert itself in any great degree, in spite of the fact that all hope of honor and advancement was now at an end. Vasilici's attitude had doubtless something to do with Ellerey's state of mind, personal antagonism rising above ambition; but this would not have been the case probably had Ellerey been forced against his will into any other service than that of Princess Maritza. There was a charm for him in her name, the memory of her had dwelt with him and lent a halo of romance to his present position. He saw her again with her hair streaming in the breeze, and felt again the subtle strength and vigor that were in her. Had he not thought then that it would be good to fight in her cause? Why should he rage at the circumstances which had forced him into it?

When he entered the tower Grigosie was asleep, and he lay down to snatch what rest he could before relieving Anton and Stefan.

When they went on duty, Grigosie watched by the path, Ellerey on the plateau. "They will wait for Vasilici," Stefan said, when he reported that all had been quiet so far.

Ellerey paced up and down, pausing at short intervals to listen. Not a sound broke the deep silence. The great world seemed to lie still and motionless under the glow of the moonlit night and the pale glimmer of the stars. It was a time to dream of life and realized ambition, not to ponder on lurking death and failure. He walked presently to the head of the zig-zag path.

"Your castle has proved a refuge after all, Grigosie. How came you to be prophetic?"

"I did not believe my own prophecy."

"Yet you hid the cartridges."

"Believing, perhaps, that they would never be wanted," Grigosie answered. "I am full of strange thoughts and superstitions to-night, Captain, and cannot talk."

"It is the moon and the stars, Grigosie."

"Madmen's time, when everything is distorted," answered the lad.

"And lovers' time too, Grigosie."

"Which are you, madman or lover?"

"A little of both, I think," Ellerey answered.

"And below us death is waiting," said Grigosie.

"I don't think death is coming to us this time," replied Ellerey.

The boy did not answer. Several times during those watching hours Ellerey went to the head of the path, but Grigosie never spoke, never turned to him. His thoughts and superstitions occupied him; and with the light of day Ellerey noticed that there was something in his face which was new. He had changed during the night. Something--was it his courage?--seemed to have left him, but in its place there had come an addition to him, to his expression, almost to his character, Ellerey fancied. He watched the lad enter the tower, saw him cast himself wearily into his corner, and would have followed him had not Stefan detained him.

"I was right, Captain. Vasilici is coming. They are gathering in the pass waiting for him."

A little later a shout proclaimed the arrival of the chief, and Ellerey saw his huge frame in the midst of his followers. His right hand was swathed in a handkerchief and rested in a sling, and savage ferocity was in his face as he looked up toward the castle. His orders, and he appeared to give many, were promptly obeyed, and he struck one man viciously, perhaps because he dared to offer advice unasked.

It was evidence of his power among them that no one interfered, nor did the victim himself retaliate. Men began to climb the opposite slopes, while others massed themselves at the foot of the zig-zag pass.

"They are going to attack us at once, Captain," said Stefan. "It is to be hot work for us to-day."

At the head of the path the little band of defenders waited.

"Every shot must tell," Ellerey whispered, "and keep well behind the stone-work, all of you."

The path was narrow with deep sides. The brigands came up it boldly enough until the last bend in it showed them the stone-barred gateway. Then they halted, and the foremost leaned back upon those behind who pushed them on and shouted: "Forward!" Two men fired blindly at the stone wall, and then rushed upon it, never to reach their goal. Only two shots rang out, but both men threw up their arms and staggered backward upon their companions. Not more than two abreast could come up the narrow way, and twice again a speedy death crowned the temerity of those who rushed to the attack. Those behind shouted to be let up to the front, and those before made every effort to let them come. The spirit of the brigands seemed to die out of them as their eyes fell upon their dead companions and that silent death-dealing barricade. Then one fellow suddenly picked up a corpse, and holding it before him as a shield, dashed forward with a shout.

"Let him come," whispered Ellerey. "Shoot at those who follow."

The man rushed to the wall until the dead body struck the stonework. Success for a moment seemed to be his. He had plugged one narrow slit through which the bullets came, and he cheered his comrades on. They came, but only to have their leader fall back into their arms. Through the slit Ellerey had driven his sword with all his strength, piercing the living through the dead. It had been an ugly rush, but for the present it was the last.

"They'll try some other plan before attempting this way again," said Stefan.

"Is there any other way?" Grigosie asked.

"For mountaineers there may be. These fellows can walk in places where we should never venture and only expect to find flies."

From the opposite mountain a desultory fire was maintained upon the plateau, which could only do harm if the defenders were careless. For the rest of the day the brigands held aloof, standing or sitting in parties in the pass and watching the castle. Vasilici strode from one group to another, but no movement followed. There was no sleep for the defenders that night, and at dawn, in spite of Stefan's forecast, another attack was made upon the gate. It was as unsuccessful as the first, nor was it made with such determination. The obedience to orders was only half-hearted.

Later in the day it became evident that a council of war was being held. The murmur of the men's voices reached the plateau, but no words could be distinguished. An oath from Vasilici sounded clearly now and again, but that was all. Some persuasion was apparently pressed upon the chief which he jeered and laughed at, but there was a shaking of heads when he pointed to the zig-zag way. His followers were not inclined to try that road to victory again. They had had their surfeit of it. Vasilici was quick-witted enough to see that he must listen to counsel, and with lowering visage he turned first to one and then to another as they spoke. Presently one speaker seemed to please him, for his features relaxed into a grim smile. A movement ran through the whole assembly, men turned to one another and nodded their satisfaction. Some definite conclusion had been arrived at.

"They seem to have hit upon another way of getting at us," said Stefan.

"Is there another way?" asked Grigosie, repeating the same question he had asked before. No one answered him, nor did he seem to expect an answer. He stood watching the now moving mass below, little interest in his eyes. His alertness had departed.

Vasilici had disappeared into some pathway at the foot of the opposite slope, and then the crowd fell aside for one man, who, standing alone, took off his neck-cloth and waved it toward the plateau.

"A parley, Captain. Shall I answer?" said Stefan; and then, having permission, he shouted: "Hallo!"

"I would speak with your Captain," came the answer.

"I'm a mouthpiece, comrade, same as you are. Speak on."

"I am commanded to offer you your lives and freedom on one condition."

"And the condition?" Stefan shouted, prompted by Ellerey. "You are free to leave the pass unmolested if you will deliver up the youth who is of your company."

"We'll see you--" Stefan began, without any prompting.

"Word it as you will," said Ellerey, "the coarser the better, perhaps, for such a devilish suggestion."

"Wait!" exclaimed Grigosie. "Ask for time to consider."

"Who wants to consider such a thing as that?" growled Stefan.

"We gain time," said Grigosie, turning to Ellerey. "Say you will consider the suggestion and answer them tomorrow. We sorely need rest; what does it matter how we gain it?"

"My gorge revolts against their even fancying that we should consider such a thing," said Stefan.

"Command him, Captain," pleaded Grigosie. "In war and love everything is fair."

Ellerey gave way and Stefan shouted the answer.

"Until to-morrow," came the answer. "The youth once in our hands, you are free to depart. If he is not given up to us we will have our revenge, though half the sons of these mountains fall in the gaining it; and the longer that revenge is delayed the fiercer shall it be when it does come. Until to-morrow. There shall be peace between us until then."

"But we'll keep watch by the gate for all that," growled Stefan, who was not in the best of tempers at having to answer the brigands in this fashion.

"There is another way, you see," said Grigosie. "I have got an answer to my question."

"Well, lad, when you alone are in their hands, the rest of us will have said his last prayer, or growled his last oath, whichever pleases him best at the hour of departure."

"The question is not so easily settled, Stefan," Grigosie said. "Send Anton to the gate, Captain, while we discuss it."

Ellerey laughed at the lad's strange mood as he entered the tower with him.

Stefan followed them and stood in the doorway.

"The question is worth consideration, though you may not think so," Grigosie began. "You have been deceived, Captain, and also those who served with you."

"Enough of that, lad. It is past, and the present is our concern. If we come out of this with our lives we may talk of punishing those who deceived us."

"Should it not be a bitter punishment?" queried the boy.

"As bitter as the death to which they have brought us face to face," said Ellerey fiercely, his whole being roused for a moment at the thought of the outrage practised upon him.

"But that revenge seems out of your power," Grigosie went on. "For you and Stefan there is almost certain death to-morrow or a week hence, it may be."

"It is very likely. I have looked death in the face before, and so has Stefan there. When we look into his eyes for the last time I warrant we shall not change color."

"Except with the heat of our final struggle," said Stefan from the doorway.

"Your comrades have gone. You two stand alone," said Grigosie.

"With you and Anton," said Stefan.

"And we wish for no better companions," added Ellerey. "Vasilici's knife would have written finis to my history had it not been for you, Grigosie."

The boy colored a little with pleasure.

"Still you forget, Captain, that Anton and I were not of your choosing. We forced ourselves into your company."

"What of it? I am glad, I--" and then the look in Grigosie's eyes stopped Ellerey suddenly. Stefan, too, started from his leaning position and stood upright in the entrance, looking straight at the boy.

"By your leave, I would become the hostage for your safety," said Grigosie. "I asked you to take me with you; now I ask you to give me up."

"Plague upon you, lad, you almost anger me. You are beyond my understanding," was Ellerey's answer, but he still looked fixedly at him.

"Since I have deceived you it is fitting that I should pay the penalty," said the boy quietly. "I would sooner meet death at their hands than at yours. Grant me this much, and make an end of it."

"You!" exclaimed Ellerey. "You deceived me! I do not believe it."

"It is the truth. Stay, I would not have you think too ill of me. It was not done wantonly. Those who made me believe that there was a good chance of success mis-led me, but if I thought you too would reap the benefit, it is none the less true that I deceived you. I came not from the Queen; I came to work this very thing that has happened, the delivery of the golden cross instead of the bracelet. I have played my hand and lost. Mine should be a bitter punishment; you yourself have said it. Grant me this only, that I receive it from the brigands yonder, and not from you."

Ellerey hardly seemed to hear the boy's latter words. The sudden confession was all his brain seemed to have the power to take in. Stefan remained motionless, statue-like, still staring at Grigosie. For a space there was silence in the tower. Then Ellerey turned sharply upon the boy and laid his hand roughly on his shoulder, so roughly that he winced a little, but showed no sign of fear.

"You lie, Grigosie, confess that you lie. The box containing the token has never left me, night or day. As I received it from her Majesty so it has always been, so I delivered it. Of course you are lying."

"You slept soundly, Captain, the night you drank from my wine flask."

"Was it then, you scoundrel?"

"It was then."

Deep down in every man is the instinct of the savage, the acceptance of the law which demands an eye for an eye and a tooth for a tooth. Given occasion great enough, it may rise even in the man who has all his life studied to curb his passions, and in his judgments to be merciful. Ellerey was of the rough and readier sort. He was a disappointed man, one who nursed the thought of revenge against those who had injured him. He was a soldier among soldiers who had much of the barbarian in them. He was an adventurer among adventurers. If the youth of this deceiver and betrayer appealed to him for a moment, the thought was sternly crushed. If the thought of what they had come through together came into his mind, there also came the knowledge that he had committed the unpardonable sin. He had betrayed his comrades.

"Heaven forgive you for making me your judge," Ellerey cried; "but what is there except death for the traitor?" and his sword rang from its scabbard as he spoke.

He paused a moment and looked toward Stefan.

"It's hateful, but it's just," muttered the soldier in his beard, and he did not move from the doorway. He only lowered his head so that he might not see.

"I admit the justice," said Grigosie; "but will you not grant my request and deliver me to the brigands? So you shall escape."

"Escape!" cried Ellerey. "For what? Is there any truth and honor in the world? I have not found them, and the end may come when it will. It is an easier death you shall have from my hands than you would have from theirs."

The sword was ready, and Stefan turned in the doorway just in time to see Anton and to catch his uplifted arm as he attempted to rush past him toward Ellerey. Not a word spoke the soldier, but he fiercely twisted Anton's aim, and the knife he held rattled to the floor.

"As my fathers faced death, so can I, unflinchingly," Grigosie cried. "Strike, Captain! God knows it was not such work as this I thought to find for the strong arm of Desmond Ellerey."

As he spoke, he tore his shirt open at the throat to receive the blow. His cap fell from his head, and curls, the hue of copper, slipped loosely down upon his forehead, while the open shirt just revealed the curve of a white bosom.

"A woman!" exclaimed Stefan, letting go of Anton in his blank astonishment.

Slowly Ellerey's sword was lowered, and for a moment he did not speak. Then almost in a whisper he said:

"Maritza! Princess Maritza."

CHAPTER XVII
THE TRUE WORTH OF BARON PETRESCU

There was excitement in Sturatzberg. Rumor flies fast, and the moment it was whispered that the city gates were watched, that Captain Ellerey, of his Majesty's Horse, was to be arrested, men began to stop and gossip at street corners, and women to stand upon their thresholds ready to give, or to receive, information. Strange stories grew current in this manner, which served to keep the excitement alive until more definite news were forthcoming. There was unwonted stir in the secret societies and clubs, sympathy being with Ellerey, since he had in some manner offended the Government. They did not stay to inquire what he had done, or, indeed, to think whether his action would tend to further any scheme of their own; it was enough that he had shown defiance to the powers that be. Every hour fresh rumors were started and eagerly discussed and as eagerly denied. Only two things were definite: there was much coming and going at the palace, and Captain Ellerey was not to be found.

Those who lead rebellion, or pull the wires of conspiracies, are seldom open with those they lead, any more than the policy of King's Ministers is wholly spread before the people. There were leaders in Sturatzberg who knew many things, who shrewdly guessed at more, and their knowledge was not reassuring.

Lord Cloverton did not expect the immediate arrest of Ellerey after the failure to discover him at the Countess Mavrodin's. He had fully believed that he was there, and had purposely kept the Countess driving in the Bois until such time as the search should be accomplished. The failure was disappointing, but his interview with the Countess would bear fruit. Ellerey would have to move cautiously, and time was therefore gained. The gates were closed that night, and no Captain Ellerey had passed through them. Countess Mavrodin's house was watched, and no one had left it. So the Ambassador met the morning with a smile; so far his prompt action had saved the situation. A few hours were destined to bring him surprises. First came the news of the return of Captain Ward's cloak. The messenger who brought it was promptly taken before the Ambassador and sharply questioned. He had received it from Captain Ellerey himself an hour before midnight, he said.

"Why were you chosen as a messenger?" asked Lord Cloverton.

"I cannot say. I brought it because I was paid to do so."

"You seem very certain of the time. Did Captain Ellerey tell you the hour?"

"No, sir; the clocks were striking the hour as he spoke to me."

"What is Captain Ellerey like?"

The description given seemed satisfactory until after the man had been dismissed, and then Lord Cloverton recognized that it would fit many men. The cloak was Captain Ward's, but there was no certainty that Ellerey was the man who had given it to the messenger. To-day the city was being searched; the return of the cloak went to prove that Ellerey was still in Sturatzberg; had that been the intention in returning it? The smile of satisfaction slowly faded from the Ambassador's face, and he began to grow feverish for further news. Later he was with the King when the Countess Mavrodin begged for an audience.

"She may unwittingly enlighten your Majesty," said Lord Cloverton, He could not believe that his cleverness would not be sufficient, sooner or later, to make the Countess betray herself, although the past was utterly barren of result.

So Frina Mavrodin was admitted. The presence of the British Ambassador did not disconcert her. She went to the point at once.

"Is it true, your Majesty, that my house was searched yesterday by your instructions?" she asked.

"Countess, how can you think that?" said the King. "It is true that I commanded the arrest of Captain Ellerey, and that command may have been used to open your doors, as it would serve to open any door in Sturatzberg."

"I have heard of no other house being entered by force," the Countess answered. "Naturally, I seek to know why I am suspected."

She puzzled Lord Cloverton more than ever. This was a bold stroke to disarm suspicion.

"My dear Countess," said the King, blandly, "would you hold me responsible for the actions of my officers? Believe me, the city is being searched in every corner for this rebel Captain. It is pardonable if in the search some annoyance is given to innocent persons, is it not? Their loyalty should overlook the offence."

"True; but your Majesty, I would humbly submit, overlooks one fact of the gravest importance to me. That my house is searched for a rebel is nothing; but when it is searched for a man who, at Court, has been somewhat in my company, the action affects me curiously. It is not a question of loyalty, but one which concerns my fair fame."

"Surely, Countess, you exaggerate."

"Indeed, your Majesty, I do not, as Lord Cloverton can prove. Only yesterday, in the Bois, he made it evident that Court gossip linked my name with Captain Ellerey's, and even suggested that I might render service to my country and this Englishman at the same time by saying all I knew. Is it not so, my lord? You were very anxious to save your countryman and get him out of the city?"

This was more than the Ambassador had bargained for and an answer did not come readily to his lips.

"Is it not so, my lord?" the Countess repeated. "I admit, Countess, that, fancying there was some tender understanding between you and my countryman, I was willing, if possible, to render you a service. I seem to have heard that love has been accountable for strange, and even foolish actions. This is the beginning and the end of my offence."

"Are you sure of that?" she said. "Forgive me if I am mistaken, but the searching of my house was strangely timed with our drive in the Bois."

"Oh, Countess!" the Ambassador exclaimed. "Surely you forget that I only availed myself of your courteous invitation."

"Which I could do no less than give since you explained that you had foregone your afternoon sleep to meet me there," she replied quickly, and smiled, the smile of a very charming woman of the world, as most people considered her; but Lord Cloverton seemed to catch some meaning behind the smile, and the King felt that he ought to come to his rescue.

"We have both fallen under the Countess's displeasure; how can we prove how unjustly? I will reprimand my too zealous officers, and they shall make you an apology."

"Your Majesty is good," she answered. "For myself it is no great consequence, but had you witnessed the consternation of my servants, you would have understood how serious a matter it was in their eyes."

"Subjects and servants alike, Countess, are our masters," said the King.

Frina Mavrodin departed full of thanks and wreathed in gracious smiles. When she had gone, the King and the Ambassador looked inquiringly at each other.

"I think your suspicions were unfounded, my lord," the King said.

"I missed the centre of the target, your Majesty, but I believe I aimed at the right mark. She is a clever woman; I admire her more every day."

Lord Cloverton spoke the truth; he did admire her. Like all great men, he was quick to recognize the sterling worth of his adversaries, and it was borne in upon him more and more that in this crisis he had a clever and beautiful woman to deal with, and what antagonist could be more powerful? He began to rearrange his thoughts upon this basis, passed in review all the seemingly trivial incidents with which Frida Mavrodin had been connected, and found many new meanings in them. The possibility that her influence might be paramount in Sturatzberg dawned upon him. Such a subtle power at work would explain many things, and the Ambassador determined to watch her more closely than ever.

All that day search was made for Captain Ellerey throughout the city. Many places, known to be haunts of the dissatisfied, were entered, but were innocent of even the appearance of evil. There were too many ready to bear warning for such places to be taken unawares. But no other houses of such importance as the Countess Mavrodin's were disturbed. There was no result. No one had seen Captain Ellerey; indeed, few people appeared to know him, or to have heard of him. This Lord Cloverton did not believe. He thought he recognized Frina Mavrodin's influence at work in such ignorance.

It was on the following day that Monsieur De Froilette called at the Embassy, and was shown into Lord Cloverton's room. With this new train of thought in his mind, the Frenchman's importance in the politics of Wallaria appeared to sink into insignificance.

"You are welcome, monsieur. Is this a friendly visit or--"

"Friendly, certainly, but something more," De Froilette answered. He had not come to the Embassy without due deliberation. He had had an audience with the

Queen that morning, and there was something in her tone which decided him to make his own interests doubly secure by giving help to the British Ambassador--such help that might count for much when the time for settling accounts came, but which should not materially hasten that time.

"I had begun to think you had forgotten your promise," said Lord Cloverton, "News of Captain Ellerey would be very useful to--to the Government of this country. You had a servant watching him, I think."

There was something resembling the Queen's tone in the Ambassador's--a want of appreciation of his position and importance.

"That is so," replied De Froilette quietly. "I understand you--that is, the Government--have done your utmost to find this Englishman, and have failed."

"At present, monsieur, at present."

"Which is hardly wonderful," continued De Froilette. "I have so constantly observed that you--the Government, I should say--concentrates its energies in the wrong direction; is it not so, my lord?"

"An opinion which may--observe, I do not say which does, but which may--arise from an entirely wrong conception of the Government's aims."

"*Ma foi*, that is so!" laughed the Frenchman, conscious that the Ambassador was annoyed. "Of course, in my ignorance I have supposed that the Government, in searching for this Captain Ellerey, really wanted to find him. Foolish of me! It was a mere blind, a strategy, to mislead. The Government is really looking for some one else. Pardon me, my lord, for taking up your time." And De Froilette rose to go.

"You are too hasty, monsieur; pray be seated again. It is Captain Ellerey we want."

"Ah! Then I am not deceived," said De Froilette, sitting down again. "Tell me, why do you so persistently look for him in the wrong place?"

"Can you show us the right one, monsieur?"

"Send your troops out by the Southern Gate and bid them march toward Breslen, and let sharp eyes watch the depths of the forest. They may be rewarded by seeing men gathering to a centre there. Find that centre and you shall find Captain Ellerey."

"Is it your timber business which teaches you so much?" inquired Lord Cloverton with a smile, some contempt looking out from behind it.

"You laugh at my trade, but it may prove useful even to you. You watch the city gates, you search every street and corner of Sturatzberg, and behold your bird is flown and is many hours upon his journey before you even start in pursuit."

"This is most interesting, monsieur, but--"

"But you do not believe it," interrupted De Froilette. "I have had a message from this Captain Ellerey. My servant watched his lodgings. Early in the morning a boy brought a message to the Captain's servant. Francois, my man, entered the house and got into conversation with this servant, a rude soldier with small understanding, but with stanch love for his master. Put upon his guard by Ellerey, doubtless, he conceives the possibility that Francois may be playing the spy, and falling upon him unawares he gags and binds him and locks him in a cellar. The next day Captain Ellerey, a band of horsemen with him, meets a woodman in the forest toward Breslen, and by him sends me word that my servant is gradually starving behind his cellar door, of which the woodman gives my the key. I go to the Captain's lodging, and there is Francois. ***Pauvre garcon***, he was hungry, my lord; and, ***ma foi***, he will be very terrible the next time he and that soldier meet."

"On the Breslen road, you say," Lord Cloverton remarked thoughtfully. He had made up his mind quickly.

"Probably in Breslen itself by this time. I understand there is much dissatisfaction there."

"And Captain Ellerey's object, monsieur?"

The Frenchman shrugged his shoulders as though such a consideration had not occurred to him.

"Is my opinion worth anything, my lord? I am not in the councils of the Government. I know little of the State's difficulties, the plots which threaten, the particular points of danger; but as a private person I should incline to the belief that it has to do with the Princess Maritza. I have already told you that she is, or was, in Sturatzberg You do not believe it. That is a pity."

"I am beginning to believe it, monsieur," the Ambassador answered, "and I thank you for coming here to-day. The gates of Sturatzberg are not so well guarded as they should be."

"That is not my affair," said De Froilette with a smile. "I have given my information to you because I know the prestige of Lord Cloverton and his value to the peace of Wallaria."

With these parting compliments the Frenchman bowed himself out, feeling that he had established his position with the Ambassador, and put him off the real scent at one and the same time. The pleasant security of the latter feeling was destined to be quickly and rudely dispelled. Some troops certainly did leave the city and go toward Breslen, but many more set out in the opposite direction and stretched across the country which lay between Sturatzberg and the mountains. Lord Cloverton, in advising the King, was still convinced that the most imminent danger threatened from the brigands in the hills.

The despatch of the troops did not surprise Frina Mavrodin. That they should go chiefly toward the hills seemed only natural, seeing that the brigands lay there. The time since she had returned to find that her home had been searched had passed in a whirl of conflicting emotions. For a few moments after dismissing Hannah she had stood upright, immovable, with a sense of being alone in the world. All the interests and hopes of her life seemed to slip from her and fall into a heap of dead ashes at her feet. The Princess had gone. Doubtless she had meant to go when Frina had left her that morning, and had got her out of the way on purpose. It was Dumitru who had suggested her going into the Bois; it was Dumitru, probably, who had persuaded Maritza that the time to act had come. Not for a moment did Frina suppose that Dumitru was cognizant of the fact that her house would be searched; she did not believe that they had gone to escape discovery. If such had been the case she would have been taken into their confidence. No; the departure had taken place for the furtherance of plans in which she had no part, and which she promptly linked with the disappearance of Captain Ellerey. It never occurred to Frina to set watches to warn the Princess should she return. She would not return. For good or ill she had begun the final move toward her goal. What were her plans? What chance had they of success? Frina knew what secret societies nursed the cause of Princess Maritza in the city. She knew to a unit what support could be depended upon, knew the exact value of it, the strength and the weakness of it. The cause had looked to the hills for support, not without reason, perhaps. Were not the men gathered there rebels, ready to strike a blow at the Government? This had always been Maritza's argument, and there had been some signs that she was right. Frina knew that the material for revolt was to hand, but a resolute leader had been lacking. Now this want had been supplied by Captain Ellerey. It was round Ellerey that the whirl of Frina's emotions centred. Her relief that the Princess had gone before the house was searched gave place to the apprehension that she had gone to join Captain Ellerey. She saw only a rival in her late guest. It was her love for the man which ruled Frina Mavrodin's actions, not her love for the cause. It was in this spirit that she made her complaint to the King, for the time might come when her house would prove the only safe refuge for Ellerey. It was in this spirit that, with her maid in attendance, she presently went to visit Baron Petrescu.

The Baron's wound had not proved serious, but it had kept him to the house. The Countess found him lying on a sofa, from which he half rose as she entered. She hurried forward to prevent him.

"This is good of you, Countess," he said. "Strangely, you were in my thoughts when you were announced."

She inquired about his wound and expressed her regrets in a few prettily turned sentences. "It was nothing," said the Baron. "The greatest hurt was to my pride."

"And, of course, you long for an opportunity of wiping out the defeat?" said Frina.

"Curiously enough, that idea has not risen uppermost in my thoughts," Petrescu answered. "I owe the Englishman an apology for the attack which was made upon him directly he succeeded in wounding me. He is a gentleman and a gallant swordsman, and I writhe under the fear that he believes that attack was of my contriving."

There was the genuine ring of truth in the Baron's words. Frina Mavrodin was not surprised. She believed that she thoroughly understood him, or would not have visited him.

"You would befriend Captain Ellerey were it in your power?" she questioned.

"Gladly, for his own sake and for yours. Pardon me, Countess, if my own confession slips out with these words. Those who love recognize love quickly."

"Was that in your mind when you forced this duel upon Captain Ellerey?" she asked.

"I have tried to believe that love for the cause stood first, Countess. Please question me no further. I take refuge behind the punishment I have received. That I have not forfeited all your esteem is proved by your presence here. Tell me how

I can serve you."

"Like many others, Baron, you jump to a conclusion too quickly; but let it pass. There is weightier business in hand," and then she told him all that was known about Ellerey, and of the disappearance of Princess Maritza. "Knowing that the Princess always had it in her mind to use Captain Ellerey when the time came," she went on, "I have little doubt she has joined him in whatever mission he has undertaken. What art she will, or can, use to turn him to her service, I do not know."

"He is not the man to be lightly turned from the cause he has espoused," said the Baron thoughtfully, "and that cause is not ours."

"Love might prove incentive enough," said Frina.

Petrescu turned to her quickly. The look in her eyes told him her secret plainly enough, but her words were sufficient to have a quickening influence on the hopes which had died within him.

"I may be jumping to a rash conclusion," Frina went on hastily, "but if I am right--indeed, whatever art is used, what hope is there of success?"

"None, unless those in the hills are with us," replied the Baron decisively. "Here in Sturatzberg we have much enthusiasm, much talk, much jealousy; but I doubt the fighting temper behind it. The Princess has moved too soon."

"Is there any chance of her being able to persuade the brigands?"

"Where men are concerned I dare not limit the power of a woman," he answered; "but since the Princess has moved, we are bound to be on the watch. Failure will be disastrous to you and me, Countess."

"It will probably mean death to Princess Maritza, to Captain Ellerey certainly."

"I understand," said the Baron. The hope that was in him died, and it is doubtful if the woman ever gave him full credit for what his words cost him. "I understand. To-morrow I shall be out again. Command me and trust me. There shall at least be one arm to strike a blow in the Englishman's defence, and back to back, Countess, he and I would render no mean account of ourselves." She had taken the hand he held out in token of her thanks and the compact between them when the door was suddenly opened and a man entered hurriedly. He stopped abruptly, seeing that his master was not alone.

"I have no secrets from this lady," said the Baron. "You may speak freely."

"The city is in excitement," said the man. "Some horsemen have ridden in saying that Captain Ellerey is in the hills surrounded by the brigands. Instead of being on the King's service, as the men supposed, he carried the token of Princess Maritza's house. The brigands immediately attacked the party."

"Yes, and then?" exclaimed Frina.

"These men deserted, my lady, and left the Captain and two or three companions to their fate. These fellows are boasting loudly of their loyalty to the King."

"And the others, are they dead or captured?" asked the Baron quickly.

"It seems they managed to gain some ruin in the hills, and are there making a last stand."

The Baron dismissed the man, and then turned sharply to the Countess.

"You must go quickly and learn all the news," he said. "My wound shall be made to serve a useful purpose. It shall be sufficient to keep me free from visitors for some days to come, but it will not prevent my leaving Sturatzberg to-night. I have a few men I can rely upon. We may not turn failure to success, but we may effect the escape of Captain Ellerey and those who are with him. Have you a trusted messenger you can send to me?"

"Yes."

"Learn all you can, then, and send word to me here before nine to-night. At that hour you may know that I have departed, and what a man may do, rest assured Countess, I will."

CHAPTER XVIII
SIX LOYAL MEN

From the Northern to the Southern, from the Eastern to the Western gates Sturatzberg was in an uproar. Excitement was in every face, and the wildest rumors were given credence. When the guards at the gates were doubled and companies of soldiers were met in the streets, it was firmly believed that the brigands were marching in overwhelming numbers upon the city. Comparatively few had heard the news from the returned horsemen's own lips, and from much reporting the tale had grown out of all knowledge. After the excitement caused by the search for Captain Ellerey the city was ready to believe anything.

As the Baron's servant had related, the horsemen were loud in their boasting of loyalty. They had followed Captain Ellerey because they believed they were on the King's service, they said, and never for a moment had they supposed otherwise until they had seen the golden cross in Vasilici's hands. This was the story they told the King when they were taken to the palace, with much more concerning their own valor when the brigands rushed upon them. They disagreed somewhat concerning one another's valour, each one striving to impress the King in his own favor; but they were of one voice regarding Ellerey's treachery and the deceit which had been practised upon them. "What message or token could you suppose I was sending to the brigands?" asked the King.

"It was not for us to inquire, your Majesty," they answered. "We knew Captain Ellerey, and we obeyed him."

In the main their story was true. If Ellerey had mentioned the Queen as their employer they had considered the King and Queen as one, and no question was put to them to make them differentiate between them.

They were dismissed, and the King was for some hours closeted with one or two of his prominent Ministers. They were men the King trusted, but it was doubt-ful if their opinion ever weighed with him to the same extent that Lord Cloverton's did. The news astonished the Ambassador, but was reassuring. Whatever the cause, the Queen's plans at any rate had miscarried, and the brigands were evidently not to be tempted into the service of Princess Maritza. For the moment there was no danger to be apprehended from them.

"I think we may leave this turbulent Captain and his companions to Vasilici's tender mercies, my lord," said the King. "All we have to guard against is a riot among the dissatisfied in Sturatzberg."

Perhaps the Ambassador felt sorry for Ellerey, but there was nothing he could do.

"Has your Majesty ever supposed that Princess Maritza is, or has been lately, in Sturatzberg?" he asked after a pause.

"It is impossible. Your Government has sent her visiting your colonies, a deli-cate attention, which, no doubt, she appreciates."

"Just so, and yet I had a strange story brought to my notice. I heard that she had managed to escape the delicate attention of my Government and had returned to Wallaria. Needless to say, I did not believe the story, but the deliverance of her token certainly lends credence to it."

"She might send her token," said the King; "she would not venture herself in the country, much less in Sturatzberg."

"That was my opinion," answered Cloverton.

"Do you mean that it is not your opinion now?"

"I am in a transitional stage, your Majesty, and have not yet decided."

So there were troops of soldiers in the streets lest rioters should gather together and do damage. No one imagined there was enough power behind them to really menace the city. A few men talked together excitedly in side streets, but these dis-persed quietly after a little while without any interference from the soldiers.

The Countess Mavrodin drove in the Bois as usual. She held a little court, her carriage drawn up to the sidewalk, and she listened to and laughed at all the news. What could it all matter to her so long as she could laugh and chatter and be hap-py?

"My horses will not stand still if you talk politics," she said to one man. "They know their mistress is of the nature of a butterfly." The man was one who was likely to be well informed, and she did not say it until he had told her all he knew.

This butterfly nature of hers caused her to drive about a great deal that day. She had shopping to do in the Konigplatz, in the square out of which the Altstrasse ran and in the Bergenstrasse nearly as far down as the Southern Gate. More than once she caught sight of a group of excited men at a street corner, and once or twice she noticed that a man would walk leisurely toward them, pause a moment, and then pass on. Whenever this happened the little crowd dispersed immediately as though some urgent business had suddenly occurred to each member of it. It was late in the afternoon when the Countess returned home, and before she retired to her private rooms she gave instructions for certain servants, whom she mentioned by name, to be in readiness, as she would require them presently. She had a small reception that evening and was the most brilliant, as she was the most frivolous, among her brilliant and frivolous guests. Yet before nine o'clock Baron Petrescu had received some closely written sheets in her handwriting, and knew much of what had happened in Sturatzberg that day. But not all; that was, of course, impossible. In dark corners of the city through which it was dangerous to travel after nightfall, there were dismal houses, behind the fast-closed doors of which ready orators held the attention of eager listeners. The time was near. The emancipation from their slavery was at hand. What they had heard in the city to-day was proof of it. Be ready! It was the same story wherever men were gathered together. And in the constant coming and going at the palace, the keenest eyes might easily have failed to notice some who entered and left; and within there were many passages known only to the initiated. One man passed in unnoticed, and in a side room was met by another who, without a word, beckoned him to follow.

"No further news?" asked the first.

"None," was the answer.

Along the same passage which Ellerey had once traversed was De Froilette taken, and ushered into the Queen's presence. He bowed low, but she had no thought of ceremony just now.

"Can you read this riddle, monsieur?" she asked. "All kinds of solutions come to me, madam, but none that seem to entirely fit the case."

"One thing only stands clear," said the Queen: "this Captain Ellerey is a traitor.

You were a fool, monsieur, to bring him to my notice."

"I may have been mistaken."

"May? Indeed you have," she answered. "Heaven help him if he returns to Sturatzberg; he will sorely need it."

"I say I may have been mistaken, your Majesty, and that is what I mean," said De Froilette calmly. "Francois has seen these men who have come back, and I am convinced that Captain Ellerey was as astonished to see the token as any one."

"How could he be?"

"Are you certain of the man who delivered it to him?"

"As I am of myself. Do you still trust this Englishman?"

"If he wished to deceive us he could have done so in a much more effectual way," said De Froilette, "and served his own ends better. Men like Captain Ellerey do not join themselves to such a cause as ours for the love of it, but in their own interests. I have put down his somewhat off-hand treatment of me to his feeling of security in being your Majesty's trusted messenger."

"So Monsieur De Froilette, ever so suspicious, has lived to become weakly confiding."

"I have another reason to urge," the Frenchman went on. "I believe Princess Maritza has been in Sturatzberg."

"Have you seen her?"

"No, but Francois says he did. He may have been mistaken, but the delivery of her token goes to confirm Francois. Now, your Majesty, one of Ellerey's companions may be a partisan of the Princess, and may have changed the token. The fact that I have led the Princess, while she has been in England, to believe that I have worked in her cause, might induce her to think that the golden cross would be acceptable to the brigands, that they would welcome the message it held."

"Had she trusted you in any degree, monsieur, she would have made her presence known to you."

"She may have come to watch me, and even then she could hardly discover my real object. I have worked in your service too secretly. Even Lord Cloverton trusts me."

"I would Lord Cloverton were removed from Wallaria either by his Government or by--"

"Ah, madam, death seldom strikes where we would have it. If heaven were pleased to remove him we should have one obstacle the less in our way; but many would still remain. Death would have to be busy to make our enterprise sure."

"Lord Cloverton stands by most of those obstacles to give them strength," answered the Queen, her hands tightening a little. "The King would be pliant in my hands were this man not beside him to stiffen him. Is there any other man in the world who would have dared to put me to the test he did? I hate him."

"It is fortunate he has done so; he will not dare to repeat the offence," said De Froilette.

"I am not sure of that."

"If he does, the bracelet is mislaid," said De Froilette. "The mere fact that it has not been delivered will prove that you never sent it. For the moment we are powerless to act, but another token will be sent presently, another messenger found to take it. Have we not the assurance of Russia that the moment the standard of revolt is raised she will find plausible excuse to cross the frontier? Has not your Majesty rather hoped to succeed without the help of Russia?"

"The possibility may have occurred to me," answered the Queen.

"These rebels who would help you to occupy the throne of Wallaria alone would be difficult to rule without an army at your call to cow them into submission."

"We are looking to the future; it is the present which concerns us, monsieur."

"We can only wait and watch events," said De Froilette. "These deserters declare that they rode out with Captain Ellerey in the belief that they were upon the King's service. Your Majesty is not mentioned by them. We are safe so far."

"Some one, monsieur, holds my token; until that is in my possession again there is no safety."

"It is mislaid," said the Frenchman; "if that will not suffice, it has been stolen; if that is not enough, pick out some servant you can spare and accuse him of the theft. The sufferings of one man must not count beside the safety of a cause involving many lives."

"You seem to forget that Captain Ellerey knows the truth," said the Queen.

"You were alone when you told him of his mission. You have told the King that your conversation related to the Countess Mavrodin--hold to that story. Is the word of a traitor, struggling to shield himself, to be taken against yours?"

"I act more readily than I lie, monsieur."

"Pardon, madam, a lie is a vulgar cowardice; we are dealing with secrets of the State."

"I am woman enough to find small difference between them."

"And Queen enough to forget the woman when the sovereign must use diplomacy," answered De Froilette. "Besides, we rush far out to meet trouble. What can three or four men accomplish against an army of mountaineers fighting in their own hills? By this time Captain Ellerey lies food for the preying vultures. We are quite safe, your Majesty."

De Froilette left the palace unnoticed as he had come, and returned quickly to the Altstrasse. Francois hastened to attend him.

"There is nothing to report, monsieur," he said, in answer to his master's look of inquiry. "The city is quieting down. Is monsieur in any danger?"

"Perhaps, Francois, but it does not trouble me. I have been in danger before. Many channels of information are open to a timber merchant, and those in authority find me useful."

"We can wait, monsieur, but those who are expecting us to speak the word, will they wait?"

"I think so, Francois; still, you may have everything ready for a hasty departure. And if by any chance circumstances should necessitate our leaving separately, you must look for me in London at the old address."

Such instructions caused the servant no surprise. His master had usually managed to steer successfully through the troubled waters he encountered, but on many occasions such preparations for rapid flight had been made.

"Did you call to inquire after Baron Petrescu, Francois?"

"Yes, monsieur; his wound is giving him increased trouble."

"I rejoice to hear it. We can well dispense with his crowing in Sturatzberg just now. A walk through the city in an hour or so, Francois, might be good for your health." The servant smiled, falling in with his master's humor, and went out. The streets were quiet when he traversed them an hour or two later. A few soldiers were in the Konigplatz and at the top of the Bergenstrasse, but, except where some entertainment was going forward, and carriages and servants were congregated without, the city was unusually lifeless. Perhaps the presence of the soldiers drove law-abiding citizens home early lest they might come under suspicion, and the lawless were evidently not inclined to run risks. Francois stood for a few moments outside the Countess Mavrodin's watching the arrivals, among whom he recognized many notabilities, including the British Ambassador; and then he went for some distance down the Bergenstrasse before returning home. Had he traversed this street farther he would probably have been convinced that the exciting news of the day was already forgotten, for he would hardly have heard the laughter and songs which came from the Toison d'Or unless he had actually gone up the narrow court in which it stood. The door was shut, but the light shone dully through the red blinds which were drawn across the windows. They were like two huge eyes bleared with strong drink, and as a late comer pushed open the door at intervals and disappeared within, a watcher might have had the sensation of seeing an ogre swallowing his victim. Another thing might have struck him. There were many late arrivals, and they all came singly, entering swiftly and letting the door swing quickly to behind them. The tavern was, surely, fast becoming overcrowded, for no one came out.

But there was much room in the Toison d'Or, and the chamber in which Ellerey had waited for the token was thrown open to-night. It was crowded with men eager to listen to the horsemen who had ridden into Sturatzberg that day. They were the centre of attraction, and had long ago become talkative and more than ordinarily boastful. They shouted answers to every question, and were regaled with tankard after tankard of liquor. They drank deep healths to the King, and swore to their unswerving loyalty with many a strange oath. They sang snatches of ribald songs at the bidding of any man who had the wherewithal to pay for wine--snatches only, which became less coherent as the evening advanced. They cursed the traitor Ellerey, and made jests upon Maritza, "who was called 'Princess' by some fools and vagabonds."

"Down with her, and all who have a word for her!" cried one of them, trying to rise to give vehemence to his words, but falling back helpless into his seat.

"Curse her again, comrade," said a thin, morose-looking man in his ear. "Don't go to sleep yet. Curse her again. We like to know the true ring of your minds."

It was beyond the soldier's power to reply, but the other soldiers did it for him, vying with one another in their language.

"That's right," said the thin man. "You are all agreed. She is a pest in the land, this Princess, an evil to be trodden down, one to be killed if opportunity occurs, and the fact of her being a woman shall win her no mercy. You are all agreed on that?"

"No mercy!" shouted one soldier.

"Less because she's a woman," growled another.

"Down with her," said a third in a drunken whisper.

"One more drink round, landlord," said the morose man. "We'll drink it standing. Those who cannot stand, let their comrades hold them up. This is a loyal and sacred toast for the last. Not a man shall sit down to it. Tankards round, landlord!"

The soldiers struggled to their feet obediently, but each of them had to be held up on either side, and they laughed at their drunken inability. Seizing a tankard, the thin man sprang upon a chair.

"See that none fail to honor my toast!" he cried. "Let it tell its tale to Sturatzberg before the dawn. Here's to our Sovereign Lady, Princess Maritza!"

Too drunk to understand the purport of the words, the soldiers raised their tankards to drink, and then let them fall to the ground with a clatter, the untasted liquor splashing upon the floor. Each man jerked forward where he stood, and, when those who held him let him go, fell down with a thud. A groan or two, a convulsive movement, and then they lay still, while something mixed with the spilt liquor and dyed it to a darker hue. The six men who had stood immediately behind them wiped their keen long knives and sheathed them again in silence.

"Go quickly!" shouted the man, still standing on the chair. "See that the Bergenstrasse is clear. They shall rest there to-night, and Sturatzberg may find them there presently and read the lesson as it will."

In the early hours of the morning, when the guests were leaving the Countess Mavrodin's a man rushed past them into the hall.

"Is Lord Cloverton still here?"

The Ambassador came forward at once.

"What is it?"

"The men who returned to-day--the soldiers."

"What of them?"

"They have just been found lying side by side in the Bergenstrasse, dead--murdered!"

CHAPTER XIX
IN DESPERATE STRAITS

Desmond Ellerey stood with his sword lowered and his head bowed. As he spoke her name a flush came into his cheeks. His anger at Grigosie's deceit had been great, stern, cold, and judicial--only in such a spirit could he take vengeance on the lad; now it was shame which flamed into his cheeks. He had drawn his sword against a woman--in another moment the blade would have been dyed in her blood--the very thought of it was horrible.

In Maritza's face there was no look of triumph. If for a moment it had lightened her eyes, if the woman's power over the man defiantly proclaimed itself as she tore open her shirt to reveal the truth, it was gone more quickly, more completely, perhaps, than Ellerey's anger.

The Princess was the first to break the silence.

"You will not strike?" she said, closing the shirt again with hasty fingers.

"Regrets are useless. I had hoped to succeed. I will tell you why when you choose to listen to me. To-morrow you can deliver me to the brigands; until then I am Grigosie again."

As she picked up her cap and drew it over her curls Ellerey looked up. It was a relief to see the lad before him as he had always known him.

"And Grigosie talks folly," he said. "I would far sooner take his life myself than deliver him to the tender mercies of the brigands." A cry from Stefan, which was half an oath, startled them, and in an instant Ellerey had sprung to the soldier's side. Anton at the same moment seized his knife, and all three men were in the doorway slashing and thrusting furiously at those without. For a moment there were only two or three, who had approached silently, but their shouts upon being discovered brought a crowd rushing to their assistance.

When Anton had deserted his post to come to Grigosie's help, the temptation to secure an easy victory had been too great for those who watched the plateau. Vasilici may have given no orders that the truce should be thus flagrantly broken, but those who had seized the opportunity knew well enough that success would win easy forgiveness.

As it had been at the gate guarding the zig-zag path, those in front, wounded or dying, were thrown back upon their companions, impeding the rush which must have effected an entrance. Perhaps there was still a desire among most of them to let any comrade who would force himself into the forefront of the attack. The prowess of the defenders had already taught them a salutary lesson.

"Quick, Stefan; see that the door will close and fasten," whispered Ellerey. "When it is ready, shout; give us a moment to thrust back the foremost of them, and a moment to get in, and then we'll shut them out, if we can."

Stefan made a sharp cut at the first man within reach of him, and then slipped back into the tower. He shouted almost immediately, for Grigosie was already at the door, and had seen that it was in working order. At the shout Ellerey and Anton made a dash out as if in a last attempt for freedom. A slash to right and left, a cringing back of those in front gave them the opportunity and the time they wanted. In another instant they were within the tower, the door was shut, and the great bolts in it shot home.

"It's not likely we'll be using this way out for a while," said Ellerey, "so we'll pile everything against it we can to strengthen it."

They worked with a will, and while the brigands beat at the door without, they barricaded it within; and having heaped up against it everything they could lay their hands on, they drove in some wooden stakes at an angle to hold the obstruction in its place and resist the pressure.

"That will stop them for a little while," said Ellerey.

No one answered him. As soon as the work was accomplished Grigosie turned away, and Stefan, wiping the sweat from his brow with the back of his hand, looked with unutterable fierceness at Anton.

"You--you----" And then he burst out with a mighty oath. "There's no word in devil's or man's vocabulary to call you by. You're to thank for this. Weren't you ordered to keep guard by the barrier yonder?"

"Let him be, Stefan," said Ellerey, laying his hand on the soldier's arm. "He did rightly in leaving it. He came to protect his mistress."

Stefan glanced at Grigosie, whose back was toward him, and muttered something deeply; oaths they may have been, but the words seemed to lose themselves in his beard. Anton said not a word. He looked at Ellerey, and it was a look of which it was difficult to read the meaning. It was one of wonder rather than of gratitude. Perhaps he was trying to understand the real character of this strange Englishman. The brigands still continued to hammer at the door, but it showed no sign of giving.

"It will hold for a time," said Ellerey, "but we must see what can be done to interrupt their attentions as much as possible. A shot or two from the chamber above might help them to become quieter. Come, Stefan, and let us see what we can do."

In the chamber above there were narrow slits in the walls, and the top of the zig-zag was commanded from this vantage place, but those immediately below were out of danger. Some men were standing by the broken-down barrier, and Stefan wanted to fire at them, but Ellerey stopped him. Their ammunition was too valuable to throw away. A cartridge presently might be worth much more to them than one man's life just now.

"Those at the door below are the danger," said Ellerey.

"There's a good deal of loose stonework on the roof," said Stefan. "A piece of that heaved over at intervals might give them something to think about besides hammering at that door."

"They shall have a lesson at once," said Ellerey, climbing carefully up the broken stairway which led to the roof. It has been said that a turret had fallen in, breaking part of the stairs away, but the roof could easily be reached. There were many fragments, some large, some small, lying there, and one piece of considerable size Ellerey and Stefan managed to get on to the wall of the parapet immediately over the door. The manoeuvre was apparently unnoticed, for there came no warning shout to those below.

"Over with it," said Ellerey.

It did its work effectually. There were groans and execrations, and several bullets struck harmlessly about the stonework from whence this message had been hurled, but the hammering at the door ceased, and the besiegers retired to a safe distance.

"We must keep watch from here, Captain," said Stefan. "Help me to mount another piece upon the wall. It can rest there until they get courageous again and ask for it to be thrown upon them."

Ellerey did so, and, leaving Stefan there for the present, returned to the basement of the tower.

Anton was standing in exactly the same place as when Ellerey had mounted the steps, but the expression on his face had changed. It was quite evident that in the interval some words had passed between him and Grigosie, and that, whatever the subject of the conversation, Anton disapproved of it. Grigosie was leaning against the wall counting the cartridges he still had in his possession.

"We have stopped their hammering for a while," Ellerey said. "While the loose stones on the roof last, we have another weapon of defence."

"Do I relieve Stefan?" asked Grigosie.

"No; Anton. Rest while you can. There will be little enough sleep for any of us."

"And little enough food, too," said Grigosie, when Anton had cast himself down in a corner.

"We are truly in a sad case, Princess."

"Grigosie, please; let me remain Grigosie. It will be easier for both of us."

She crossed over to the steps which led to the upper chamber and sat down.

"As you say, our position is hopeless," Grigosie went on. "In Sturatzberg there are some who would strike a blow for Maritza, but no one knows of Grigosie. It is a poor end to make, Captain. I have had my moments of despair, but whenever I have thought of failure, I have never pictured such a miserable failure as this. I was prepared to face death and disaster, but if death came, I meant that it should be glorious, that it should come in a fashion to set Europe ringing with the news. It was a magnificent setting I had arranged for myself--the going down of a sun in purple and red and gold."

"Even as it is we make a mountain legend of it," said Ellerey, with a short laugh; "and legend lives long, longer than fame, often. You have a fair chance of being remembered by the generations to come."

"I have brought you to this, so it is your privilege to laugh at me," she said.

"At least, we can be honest with each other now," said Ellerey. "At the best we can only keep these wolves at bay for a few hours. Though these old walls stand, we have little food, little ammunition. Death has no very great terrors for me. I seem to have lived my life for the express purpose of showing how a man can fail, and, having been unjustly robbed of my honor, you succeed in robbing me of my self-respect by making me lift my hand against you--a woman."

"I am sorry. Question me as you will."

"How could you hope for anything else but failure from such a mad enterprise?" he asked.

"Captain Ellerey, do you remember what I said when we met on the downs that day?"

"Every word."

"That I spoke truly you now know. You know how my claim stands, and whether you love my cause or not, you must recognize the justice of it. While I was in England, kept there to be out of the way, my friends were working in Sturatzberg. My adherents, my well-wishers, are in every grade of society there, but there was one man on whom I thoroughly depended. He was in constant communication with me, and one of his great schemes, a plan which he swore was ripening every day, was getting the brigands to espouse my cause. To these hills have flocked all the malcontents of the country. They are not robbers; they are political outcasts many of them, and should welcome one who is by right their ruler. So said this man, so he swore they were ready to do, but constantly advised a little further delay. You cannot understand what this waiting day after day, month after month, meant to me. Impatient in heart, I was yet patient in action. I might still be quietly waiting but for two things. First I learnt that to be put further out of the way I was to visit England's colonies, a pleasure trip graciously arranged for me by your Government; secondly, I was informed that the man I trusted was scheming for his own ends more than for mine. It was the parting of the ways, Captain Ellerey, and I had to choose. Another stepped on board the vessel placed at my disposal in my stead, and while she was taken to the colonies I came secretly to Sturatzberg. There I have since lived, watching and waiting, in the house of the woman who devised and helped me to carry out this plan."

"A woman!" Ellerey exclaimed.

"Countess Mavrodin, whose power is only the greater because no one has any idea of its existence. My first work was to watch the man whom I believed had been working for me. I quickly found that my interests were not first in his consideration, but I learned also that he feared his own schemes would fail should some unlucky chance bring me to Sturatzberg. In this fear I saw my hope. Was this unnatural?"

"Is this man De Froilette?" asked Ellerey.

"He is the man. Unconscious of my presence in the city he continued to work against me. Queen Elena had now become his dupe. The men in the hills would help to set her alone upon the throne in Wallaria, and the King once got rid of and the country in insurrection, De Froilette would have sold it to Russia--more, would have aspired to the hand of the Queen. Perhaps he loves her, perhaps he only loves the power he would gain. His conspiracy was well laid, and he only wanted a man to lead, to bear the brunt of the fight, to pay the penalty should failure come, while he remained an uninterested citizen ready to be the first to cry out against the rebellion if necessary. His choice fell upon Desmond Ellerey."

Ellerey did not answer. This recital was making many things clear to him.

"I knew something of this Captain," the Princess went on. "In my heart I had long ago chosen him to lead my cause. I tested his courage on the night I believed he had received the token. It was I, Captain Ellerey, who ran with you along the deserted streets from the Altstrasse that night; it was I who, when only numbers had succeeded in binding you, came and looked into your eyes and was satisfied."

"Yet you didn't trust me enough to whisper your name," said Ellerey.

"At Court you came under the influence of Frina Mavrodin," she went on hastily. "Perhaps, even with her, my cause took second place then. You were stanch to the mission you had undertaken; she could not turn you from that, although she influenced you in another way."

"What do you mean, Princess?"

"I have heard her speak of you, I have noted the light in her eyes; do you think I could be deceived?"

"And do you think, Princess, that I have no memory? Since that morning on the downs---"

"Her success did not help my cause, therefore what was it to me!" cried Maritza, suddenly starting to her feet. "It was time for me to act. You know the rest. There are spies everywhere, and I knew when the token was given, how it was sent, and enclosed in a similar fashion I had my own. De Froilette was afraid of me, therefore it was possible that the brigands, or some of them, at least, were ready to take up my cause. The wine that night made you sleep heavily, and I changed the tokens. There is a loose brick in yonder corner, under it lies the Queen's bracelet of medallions. So, Captain Ellerey, you have me in your power. I brought you to this strait-- the remedy is in your own hands. Deliver me and the Queen's token into Vasilici's hands, and--who knows, you may yet win place and power in Sturatzberg."

With an impatient gesture, Ellerey walked across the chamber, and as he did so Anton raised his head.

"What, old watch-dog, so you think as basely of me as your mistress does," he said, noticing the sudden movement.

Anton did not answer, but waited, resting on his elbow.

"No man loves being fooled, Princess," Ellerey went on, turning round hastily, "and that I have been by the Queen, by De Froilette, and by you, but of them all you only have insulted me. What contempt must you have for me to think even of such a thing! Let me be as short and brutal. If by the sacrifice of a dog to those wolves without I could purchase my freedom, I would not buy it at the price. I will wake you presently, Anton. You, at least, I can understand," and Ellerey mounted the steps and disappeared into the upper chamber. He went no farther for a time, but sat on some fallen stones to think, and his thoughts were not of how to escape from his enemies, nor even how to hold them at bay as long as possible, but of two women. One, a woman of the world, for so she seemed, the centre of attraction, beautiful, witty, frivolous, shimmering in silk and lace and jewels, jewels that were no brighter than her eyes. He had not mentioned her among those who had fooled him. She had not done so. She had been a pleasant companion, a true comrade, perhaps; indeed, was ready to give him even more than friendship. He might have loved her but for the other woman, whom he saw again as in a vision, standing on the summit of the downs, talking of empire and power, stirring his soul from its lethargy and bidding him play the man. If she had stirred him then, how much more did she make his pulses throb now, now that she had shared his dangers and braved so much! Had she any memory such as his, of that breezy morning long ago? And then the horror of the present overwhelmed him for a time. He was powerless to help her.

"There is no future for us beyond tomorrow, or the day after," he murmured. "Fate has strangely linked me with these two women, and made sport of me. One might have loved me perchance, and will regret me; the other I love, and she cares not, and I am likely to lay down my life in a last endeavor to save her. Thank God for such a death! A man could scarcely die a better one, although Stefan would hardly think so," and he climbed to the roof to talk to the soldier there.

Princess Maritza stood for some time where Ellerey had left her. She too, perhaps, forgot the present for a little while, and her thoughts sped to Frina Mavrodin, Then she crossed the chamber quickly.

"Dumitru, are you asleep?"

"No, Princess," the man answered, starting up.

"Lie down again, Dumitru, and listen. If he comes, be asleep, as I shall feign to be; but listen, and if you do not understand, question me until you do."

"You distrust this Captain, Princess?"

"No; he may yet do good work for us."

For a long time she continued to speak in a whisper.

"It is madness," murmured the man.

"Wise men would call all I have done madness," she answered. "Listen, Dumitru, there is more."

When she had finished there was silence.

"You would have me play the traitor," said the man, slowly.

"He is never a traitor who obeys the word of his sovereign," she answered.

"But, Princess---"

"Am I your sovereign, Dumitru?"

"My beloved Princess, indeed."

"Then obey, Dumitru. Act promptly when I give the word. It shall be soon. Perhaps to-night."

CHAPTER XX
TREACHERY OR SACRIFICE

All that night the stone, menacingly balanced on the wall above the door, remained in its place. The brigands had no desire to court a useless death, and they could afford to wait.

At dawn Ellerey ascended to the roof of the tower and found Anton pacing its narrow limits to keep the warmth in his limbs.

"Nothing happened, Anton?"

"Nothing, Captain."

"You have helped your mistress into a desperate strait. How could you hope for anything else but failure?"

"The Princess has told you, Captain?"

"Aye, man, but that was a woman's hope--a brave one if you will, but there was no weighing of chances, no counting the cost in it. Was there nothing more than this desperate hope at the back of your mind, no sane man's reasoning to see the peril of it?"

"I am but a servant to obey," Anton answered. "Yet desperate ventures have succeeded, and we had honesty on our side, Captain. Ours is the just cause, and that counts for something."

"No wonder Princess Maritza's history is one of failure if her counsellors have advised after this manner," said Ellerey.

"Are you certain she has failed, Captain?" Anton asked, turning quickly toward him. The earnestness of the question, added to its seeming absurdity, was startling. Could there be any doubt of the failure?

"Can your eyes penetrate beyond the spur of the hills yonder and see an army marching to our rescue, or your ears catch the welcome sound of tramping feet?"

Ellerey said, pointing to the head of the pass.

"No, Captain."

"Is there any hope that a single man has set out from Sturatzberg to help us?"

"I know of none," was the answer.

"And about us the plateau is full of men, and below us in the pass men wait-- enemies all. Outside this tower there is certain death for us, and within there is food enough to satisfy one man for a day perhaps."

"I know, Captain, and yet the Princess may not have failed."

Ellerey did not answer. He leant against the parapet watching the day grow brighter, and Anton resumed his quick pacing to and fro.

The men on the plateau and below in the pass were beginning to stir. Sentries were changed. There was the murmur of voices, and presently rising curls of faint blue smoke from fires cooking the morning meal. There was sunlight on the higher slopes, and the song of birds in the air, a welcome new day to myriads of creatures on the earth. To the man looking out across the panorama of mountain peak and gorge everything seemed a mockery. There was something cruel in gladdening the eyes with the beauty of earth and sky when in a few short hours those eyes must close forever. In the full possession of his life and strength the man rebelled against his fate. It was the end of a rat in a trap--ignoble, inglorious. That he would fall in striking a last blow for a woman who cared naught for him had little attraction for him just now. If he could save her, if his death could bring some good thing to pass, it would be different.

Once or twice Anton stopped in his pacing backward and forward to look steadily toward the head of the pass.

"Can you hear the tramping feet?" Ellerey asked when he stopped again.

"No, Captain."

"Can you see anything?"

"No, Captain; but it is too good a morning to accept failure."

"The sun doesn't put on mourning for every miserable dog that dies." And then, as Anton resumed his walk without a word, Stefan's voice was heard calling Ellerey to breakfast.

All the stones which had once served for seats and a table had been piled up against the door, and the food was spread in a little circle in the centre of the floor.

It was Stefan's arrangement. He had refused all help from the Princess, gruffly but firmly, although the gruffness may have been something less than his usual manner and intended for courtesy. Maritza stood with her hands behind her watching him, a smile upon her lips.

"There's more table than breakfast, Captain," he said as Ellerey came down; "but it's as well to have things orderly. There's little enough to say grace for, but there's a lesson in the display, for all that. It represents all that stands between us and starvation."

"With care, Stefan, we can live for--" And then Ellerey paused.

"Quite so, Captain. I've been trying to fix a limit myself and failed."

Ellerey looked at the scraps of food. At any other time he would have spurned them as a meal of any sort; but in such a case as theirs was, morsels of food bulk large with possibilities.

"To-day and perhaps to-morrow," he muttered.

"Yes, we'll be quite ready to welcome a change of diet by to-morrow night," said Stefan, "and for my part I shouldn't quarrel with any kind of food and drink which happened to arrive sooner. There's no drawing from the mountain stream now and the flasks hold little."

"Much may happen in two days," said Maritza quietly.

"True. They may storm the tower successfully and put us beyond the want of food before to-morrow night," Ellerey answered.

They ate their small portions in silence, and having eaten them remained silent. Each one was conscious that there was something to be said, yet each one waited for the other to say it.

"Captain." It was a relief to hear Stefan's voice, and Ellerey looked up. "Captain, I make no claim to be much of a man at giving advice. I've seldom been asked for it, and I've usually been in a large enough company for it to be done without; but as we are, I take it each one of us becomes of more importance than under ordinary circumstances."

Ellerey nodded.

"Well, then, my case is this: Years ago someone found me in the streets, and for some reason known only to themselves decided that I should live. I may have been hungry then--I don't remember--but I've never been hungry since. I may have had to steal my victuals, but anyway I've got them. It follows, therefore, that in fighting hunger I'm not to be depended on. The weapons in use for such a fray are new to me, and I don't know how to handle them. I'm afraid of the enemy."

"Well, Stefan?"

"Now death, I suppose, is as certain within the next few hours as anything well can be, and I should like to meet the kind of death I understand. Let us fix a time for hauling down the barricade, and then make a dash for it. We'll get as far as the path, perhaps--there is just a chance that some of us may get farther; but anyhow, we die in the open."

"Have you thought of the Princess?" Ellerey asked.

"The circumstances don't make it easy to forget her," Stefan answered.

"Nor difficult to hate her," said Maritza.

"I took a kind of liking to Grigosie which somehow keeps me back from hating her," Stefan went on, speaking to Ellerey and not looking at the Princess. "I don't suppose, however, that she knows much more about starvation than I do, and dying in the open may suit her case as well as mine."

"But a woman, Stefan?"

"I've naught to do with women, Captain, and I see none in our company. I only see two good comrades before me, one lacking a bit of muscle it may be, but lacking no courage. He shall go between us, and Anton shall cover our rear. There's such pleasure in the thought of striking another blow that there's even a hope in it that we may win though."

"Stefan is right," Maritza said. "Let us make the attempt to-morrow."

"Why not to-day?" Stefan asked.

"The food is not all gone," she said; "besides, the day holds possibilities. Let us wait a day, Captain."

"If the attempt is to be made, why not make it to-night? The darkness will help us," said Ellerey.

"I prefer dying in the sunlight," said Stefan, "but so long as I die in the open the stars will serve."

"In the night if you will, but not to-night," pleaded Maritza, laying her hand on Ellerey's arm. "Let it be to-morrow night.

"Hope dies hard with you, Princess."

"I have a fancy to look upon another dawn," she returned. "Perhaps to-morrow is the anniversary of some great event in my history, and that is why I long to see it. I do not know, but in us all there is a vein of superstition. I will go and relieve Anton."

Stefan watched her as she went up the stairs and disappeared into the upper chamber.

"If anyone could make me change my opinion of women, she would," he said; but Ellerey took no notice of the remark. He had commenced walking up and down, deep in thought.

The day passed quietly. The brigands made no attempt to storm the tower, and the huge stone above the doorway remained balanced on the wall. But to those within the hours dragged heavily. Stefan spent his time feeling the edge of his sword and seeing that the revolvers were in good order and loaded. The occupation seemed to bring him nearer to his emancipation. Ellerey walked from wall to wall, turning with the regularity of a wild beast in a cage. A dozen times or more he climbed to the roof, but hardly spoke a word to whoever happened to be sentry there. Maritza lay down and appeared to sleep a good deal when her duty on the roof was over, for she demanded to take her turn with the rest; and Anton was restless and nervous. He lay down, but he did not sleep; his eyes were constantly on the Princess.

"You know what we have decided?" said Ellerey to him during the day.

"Yes, Captain."

"You have no better plan?"

"No, Captain, so that I die with her I am content." The day drew slowly to its ending. A camp-fire blazed upon the plateau, and two in the pass below, around which the besiegers gathered. Still there were no signs that an attack was meditated, and Ellerey watched the moving figures for a long time and marked the position of the sentries. Such knowledge might prove useful to-morrow night. And he determined which direction to take should Providence so far favor them as to allow them to gain the pass. It was a relief to find even this employment to occupy his mind.

After the weary day the night was almost welcome. First Stefan, then Ellerey, had watched through the early hours; now Anton paced the roof restlessly while Maritza still slept. She was to go on duty at dawn, so might she see the new day break as she wished. When Ellerey came down, Stefan was sleeping heavily, and the Princess lay in her corner with her arm under her head, a picture of graceful repose and rest. The thought of the certain death that awaited her made Ellerey sick almost, and with a shudder and a curse at his own impotence, he cast himself down. For a time he tossed and turned restlessly this way and that until, utterly wearied out, sleep fell upon him and held him fast, smoothing the care from his face with pleasant dreams. Now he climbed a stretch of sunny, wind-swept downs, the song of a lark and the sighing sound of the long waving grass in his ears; now he heard the rustle of silk beside him and a sweet low voice and pleasant laughter answered him, a little foot stepped out bravely beside his own, and a little hand rested confidently in his. There was music and laughter about him, and then a sudden pause, and darkness, and out of it a sharp crackling sound.

"What was that?"

Ellerey had started up only half awake. It was Stefan's sudden question which thoroughly aroused him. The dawn had come and a dim light was in the chamber, strangely dim and sombre after the light and movement in his dream. He looked across at Maritza's corner and saw that it was empty.

"We have slept soundly, Stefan," he said, springing to his feet. "The Princess has gone on duty."

"It sounded like revolver shots to me," the soldier answered as he followed Ellerey quickly to the roof. They stepped from the broken stairs into the open, and then stood still, turning to look at each other. There was no one there. The stone still rested on the wall, and a rope which had been in the lower chamber lay sprawling over the roof, one end of it hanging a few feet over the parapet. Both men ran to the wall together. The plateau was empty, not a man remained there. No sentry paced along the edge of it, no one stood there at the head of the zig-zag path.

"Gone!" Ellerey exclaimed. It was not of the brigands he was thinking, and Stefan knew it.

"By that rope. And Anton, too. Maybe we woke none too soon, Captain." And then, as Ellerey turned questioning eyes to him, he added: "There's the look of treachery in this."

Ellerey did not answer, but the question asked a moment later showed the direction his thoughts were taking.

"Have they really gone?" he said, pointing to the plateau.

The soldier shook his head doubtfully and then suddenly leant forward, his hand stretched out toward the pass before them. "Look yonder!"

The light was growing stronger every moment, and the moving figures in the valley could be seen distinctly. There was more going forward there than the awak-ening of a camp to a new day. The men were moving in orderly groups, and there was no curling smoke from newly-lighted fires. "They are on the march, Captain: and--look, is not the lad in the midst of them?"

Ellerey's eyes might not have served him to pick out the slim figure, but thus directed he had no doubt it was the Princess in the midst of the men who marched quickly along the pass for a little way and then turned aside and seemed to be swal-lowed up in the foot of the mountain opposite.

"She could not have gone of her own accord, Stefan. They must have found means to capture her."

"Anton may have helped them, perhaps."

"No; he was faithful--my life on that. Great heavens! She is in their power, in Vasilici's power, and we stand here doing nothing."

"She may have gone willingly," said Stefan, as Ellerey rushed toward the steps; "besides, what can we do?"

"Come or stay as you will!" Ellerey shouted as he disappeared.

"She went willingly," Stefan murmured, lingering behind for a moment to look at the rope. "At least, she climbed down to them, not they up to her. I never trusted Anton. If I hadn't taken a liking to Grigosie I shouldn't trust the Princess. She's a woman."

Although only a few moments had elapsed, Ellerey was already throwing down the barricade at the door in the lower chamber of the tower. Stefan first looked at his weapons and then went across to the corner which the Princess had occupied. Ellerey did not notice him, and he rose from his knees there only as Ellerey had sufficiently thrown down the stones to draw back the bolt and open the door wide enough to get out.

"One moment, Captain. I am with you, but be prepared for attack." Ellerey, sword in one hand, revolver in the other, rushed out on to the plateau, Stefan at his heels. No shout rang out, no man sprang from his hiding-place among the ruins to bar their way. Even the valley was empty. The last of the men who had encamped there had been swallowed up by the mountain opposite.

"Captain, the token which the Princess said was hidden under the loose brick yonder is gone."

The sword which Ellerey held ready to defend himself fell suddenly, almost as it had done when he recognized that he had raised it against a woman. Shame had sent the color to his cheeks then, and the color came into his face now, anger bringing it there. Had she deceived from first to last, played carelessly with all the finer feelings that were in him, using them boldly and deliberately for her own end? These were the thoughts which ran swiftly through his mind, and well might they stir him to anger. Then came the reaction, suddenly, swiftly. No, she could not have deceived him in this manner. There was some reason for her going, something unforeseen had happened. After all they had come through together, she could not be guilty of treachery.

"You found nothing else?" he asked hoarsely.

"Yes, this. A piece of stone lay upon it to keep it in its place close to where she slept last night."

Ellerey seized the scrap of paper Stefan held out to him.

"I have brought you to this," he read, written faintly in pencil; "I have thought of a plan to save you. At dawn I shall have gone, but so will the brigands. You will be free to go to Sturatzberg, if you will, or across the mountains northward to safety. I wonder which way you will take? Mine is a desperate venture. If I fail, think of me sometimes, for to me also there has often come the memory of that breezy morning in England--Maritza."

"Look, Captain!" Stefan cried.

On the slope of the opposite hills, where the path rose over a spur, a party of the marching brigands had come into view. The sunlight had come, and it touched the men as they went. The distance was too great to distinguish the slim figure in the midst, but one spot of white showed clearly, quivering as the sunlight touched it. For a moment it disappeared, then it fluttered again, and, as Ellerey looked, a crowd of conflicting thoughts and emotions were in his brain. This was not treachery, but sacrifice.

"A waving handkerchief, Captain; a signal of farewell," Stefan murmured in a low gruff voice.

CHAPTER XXI
THE RESCUE

The white signal had gone, but Ellerey's eyes remained fixed upon the moving black line until a fold in the hills hid it from sight. Something seemed to have gone out of his life, suddenly as a candle is blown out in a room. Then he turned and held out the paper to the soldier.

Stefan read the pencilled lines, turned the paper over meditatively, and then read them again. The words seemed to burn their way into his brain as they had burnt into Ellerey's, but the effect was somewhat different.

"It is not like a woman, is it?" said Stefan.

"Very like, I think."

Stefan shook his head, as though he regretted his companion's ignorance.

"I took a liking to Grigosie," he said. "I saw the making of a grand comrade in Grigosie. I can understand his doing this kind of thing, but not a woman."

"The fact remains that she is a woman," said Ellerey.

"Wonderful," answered the soldier, as he handed back the paper. "It would appear that the making of a man rests much in his clothes. I've never known good come from a petticoat. Grigosie didn't wear one. Maybe he recognized that he was a man, hidden by a cruel mistake in the shape of a woman. Ah, Captain, women have had the spoiling of many a good man I've drunk with and fought beside. I wish you a better fate than theirs."

"This does not look like treachery," said Ellerey. It was evident that he had not been attending to his companion, but had been following out a train of thought of his own, and now put his decision into words.

"We're standing here like two fools, at any rate," Stefan said. "We ought to know the value of precaution by this time. What is to be done, Captain? Are you for Sturatzberg, or for crossing the mountains northward? It's a speedy making up our minds that is needed if we are not to starve."

Ellerey was still following his own thoughts.

"What can her plan be?" he said. "What hope for her cause is there in these hills? What mercy can she expect from Vasilici?"

"As Grigosie, none; as a woman, she may persuade these men to anything," Stefan answered. "Some power she has, or why did they not kill Grigosie at once?"

"It is a terrible thought, Stefan, but may they not have reserved her for Vasilici's vengeance? Did they not cry to us that we might go free if the lad were given up? She heard that; she argued with us, you remember. She has sacrificed herself for us."

"Well, Captain, shall we follow? Give me but leave to kill something on the way and get on friendly terms with my stomach. I care not which road we take, nor to what it leads us."

"We will follow her," said Ellerey.

"I'd never leave so good a comrade as Grigosie in a tight place," murmured Stefan. "Keep watch, Captain, while I gather up what we take with us, and fill our flasks at Grigosie's fairy fountain yonder."

When Stefan returned, he found Ellerey standing on the edge of the plateau looking down into the pass.

"What is it, Captain?" he called out as he came. "They have not kept their promise, Stefan, that is all," Ellerey answered, pointing down into the valley.

A savage oath burst from Stefan's lips. "They've played the lad false in this, they'll play him false in all," and the tone in which he said it revealed for a moment the real heart of the man hidden deep down under this rough exterior.

From a hidden pathway at the foot of the hills the brigands came out singly, fourscore of them at least. Each man looked up at the plateau as he issued from the path, and the manner in which his eager steps gave way at once to an easier and more slouching gait showed plainly enough that the object of their coming had been attained, that no further hurry was necessary. Some went to the places where the fires had been, and kicked the ashes together; while others stacked their arms, and sat down in twos and threes along the pass.

"Those were revolver shots that woke us, Captain," said Stefan thoughtfully. "I expect Grigosie meant to rouse us as soon as we could no longer prevent his going, and intended us to make the best of our chances."

"And we've missed them," said Ellerey. "I fancy this is meant to be our last adventure, Stefan."

"They'll come up the path presently, and the sooner the better," was the answer. "A few of them shall finish their adventures along with us; but we'll fight our last fight here, Captain, not in the tower yonder."

"I have a sudden lust for life, Stefan, a longing to be face to face with Vasilici once more," whispered Ellerey, as though he imagined the men in the valley below might hear his secret. "If we wait until sundown we might get through them in the darkness."

"Our original plan," Stefan answered. "I am with you, Captain, and if you will watch those blackguards yonder, I'll turn my attention to a bird that's hovering on the mountain above. Heaven grant he comes within range, and an empty stomach does not put my eye out."

But the bird seemed to have no more intention of serving two hungry men for food than the brigands meant to throw away their lives by an attempt to win the plateau. They posted sentinels, one near the foot of the zig-zag path, and one beyond the camp-fire toward the head of the pass; the rest sat or stood at their ease between these two points, and, unless they changed their plan at night, Ellerey perceived that, if the sentry at the foot of the path were once silenced without being able to give warning, the road to the way taken by the Princess and her captors would be clear. He studied the shape of the hills and the distance carefully, so that he might the more easily find that road, and he noticed how long a time elapsed between the relief of the sentries. If they attacked the man soon after his coming on duty, so much the longer start would they obtain.

The day wore on, and he and Stefan finished the scraps of food which were left, and thanked their good fortune that they had not the terrors of thirst to face. Stefan still watched the mountains above for a bird, and Ellerey planned the work of the night in every detail, explaining some new point to the soldier every time he approached him. He had paid little attention to the men in the valley below for some time, when he was startled by a single shot, which rang out clearly in the still air. For a moment he thought that Stefan had got his bird at last, but the next instant the soldier was beside him, as startled as he was. It was the sentry toward the head of the pass who had fired, and he now came rushing toward his companions, who quickly seized their weapons.

"Do I hear horses?" exclaimed Stefan excitedly. "By the father and mother I never knew, there are horses galloping up the pass. There are several of them, and they come quickly."

The brigands were evidently unprepared for such an attack, and did not appear to have a capable leader among them. They had not come there to fight, only to starve two men into surrender, and as they ran together there was a general movement toward the path they had come.

Into the pass galloped some two dozen horsemen, who, at a sign from their leader, drew rein upon seeing the brigands, and turned to shout to others who had not yet come into view.

"An advance guard only," muttered Stefan.

The brigands evidently thought the same, and those who could not reach the mountain path in time began a hasty retreat up the pass, firing in a desultory manner as they went. They had no intention of attempting to hold their position; safety was all they cared about. The horsemen paused a moment to fire a volley, and then charged, but there was little fighting. Two or three of the brigands were cut down, and one horseman pitched forward suddenly as a bullet brought his horse to the ground, but that was all. The brigands scrambled into the mountain paths or up the mountain slope out of reach, and the leader of the troop checked any pursuit of those who were fleeing rapidly up the pass.

"Is this a rescue, or have we only changed our enemy?" said Ellerey.

"They are dismounting, and will come up the zig-zag way; we had better meet them at the top of it," said Stefan.

Only one man came up to them.

"There is not much distinction to be had from routing such an enemy, Captain Ellerey," he said. "Baron Petrescu!"

"At your service, although barely recovered from the effects of our last meeting. Time pressed, so I did not wait for a doctor's certificate of fitness."

"I thank you, but I hardly understand the situation, Baron," said Ellerey.

"And that is not to be wondered at," was the answer; "but there will be time to explain presently. Enough that we can shake hands over a past quarrel for which I have paid the penalty, and know that we stand together now."

Ellerey took his outstretched hand without a word.

"The Princess is with you?" Petrescu asked.

"She was until this morning."

"Killed!" cried the Baron.

"No; and yet I do not know that worse has not happened to her."

"While you explain, Captain, have I your leave to go down and make the acquaintance of our new comrades?" said Stefan. "My stomach yearns toward them, and their victuals and drink."

"I had forgotten," said the Baron hastily. "You can explain while we eat and drink, Captain."

"A few moments will make no difference, Baron," said Ellerey, nodding a consent to Stefan, who went down into the pass quickly. Then he went on: "Do you know the Princess's plans, Baron?"

"I thought I did, but her sudden disappearance from Sturatzberg was unexpected by me; still, I know enough of your mission to guess her reason for joining you."

"Then, Baron, you know my position. It was not Princess Maritza's cause which brought me to these hills. I am the victim of a conspiracy; but at the same time, my only thought now is for the safety of the Princess." The Baron nodded, and glanced swiftly at his companion.

"I understand, Captain."

Shortly Ellerey told him what had occurred since Princess Maritza had joined him at the Toison d'Or, reserving nothing, not even his own anger at the deceit which had been practised upon him.

"It was a desperate enterprise, doomed to failure from the beginning," he went on; "but as it was, only one course was open to me, to protect the Princess to the best of my ability. Our food was gone, and we had determined to make a dash for safety after dark to-night. That we did not do so last night was by the Princess's desire. Her going must have been in her mind then."

"She took the bracelet of medallions with her?" said Petrescu thoughtfully.

"She told me it was in the tower yonder; it is not there now, so I presume she took it."

"It may possibly secure her safety."

"Vasilici is a truculent villain," Ellerey answered. "He is not likely to forget, or forgive, that shot which saved my life."

"Then you would follow her?"

"Stefan and I had decided to do so when those fellows stole back to prevent us. We should have taken our chance after dark to-night."

Petrescu was thoughtful for a time.

"I hardly know what course to advise," he said presently. "We may not be able to help her much in these hills, while in Sturatzberg we might stir up the people in her cause."

"At least I have small power in the city," said Ellerey, with a smile. "Those who trusted me very naturally think me a traitor, and I should quickly be delivered over to enemies who would make short work of me."

"Yet you have powerful friends there."

"Indeed?"

"When the men who deserted you rode into the city with stories of your treachery, Captain Ellerey's name suddenly became known to hundreds who had never heard it before, and to each one of them he became a friend, since his fate was linked with Princess Maritza's."

"Would such friendship protect me from my enemies?"

"At least many a hiding-place in the city would be open to you, and some men might sooner give up their lives than betray you. There is one proof of the truth of what I say. The men who deserted you all died a violent death that night. They were found lying side by side in the Bergenstrasse, in spite of the fact that the city was patrolled by troops."

Ellerey looked at him inquiringly.

"No, Captain, I was not privy to their assassination, although I might make a shrewd guess in what quarter the plot originated."

"Then Sturatzberg is in uproar?"

"No; it is strangely quiet, all things considered--that quiet which presages a storm. The King would strike if he knew where to strike, but he hardly knows who are his enemies."

"The sight of me would give him some idea where to aim a blow," said Ellerey.

"Yes; and yet he might think twice before striking it. You have powerful friends, one very powerful friend--one very powerful friend."

"You do not mean her Majesty?"

"I think you know I do not, Captain Ellerey," the Baron answered. "It was the Countess Mavrodin who bid me come."

"I know that the cause of Princess Maritza is dear to her," said Ellerey quietly.

"It is, and to me," said the Baron; "and yet we are probably not doing the best for it by bringing two dozen horsemen into the hills. There are no more behind. Our calling back as though there were was a stratagem to strike greater terror into the brigands. No, Captain, the Countess bid me come to rescue the Princess, and you, to aid your escape out of Wallaria if need be, and her command is my law. Do we understand each other, Captain Ellerey?"

They looked into each other's eyes for a moment.

"Do you understand why I forced a duel upon you?" Petrescu went on. "I might tell you that I believed the Queen's token was in your possession; it would be true; but that was not uppermost in my thoughts when we stood face to face. Therefore, when I come to you at her bidding, you may well trust me, since I have little to win by it."

"Only partly do I understand you, Baron."

"You Northmen, in spite of your many virtues, are slower to understand than we Southerners are. Would you have me pluck the fruit for you as well as show you the tree? Sturatzberg may be in open rebellion before a week is out, and Frina Mavrodin may have to leave it. I will say no more. Even my generosity has a limit."

Ellerey could not fail to understand his meaning.

"You had better read that, Baron," he said, handing him Maritza's letter.

Petrescu took the scrap of paper and read it carefully.

"I met Maritza long ago in England," he said as Petrescu looked at him. "She has remembered it, you see, and I--I came to Sturatzberg."

"Then the Countess is--"

"My friend, but Maritza---We waste precious time, Baron; I must follow Maritza."

"I understand. Come and eat. We must lose no time."

It was arranged to leave some of the men in charge of the tower and of the horses. They were to wait there six days, and if by that time Baron Petrescu and his party had not returned, they were to go back to Sturatzberg, taking a circuitous road to avoid the soldiers encamped in the plain. Stefan was left in command of these men, since he had had experience how the plateau could best be defended in case of need. That the brigands would attack them, however, seemed unlikely, for they had evidently fled in the belief that the men they had seen were only an advance guard.

Night was falling when the party, well armed and full of excitement, set out. There was a silver light behind the distant heights, herald of the moon, so there was little need to wait for the dawn; besides, one of the brigands had only been slightly wounded, and was pressed into their service as guide. He loudly declared that he had no idea where his chief was hiding, until the Baron held a revolver to his head, and gave him half a minute to find whether his memory could not be jogged sufficiently to serve him better. Before the thirty seconds had passed, it had worked to good effect, and he set out with a man on either side of him who had strict injunctions to see that he should be the first to pay for any treachery which might happen.

"Some of the brigands cannot be far in front of us," said the Baron; "and this fellow will know their likely haunt and give us warning in time. If he forgets to do so, the sun will rise in vain to-morrow for him."

They tramped silently through the night, often in single file, for the way contracted often to the narrowest of defiles. That they had started right Ellerey knew, and he was inclined to think that so far their guide had not misled them. There seemed to be no other way by which they could have come.

Just before dawn the brigand stopped; his memory had been excellently aroused.

"We approach an open space where my people sometimes halt," he said.

Two men were sent forward to reconnoitre, but found the place empty, and here they halted.

"How much farther to where Vasilici is?" asked Petrescu.

"We should reach the place by noon," the brigand answered; "but he may have moved. My comrades will have told him of your coming to the pass."

"I dare say you will remember where he is likely to have removed to," the Baron returned, "since your miserable life depends upon it."

They were just preparing to continue their journey after a short rest and hasty meal, when they heard the sound of falling footsteps coming rapidly toward them. Only one man, and he was running with that easy, measured stride which a runner falls into when his journey is likely to be a long one. A moment later he ran into the midst of them.

"Stop!" cried several voices.

The man, with a glance to right and left of him for a way of escape, stood still; but in an instant a knife gleamed in his hand, and in that moment Ellerey recognized him.

"Anton!"

The man turned toward him and lowered the knife at once. "The Princess, Anton, where is she?"

"Yonder; alive," Anton answered. "Give me a moment and some drink. I have a message."

"For me?"

"For all, Captain, who love her."

CHAPTER XXII
IN VASILICI'S STRONGHOLD

Although Anton had declared to Ellerey that there was no certainty that the Princess had failed, he did not believe in his own optimism. True, death seemed certain in the tower, but it had been kept at bay until now almost miraculously, it seemed to him, and a faith in Captain Ellerey had grown up in him. The Princess's resolution to deliver herself to the brigands appeared little short of madness to Anton; he even considered whether he would not be acting in her best interests by disclosing the plan to Ellerey; and he felt a traitor even when he carried out her commands.

During his long hours of watching on the roof, it had been comparatively easy to communicate with the brigands on the plateau. Having attracted their attention, he dropped a paper, wrapped round a piece of stone, telling them who the youth really was, that she was ready to go with them to Vasilici, on condition that her companions were allowed to leave the hills unmolested; that she had in her possession the token which Vasilici expected and was, moreover, the bearer of a message which those who were with her would not allow her to deliver. The brigands accepted the terms, and although they broke faith and came back to secure the two men in the tower if possible, they made no attempt to injure the Princess when she climbed down the rope after Anton and stood in the midst of them. She was not wrong in thinking that she was far too valuable a prisoner not to be taken with all speed to Vasilici. As the brigands surrounded her, Anton caught the rope, and, with a quick, dexterous turn of his arm, sent the end of it flying upward to the roof.

"You may trust us," said one man, trying to keep the anger out of his voice.

"I do," Maritza answered; "but nothing was said about the rope, and a small matter may make a difference in such a treaty as ours."

As they descended the zig-zag path, Maritza fired three times into the air, causing the men near her to start back.

"They are sleeping," she said, nodding toward the tower. "That is to wake them, and let them know of the treaty."

"I must ask you for that weapon," said the leader, but in spite of himself he spoke with a certain deference. "It is a dangerous plaything in your hands."

"It is empty and of no further use to me," she answered, with a smile, handing him the revolver. "Keep it, my friend. It has my initials engraved on it, and may serve you as a boast some day when you entertain your fellows with tales of your adventures."

Having arranged which men should gradually fall out in twos and threes and presently return to the pass, the brigands made haste to march, and they did not interfere when Maritza waved her handkerchief to the two solitary figures standing on the plateau. It would show that the Princess was safe and allay any suspicions they might have; they would probably not hurry their departure, and were likely to fall into the hands of the men returning to the pass. Nor did they make any objection to Anton walking beside the Princess; there was so evidently no idea of attempting to escape. "How long a march have we before reaching Vasilici?" Maritza asked, turning to a man who walked near her.

"We shall reach him to-night," was the answer, "unless we make a long halt on the way."

The man did not look at her as he spoke. He had been specially told off to keep near her and to listen should she talk secretly with her fellow-prisoner. His companions immediately near straggled a little as they marched, and presently he drew nearer to Maritza, and she noticed it.

"Take no heed of me and do not look at me," he said. "Have you a hope of winning over Vasilici?"

"I have a message for him."

"A doubtful protection," was the answer.

"Perhaps so, but I have friends in his company."

"You were ill-advised to make this journey; I have warned you." And still keeping his even pace, the man moved farther from her side.

This whispered conversation set many thoughts surging through Maritza's brain--not new thoughts exactly, for there were few contingencies she had not provided for when she determined to place herself in the hands of the brigands, but thoughts which began to cut deeper, as it were, into a channel already made. This man's action proved that he was not altogether indifferent to her, and it was hardly likely that he was the only one among Vasilici's followers who might be ready to speak a word for her, perhaps even strike a blow for her, could she stir them sufficiently. Brigandage was not the natural calling of many who had flocked to Vasilici's standard, nor were they likely to rest contented with Vasilici's leadership for long. Were they not even now waiting for a message from the Queen, to whom in the future they would look for favor?

At noon, when a halt was called, this same man saw that Maritza had sufficient to eat, and replaced the flask of wine given her by another, saying that it was better and that she would want all her strength. He took no notice of Anton, who, by the Princess's instructions, spoke to no one unless he were spoken to. She wanted to draw as little attention to him as possible, and sought by various means to show that he was a servant only, and not a very highly valued one. She felt that his insignificance might render him trebly valuable under certain conditions. So utterly absorbed was she by her thoughts that the length of the march did not greatly fatigue her. She failed to recognize that the way was often rough and difficult, and that the pace of the whole band had slackened somewhat as the day advanced.

It was late in the afternoon when they entered a narrow defile between two precipitous mountain walls, which looked as though some huge giant had cut out one slice from the top to the bottom of the mountain. Perhaps through many ages a rapid narrow torrent had rushed here cutting slowly but surely deeper. There was no water now, but the way was paved with loose pebbles, which made progress slow and tiring. It was not a way one would choose, and since near the entrance there were other paths more inviting, Maritza concluded that they were nearing the end of the journey. For a moment on entering the defile her heart sank within her. It was like leaving the open world and the sunlight to creep into the dark unknowable, where some horrible fate might await her. Would she ever step freely into the open light of day again? Her thoughts sped backward to the tower standing above the pass and to the man she had left there. Which road had he taken--the way to Sturatzberg, or the path across the mountains northward which led to safety? If to

Sturatzberg, why had he gone there? Her hands clenched a little as an answer came quickly to her question, but she murmured to herself: "What is it to me? I am Maritza, the lawful ruler of this land. What is anything to me but the memory of my fathers and the battle for my rights?" The thought brought back her courage, and made her calm.

They had not proceeded far along the narrow defile before they were challenged by a sentry posted upon a narrow pathway which seemed to have been scooped out of the solid rock above the rough road they were traversing. The challenge was a mere form, for he could not fail to recognize many of his companions, but his gun was not lowered until the pass-word had been shouted back. This was evidently the brigand's stronghold, and it was well guarded. In a retreat so defended by nature, the brigands could defy any army sent against them, and for the first time Maritza understood why no effort had been successful in dislodging them.

At the end of the defile they were challenged again, this time by a small body of men on guard there, and having answered and been allowed to pass, they emerged into a large circular hollow in the hills. On every side it was enclosed by precipitous walls in which, here and there, were narrow openings, evidently paths similar to the one they had travelled. The hollow was covered with tents and wooden huts, the latter put together with a solidity which showed that they were permanent structures, and suggested that whatever enterprise the brigands entered upon, this stronghold was never left undefended.

The party was evidently expected. The news that Princess Maritza had determined to place herself in his hands had been quickly carried to Vasilici, and with a few of his leading men he was seated in front of a long wooden shed when his captive was brought into the hollow. His arm was still in a sling, and his expression was morose and fierce, although a grin of satisfaction lightened his face for a moment when he saw the trim, youthful figure and knew that the cause of his bandaged arm was now in his power. Perhaps in the back of his mind he had already begun to devise fitting tortures for his enemy. During the long march Maritza had pictured this moment, and had determined how to act; but the real scene was rather different from the picture she had imagined. As the men who had brought her fell back, leaving her alone, with Anton a few paces behind her, she glanced round at the crowd and said:

"Which among you is Vasilici?"

His appearance sufficiently marked him out from his companions, but Maritza was quick to perceive that there was a half-concealed smile on the faces of some of the men near him when she pretended not to recognize him. Perhaps Vasilici saw the smile, too, for, although his face darkened, he answered the question without any sudden outburst of anger.

"Greeting," said Maritza. "I would be seated while I talk. The journey which I have undertaken into these hills has been a hurried one over a rough road; and, besides, it is not usual for a sovereign to stand in the presence of her subjects."

Vasilici burst into a loud laugh, which found an echo among many of his followers, but not all. Even while he laughed, and before he could say a word to prevent it, one man had stepped forward and placed a rough stool beside Maritza.

"Carry it nearer, Anton; that will do." And then she seated herself, Anton standing behind her.

"Thus we can talk more easily," she said after a pause. "Are all your leading men here, Vasilici--all those who form your council? for what I have to say concerns all."

"In these hills my will is law," was the answer.

"So long as you please your followers, or the majority of them; I understand," Maritza said quickly. "Absolute power lies in the pleasure, or the fear, of the majority."

"Not here," said the chief, raising his voice angrily. "I alone am the law."

"Then indeed are you great among the kings of the earth."

Her question had forced him to exalt himself, and this was not pleasing to all those who stood about him.

"What you have to say, say quickly," Vasilici went on. "The death of good comrades lies at your door, and punishment is swift here. We move too rapidly to burden ourselves with prisoners."

"I will be brief," said Maritza. "For a long time you have been intriguing with Queen Elena, through a servant of hers, one Jules de Froilette. By him you have been told to expect a certain token from her Majesty, upon the receipt of which you were to sweep down upon Sturatzberg, join yourselves with those who espoused her cause in the city, and set her alone upon the throne of Wallaria. That token was brought to you by Captain Ellerey."

"It is a lie," Vasilici burst out, "and you know it. He delivered the golden cross, the sign of your house, if indeed you be the Princess Maritza as you say."

"Captain Ellerey brought the Queen's token," Maritza went on quietly, as though there had been no interruption, "and delivered it as he supposed. He was as astonished to see the golden cross as you were."

"Then you--"

"Yes, I changed them. There is the proof." And she tossed the sealed box carelessly into Vasilici's hands. He cut it open quickly, while dead silence reigned around him, and then held up the bracelet of medallions that everyone might see.

"By this message you accuse yourself," cried the brigand, standing at his full height. "Now, hear your punishment."

"Wait!" said Maritza; "there is more to tell."

Absolute as he had proclaimed himself to be, Vasilici nevertheless glanced at those about him and, seeing that they were inclined to hear all the Princess had to say, waved his hand for her to continue. The fact that the chief was not quite so strong as he said was not lost on Maritza.

"It is true that I changed the token," she went on, not addressing herself especially to Vasilici, "and if I had a hope that there might be men loyal to me in these hills, for so this miserable scoundrel De Froilette has told me, that was not my only reason for changing it. De Froilette never told you that there was a time when he espoused my cause; he has never said how he would come fawning to me to-morrow were it in his own interests to do so; he has never explained what is to follow your devotion to the Queen. Rewards, place, honor, he has promised them all; yet on the frontier at this moment lies a Russian army only waiting this De Froilette's word to enter Wallaria and secure every benefit which you have pledged yourselves to fight for."

"The proof! The proof!" shouted many voices.

"What proof can I carry of such a scheme? Send for De Froilette on some pretext or other and question him, or send to the frontier and spy upon the army that waits there. You have the Queen's token; I have delivered it. Go out and meet the King's army, which lies ready to contest your way to Sturatzberg, if you will, but remember this: if you win your way to the city, if you succeed in overthrowing the present Government and setting Queen Elena alone upon the throne, you will not have advanced the cause of your country one step. You will be forgotten as soon as your work is done, and be under the firm hand of the Muscovite. You will have fought your enemies' battle for them and sold yourselves into slavery. You will have played into the hands of this Frenchman, De Froilette, who is serving his own ends only, who cares nothing for Wallaria, whose reward lies ready for payment in Russian coffers, who is as false to Queen Elena and to you as he has been to me."

There was a low murmur among the eager crowd as Maritza stopped abruptly, and those sitting and standing near Vasilici turned to one another and whispered together. Whatever hopes lay in the hearts of these men, selfish hopes for the most part, perhaps, yet with some patriotism in them, too, it was evident that the accusation against De Froilette was not entirely a surprise. There were men there who had never trusted him, and Maritza recognized that her words were not without weight. While they still whispered, and even grew quarrelsome over their opinions, she rose from her seat.

"For a long time I have been in Sturatzberg watching events," she said, raising her voice a little and obtaining instant attention. "There are many there who love my cause, some because of my right, some because they have learnt that Wallaria is merely the plaything of the nations. Are there not here about me many who love their country, who have fled from tyranny to the freedom of these hills, not to defy just laws, but to withstand oppression? I tell them that Queen Elena's promises are valueless. I tell them that every move the Queen has made is known in Sturatzberg, discounted and guarded against by the Ministers of foreign powers who rule the King. I tell them that the token of the bracelet of medallions has no power to help them to freedom, that from first to last they have been deceived. I might point to the golden cross and tell them that it is the sign of this country's salvation; but Vasilici, who stands for chief among you, has spurned it. I might stand here and cry to you that he is no chief worthy to lead an army of patriots, that there is another now among you whose right it is to lead, who has the power to win success; but men who bow to windy words are no countrymen of mine, and I scorn to tempt them to such false loyalty. Judge for yourselves and choose. There stands Vasilici, a brigand, King of these hills; and here stand I, Maritza, Princess, daughter of Wallarian kings, come among you of her own free will. I promise you not success, that knowledge is in the mind of God only; but this I do promise: I will lead you toward success, and, if we fail, die fighting in the midst of you. Choose, therefore, Maritza or Vasilici."

The stroke was a bold one. Brave men could understand the daring of flinging down such a challenge to a man like Vasilici, here in his own stronghold. It appealed in a manner that nothing else she could have done would have appealed, and she enhanced the force of her words by her apparent indifference as to what their decision might be. She resumed her seat as abruptly as she had risen from it, and beckoned Anton to approach her.

"Princess!" There was reverence in his tone as he bowed before her.

"Listen," she said quickly. "You marked well the way we came?"

"Yes, Princess."

"There is division among them, and for the present we are safe, perhaps, but the issue is doubtful. If they decide to hold me prisoner for a while, if their decision be anything short of making me their leader, take the first opportunity to escape back to Sturatzberg as swiftly as you can, and tell them what has happened in the hills. Wherever there is a man who loves me, tell him the story, tell Countess Mavrodin, tell Captain Ellerey if he be in the city. Give me but a score of men to shout my cause, and there are many here who will gladly add their voices to such an acclamation. Tell them that."

No shout, not a murmur, even, had followed Maritza's challenge. Those who hated her most were astonished into silence. Vasilici's face grew a shade more savage, but he was quick to note that the Princess had not appealed altogether in vain. He did not turn to those about him at once and mock her pretensions. It was not the moment to assert an authority which he well knew some of those with him in the hills resented. For a time he made no effort to suppress the whisperings on all sides; he had to determine on some counter-stroke. Suddenly he turned toward Maritza--

"Princess," he said, "I love a courageous foe. All here shall be your judges, not I."

"I am content," she answered.

At a sign from the chief, food and wine were brought to her, while the brigands gathered together and listened eagerly to this counsel and to that. There were many who, like Vasilici, had taken to the hills merely to swoop down upon the defenceless for pillage and for ransom, who cared nothing who might sit upon the throne in Sturatzberg, and among these there was a certain resentment that latterly there had come a change into the councils, that the organization was in danger of growing into a political one. What rewards in the city could compensate for the loss of their freedom in the hills? This faction was strong, but hardly strong enough to make it possible for Vasilici to break with his other followers. The chief knew it was the time for plausible arguments rather than domineering demands, and these he well knew how to use. He listened to the counsel of others, and he advised, and gradually there arose a large majority in the camp to whose decision the minority bowed because their opinions were subtly provided for.

There was a smile upon Vasilici's face as he stood forward to speak from which Maritza argued no good.

"Princess, I am but the mouthpiece, not the judge," he said. "It is true that there are many political refugees among us to whom you appeal personally, even if your cause does not; but chiefly we are not political. We are against all kings and the laws which make men either rich or poor, and we have set up in these hills a kingdom of our own of which I am at present the head. We take our living where we find it. Such a leader as you would make should draw men to your cause; but are they drawn? Is there any real force in Sturatzberg to rise and fight at your bidding? We doubt it. We are not patriotic enough to throw our lives away upon a dream. Yet you may be right, and the time may come when the golden cross will send us to fight your battles; but that time is not yet. We want more certainty before we espouse so desperate a venture. Those friends you have in the city yonder should, however, be strong enough to insure your safety if their loyalty is as you say, and for them the time has come to prove that loyalty. For us, we have to live. It has been decided, therefore, to hold you to ransom. We shall despatch messengers to the troops which lie in the plain, and for a price we shall deliver you to them. I doubt not you will receive as great courtesy from them as from us."

Maritza did not answer.

"You are content, Princess?" said Vasilici.

"I am disappointed," she returned. "I perceive that they were only the cowards who fled from Sturatzberg to these hills; the brave hearts remain in the city."

"We move to-night," said Vasilici, turning to those about him. "Let the messengers start at once."

"Remember, Anton: to Sturatzberg with all the speed you may. Now leave me alone," whispered Maritza.

To the good offices of the man who had shown kindness to the Princess, Anton owed his ability to slip past the guards as soon as night had fallen, and he had travelled a long way when he fell in with Ellerey and Baron Petrescu's party at dawn. He told his tale quickly.

"Only in Sturatzberg can we help her," Anton declared. "It is useless going forward. She will certainly be delivered to the soldiers."

His counsel prevailed, and they returned as quickly as possible to the castle in the hills, taking the brigand who had been their guide with them. They could not let him go and divulge their plans. Before another dawn came they were riding as swiftly as the rough way would permit in the direction of Sturatzberg.

CHAPTER XXIII
THE TEMPTATION OF FRINA MAVRODIN

Lord Cloverton pushed his chair back from the table, and with his arms folded gazed abstractedly at the ceiling. Captain Ward sat opposite to him, turning over a pile of papers, noting their contents, and placing them in order.

"De Froilette was right after all, Ward. Princess Maritza has been in Sturatzberg."

"And will be again almost immediately, now that the brigands have delivered her up. She is likely to be brought into the city to-morrow, I understand."

"Yes, and lodged in the palace under safe keeping, and then--then, Ward?"

"She must bear the consequences of her folly," Ward answered. "Has England any part to play in whatever treatment she may receive?"

"No, I think not. One may pity the woman, but even a woman must pay the penalty of her actions. Still the death or banishment of the Princess may do little to relieve the situation; indeed, may only intensify it. There have been other influences at work, and we are as ignorant of them as ever we were."

"I see you have some scheme maturing, my lord," Ward said with a smile.

"It might mature at once did I know what had become of Captain Ellerey. Would he seize the opportunity and escape out of Wallaria, think you?" "Not if he thought anyone who had a right to his help needed it. He is the kind of man who would return, no matter what the danger might be," answered Ward.

"I believe some friendship of the sort does bind him to Sturatzberg," said Lord Cloverton, "and I should be happier if he were in Princess Maritza's company. I should know how to act then."

The door opened and a servant brought in a card.

"Ah, now we may hear news," said the Ambassador. "De Froilette, the timber merchant. Show him in. You need not go, Ward."

De Froilette came in quickly and was cordially greeted by the Minister.

"My secretary, Captain Ward; you may safely speak before him, monsieur."

"It is no secret information I have to give," said De Froilette. "I came rather impudently to give myself the pleasure of laughing at your lordship."

"You have seen fit to praise me so often, monsieur, that I can no doubt bear your ridicule with the same equanimity as I accepted your praise."

"A witty retort to my pleasantry, my lord. You did not believe me when I said Princess Maritza was in Sturatzberg. You see I was right."

"Monsieur, I grant your information was valuable; my policy might have suffered considerably by my disbelief. I have learnt a lesson and wish to profit by it. Can you tell me where Captain Ellerey is?"

"No, my lord; but I can tell you where to watch for him."

"You will help me by doing so," said Cloverton.

"In Sturatzberg, my lord," said De Froilette.

"Do you imagine he will return to the very centre of his danger? I am inclined to think he has crossed the hills and taken the quickest way out of Wallaria."

"You do not know the man, and you forget he is an Englishman," said De Froilette. "They are desperate fellows, these English adventurers. They have no eyes for danger, and are lacking that diplomacy which makes men feel that it is honorable to retreat sometimes. He is one of those who love their sword and would fain die with their boots on. Besides, he is in love."

"Ah, now you interest me, monsieur," Cloverton exclaimed. "I have been wondering whether he had not some weak spot."

"I heard him once speak of Princess Maritza," De Froilette went on. "He had met her in England; and I read the story behind his careless words. Here in Sturatzberg the Princess must have seen him, and for love of her he espoused her cause. She is being brought to the city, and he will surely follow her. Seize him, my lord, and you nip the rebellion in the bud."

"You think so," said Cloverton reflectively.

"I am certain of it," was the answer. "I am even bold enough to give advice. The King can afford to treat the Princess leniently. She has no strong personality to guide and counsel her; alone she is no danger, or the brigands would not have given her up. But this mad Englishman has the power to keep her cause alive. The King cannot afford to pardon him. Kill him, my lord, as quickly as you can. With her lover dead, the Princess will have no heart to plot."

"I think you are right, monsieur. I shall advise the King."

"And I will do my part in watching for Ellerey," said De Froilette. "You will be serving the State, monsieur," said the Ambassador; "but are there no others who are dangerous?"

The Frenchman was thoughtful for a moment.

"No, I think not," he answered. "There are some who talk loudly in the back streets, but their talk serves them instead of fighting, and does no harm."

"Quite so, monsieur; but I was not thinking of them," Lord Cloverton returned. "There is one curious feature in the situation. The brigands, it is true, have played into the hands of the State, but there seems little doubt that they were waiting for a message from Sturatzberg and were prepared to act upon it. They did not receive the message they expected, and so became revengeful. Now what message did they expect, and from whom was it to come?"

De Froilette shrugged his shoulders.

"Perhaps Captain Ellerey betrayed his trust and delivered the wrong message," suggested the Ambassador.

De Froilette looked at him in astonishment.

"By doing so he may have unconsciously served the State," Lord Cloverton continued, "and perhaps--of course, monsieur, one has to guess rather wildly some-times--perhaps balked the intentions of those Russian troops which, for no apparent reason, have been gathering on the frontier."

Then De Froilette laughed.

"You are prepared for all emergencies, my lord; it is wonderful, your foresight; but I conceive that you are making something out of nothing. The diplomatic brain is so fertile it surpasses me."

"It is a soil which so many persons throw seed into, monsieur," was the answer. "Those who deal in timber are not the only merchants who scent danger to their interests in the political ferment of the times. But your advice is good; I shall advise the King. When Captain Ellerey comes he may tell us more." And the Ambassador rose, putting an end to the interview.

When the door had closed upon the Frenchman he resumed his seat and smiled benignantly. The smile invited comment from his companion.

"Personal enmity as regards Ellerey," said Ward, "and astonishment at your accurate knowledge."

The Ambassador nodded.

"He should be watched," said Ward.

"That is no longer necessary," was the quick answer. "Whatever power he may have had is gone. He is chiefly concerned about his own skin nowadays, and it would not surprise me to hear that business had suddenly called him away from Sturatzberg. Still, I thank him for giving me an idea. I shall see the King."

De Froilette went quickly back to the Altstrasse, and it would appear that Captain Ward's estimate of his attitude was near the truth. He sent for Francois at once.

"The net is being drawn in, Francois," he said.

"Are we within it?"

"We shall easily escape," was the answer. "Is everything ready to depart at a moment's notice?"

"Yes, monsieur."

"Good. You carry a revolver, Francois?"

The man showed it to him.

"Good again. Captain Ellerey will return to Sturatzberg--may have done so already. That he has played us false we know, that he can give evidence against us is certain. Revenge and safety, therefore, lie in the same direction. Watch for him, Francois, as I shall, and silence him."

"And his servant?" asked the man.

"If your private quarrel with the servant leads you to do so, no harm will be done." And with a wave of the hand he dismissed him.

The news that Princess Maritza was in the hands of the King's troops and was being brought to Sturatzberg had reached the city early that morning, but the news was not immediately known to Frina Mavrodin. It was being conveyed to her by a trusted messenger who had much to do on his way, and the fact that she had lately kept much at home accounted for her not hearing it from any other source.

The days of waiting are ever the longest days to live through, and the hours had dragged heavily for Frina Mavrodin since Baron Petrescu had started for the hills. Hardly anyone saw her except Hannah, and the old serving woman pitied her, judging her distress by her own. She little knew the terrible struggle which raged in the breast of this beautiful woman, how all that was good and bad in her, all those latent forces which lie in the heart of everyone, sprang into life and fought equally for the mastery. It was not the Princess who was first in her thoughts from dawn to dark, or whose image passed incessantly through her restless dreams. It was the man who was beside the Princess, who had fought desperately for her whether he loved her cause or not, who was hourly under the spell of her enchantment. The potency of that spell seemed to grow the more she thought of it, and all the charm which some had professed to find in herself seemed to sink into insignificance. It was not sufficient to win the love of this man. And those waiting hours, too, are hours of danger. Troubles or desires, or whatever thoughts assail at such a time, lose their proportion, and idleness lends vitality to the evil lying dormant. Was there no way to win her desire? Between it and her stood only the Princess, an enemy to the State. Might she not be swept out of the way? How easy such a thing seemed to be. She had only to speak a few words to dash to the ground all Maritza's hopes of success. Why not speak them? In love and war all means are fair. And then arose the good in her, and she turned away in horror from the very thought of such treachery.

It was in a fierce moment of her struggle that the messenger arrived. Dumitru, travel-stained yet unweary, more keenly alive now perhaps than he had even been as Anton in the hills, came to her.

"What news? What news?" she cried, springing up.

"The worst, Countess."

"Dead?"

"No; the Princess lives."

"Yes, yes; and those who are with her?"

"Are on their way to the city," Dumitru answered. "We could not enter openly; we had to delay, and exercise the greatest care. Baron Petrescu will come to-night if possible, but extreme caution is needed. I came on. I am of no importance and pass unnoticed. I have visited a score of places in the city already, and I have much more to do before sunset."

"Does Captain Ellerey return to Sturatzberg?" asked Frina thoughtfully.

"Aye; and he is a man whose equal these eyes are never likely to see again. He is fit to be a king."

"A king!"

"Yes, a king, and though he be a foreigner, I for one shout for him."

"A king, Dumitru; tell me, does he love the Princess?"

"Surely he must, since for her cause he has shown no great affection. He will be here to strike one more good blow for her, and, loving her, may learn to love her cause too. We may yet triumph, Countess. But listen. The Princess has been delivered by the brigands," and Dumitru told her the whole story quickly. "To-night she will be brought back to Sturatzberg," he went on, "although it is given out that she will not come until the morning. The gates will be shut, and when the streets are quiet they will be opened again. Not many soldiers are with her, and those within the gates will hold all danger cheap. The city will be hushed and still, but there are many who will not sleep. A signal will blaze forth in the darkness and a few may fall in the streets, but the Princess will be free. You will be ready to receive her, Countess?"

"Here?"

"Is it not the safest refuge in Sturatzberg?" asked Dumitru. "There are hiding-places here, and you are not a suspect in the city."

"And afterward?" said the Countess.

"I know not. A small success in the city would perhaps raise the country; the afterward is for the Princess to decide. She will have to consider the welfare of those who strike to-night. You will be ready to receive her, Countess?"

"Yes," Frina answered, and Dumitru went to pursue his way through the city, calling men to arm and prepare, little dreaming what thoughts troubled the beautiful woman he had left.

The frail little hopes she had found consolation in vanished at Dumitru's words. Desmond Ellerey loved Maritza. Dumitru had said it, and had he not had ample opportunity of judging? Now Maritza was to come a fugitive to her house; her very life perhaps lay in her hands. How easy it would be to speak the few words which would tell her enemies where she was hidden, and who would know, who would guess, that it was the Countess Mavrodin who had betrayed her? Such specious arguments did the evil that was in her whisper in her ear, and she could not shut the whisperings out. All day long her restlessness increased. Her solitude became unbearable. She longed for the world of men and women, hungered to hear laughter and the sound of voices--anything to distract her from her thoughts. That evening she went to Court, beautiful, reckless, heartless to all seeming, ready to be flattered and to flatter--a dangerous mood for such a woman to be in.

So, all unconsciously, she was driven forward by destiny. She was in a mood to be tempted, and the greatest temptation of all was lying in wait for her.

She had shown such marked preference for Captain Ellerey when he came to Court that a host of her admirers had perforce to stand sullenly aside. To-night they gathered round her, each one in his turn receiving some little favor which buried in oblivion all past disappointments; such virtue lies even in the least of a beautiful woman's favors. Frina Mavrodin had always had the subtle power of making her companion of the moment believe that he was the one person in all the world she would wish to have beside her, and this power she exercised to the full to-night.

Lord Cloverton, covertly watching her, was constrained to admire her, and even his old blood tingled with a remembrance of youth as he did so. But he did not approach her. It was not his part to play the tempter to-night. He had arranged otherwise. Presently he saw the King enter the room alone, and look round in search of some one. His eye fell upon Frina Mavrodin, and he went toward her. Perhaps, too, in his veins the blood tingled a little.

"An hour of ease which so seldom falls to me renews my strength to-night, Countess, and youth and beauty draw me like a lodestone," said the King.

"Your Majesty is pleased to flatter me," she answered with a sweeping curtsey.

"That would indeed be impossible. I am honored, doubly so, if you will take my hand in the dance."

It was a set dance, stately in its measure, and those who watched remarked how the grace of the woman seemed to lend grace to the King's movements, who danced but seldom, and that, in truth, somewhat awkwardly.

The King thanked her as he led her to a seat when the dance was over. It was in the alcove where she had so often sat with Ellerey, and the coincidence impressed her.

"There should be brighter times at hand for Wallaria, Countess," said the King. "The Princess Maritza will enter Sturatzberg--a prisoner--to-morrow."

"So I have heard, your Majesty."

"And you loyally rejoice with us, Countess?"

The question was so marked in the intonation of the King's voice that Frina Mavrodin was on her guard in a moment. "She is a woman, your Majesty, and, since I am no politician, I pity the woman."

"I am not without pity, either, Countess," was the answer. "The Princess has been ill-advised, and the onus lies with those who have advised and supported her. It is upon them punishment should rightly fall."

"And who are they?" asked the Countess.

"That is a question to which there is no complete answer," said the King. "There is only one I can name definitely. But there is one person in Sturatzberg who could answer the question, so I am informed, and so I believe."

"And he will not answer?"

"She has not yet been asked," the King returned.

"A woman, your Majesty?"

"A very beautiful woman; yourself, Countess."

Perhaps Frina Mavrodin was prepared for the King's words. She did not start, the color did not rise to her cheeks. She remained silent for a few moments, feeling that the King's eyes were fixed upon her.

"I can guess who was your Majesty's informant," she said quietly. "Lord Cloverton. He has always credited me with a power I do not possess, and has often set traps for me. They were subtly hidden, well devised to catch a schemer; but, being innocent, they failed to ensnare me."

"We ourselves have eyes, Countess; it is not necessary that the British Ambassador should see for us."

"No, your Majesty; but we, the Court, sometimes fancy that he attempts to take that duty upon himself," Frina answered.

"Then you will not help me, Countess?" said the King with a smile.

"In any way I can, your Majesty."

"But not in the way I want. It is a pity. You will force me to harsh measures. There is one other I may constrain to tell me, unless he values his secret more than life."

Frina looked at him, a question in her eyes, but her lips gave it no words.

"A brave man," said the King, "although circumstances have made him my enemy. You might save him."

Still Frina was silent.

"Probably Captain Ellerey will not speak, therefore it is certain that Captain Ellerey must die," said the King slowly.

"Is he in Sturatzberg?"

"Ah, Countess, you must not try and surprise my secrets; but rest assured he must die unless you choose to save him."

"How can I save him?" she asked.

The King suddenly laid his hand on hers, which were folded in her lap. "To-morrow, early, send me by a trusted messenger the names of those who are foremost in Maritza's cause, the names of the societies whose plans and aims they govern, and, so far as is in your knowledge, the plans which they have formed. On my royal oath, none shall know from whom I received this information, and Captain Ellerey shall be free to leave Wallaria."

"He is a brave man, and I would help him if I could," she said.

"You can, Countess; if you love him, you will."

"Your Majesty is strangely at fault; Captain Ellerey is nothing to me."

"I have touched your hand, Countess, as you asked a question concerning him, and felt the quiver in your frame. Your heart would not answer as your lips do. Remember this: he dies unless you save him."

"But I am powerless, your Majesty."

"Then, Countess, his case is hard indeed. There are some hours before to-morrow; use them to understand how powerful you are in this matter."

"So far I will obey your Majesty."

"Always remembering, Countess, that if you cannot save him no power on earth can;" and, with a bow, the King left her alone.

Here was the opportunity she had dreamed of. No one would ever know. What to her were Princess Maritza and all her followers in comparison with Desmond Ellerey? There was a look of determination in her face as she left the alcove quickly. The few hours before tomorrow seemed all too short for her.

CHAPTER XXIV
HOW MARITZA ENTERED STURATZBERG

It was a dark night without a moon, and only a faint star or two glimmered in the sky. The smell of rain was in the air, and there was a closeness in the atmosphere which made the effort of breathing a conscious one. It was still early as Frina Mavrodin was driven rapidly homeward. She left the palace immediately after her conversation with the King. The few hours before to-morrow were best spent alone. A wild confusion of thoughts surged through her brain, but one thought was ever dominant--how could she save Desmond Ellerey without betraying others? For while the King's suggestion was a subtle and potent temptation, it had the effect of steadying the Countess. Such an idea as a wholesale betrayal of those who had trusted her had never occurred to her; her only thought had been how to raise a barrier between Maritza and Desmond Ellerey, how to act so that they might be effectually separated forever. Such plans as had come into her mind may have been mean and unworthy, but the circumstances had excused them. The King's words had robbed them of all excuse, had shown her that base treachery belonged to them as surely as to the larger scheme which he had suggested. It did not occur to her to blame him for the suggestion; politically, perhaps, he was justified; but that he could believe her capable of such treachery showed her that, between her private jealousy and her political position, there was no room to draw even the finest of lines. So the few hours before to-morrow were not to be used, as the King supposed, in a struggle between her honor and her desire, but in concentrated thought of how his Majesty might be outwitted. Desmond Ellerey must be saved, but neither the Princess nor her followers must be sacrificed to save him. Her own desire must stand aside, whatever the suffering might be. Thus, through the fierce fire of temptation Frina Mavrodin came forth a stronger woman, a keener slave to duty, because that duty must cost her so much. And having shaken herself free from the fetters of selfishness, her thoughts and conceptions became more acute.

It was hardly possible that Desmond Ellerey had yet returned to Sturatzberg. No one could know his movements better than Dumitru, and he had shown no fear concerning him. Even if the King possessed information which might point to the probability of his arrest, Ellerey's courage and resourcefulness were factors to be reckoned with before his arrest could become an accomplished fact. That in Maritza's defence he might prove reckless was true, but he would hardly do so until every other means had failed. No; the King had played upon her fears, and she had fallen a victim to his cunning. She had plainly shown that Ellerey was dear to her, that she was prepared to sacrifice much to secure his safety; she had, moreover, given the impression that she could betray many in Sturatzberg if she would, and therefore, should the rescue of Maritza prove successful, she herself, and her house, and all who belonged to her would be closely watched. She had, in fact, undone what she had so persistently taken pains to accomplish; she had given cause for suspicion; she had rendered her house by the river an unsafe place of refuge. How was she to retrieve the position? Entering her house she gave rapid instructions to certain of her servants, and then went to her own rooms and sent for Hannah. The old serving woman came quickly, and to her Frina made her first confession.

"I have been cross, Hannah, sometimes," she said; "forgive me."

"Oh, no, my lady, you have only been troubled. We all have our own way of showing grief."

"True, Hannah, and I have had troubles which you cannot know of. Your quick pardon teaches me a lesson."

"O my lady---"

"Listen, Hannah, there is much to do and little time to do it in. To-night, perhaps, the Princess will return."

"Here!" Hannah exclaimed.

"Yes; but she will be a fugitive from her enemies, and how long this house may be a safe refuge for her I cannot tell. Come with me. I will show you a means of escape should the worst happen--a stout door which will hold back pursuers for a long time. It opens from a room which shall be yours for the time. The key shall be in your possession. Study to look innocent, Hannah, when you are questioned, and in a crucial moment you may prove a far better defence than a dozen armed men. Come."

As Frina Mavrodin had driven through the city there were many people in the streets. The cafes were still full, and there were no signs of any unusual excitement. A few may have discussed Princess Maritza over their coffee, liquor, or syrup, but in most cases it was with casual interest, or with a remark that, if they "were abroad early enough, they might walk down to the Southern Gate to see her enter." What had her fate to do with them? Though the times were troublous they would go their way to-morrow as they had done to-day, as they would every day until their own small circle of interest were touched. They had as little sympathy with the agitator as they had with the Government; neither the one nor the other did anything to affect them materially. So these law-abiding citizens, law-abiding only because there was no temptation to be otherwise, perhaps, finished their coffee and went home, and the streets of Sturatzberg grew quieter, and, with the closing of the cafes, darker. The city gates were shut, and if a few soldiers appeared at the corners of streets, they caused little interest to the people going home. Since the murdered bodies had been found lying in the Bergenstrasse, it was only right that the city should be well guarded.

The soldiers themselves grumbled somewhat. Fighting was their trade, and they were discontented at being made a city watch. Beyond a late reveller or two no one was out after midnight. What was the use of all this precaution? In the smaller streets there was even greater silence. Where one might have expected to find whatever dissatisfaction existed in the city, there was only the greater peace. Hardly a light shone out from any of the dark buildings, no one lurked in shadowy corners, and although the soldiers had been ordered to be especially careful tonight, there seemed to be even less than usual to demand their attention. They believed that the Princess Maritza was to enter the city at dawn.

At the guard-house of the Southern Gate the men were alert. An hour ago their officer had told them what was to happen, and the news was presently conveyed to the soldiers at the corners. The officer of the guardroom kept a steady watch upon the slowly passing minutes, while outside the city a small army had approached under cover of the darkness.

Without and within there was silence. Yet wakeful and watching men may be as silent as those who sleep. Throughout the day a man had passed from one narrow street to another with quick and stealthy steps. Into this house he went, mounting the stairs swiftly, and disappeared for a few moments into some upper room; then as swiftly he came down again, and, gliding up alleys and half-deserted streets, entered one little cafe after another, and mounted to many a room whose occupants listened eagerly to his words and made a sign that they were understood. Long before darkness had fallen upon Sturatzberg there were many cafes doing little business to all seeming, which, nevertheless, were crowded with men hidden away and waiting.

Such a crowd waited in the long room at the rear of the Toison d'Or. The men who composed it had gathered there one by one, as they had done that night when they came to drink with the soldiers who had been found dead in the Bergenstrasse next morning. Many of the same men were in the crowd, many also of those who had once chased Ellerey so furiously through the garden of that other tavern where was the door in the wall. They greeted each new arrival with a nod, and for the most part were silent or spoke only in whispers.

"At what hour?" asked one.

"Two hours after midnight."

"Are our numbers sufficient?"

"Quite sufficient," answered another. "At a dozen places I have had our brothers gathered, close to the spot from which they will make their rush upon the troops. The attack will come from all sides at once, and the soldiers will be taken by surprise. We cannot fail."

"Does the Princess know, Dumitru?"

"Not certainly, but she will be expectant and ready. You understand whose command you have to obey, and the signal?"

The men about him nodded and smiled with quiet confidence, while Dumitru passed on to others to answer similar questions. He was of much importance among them to-night. They felt that he was but the mouthpiece of the Princess, that she was their real leader, that the time they had waited for and plotted toward had really come. A few nervous ones there were among them who calculated what the price of failure would be, and had planned what they might do for their own safety in such an event; but the majority of them were enthusiasts who rejoiced that the hour of action had arrived at last.

"After to-night, Dumitru, there will be no turning back," whispered one man, who, standing on a chair, had called for the toast to Maritza on that night fatal to the deserting soldiers. "The next few days will make the name of Sturatzberg ring through the world, and our deeds strike terror into the heart of the nation."

Dumitru nodded and passed on, but he too kept eager watch upon the time, even as did the officer at the guardhouse.

The crowd became more excited and restless as the hands of the clock crept farther and farther from midnight. "Surely it is time now," they whispered at intervals. And the leaders had some difficulty in restraining them. As it was in the Toison d'Or, so it was in many a dark house where men lay hidden and waiting.

From the watchman over the gate word was sent to the officer that the prisoner had come, and at his command the gates silently swung back upon their hinges. It was a large body of men that entered, having in their midst a slim boyish figure mounted on a charger. So Maritza entered Sturatzberg.

The men at the word of command halted to right and left, and only a few, comparatively, continued their silent march along the Bergenstrasse. With the city full of troops what chance of escape had that lonely prisoner, who spoke no word, yet furtively glanced to this side and that, and studied the attitude of the men nearest to her? She noted that soldiers stood at attention at street corners, a few here, a few there; that of all other signs of life the streets were empty. She realized that she had been brought in at an unexpected hour, and the silence over the city fell upon her soul. Hopelessness and despair seized her, and a wild thought prompted her to make a sudden dash for freedom. Death might come, but such a death was preferable to the fate which must await her at the end of this journey. Her fingers had tightened on the reins, when the silence was suddenly broken, and, with a swift hiss, a streak of light cut through the darkness skyward, paused a moment, and then, with a muffled detonation, burst into globes of light which floated downward. The foremost of the troop reined in their horses sharply at the unexpected flight of the rocket, causing some confusion among those behind. Then came a quick command from an officer which was half lost in the great shout which rent the air on every side--

"For Grigosie! Grigosie!"

Had the cry been for Maritza the soldiers might possibly have understood better what this sudden stopping of their progress meant; but, as it was, a black, rushing mass was upon them before they had time to draw their weapons. The attack was so fierce, so sudden and overwhelming, that when the meaning of it had thoroughly dawned upon the soldiers, they had enough to do to protect themselves without giving much thought to their prisoner. There was hardly a trooper who was not in a moment separated from his fellows by a swaying mob, whose one object seemed to be to force the soldiers apart and prevent any concerted action. The ring of steel and the crack of revolvers mingled with groans and curses and sharp cries which blades thrust home drew forth. Here a horse fell prostrate on its knees, bringing its rider head foremost into the arms of his assailants; and there some plunging charger, dexterously managed, beat down and trampled on a writhing mass of limbs. Shouting came from a distance, as the soldiers from the various street corners came running into the Bergenstrasse to the assistance of their comrades, and, since they ran compactly and with bayonets fixed, the mob gave way before them. An officer, whose plunging horse cleared a path before him, slashed right and left as he came, and shouted: "To the prisoner! Secure the prisoner!" and desperately he struggled toward the slim figure carried this way and that by the swaying, fighting crowd. At his shout the crowd threw itself more savagely upon him. The greatest danger seemed to centre in this man, and bullets sang about him, and steel struck at him from every side.

"Quickly, Princess!"

A strong arm was about her and drew her swiftly from her horse. In a moment a ring of men had formed about her as they pushed their way through the crowd. Two soldiers who sought to stop them fell back groaning, and were trampled under foot; and then the little band with the slim figure in the midst of it was outside the mob, and at the entrance to a narrow, dark street.

"Hold this street with your lives!" cried one. "This way, Princess," and with half a dozen men to guide and guard her she ran forward, the din of the struggle in the Bergenstrasse growing fainter and fainter as they went.

Another rocket hissed skyward, and then tactics changed. The crowd knew what the signal meant, and instead of throwing themselves fiercely on the soldiers, they began to draw back to side streets, fighting desperately at corners for a few moments and then fleeing, breaking up into small knots and turning by twos and threes into alleys and dark passages into which the soldiers did not deem it wise to follow them. Fully an hour passed before the Bergenstrasse was cleared, and many a dark form lay stretched in the roadway, and not a few who wore the King's uniform. Some lay quite still, their troubles and ambitions over; some attempted to crawl away and hide themselves; while others, too hurt to move, groaned and cried piteously for help. The inhabitants of the Bergenstrasse had been rudely awakened, but for a long time none ventured out to render any help to the wounded, lest the soldiers should attack them.

Meanwhile, running feet woke the echoes of the quieter streets and distant parts of the town--men speeding toward safety. More troops would march from the castle presently, and it would be dangerous to be found in the streets to-night. Doors in dark streets opened and quietly closed again; weapons were carefully hidden away under loose boards, and their owners became harmless citizens again.

One little band of men held together, running lightly, and certain of every corner they turned. Some of them were those who had guided the Princess to safety, and now they were bent on carrying the good news to others who were waiting eagerly to hear it. The foremost stopped at a door and gave a peculiar knock. It was opened immediately, and the custodian asked no questions as the men filed in and went quickly to the rooms looking on to the garden, where, not so long ago, they had helped to put an end to a duel. As they entered the long room, which was only dimly lighted, they paused. It was easy to see that there was consternation among the men gathered there, and strangers were present. "Well?" cried a dozen voices.

"She is safe."

"Safe! Gone to her death and destruction," was the answer. "The Countess is a traitor."

"It's death to the first man who repeats that accusation," thundered one of the strangers, his hand upon his sword hilt, and as the men drew back before such sudden fury, they noticed that the other stranger, a bearded soldier of huge proportions, grasped his sword hilt too.

The men who had run from the Bergenstrasse waited for an explanation.

"Are we not all friends here?" exclaimed Baron Petrescu hastily. "There is some mistake. Tell us your story again," and he turned to a man who had only ceased speaking as the newcomers had entered. He had come in breathless haste at the very moment that Petrescu had brought Desmond Ellerey and Stefan through the garden. Willing hands had opened the low door in the wall for them, forewarned of their coming by Dumitru. Ellerey's fame had run before him, and eagerly was he looked for and recognized as the leader of the rebellion which must quickly follow the work going forward in the city to-night. He had come; the conspirators had succeeded in rescuing Princess Maritza; and now came this man with a tale which filled their hearts with consternation.

"I had it from one who fills a chief servant's place in the palace, and who is one of us," said the man, speaking rapidly. "He was delayed in coming to me, or I should have been here earlier. The King sought out the Countess, danced with her, and then, seated in an alcove, behind some curtains of which this man was hidden, the King persuaded her to betray those who favored the cause of the Princess, and the Countess was tempted, and promised. Early to-morrow she is to send the information to the King by a trusted messenger, and the King has given his oath that no one shall know from whom it comes."

"I do not believe it," said the Baron. "She may have promised, but she had some reason for doing so."

"She had, Baron. The King persuaded her that her act of betrayal should be the salvation of a rebel."

"What rebel? Princess Maritza?" asked Petrescu.

"No, Baron; Captain Ellerey."

"It was indeed a subtle temptation," and Petrescu turned slowly to look at his companion.

"The truth shall quickly be put to the test," said Ellery. "Give me wine, a full measure, to put new strength in me. Is mine to be the only voice raised in her defence? Are you all so ready to believe evil of the woman who has served your Princess so well? I stake my honor that with her Maritza is safe."

"True; but speak less harshly, Captain," whispered Petrescu. "These men are our friends; do not anger them."

"He from whom I had the news ever speaks the truth," said the man who had told the story. "He has never failed us in the past."

"Has the Countess ever failed you in the past?" Ellerey cried. "Shame on you all for the thought. Her loyalty shall be proved on the instant."

"You can do nothing to-night," said Petrescu.

"Soldiers are in every street," said a chorus of voices.

"Therefore give me wine to renew my strength," Ellerey cried, and he seized the tankard held out to him.

"It is madness to go now," said Petrescu.

"For you, perhaps, for you, but not for me. Man--man, do not you understand? Besides the woman whose truth I would vindicate, is not Maritza there? She once gave me life yonder in the hills; even less than love would repay such a debt as that. To-morrow, comrades, we may fight side by side in the streets of Sturatzberg, but this hour is my own. Let me pass. It is death to rebel or soldier who seeks to stay me to-night." And throwing down the empty tankard, he went quickly to the door, followed by Baron Petrescu and Stefan.

CHAPTER XXV
'TWIXT LOVE AND PITY

L ong before midnight Frina Mavrodin had completed her work of preparation. The servants who were in her confidence had been told of the coming of the Princess. Some were at the main entrance ready to admit her if she came that way; others were waiting at a small door which opened from the garden into a side street. They were instructed to show surprise, but not consternation, should any officer of the King demand admittance, and servants were stationed on the stairs and in the corridors, a signal arranged between them, so that news of any such demand might be immediately conveyed to the Countess silently, and without any man rushing to her and causing suspicion to those who entered.

"If Captain Ellerey comes, let him pass to me at once," she said. "And at the usual hour put out all lights that shine upon the street. This house must seem to sleep, no matter how wakeful it may be."

Only a dim light burned in her own room, which looked toward the garden, and here the Countess paced up and down with slow, thoughtful steps. She had changed the dress she had worn at Court that night for a soft, loose gown of delicate rose color, caught in at the waist by a silken girdle of a deep shade of the same color. A filmy cloud of lace was about her throat, and fell over her shoulders and from the short loose sleeves.

Once or twice she stopped before a glass to set a wayward tress of her hair in its place, or to arrange the falling folds of the lace, and perhaps lingered for a moment in contemplation of her own reflection, half conscious that she looked fairer dressed as she was than in Court attire of costly silks and flashing jewels.

Many times she paused at the open window, drawing aside the curtains to listen for footsteps in the garden, and she listened often for footsteps in the corridor.

Princess Maritza was coming; perhaps Desmond Ellerey would come, too.

How to outwit the King should Desmond Ellerey fall into his hands, she did not know. She thought of little else as she paced the room, but no solution of the problem came to her. If he should be taken, it seemed as if he must suffer for the cause into which he had been pressed. If by her betrayal of others he only could be saved, she knew now that he must perish. There was no thought in her mind of writing out a list of names to send to the King to-morrow. She put her hands before her eyes to shut out the hideous vision which rose before her-- Ellerey standing with folded arms, facing a dozen loaded muskets waiting for the order to fire; but even in her vision the face of the so-called traitor, firm, resolute, determined, in this supreme hour, as it had been throughout his life, as it would be in reality when such time came, thrilled her soul and made him only the greater hero.

"Oh, to be at his side then!" she exclaimed in a low voice. "What would I not give to share that death with him?"

But Ellerey was not yet in the King's hands, that seemed certain. She felt convinced that some time before the dawn she would see him; that he would enter the house to stand by Maritza's side to the last. Had she not power to save him then? There was a way of escape for the Princess; that same way could Desmond Ellerey go. He and Maritza should go together to find in some other land a quiet haven of happiness.

"Yes," she murmured, her little hands clasped so firmly behind her that the rings cut into the flesh, though she hardly noticed it; "yes, that is how it shall be. Even if my life pays the forfeit, they shall go together. Perhaps, when his happiness is greatest, he will sometimes think of the woman who helped him to it."

There were hurried steps in the corridor, and the next moment Princess Maritza and Dumitru entered.

"So far the fates are with us, Frina," said the Princess, taking the Countess's hands in hers and kissing her; "but I little thought to use your house again as a refuge."

"It may prove an insecure retreat," Frina answered. "There is no escape from this room. I have arranged another place for you. Come, and come quickly."

"Are you suspected, Countess?" asked Dumitru anxiously.

"I fear so, but they will hardly trouble me to-night. Still, I do not feel that you are safe in this room, Maritza."

Frina led the way down several corridors and up and down short flights of steps until she came to the room where Hannah waited. The old serving woman came hurriedly forward as the door opened. For a moment she did not recognize Maritza in her boy's dress, and it was not until she spoke that the old woman's arms were stretched out with trembling eagerness toward her, and her joy found its expression in tears.

"O my Princess! O my dear lady!" was all she could say.

"Dumitru has brought her back, you see, Hannah," said the Countess, "You owe Dumitru some apology for the hard thoughts you have had of him. Go with him while I speak to your mistress a moment."

"Gladly, now she has come back," said Hannah; "and then I'll be looking out decent garments for you, Princess. I should not wish all the world to see you as you are."

"This is a safer retreat for me, is it?" said Maritza, glancing round the room when Hannah had closed the door. "It is a corner of your house I do not know, Frina. Thanks for your great care of me. It is not long that I shall trouble you."

"What do you mean?"

"Mean! Why, that the days for sitting idly down to wait are over. There has been deadly work in the Bergenstrasse to-night, and to-morrow the King will seek to avenge it! Do you suppose I shall leave them without a leader? Before dawn, those who love me will be preparing for the final struggle. To-night's work will convince many who until now have wavered. Rest assured, there will be a goodly host about me when the King sends to take me."

"It is madness, Maritza!" exclaimed the Countess. "What can these men, un-trained, undisciplined as they are, do against the troops which even now doubtless are pouring into every street? Wait."

"My dear Frina, you are a woman; I, in heart at least, am a man. Hundreds are in jeopardy because of me to-night; would you have me desert them? You were wont to be of better courage."

"But wait--wait for counsel and advice."

"From whom?" asked Maritza.

"From Desmond Ellerey."

The two women were looking into each other's eyes; neither fully understood the struggle in the other's heart, yet each of them knew something of the other's secret. For some moments there was silence.

"Is Desmond Ellerey here?" asked Maritza presently.

"No; but he will come. Something tells me that he will come. Wait until then, Maritza. That door," Frina went on, pointing to one which was hardly discernible from the panelled walls of the room, "opens into a passage which leads to a small building by the river, where there is only rubbish. No one is likely to search there. Hannah has the key, and it is a way of escape if they come to this house. I implore you to wait for Captain Ellerey. Has he not struggled for you? Is he not returning to Sturatzberg to stand beside you in the hour of your need, rather than take the road to safety as he might have done? Have you not a hundred times in your heart chosen him the champion of your cause?"

"If he comes to-night he may help me, but I cannot wait," was the answer. "The people call for me; they shall not call in vain."

"Maritza! Maritza! I tell you it is madness. Be persuaded. Think of your love for him; think of his love for you. Ah, you must be ruled by me in this," the Countess went on desperately. "I might let you go to your death. I have been tempted to let you go. Yes, it is true, look at me as you will. Mine has been the waiting part, and temptation comes easily then; more than once it has nearly conquered me. Only to-night the King persuaded me to betray his enemies to him; I am to send a list of them to-morrow; no, it is to-day--in a few hours."

"You have promised to do this?" said the Princess, laying her hand sharply on her companion's arm. "I promised to think of it--aye! and when I made the promise I meant to think of it. Shall I tell you why?" And Frina looked straight into Maritza's eyes. "The King made me believe that Desmond Ellerey was already in his hands, and he swore to spare him if I would do his bidding. It was the keenest temptation he could have assailed me with. Do you understand, Maritza?"

"And you will send that list?" repeated the Princess.

"Can you ask the question now? No, I have fought my battle and won. What is to come will be easy after the stress of that fight. But that the King should so tempt me shows that I am suspected; therefore you are here in this room with the means of escape at hand. Wait for Captain Ellerey, Maritza. For the present, at least, I believe your cause is lost; but a way of escape, desperate though it be, still lies open, and you will take it with the man you love to defend you. Wait, Maritza."

The hand that had rested on Frina's arm stole slowly round her, and the Princess kissed her.

"I understand," she whispered. "I have had my struggle, too. I have never forgotten that meeting long ago in England, and now--now I love him. Ah, Frina, you may pity me. Many a time in the hills I longed to cry out to him to take me northward into safety, to give me love instead of helping me to a kingdom. And then would surge into my soul the memory of my fathers, and I felt myself a coward. If you have been tempted to treachery, so have I. I have my mission to fulfil, my work is before me, and there is no place for love in it. If ever I call any man husband, he must be a king who will satisfy the State."

"But he loves you, Maritza."

"Do not make it harder for me, sister of mine. Fate deals ungently with us both. If Desmond comes before daybreak, bring him to me, and he shall give me counsel. Should I taste failure, should I--should I never see him again, say to him--"

"Maritza!"

"Yes, speak my name and say that you loved me, too. If I understand him he will love you for that. I am very weary and have much to do to-morrow. Send Hannah to me and let me sleep."

In silence the two women kissed each other, and then Frina returned to her room while Maritza threw herself on a couch, Hannah watching beside her. Dumitru stood sentinel outside her door.

For Frina there was no sleep, only a restless pacing to and fro, and a longing for to-morrow--the end, surely the end would come to-morrow.

The dim light in her room grew dimmer, paling before the coming day. A bird in the garden whistled a long note, and after a silence it was answered from another part of the garden, and then quickly from another. A star gleamed low in the ever-lightening purple of the east, the herald of the dawn, and from her window Frina watched it, wondering. There was mystery in the breaking of a new day; would her eyes behold its setting? What thoughts would be in her brain as the golden light faded once more into the black pall of night?

She turned from the window sharply as she heard quick footsteps in the corridor.

Long hours had she waited for them, and now they had come. Her heart seemed to throb violently to a sudden standstill, and having taken one hurried step toward the door, she paused as it opened, and Desmond Ellerey stood before her.

Looking forward to this meeting it had seemed to Frina Mavrodin that in it her life must reach a crisis; but the reality fitted none of her preconceived notions of what this meeting would be like. Ellerey's dress was travel-stained; there was a rent in his sleeve, and he looked as though he had come through some struggle. She noted all this, but it was the expression on his face which fixed her attention. It was stern, unyielding, desperate; and her frame stiffened, and a flash came into her eyes as though she were angry at his intrusion.

"The Princess, Countess?" said Ellerey.

"Is sleeping," she answered.

"I would see her."

"She has need of your counsel. Come."

She swept past him without another word, without looking at him even, and led the way.

Dumitru stood at the door, doubly alert at the sound of approaching footsteps. One hand was thrust inside his cloak, and it was easy to guess what his fingers played with there. He smiled as he saw who the newcomer was.

"Welcome, Captain," he whispered.

"Is all well?"

"Sleeping," was the low answer.

Frina opened the door softly, and then she motioned Ellerey to enter; but he came no farther than the threshold. The Princess lay on a couch sleeping peacefully, dreaming pleasantly it may be, for her lips were half parted in a smile. One arm was thrown above her head, her fingers thrust through her bright curls, and over her feet Hannah had spread a leopard-skin rug. A lamp was still burning on a table, and the glow from it lit up the graceful figure. For some moments Ellerey gazed upon the sleeper, taking in the whole picture.

"Shall I wake her?" asked Frina. "No, let her sleep awhile," said Ellerey, as he went back into the corridor. Then he turned to Dumitru. "Is there a way of escape open?"

"Yes."

"When will you go?"

"When the Princess commands, unless it should be necessary suddenly," Dumitru answered. "There are servants watching who will let me know. The Countess has arranged." He knew nothing of the tale which had been told concerning the Countess.

Frina had closed the door and stood beside them, but she did not speak. As Ellerey turned and showed that he had no other question to ask Dumitru, she led the way back, but at the door of her room she paused.

"You have come to protect the Princess, Captain Ellerey. You are welcome. Use my house and my servants as you think fit."

"Countess, will you give me leave to speak to you a few moments? You must."

He followed her into the room and closed the door; then Frina turned, facing him, and waited.

"To-night, Countess, I entered Sturatzberg by a way you know of, doubtless, to hear two things. One that Princess Maritza had been rescued and brought to your house; the other that you were a traitress."

Frina started, but Ellerey went on quickly--

"Hear me to the end. Heaven knows I am in no mood to take you unawares. The man who brought this tale of you came from the palace. Why you should have been spied upon I neither know nor care; but every word you said to the King last night was heard, and out of them came this story, that you had agreed to betray to his Majesty all those who favor the cause of Princess Maritza. No; hear me out, Countess; I swore it was a lie. Petrescu, Stefan, and I came together. Do you know, Countess, that this house is surrounded, watched by the King's troops? Every way of entrance that the Baron knew of was guarded, and only after long waiting have we managed to scale the garden wall and get in unseen. What does it mean? Is the Princess trapped? If she is, who has betrayed her?"

She was silent, but her eyes did not fall before his.

"For heaven's sake, speak, Countess!"

"The tale is untrue," she said in a low voice, "and yet--"

"Yes, yes; tell me. I have pledged my honor; trample on it if you will, only tell me the truth now."

"I have been tempted," she said. "Yes, you shall hear the truth. I have been tempted, perhaps even I have stumbled, but I have not fallen. I am a woman first, then a conspirator, and I have had many idle hours. Look into my eyes, read my secret if you can and judge me. I was tempted, and the King's words seemed for a moment to help my decision. I did not promise to betray, but I did promise to think of betraying."

"To gain time, that was it, merely to gain time," said Ellerey.

"No; I think when I promised I had almost decided to act."

"Ah, how could you!" Ellerey exclaimed.

"You have heard the story; were you told the bribe the King offered?"

Ellerey did not answer, but Frina understood in a moment that he did know.

"Yes, Captain Ellerey, that tempted me; but with it came a clearer knowledge, and I saw that for me only one road lay open. I have taken it. Maritza is in a room from which there is an escape. The King suspects me. He has surrounded my house with soldiers; presently they will hammer at my closed doors, and I shall stay to face them; but Maritza will have gone, and you will go with her. She would stay in Sturatzberg to fight with those who love her cause; only you can persuade her to go. Do you understand, only you? Go now and wake her. Hannah has the key of that secret way. If in my temptation I have been trapped into showing that I have power in Sturatzberg, that I have knowledge of this conspiracy and the conspirators, I have opened the way of escape too. I am prepared to meet the King's wrath. Go to Maritza, and think less hardly of me."

Ellerey stood with lowered head, his hands pressed before his face.

"What can I say, Countess? God has brought into my life two noble women. I am powerless to help the one; to the other it seems I have only given sorrow."

"You must not say that," she said softly. "You are powerful to help her and to counsel her. As for me, I am a weak woman; if fault there was it was mine. Go now--now that I am forgiven--to Maritza. She expects you. I told her I would send you."

The door was suddenly burst open and Stefan entered.

"Quick, Captain. They demanded admission, which was refused, and they are breaking in. The Baron and those with him will hold them as long as possible."

"The Princess!" Ellerey exclaimed.

"She has been warned," said Stefan.

"She will get away. She will have time," said Frina. "They will not find her room easily."

"Whatever is done must be done quickly," said Stefan from the door. "Even now they drive the servants up the stairs, and the good fellows fight every inch of the way."

"By the river is a house," exclaimed Frina--"only rubbish is in it. Maritza will come that way. Go to her. The window. You can easily drop into the garden."

"And you?"

"I shall stay here."

"You cannot; you must not."

"Quickly, Captain," said Stefan.

"Go, go!" Frina cried. "You must be with her. She will need all your love and courage to-day."

"But you--what will you do?"

"I, too, may find a way to help her."

He caught her hand and raised it to his lips.

"God keep you," he whispered.

"And you, Desmond."

Then he sprang to the window.

"Do I come?" asked Stefan.

"No," Ellerey answered. "The Countess is in your keeping. Guide her to safety."

"I will do all a man may do," Stefan answered, as Ellerey swung himself free by the stout branch of a creeper near the window, and dropped into the garden.

CHAPTER XXVI
REBELLION

The servants, heartened by Baron Petrescu, contested the stairs step by step. With all the odds against them not one turned to fly. They were fighting for the mistress they loved, and were staunch to a man. Some fell, staining the thick carpet with their blood, yet even in dying struck one more blow as the soldiers trampled over them. Meeting with such unexpected resistance made the soldiers savage, and there was no quarter given or asked for. In the forefront of the battle Petrescu's sword did deadly work, for so mixed up were besieged and besiegers that those behind dared not fire. It was a hand-to-hand struggle, steel to steel, and although there could be no real doubt of the issue, the Baron knew that the longer he could hold the soldiers in check, the more time would the Princess and the Countess have to get away.

Stefan was silent until the sound of Ellerey's quick steps in the garden had ceased.

"Where does that lead to, Countess?" he said, pointing to a door at the other end of the room.

"To my bedroom."

"And from there?"

"There is a door on to a landing seldom used," she answered.

"That is our way, then," said Stefan. "I shall stay here. I am safe from them. It is only the King who would dare--"

"The gentlemen fighting yonder are in no tender mood; I know them. Besides, the Captain left me in command, and you must obey, Countess. This is war time, and I am only doing my duty. So we'll lock this outer door, and we'll put as many more between us as possible. Is this your cloak?"

"Yes," Frina answered.

In a moment Stefan had ripped a piece from the edge of it and stuck it in the creeper at the window, and thrown the cloak into the garden below. Then he tore down one of the curtains.

"They'll think we've gone that way, maybe. Come, Countess, you can get another cloak as we pass through your room."

There was strength in this great bearded soldier, and besides, Desmond trusted him, so Frina Mavrodin obeyed.

At every point the servants were driven back, and the soldiers spread through the house, cutting down anyone who opposed them, but not making any particular effort to pursue those who got out of their way. They were there to take the Princess Maritza and the Countess Mavrodin. Such were the orders the officers had received. But long before the servants had given way on the stairs, Hannah had opened the door leading to the passage, and the Princess and Dumitru had gone together swiftly, while Hannah waited for the coming soldiers, her heart growing the lighter the longer that coming was delayed. She had locked the door again, but kept the key lest others should want to use that way of escape presently. The soldiers rushed in at last, and Hannah's face assumed an astonished look as if they had roused her from sleep. "Who are you?" demanded one man sharply.

"I might as well ask that question of you," she replied curtly. "What's come to the city that a band of ruffians break into an old serving woman's room before she's scarce awake?"

"Do serving women sleep on couches only in this house, and are they pampered with leopard skins for covering?"

"How they sleep, and what they're covered with is none of your affair," Hannah said.

"A soft tongue will serve you best," replied the man. "Tell me who slept on that couch during the night?"

"And how she slept and what she dreamt about, I suppose. Well, I had no dreams of such a rough awakening as this."

Other men were turning over the things in the room, and presently one espied the door. He called the attention of the others to it at once.

"Open it," they cried.

"It's locked."

"The key, woman--quickly," said one who seemed to command.

"It's likely I shall let you pry into my cupboards, isn't it?"

"This is no cupboard. Give me the key."

"I haven't got it," said Hannah, and with a sudden swing of her arm she sent the key flying through the open window with unerring aim.

"Curse you!" cried the man.

"In the time you take to find it you may learn better manners," said Hannah defiantly.

Brave, staunch old soul, full worthy of that far-off Devon county which gave her birth. The man followed his curse with a blow--a heavy blow, striking with the hand which held his sword, and the woman fell with a thud to the ground, to lie there until Stefan and the Countess, stealing from the house presently, covered the dead serving woman with the leopard skin.

To find the key was hopeless, and the door was a stout one. It resisted the soldiers' efforts for a long while. When at last it yielded they rushed along the passage to the small house by the river, but, save for rubbish, it was empty. No boat lay upon the water. There was no sign of the fugitives. "They must have come this way," said one man. "Had not that old beldame resisted us we should have caught them."

"Back to the house, comrades," shouted another; "there should still be something there worth laying hands on."

Until now Ellerey had waited, hidden by the river house. He had reached it almost directly after the Princess and Dumitru had left it; but ignorant of this fact, he had waited for them. From the soldiers' words he learnt the truth. Soldiers were in the garden now, and as only a little while since he had sought to enter it unseen, he now sought to leave it, crouching from tree to tree and from shrubbery to shrubbery. His life was too valuable to be uselessly thrown away. He succeeded presently in scaling a wall and dropping into a side lane, to fall in later with a band of conspirators, some of whom were present when the tale of the Countess's treachery was told last night, and who were now quietly making their way to an arranged meeting place.

"But the Princess, comrades?" said Ellerey. "My place is beside her."

"Fear nothing, Captain. She will come and help us to make this day a glorious one in Sturatzberg." The morning was advancing, but people who respected the law kept within their houses, and left their doors fast barred. From early dawn the soldiers were in the streets, and it was evident that to-day the ordinary business of life must be suspended. As the hours passed there were sounds of fighting on every side, the fierce rattle of musketry at street corners, flying men charged by the soldiers, turning sometimes into every alley and place of refuge which offered, turning sometimes at the shout of one determined leader to withstand the charge, to be cut to pieces or to bear the soldiers back, leaving many a King's man and King's enemy lying dead or writhing with their wounds, their enmity forgotten in their common suffering.

In one side street, soon after such a skirmish had swept it from end to end, a dark figure glided from door to door. He had not fought; he seemed unwilling to do so, for at the sound of approaching conflict he was in readiness to retreat and hide himself. More than one wounded man in the roadway pleaded for help, or cried for water, but he was deaf to their entreaties. He was making all speed to some point, and would allow nothing to hold him back. Now he ran forward a few paces, now stopped and turned hastily into an alley and went quickly on again. He came at last to the house of Frina Mavrodin, when it was close on noon. The door at the chief entrance had been torn from its hinges, there was nothing to bar his entrance. The servants who had escaped death had fled, or lay hidden in secret places in the house. The soldiers had deserted it, finding their quarry gone, to go and help their comrades in the streets. At the moment the street was empty, and the man slipped across the threshold, stepping over the dead which lay in the hall, grim witnesses of the fierceness of the fight there. The man passed from room to room rapidly, his ears intent to catch every sound. It was clear that robbery was not his object, for there was none to stay him taking whatever he would. He passed on, touching nothing, and, by the way he glanced down this corridor and that, it was evident that the house was not familiar to him. Chance directed his footsteps and brought him to the room where Princess Maritza had been. The broken door at the further end attracted his notice and he entered the room, stopping for a moment to look into the face of Hannah. The leopard skin had not been thrown over her yet. She was the first woman lying dead he had come across, and he grew excited. She had been killed because she stood in the way, and she would not have stood in the way unless she had had someone in imminent danger to defend. She must have been with the Princess, he argued, and if so, this must be the way they had taken. He went quickly along the passage and up to the house by the river. Someone had certainly been there, but which direction had they taken afterward? He glanced to right and left, and stood for some time looking across the river.

"He would not leave the Princess, and he would take her as far as possible from these fighting madmen in the streets," he mused. "Surely he cannot escape such a day as this."

The man went slowly back along the passage again, and then he stopped suddenly. The sound of voices reached him distinctly.

"Brave woman," he heard one say. It was a woman's voice and the man's heart beat high.

"Cowards to treat her thus," came the muttered answer in a man's lower tone.

There was a moment's silence. "Help me to cover her," said the woman.

There was a turn in the passage, and the man standing waiting there could not see into the room. But the passage was dark, and if those in the room came that way they were not likely to see him, and his mouth widened into a malicious smile. Would they come? He had hardly whispered the question to himself when it was evident that they had entered the passage and were approaching. The waiting man drew back against the wall, a knife in his hand, and if this failed his other hand grasped a revolver. They came slowly, cautiously, and just before the turn paused. It was clear that they meant to be careful, for the man said, after a moment's hesitation--

"It is clear."

Then he came, but alone and swiftly, with his sword in his hand. The waiting man had not recognized Stefan's voice, nor, had he done so, would he have feared detection. Stefan's eyes and ears were quick, however, and in that pause he had held up a warning finger to his companion and had then sprung forward.

"I took you for your master," cried the waiting man when he saw that he was discovered, "but---"

The cruel blade flashed swiftly down, but fell on Stefan's sword only, and then before his fingers could pull the trigger of his revolver, the sword point was thrust through his throat, and the man, who had so stealthily waited for his victim, fell back against the wall, upright for a moment, and then collapsed, only a gurgled sigh sounding in the silent passage.

"My ancient friend of the cellar," said Stefan, bending over him. "Waiting for the Captain, eh? Well, you did your best, Master Francois, and so I will report to your master, should I find him. Come, Countess, the light is too dim to see the unpleasant sight," and the soldier held out his hand to her.

Frina shuddered a little as she stepped past the fallen man, and she and Stefan went slowly out of the passage together. The soldier's eyes were searching and keen as they went. The servant was dead, but the master might not be far off, and he would be even a more dangerous enemy. They passed stealthily from street to street, much as Francois had done a little while since. Stefan had a plan, a goal to win, but he did not speak of it to the Countess.

Suddenly Frina stopped. They were at the end of a deserted alley, but the roar of voices came from a distance; then the sudden rattle of musketry, the harsh and discordant music of battle.

"Which way now?" she asked.

"To safety," said Stefan.

"While others fight and fall?" she said.

"So the Captain willed it."

"I will go no further toward safety--not yet. Time for that when the day is lost. Our way lies there." And she pointed in the direction from which the roar of battle came.

"Countess, I have my orders."

"And have obeyed them; now listen to mine. Yonder, where they fight, lies the Grande Place. Lead me there by the quietest way we can travel."

"That is to go to your death."

"Listen, Stefan--and look!" She pointed to the street into which the alley opened. Some men were running swiftly to the battle. "I have but to cry my name and they will come to me. Shall I cry?"

"For heaven's sake, Countess---"

"Then lead me as I say."

"I cannot. I dare not. The Captain---"

"Follow me then if you will." And before he could stop her she had darted from him.

"Stay!" cried Stefan, rushing after her. "Stay! If you will go, let me lead you."

"Show me the quiet ways if you can, but come." And though Stefan argued, though he tried to deceive her at every corner they came to, she would not be turned from her purpose. Ever, as they went, the roar of battle grew louder in their ears, and there was fear in the heart of Stefan the soldier because of the woman who walked beside him.

Francois was dead. That was one enemy the less, but of the master there was no sign. It had been as wakeful a night for Jules de Froilette as it had been for Frina Mavrodin, but he had spent it in no restless pacing up and down, nor in listening for expected footsteps. Francois he knew was prowling about the streets. In the early hours of the morning the servant had come hastily and told his master of the rescue of Princess Maritza. De Froilette had turned pale and dropped back in his chair, dumbfounded at the news, but he quickly recovered himself. Her freedom could be only temporary. There might be some street fighting, but her re-capture was certain. Francois had neither heard nor seen anything of Captain Ellerey, but he was sure to come, and the servant had gone out to roam about the city again in search of him. Jules de Froilette spent his time in busily destroying papers, now and then placing an important one aside, sometimes reading one with greater care and hesitating over it. At intervals he leaned back in his chair and remained buried in thought for awhile, and once he got up and went to a side table on which stood the portrait of Queen Elena.

"If Ellerey were out of the way we might win through yet," he mused. "I wonder what has become of the bracelet of medallions. If it were in my hands I might save the situation, or the Queen might have to leave Sturatzberg, and then who is there to protect her but me?"

The dawn found him still sorting and destroying. He expected Francois to return with further news, but the servant did not come. The Altstrasse began to wake, and grew noisy at an earlier hour than usual. The fact made De Froilette lean back in his chair in thought again. The news that the Princess had escaped was spreading--that was natural, and with the town in an uproar, rebellion in the air, there were many who would look to him for a sign. They had been waiting for it and expecting it hourly during the last few days. Had he not for a long time been fostering rebellion, a revolt that should set him in high place, that should bring him riches from Russian coffers, that should bring him love? Was not his house at this moment full of men to whom he had promised much--men who should presently help the brigands to seize the city, and then in their turn be quelled and crushed by Russia, whose army on the frontier was only awaiting the word from him? His scheme had failed through this cursed Englishman, but De Froilette had not dared to tell the waiting men so, had not dared to tell them at any moment he might be compelled to fly for safety. They were rebels, and would be quick to see treachery in any failure when they had not even been given the chance to strike a blow for success.

Presently a servant brought him coffee and some rolls.

"The city is noisy," De Froilette said.

"Yes, monsieur."

"Where is the rioting chiefly?"

"Toward the Southern Gate they say, monsieur; but the soldiers are every-where."

"What about the Northern Gate and the Bois?"

"It is quieter that way, monsieur, I am told."

De Froilette nodded and the servant went out.

The Altstrasse became quieter presently. The men had gone to swell the crowds in the Bergenstrasse, not to fight perhaps, but to hang about in side streets and seize whatever loot they could. With dead and dying men lying in the roadway, there would be much to be picked up. Many of the women had gone too, for in the Alt-strasse much of the human refuse of the city had its home, and sex counted for little.

It was toward noon that De Froilette's door opened suddenly, and a tall figure, cloaked to the eyes, glided in, closing the door. In an instant De Froilette was on his feet, and then as the man let the cloak fall apart, he exclaimed--

"Vasilici!"

"Yes, Vasilici," was the answer.

"They are not your men who are fighting in the streets, are they?" asked De Froilette, a ray of hope in his eyes.

"No; my men remain in the hills."

"We have been overreached," said De Froilette; "but only for a little while. It was a good move of yours to deliver up the Princess, although it might have been wiser to shoot her. There will be many lives lost through her today. She escaped last night. Do you know that?"

"I have heard nothing else since I entered the city," returned the brigand.

"It was bold of you to enter it at all just now," said De Froilette.

"I am used to dangers," said the brigand, grandiloquently, "and I had business with you."

"With me?"

"With you and with one other," Vasilici answered. "It was fortunate this Princess came into our hands; we learnt many things. We were to do the fighting, monsieur, but to have little of the reward; that was for the Russians lying on the frontier. It was a pretty plot you and the Queen had arranged."

"Whose tale is that, Vasilici? You are easily deceived if you believe it."

"We learnt the truth when we received this, monsieur." And the brigand held up the bracelet of medallions.

"Whoever your messenger was, he lied to you," said De Froilette. "Her Majesty shall presently convince you of that. I will return the bracelet to her."

Vasilici burst out laughing. His quick eyes had taken in every detail of the room, had noted what lay upon the table, had keenly scanned his companion from head to foot.

"We are not all fools in the hills, monsieur. I am going to deliver this to her Majesty myself. She is the other I spoke of with whom I have business in Sturatzberg. Ah, you are clever," he went on, replacing the bracelet in his pocket, "but you have failed. We are not to be sold to Russia just yet, and by a foreigner, too. Exterminate the foreigners, monsieur, that has been your cry. It is a good one. Tell me, why should you go free?"

He did not wait for an answer. With a sudden spring, his glittering dagger raised to strike, he was upon his adversary. But the blow fell limply, and his fingers relaxed, letting the knife fall with a clatter upon the table. The brigand's swaggering courage had risen as he contemplated his defenceless enemy. From the moment of his entrance, however, the Frenchman understood that he came in no friendly mood, and was prepared. As Vasilici sprang forward, two shots in quick succession startled the echoes of the room, and the tall figure swayed for a moment, then fell sideways on to the table, and slithered to the ground.

In an instant De Froilette was at the door and had locked it. There were running feet in the passage without, and cries of "Monsieur! Monsieur!"

"It is nothing," De Froilette shouted. "The weapon was loaded and I had forgotten the fact. I am not hurt. *Dejeuner* at once."

As the servants departed, De Froilette bent over the dead body.

"Fool! *Canaille!* To think to make an end of me so easily," and he took the bracelet from the dead man's pocket. "In bringing this you have served me, and I thank you. I would give you decent burial had I the leisure, but time presses. You must rest here until they find you."

De Froilette hastily put some papers in his pocket, and reloading the two chambers of his revolver, slipped that too into his pocket.

"Now if I can only see Ellerey as silent as this brute, I can laugh at them all. With the bracelet in my possession I am safe. It will buy the King's courtesy, or, if it suits better, the Queen's obedience. I thank you, friend Vasilici," and with a mocking bow to the lifeless brigand, De Froilette took up his hat and cloak, and left the room by a door concealed in the wall behind his writing table.

CHAPTER XXVII
IN PURPLE AND RED AND GOLD

The attack upon the Countess Mavrodin's house had commenced soon after daybreak. At that early hour few persons were abroad in the streets except the soldiers, who had been hastily marched to all points of vantage in the city as soon as the escape of the Princess became known; but it was not until an hour or two later that the news of the attack, and the desperate resistance the soldiers had met with, began to circulate.

When the riot, which had resulted in Maritza's rescue, had been quelled, and the rioters had melted away before the onslaught of the troops, it was hoped that a salutary lesson had been administered which would prevent any recurrence of open rebellion. That the Princess could not long elude recapture seemed certain, and her brief triumph had been dearly paid for. Citizens lying dead in the streets were a grim reminder of the reality of law and order.

The strenuous defence of the Countess Mavrodin's house had come as a severe blow to the complacency of the authorities. It seemed probable that Princess Maritza had found shelter there, that she was actually in the house when the attack was made, and her defenders had succeeded in holding the soldiers back until she had escaped. But this was not all. It was evident that it was not only upon the rabble that the Princess could depend. Her cause was espoused by Frina Mavrodin, and those who had considered her only a beautiful, frivolous woman awoke to the fact that she had power and unlimited wealth. She had played a part, she had become a Lady Bountiful in Sturatzberg, and it was easy to understand how far reaching her commands might be at this crisis. Baron Petrescu, too, had been a prominent figure in the resistance which had been made, and was still unharmed; it was impossible to foretell how many others, from one cause or another.

That the attack had been successfully resisted, in so far that the Princess had been able to escape, gave an enormous stimulus to the courage of the rebels. The death of companions last night had had a sobering effect upon some; they were inclined to argue that they had done what they had set out to do, and that for the present enough had been accomplished; but the news of the morning raised fresh passions within them, and their leaders were not slow to add fuel to the furnace. These enthusiasts declared that it was only necessary to seize the advantage already gained, to win the city and to force their will upon the country. Was not their Princess among them? Had not important persons already declared for her? Were there not hundreds of others ready to do so, only that fear of the people's fickleness and half-heartedness held them back?

So the carefully secreted arms were taken out again. There were stir and determination in every corner of the city. The word had gone forth that the day so long looked for had indeed come; that before nightfall Sturatzberg would be in their hands; that Maritza, their sovereign, would most surely come amongst them in the Grande Place to lead them, and that by noon all loyal men must win their way there. It was no mere rabble to whom this command was given. Some organization, at least, had been proceeding for a long time. Points of meeting were known. Leaders had been chosen and accepted, men who knew every alley and byway of the city, and had made a study of street fighting, the cover to be had and taken advantage of, and the narrow ways where the soldiers would manoeuvre at a disadvantage, being compelled to fight singly and hand to hand.

As the morning advanced, separate bands traversed the meaner streets, avoiding conflict for the present as much as possible. Here and there sharp skirmishes took place, but no determined effort was made to rush the soldiers, nor were the soldiers successful in dispersing those with whom they came in conflict, except, perhaps, to make them change their route. The rebel leaders had no wish to make boldly for the Grande Place before noon, that would only be to make known what their objective was. When the time came, their numbers would be overpowering, and when once the soldiers saw that they were hemmed in, many of them would be fighting with them instead of against them. Was it not common knowledge that among the troops there was dissatisfaction?

Desmond Ellerey had fallen in with one of these bands when he escaped from

Frina's garden. The leader, a lusty enthusiast, who had already looked forward to the rewards which must accrue from this day's victory, could tell him all that was to happen, but of Maritza's whereabouts at that moment he knew nothing. All he was sure of was that she would be in the Grande Place at the appointed time. He was a skilful leader. He took his followers by a multitude of back streets, avoiding every point where soldiers were likely to be. Every man was valuable, and to lose even one in a skirmish which could achieve nothing was to jeopardize the success of the rebellion to that extent. He constantly turned aside to avoid some particular corner which the scouts sent on before reported occupied; but although this often necessitated returning for some distance along the way they had come, he managed gradually to approach the place of rendezvous, until a little before noon he had brought his band into an alley opening out of one of the streets which led directly into the Grande Place.

"An excellent battle ground for us," he said, turning to Ellerey. "The space is confined, narrow streets abound for us to fight in, which will prevent the soldiers rushing us or bringing guns into action."

Ellerey nodded, but his heart was heavy. Enthusiasm might accomplish much, but he did not believe in the ability of the rebels to withstand the military force which would be opposed to them. After last night, Sturatzberg was not likely to be caught asleep. What was this day to bring to the woman he loved? If he could have known that she was in safety, he could have drawn his sword with a lighter heart, and struck boldly for her cause--died for it, if need be. But she was not safe. Unless she had already fallen into the hands of her enemies, she was coming to the Grande Place. She had promised, and that promise was the mainspring of the enthusiasm which was on every side of him. He knew her too well even to hope that she would not come. And her coming must mean death. His love made him afraid. He could not see even the barest possibility of victory, nor had he any hope that she could escape now. Love made him a coward--his vital force seemed numbed, and his hand shook. He had been an entire stranger to such a sense of fear until this moment, and it was only with a great effort that he was able to throw off the paralyzing effect it had upon him.

From the tower of the Hotel de Ville the hour of noon sounded clear and musically over the city.

"Ready!" said the leader. "But the Princess?" said Ellerey.

"She will come," was the answer. Would she? The striking of the hour was evidently the signal. The last stroke had not died away when the men moved out from the alley into the street, and went quickly towards the Grande Place. Similar bands of men came from other alleys, and from every street they poured impetuously into the Square.

No place had been assigned to Ellerey, no duty had devolved upon him, and as the forward rush was made, he contrived to keep at the side of the street, so that he might not be forced to the front of the crowd. Once in the Square he stepped aside, sheltering himself in the angle of a wall, and no one noticed his movements as they rushed past him.

There were comparatively few soldiers in the Grande Place, and for them the striking of noon had had no warning. The sharp rattle of musketry came swiftly, but in a moment the soldiers were swept back or beaten down. There was a triumphant shout at this success, but the men were well in hand. They did not attempt to follow the enemy into the side streets into which they were driven, but, having in the first onslaught seized every entrance to the square, took up their positions to hold them. For a few moments there was silence, save for the quick commands of rebel leaders, and the hurrying feet of men taking their appointed places. They were heartened and enthusiastic. They had only to hold the Grande Place for a while--comrades were marching from every quarter of the city--and the soldiers would be between two fires. So the leaders encouraged, and the men believed and were content.

Ellerey still remained in the angle of the wall, endeavoring to attract as little attention as possible. Were he seen and recognized, some position of command was likely to be thrust upon him, and this he was most anxious to avoid. His place was beside Maritza when she came. One man spoke to him, asking him what orders he had received. "To protect the Princess," he answered.

The man gave him a friendly nod, and Ellerey conceived that to certain men some such command had been given, and that his answer was a happy one.

From the opposite side of the square came the crack of rifles again, quickly answered. The rebels were well armed, and, whatever the issue, the struggle was to be a desperate one. Here was no loose rabble to turn and flee, but enthusiasts bent on disputing every inch of the way.

"Charge!" came an order from the distance, and there followed the sudden growling of conflict. Yonder the battle had begun in earnest, and a moment later a roar of triumph proclaimed that the soldiers had been thrust back. There was wisdom in making them fight in narrow streets.

It was difficult for Ellerey to remain where he was. Fighting was going forward, and the spirit of the soldier in him made him restless to take his part in it. His hand was upon his sword, when suddenly a great roar of voices from every side seemed to shake the Square. Again and again it rose swelling and breaking like storm waves lashing a shore. There was quick movement round the statue of Ferdinand, a frantic waving of arms, and then the mighty roar became articulate.

"Maritza! Maritza!"

She had come among them--a warrior, even as her fathers were: it was fitting that her name should resound over Sturatzberg.

"Charge!" Again the distant command, again the fierce cries and groaning of conflict, and still the rebel ranks remained unbroken; again the soldiers were beaten down and driven back. Maritza had come, and that meant victory. The belief was deep seated in the heart of every man.

From what point she had entered the square, Ellerey could not determine, but in a few moments he saw her. She was standing on the steps of the statue, a pathetic, yet an heroic figure. She was still in her boy's dress, her bright curls falling loosely from under her cap. She said something which Ellerey could not hear, and then the shouting broke out again. Men ran to join their comrades, impatient only for opportunity to strike a blow at the foe, leaving the Princess in the midst of a little band, evidently a picked bodyguard, among them Baron Petrescu and Dumitru.

For a moment Ellerey watched her. She had come. There was no sign of fear in her face; how should there be? Did he not know her courage? When had Maritza ever failed when the time for action arrived? Had he not full reason to know what a splendid comrade she was in a tight place? All these who shouted her name were her comrades; was it likely she would desert them in the hour of their need? And this was the woman he loved, the woman who loved him--yes, in that instant all doubt seemed to fade into knowledge. Almost he fancied that her quick glance sought him in that striving crowd, and, not finding, that disappointment touched her heart. Oh, it was good to be loved, even for one short hour, by such a woman as this.

His sword was naked in his hand as he went swiftly across the square and shouldered his way to her.

"Desmond Ellerey!" she cried, a wondrous light glowing in her eyes as she stretched out her hand to him.

"At your service and command, Princess," he answered.

In her glad cry at his coming he heard the confession of her love; he read it in her eyes, yet he did not call her Maritza. To-day, indeed, she claimed the address of sovereignty.

"I thought perhaps you would not come," she said in a lower voice. "You do not love my cause."

"To-day I stand or fall for it, Princess," he said aloud; "because--"

"Desmond!"

"Because I love you," he whispered.

It was said. It had to be said now, lest she should never know, for this day was a day of battle, and, before evening, ears might be deaf and lips silenced forever.

For a moment longer she held his hand in hers, and then, fearing, perhaps, that others about her might see some preference in her welcome, she cried aloud:

"Ah, God must surely destine me for victory. He has given me so many brave and true men!"

The roar of conflict was not confined to one side of the Square now. Street after street took up the fight. The soldiers were attacking from every quarter. The sharp command to charge rang out more often, and the sudden growl of the hand-to-hand struggles was fiercer and longer and more continuous. Here and there was an ominous bending inward of a mass of defenders, but it was straightened again by mere force of numbers.

"They want more men there," said Ellerey, pointing with his sword to one place.

Maritza gave a quick order to a man near her, and immediately other men were hurrying to strengthen the position.

"Who commands?" asked Ellerey, turning to the Baron.

"The Princess," was the answer.

"A dozen leaders fight for me," said Maritza; "but I look to you and the Baron to advise me."

"What forces have you in the city beside these?" Ellerey asked, turning to Petrescu.

"Many are hurrying to join us," he answered.

"And will have to fight their way to us," said Ellerey. "We must hold the Square at all costs, for I see no line of retreat."

"Retreat!" exclaimed Maritza. "There is no retreat for me. To-day makes me Queen in Wallaria or nothing."

"Still, Princess, a momentary retreat might save the day."

"We have no way of retreat, Captain," said Petrescu, and the look in his face told Ellerey plainly enough that, loyal as he was, he had little hope of success. "Circumstances have forced matters to an issue, and we must stand or fall as the fates decide."

The rattle of musketry was now continuous on all sides, and for those who fell there was little help or thought, friend and foe alike trampling them to death in the struggle. More than once soldiers, thrust forward by those behind them, had broken through the ranks of the defenders, only to be shot or stabbed before they could recover themselves. Again the rushes were stopped and repulsed, but still they were made with unabated fury, and Ellerey saw that each one was more determined, more difficult to meet than the last. Constantly that ominous bending inward was only straightened with great effort.

Presently he touched the Baron on the shoulder, and pointed to one street where, in the distance, mounted men could be seen.

"I have been wondering why they did not use them," said Ellerey.

"The streets are narrow for them," said Petrescu.

"True; but if only a dozen break through there will be confusion." And then, lowering his voice, Ellerey went on: "Is there no way of escape for her?"

"We may carve one for her, Ellerey, you and I; it is the only way I know of."

They had spoken in a low tone, but, had their voices been louder, it is doubtful whether Maritza would have heard them. She was absorbed in watching the deadly struggle which raged around her. She was unconscious of the bells above her, which told quarter after quarter, sounding musically over the city. Perhaps the thought came to her that these men were dying in her cause, at her bidding; but how could she blame herself? Had not thousands before them died for her fathers? Were her rights less than those of her fathers? And was she not among her subjects to cry victory with them, or to die in their midst? She asked from them no sacrifice which she herself was not prepared to make.

"Will those others who are coming never fight their way to us?" she said turning to Ellerey suddenly.

"If they can, Princess."

It was a vain hope. In every street which led to the Grande Place there had been desperate struggles. In the roadways lay the dead and dying, while others fled to find safety if they could. There was no help to come, and Ellerey did not expect it.

"Charge!"

The command rang out simultaneously from all sides, and there was the jingle of harness and the thud of horses' hoofs.

Here the attack was hurled back, horses riderless, here horse and man pitched forward to be shot and stabbed; and here the same, and here; but yonder the defenders had been driven in, and there too. A dozen horsemen were in the square, and although they fell, confusion had begun. The defense was weakened at several points, more horsemen fought their way in, and with them foot-soldiers gained an entrance. Step by step the rebels were driven backward toward the statue where Maritza stood. "Will those others never fight their way to us?" she cried in almost piteous tones.

"You cannot stay here," said Ellerey. "Come!"

Men were already rushing past them. Once beaten back, hopelessness came quickly, and many of those who had been foremost in the fight now shouted to their comrades to escape if they could. The soldiers, resistlessly pressing forward, were closing in on them when Ellerey spoke. Maritza did not answer.

"Come!" he said again, his hand on her arm.

The touch roused her.

"I have brought you to this; forgive me, Desmond," she said. Her whole ambition was forgotten for a moment in the thought of the man beside her.

Ellerey did not answer. There was no time. The soldiers were upon them. With Petrescu on one side and Dumitru on the other Ellerey threw himself before the

Princess. The final struggle had commenced, and so fierce was the resistance of these three men that the soldiers hesitated and fell back a pace.

"Fly, Princess, while there is time," Ellerey shouted.

"Victory or death, I stay" (and her voice rang clear above the uproar) "with you, Desmond."

The last words were spoken almost in a whisper, and they maddened him. Here was death, butchery, and she was in the midst of it.

"Maritza! Go, dear! Go!" he cried. "Let me hold them back for a moment. I will follow. Petrescu! Dumitru!"

So determined was the struggle round the steps of the statue that the tide of battle seemed to have turned again, and some of the rebels dashed fiercely back into the fray.

"Take her, Dumitru," Ellerey whispered. "We'll hold them while we can." Suddenly from a corner of the Grande Place, rushing swiftly through the ranks of the flying rebels, came a woman.

"Are you cowards or men?" she cried aloud as she came, and some turned at that cry and met death with a shout of defiance, while others stood irresolute until fear overcame them.

Ellerey saw her as she reached Maritza's side, and then he was conscious that a stalwart arm was raining heavy blows upon the foes which seemed to surround him.

"She would come. I could not stay her," said Stefan between his deeply panted breaths as he struck again and again.

"Fly, Maritza!"

"Frina! You!"

"Fly, Maritza!" The salvation of Maritza seemed her one thought. The hope that she might accomplish it, even at the last moment, had drawn her hither. How it was to be done she had not asked herself. Yet now she appeared to have found the way.

Even as she spoke Dumitru seized the Princess.

"Come!" he said, as he threw a cloak about her to conceal her identity. "To-day we fail; to-morrow--Ah!"

It was a short, sharp cry, a cry with finality in it. Whatever to-morrow might bring forth, he should have no part in it. His hand still grasped the cloak as he fell backwards, and Maritza was dragged down with him.

"Grigosie," said Ellerey to the soldier beside him as he saw Dumitru fall. He used the name that Stefan might understand to the full. Was there anything that Stefan would not do for Grigosie?

Frina Mavrodin stood for a moment alone above the surging, fighting mass. She had shuddered when she had passed the dead body of Francois in the passage, now she drew herself to her full height and looked down upon the battle. She stood there that all men might see her, that Maritza might escape, and then she saw Ellerey with the sweat and grime of the conflict upon him. For an instant their eyes met, her lips whispered his name, and then she threw up her arms, and with a low cry fell prone upon the steps of the statue.

Maritza, who was bending over Dumitru, turned swiftly and made one step towards her when Stefan stopped her.

"Come," he said. And this time he waited for no pleading. Drawing the cloak tightly round her, he caught her in his arms, and, in the midst of those who fled, rushed from the Square. The plan he had made earlier in the day when the Countess walked beside him he would carry out now. He had ears for no entreaty, for no threat.

"We'll win through, Grigosie," he said over and over again as he turned now into one alley, now into another, leaving the flying rabble further and further behind. "We'll win through, Grigosie. It's the Captain's orders."

Ellerey heard that cry too, and knew its meaning. There was a shout of triumph from the soldiers pressing forward, a swaying back of the rebels, and he was carried along with them unable to use his sword in the seething mass of friends and foes.

"She is dead!" someone cried; and the effect was instantaneous. Men took up the cry and shouted that Maritza was dead, and the soldiers may have thought it was so seeing a woman fall. Every rebel was at once struggling to fight his way out of the crowd, his own safety his only thought. They day was lost, it was the time to seek safety if it were to be found. The Baron and Ellerey were still side by side, and together they were forced back toward a narrow street.

"There is still a chance for you," Petrescu whispered. And the next moment he was striving madly to force his way back to the statue, to the side of the woman he had loved. Then he was cut down and trampled under foot as Ellerey was carried away in a rush of pursued and pursuers. Suddenly the pressure relaxed, the open street was before him.

"Ellerey! No matter who else escapes, seize Ellerey!" He had been recognized, and for him there was no hope of mercy. He swung round one sweeping blow of his sword and sprang forward. The way seemed clear, when a figure suddenly dashed from a doorway and fired at him point blank, twice in quick succession, crying his name to those who appeared to have lost him for a moment.

A pain like the running in of a red-hot skewer was in Ellerey's arm, but not his sword arm, and the weapon flashed high in the air and fell with relentless force.

"Quits, you devil!" he cried as De Froilette reeled backwards, cut with deadly depth downward from the shoulder. Then Ellerey rushed on again, one among hundreds seeking safety, followed by their conquerors, who showed no mercy. Suddenly an arm was outstretched from an alley and seized him. The impetus of being thus turned in his headlong flight carried him some yards down the narrow way.

"Quickly!" said a voice in his ear. "To the right, now to the left."

A guiding hand and a supporting arm urged him forward. Ellerey asked no question, never turned toward the man who ran beside him, but went on mechanically. His brain was full of a whirling nightmare. Then a door was slammed heavily, there was the sensation of rapid movement, the quick beating of galloping horses, and then faintness and oblivion.

The red sun sank westward, glowing on the roofs and spires of the city. The minutes passed swiftly, and the hours. Still in the smaller streets and the narrow alleys there were flying feet, and now and again a shriek as some poor wretch pitched forward, shot or stabbed by his relentless pursuers. Resistance there was none; that was over. The dead and dying lay in the roadways where they had fallen, the only cry now was for mercy, and that was seldom granted. The soldiers were savage too, and rebellion must be stamped out.

By the statue of Ferdinand a squad of soldiers was halted, and on the steps, just as she had fallen, lay Frina Mavrodin. She was beautiful in death, and there was a pathos in that prostrate form which appealed even to these rough soldiers. Had she not been the Lady Bountiful in that city? They were silent for the most part, or if they spoke, hushed their voices to a whisper, and used no oaths. She had sacrificed her life for the man and woman she loved. Here in the Grande Place of Sturatzberg, where a little while since fierce conflict raged; here where Maritza's cause had been fought for and lost; here where so many turned sightless eyes to the deepening sky, Frina Mavrodin had found her rest. No tramping, struggling feet had touched her, and only the blood staining the brown hair where the bullet had struck showed that this was death and not sleep. The minutes passed, and the hours, the bells sounding musically at short intervals over the city, and the sun slowly sank lower and lower into his bed of purple and red and gold.

CHAPTER XXVIII
THE DIPLOMACY OF LORD CLOVERTON

Desmond Ellerey recovered consciousness slowly and gradually. After the sensations of movement and galloping horses, there was utter oblivion for a time, followed by sharp pain which seemed to be caused by some-one bending over him--a shadowy figure whose attack upon him he was powerless to resist. Then he heard voices, and more than one shadow flitted vaguely across his vision. Presently he realized that he was stretched out at full length, and that he was in a room which had an intricate pattern on the ceiling, the lines and curves of which his eyes were trying to follow.

"Well, Doctor?"

"Nothing serious," was the answer. "A bullet has torn the fleshy part of the arm, but it would hardly account for his collapse. The man is thoroughly played out, and has had no sleep for some nights probably, and has been at high tension for a long time."

"But will he be able to travel?"

"He would be better for twenty-four hours' sleep first."

"That is out of the question," was the answer.

"Is it a long journey?" asked the doctor.

"Yes; but he will be well cared for, and will have nothing to do."

"It will pull him down a bit, but he will stand it all right," the doctor returned. "His is the sort of constitution which stands anything." At first Ellerey had only been conscious of voices, now he partly understood what was said, and half raised himself.

"Where am I?" he asked faintly.

"Ah, that's better," said the doctor; "drink this, it will start you toward recovery. No, leave that arm alone, it will be all right presently."

"It hurts a bit," Ellerey answered. "I remember; De Froilette did it. I think I struck him down; I forget what happened after that," and he drank from the glass handed him.

"Well, Goldberg, he looks better already," said the other man, coming forward and standing by the couch. "Do you know me, Ellerey?"

"Lord Cloverton!"

"I told you I would pluck you from under the wheels of Juggernaut's car if I could, and so far I have succeeded."

"I don't know how you have done it, but I thank you."

"I will leave you for a little while," said Dr. Goldberg. "How long before he starts? Delay it as long as you can."

"A couple of hours," said Cloverton.

"Very well. I will come in and see him comfortably packed up."

"I cannot go," said Ellerey as the door closed upon the doctor.

"Listen to me," said the Ambassador, sitting down on the end of the couch. "I am not going to criticize your actions, and that you are here in the Embassy proves that I still feel some interest in you. I hardly expected to save you, but Captain Ward was fortunate in choosing the right spot to rescue you, and he managed to get you here without anyone knowing. You are still being eagerly sought for."

"I should like to thank Captain Ward," said Ellerey.

"You shall before you go."

"I cannot leave Sturatzberg," said Ellerey.

"You can understand that under the circumstances I have run some risk in having you brought to the Embassy," Lord Cloverton went on. "It is quite impossible for you to remain here, and to go into the streets of the city would be to go to your death."

"Still, I must go, Lord Cloverton. You do not understand."

"Perhaps not; but I have myself to think of as well as you. For both of us it is necessary that you cross the frontier as soon as possible. In two hours we start. I am going as far as Breslen on my own affairs, and, in case of accident, an escort is to accompany my carriage, which will be closed. I have made the most of the dangers to myself, and have demanded that my person shall be well guarded. You will go with me, and for your journey from Breslen I have made further arrangements. You are unlikely to be stopped."

"But, my Lord--"

"You owe no further allegiance to the cause you have striven for. You can depart in all honor. The cause is annihilated."

"I know, my Lord, I know; still, I cannot leave Sturatzberg."

"Somehow I expected to find you difficult to persuade," said Lord Cloverton, rising. "I have no time to argue with you; I will send someone else to do that. I hope to find you more tractable when I return."

He went out of the room, closing the door gently behind him. Ellerey raised himself on the couch, wincing with the pain his arm gave him, but determined to balk the Ambassador while he had the opportunity. It was evident that if he remained there Lord Cloverton would force him to this journey, and he was too weak to offer any real resistance, but once in the streets he could hide and wait, and seek Maritza in every corner of the city until--

The door opened again, and closed. Ellerey's back was toward it, and he did not turn. It was only a servant, probably, who would go away presently.

"Desmond!"

A few hurried steps, the quick rustle of a dress, and then a figure was kneeling by the couch, and a head was pillowed on his breast.

"Desmond!"

For a moment he did not speak; he could not. His confusion returned, and seemed to overwhelm him. Surely he was still dreaming?

"Maritza! You? Is it really you? How wonderful it is, this waking! Is it you, Maritza?"

"Yes, dear. Thank God for bringing you to me again."

"It is wonderful," Ellerey murmured. "Red blood is before my eyes still, and in my ears shouting and groaning. We have lived through it all, you and I--"

"And so many are dead, Desmond, have died for me. My heart is heavy and full of tears, only--only there is you, and you are here, and, God forgive me, there is joy in my soul because of this."

It was a strange, new thing for him to see Maritza weep.

"And Frina. Frina gave her life for mine, Desmond," she whispered.

He did not speak, but his fingers closed over hers, and they were both silent.

"They are looking for us in every corner of the city," she said presently.

"How did you escape?" he asked.

"I hardly know. Stefan caught me up and ran with me. I strove to free myself in vain. I pleaded, I threatened, but it was of no use. I was a child in those great arms of his. He brought me here. Lord Cloverton was very kind."

"Where is Stefan now?"

"Here still. He is going with us. Lord Cloverton says that you will not go; but you will, Desmond, won't you? I want you to take me away, anywhere, Desmond--anywhere away from Sturatzberg."

"I would not go, my darling, because you were not with me. When you came in I was making up my mind to drop from the window that I might look for you; but now--"

"My poor love, you are weak; how could you?"

"My sword arm is whole still, though it is tired--very tired."

"It shall rest now," she said, taking it and pressing it to her breast. "Desmond."

"Yes, dearest."

"Only once have you said to me: 'I love you.' Never yet have I been in your arms. Put this one-this strong one--round me now. Say 'I love you.' Tell me. Oh, how often have I longed to hear those words from your lips."

"I love you, Maritza, my Princess," he whispered, and he kissed her lips as a little contented sigh escaped them.

"How beautiful you are!" he went on, after a moment's pause. "It is strange, Maritza, but since that morning on the downs I have never seen you dressed as a woman."

"Once, Desmond."

"Ah, then you wore a mask."

"And looked through it with eyes of love, Desmond."

"Even then?"

"Yes, even then. These are borrowed clothes. Lord Cloverton persuaded some-one to lend them. He was nervous until I became a woman. Grigosie is dead, Des-mond."

"Is there no regret in your heart?"

"None," she answered.

"You lose a kingdom, Maritza."

"It is well lost for love, Desmond. I have found my king."

She was kneeling beside the couch when Lord Cloverton entered.

"Well, Captain Ellerey, are you ready to go?"

"How can I thank you, my Lord?"

"By going," the Ambassador answered, with a smile. "Sight of the Princess is evidently good medicine for you. You have both given me many anxious hours."

"You must forgive us," said Maritza.

"Princess, I am an old man; I envy my countryman his youth. But for all that, I shall find my work in Sturatzberg easier when I know you two rebels are safely over the frontier."

Dr. Goldberg came in, and with him Captain Ward.

"I owe you much," said Ellerey, grasping the latter's hand. "Thank you."

"It is but repaying the debt I incurred on the night of the duel, Captain Ellerey."

"The carriage is waiting," said Lord Cloverton. "It is in the inner courtyard. We must be silent, for the escort, which waits without, has no knowledge that I am accompanied. Now, Doctor, wrap up your patient, and help him out. Here is a cloak for you, Princess. You travel with light luggage, but that, I am afraid, cannot be helped."

"And Stefan?" asked Ellerey.

"Goes with us. He is waiting. Come!"

The travelling carriage was large and roomy, and they entered it in silence in the inner courtyard. Stefan was waiting, and saluted Ellerey, but neither of them spoke then. The windows were drawn up, the blinds closed, and then they moved out. There was a sharp word of command as they passed into the street, and so, escorted by the King's troops, the man and woman who were being searched for in every corner of the city passed out by the Northern Gate and through the Bois, and were presently driving along the Breslen road.

Lord Cloverton's arrangements had been very carefully and completely made. In Breslen the carriage drove into an inn yard, the escort remaining without, and in the yard another carriage was waiting. The driver was in possession of the papers necessary for the journey, and, unless something unforeseen should happen, nothing could prevent the fugitives reaching the frontier in safety.

"Wait until I have gone," said Lord Cloverton, "and then start. ***Bon voyage***," he whispered, as he raised Maritza's hand to his lips. "I hope we shall meet again under happier circumstances--in England, it may be. Your marriage will render a very charming Princess powerless to disturb the peace of Europe."

"Thank you a thousand times," said Ellerey. "You have given me more than life--happiness."

When the Ambassador had gone, Ellerey turned to Stefan.

"What can I say to you, old comrade?"

"Better say nothing, Captain. I'm nearer to tears just now than I ever was in my life."

"I had forgotten," said Ellerey; "you are leaving Sturatzberg."

"Oh, they're not tears of that kind," said Stefan. "I think they're happy ones, but having shed so few I'm a poor judge. I only know, Captain, it's good to be beside you again. I know it's good to have served you, and--and Grigosie, the name will slip out--and if you want to say anything, just promise that you won't send me packing as soon as we get free. I can turn my hand to other things beside soldiering."

"You shall stay with us, Stefan," said Maritza.

"I don't think I could have known any real woman before," the soldier muttered.

Ten minutes later they had passed out of the inn yard, and were galloping toward the frontier.

And in the midst of his escort, Lord Cloverton was riding back to Sturatzberg. So far he had succeeded, but he knew how often some little thing destroyed the best-laid scheme. He drove direct to the palace, and was admitted to the King. Queen Elena was with him.

"Do you bring us news of this countryman of yours, my Lord?" said the King, and he spoke somewhat curtly.

"Or of Princess Maritza?" said the Queen. "It is very strange that neither of them can be found."

"So they have not been found yet?" said the Ambassador.

"No, my Lord; but they will be. I have it on good authority, only a moment ago, that they are even now between Breslen and the frontier. It was cleverly conceived, Lord Cloverton, but it is not too late to stop them," and the King's hand was raised to strike a gong to summon a messenger.

"One moment, your Majesty."

"Why delay?" exclaimed the Queen impatiently. "Every moment is of value. Five minutes have slipped away already since this news was brought to you. Telegraph to the frontier at once. I shall not rest until Maritza is taken."

"And De Froilette, your Majesty?" said the Ambassador quietly.

"He is dead."

"I know," was the answer. "Had he been alive, he too would have been hurrying toward the frontier. Your Majesty should rejoice in his death. He was not a man to be trusted."

"My Lord, you tell us only what we know," said the Queen.

"A little more, I think, your Majesty," was the quiet answer. "A servant of mine saw Monsieur De Froilette struck down by Captain Ellerey, and, knowing the man, searched him. He carried much that was incriminating upon him." And then, turning to the King, he added: "Would it not be well to let Captain Ellerey and the Princess go?"

"What do you mean?" asked the King angrily.

"Lord Cloverton only seeks to delay that message," said the Queen. "Send it. Some of your enemies are dead, but these two escape."

"And must be allowed to escape," said the Ambassador.

"Do you threaten, my Lord?" said the King.

"I ask the Queen to support me with regard to these fugitives."

"And I refuse," she answered. "Send the message."

"Will your Majesty show the King the bracelet of medallions?" said Lord Cloverton.

The King rose angrily.

"Once before, my Lord--" and then he stopped.

"Send the message," cried the Queen.

"And then look to your own safety," said Lord Cloverton, turning sharply to the King. "Russia has plotted against you; her troops lie still on the frontier, and treachery has been beside you. By a strange chance the plot miscarried, but it was near to success. This was found in Jules de Froilette's possession," and he held up the bracelet.

The King looked at it. The Queen drew in her breath sharply, and bit her lip until the blood came. "What is the meaning of this?" said the King, turning to her after a pause.

"At a fitting time I will answer," she said.

The King sat down heavily in his chair.

"I will send no message," he said.

Lord Cloverton bowed, and placing the bracelet carefully on the table, silently left the apartment.

CHAPTER XXIX
AFTER WAR--PEACE

Peaceful times had fallen upon Wallaria. It is whispered sometimes that the relations between the King and the Queen are not of the happiest; but who that would publish such a statement can possibly know the truth with any certainty. It is a fact that the country is better governed. At nights the streets of Sturatzberg are far safer than they were formerly, and the brigands in the hills have been dispersed. Some political malcontents among them have been banished, but many have been pardoned, and go in and out of the city unmolested. The Court is still a brilliant one, but in these days there is no woman there as beautiful as Frina Mavrodin, and Lord Cloverton is no longer British Ambassador. He has been transferred to Paris, and this fact alone is sufficient to show that the Powers are more agreed concerning Wallaria. A less experienced man than Lord Cloverton is now at the Embassy, and has had no such troublous times to steer through as fell to his predecessor.

Yet Princess Maritza is not forgotten in Sturatzberg, and for a small bribe many a man will tell the traveler her romantic history, and will perhaps whisper in his ear, as though the spirit of revolution were not altogether dead in him:

"I was among those who fought that day in the Grande Place." So long as they live, Desmond Ellerey and his wife will not forget that day, but they seldom speak of it. It is quite certain that Maritza has never regretted the kingdom she lost. Love has crowned her life, and she is satisfied.

Long since has it been known that the story which drove Ellerey away from his country was a lie, told and substantiated by the real culprit to shield himself. By this man's tardy confession, Ellerey's character was cleared, and many expected him to return to England at once, but he did not do so. When his brother died, and he became Sir Desmond Ellerey, he did return for a while, however, staying for some time with his old and staunch friends, Sir Charles and Lady Martin, and his beautiful wife caused a sensation. She visited her old school, and she stood with her husband upon the downs on the very spot where they had first met. But England was not for them, they decided, and their permanent home is in Italy, in sight of dancing blue waters and under a blue sky.

And in this Italian home is Stefan, whose chief duty seems to consist in worshipping Ellerey's small son, who is going to be a soldier when he grows up and win a wife like his mother, just as his father did. It is Stefan who tells him stories of the past, Stefan who fashions wooden swords for him, and who would willingly lay down his life for his father, mother, or son.

"Once I didn't care for anybody," Stefan said to the lad one day.

"You didn't know father then."

"No; and for a long time after that I hated women."

"Until you met my mother?" asked the boy.

"Yes; and until I knew Grigosie."

"Grigosie? Who was Grigosie?"

"She was a Princess."

"My mother is a Princess. Father says so."

"And some day, when you are old enough, he will tell you all about Grigosie, too, and how it is you are not a king."

"Mother sometimes calls me her little king," said the boy.

"I don't wonder. Now it's time to mount and charge home."

So the little warrior is quickly lifted on Stefan's shoulder, and with waving wooden sword, and with curls flying, is whirled off on his willing charger.

The Codes Of Hammurabi And Moses
W. W. Davies

QTY

The discovery of the Hammurabi Code is one of the greatest achievements of archaeology, and is of paramount interest, not only to the student of the Bible, but also to all those interested in ancient history...

Religion   ISBN: *1-59462-338-4*   Pages:132

MSRP $12.95

The Theory of Moral Sentiments
Adam Smith

QTY

This work from 1749. contains original theories of conscience amd moral judgment and it is the foundation for systemof morals.

Philosophy ISBN: *1-59462-777-0*   Pages:536

MSRP $19.95

Jessica's First Prayer
Hesba Stretton

QTY

In a screened and secluded corner of one of the many railway-bridges which span the streets of London there could be seen a few years ago, from five o'clock every morning until half past eight, a tidily set-out coffee-stall, consisting of a trestle and board, upon which stood two large tin cans, with a small fire of charcoal burning under each so as to keep the coffee boiling during the early hours of the morning when the work-people were thronging into the city on their way to their daily toil...

Childrens   ISBN: *1-59462-373-2*

Pages:84

MSRP $9.95

My Life and Work
Henry Ford

QTY

Henry Ford revolutionized the world with his implementation of mass production for the Model T automobile. Gain valuable business insight into his life and work with his own auto-biography... "We have only started on our development of our country we have not as yet, with all our talk of wonderful progress, done more than scratch the surface. The progress has been wonderful enough but..."

Biographies/   ISBN: *1-59462-198-5*

Pages:300

MSRP $21.95

The Art of Cross-Examination
Francis Wellman

QTY

I presume it is the experience of every author, after his first book is published upon an important subject, to be almost overwhelmed with a wealth of ideas and illustrations which could readily have been included in his book, and which to his own mind, at least, seem to make a second edition inevitable. Such certainly was the case with me; and when the first edition had reached its sixth impression in five months, I rejoiced to learn that it seemed to my publishers that the book had met with a sufficiently favorable reception to justify a second and considerably enlarged edition. ..

Pages:412

Reference   ISBN: *1-59462-647-2*   *MSRP $19.95*

On the Duty of Civil Disobedience
Henry David Thoreau

QTY

Thoreau wrote his famous essay, On the Duty of Civil Disobedience, as a protest against an unjust but popular war and the immoral but popular institution of slave-owning. He did more than write—he declined to pay his taxes, and was hauled off to gaol in consequence. Who can say how much this refusal of his hastened the end of the war and of slavery ?

Law   ISBN: *1-59462-747-9*   **Pages:48**

MSRP $7.45

Dream Psychology
Psychoanalysis for Beginners

Sigmund Freud

Dream Psychology Psychoanalysis for Beginners
Sigmund Freud

QTY

Sigmund Freud, born Sigismund Schlomo Freud (May 6, 1856 - September 23, 1939), was a Jewish-Austrian neurologist and psychiatrist who co-founded the psychoanalytic school of psychology. Freud is best known for his theories of the unconscious mind, especially involving the mechanism of repression; his redefinition of sexual desire as mobile and directed towards a wide variety of objects; and his therapeutic techniques, especially his understanding of transference in the therapeutic relationship and the presumed value of dreams as sources of insight into unconscious desires.

Pages:196

Psychology   ISBN: *1-59462-905-6*   *MSRP $15.45*

The Miracle of Right Thought
Orison Swett Marden

QTY

Believe with all of your heart that you will do what you were made to do. When the mind has once formed the habit of holding cheerful, happy, prosperous pictures, it will not be easy to form the opposite habit. It does not matter how improbable or how far away this realization may see, or how dark the prospects may be, if we visualize them as best we can, as vividly as possible, hold tenaciously to them and vigorously struggle to attain them, they will gradually become actualized, realized in the life. But a desire, a longing without endeavor, a yearning abandoned or held indifferently will vanish without realization.

Pages:360

Self Help   ISBN: *1-59462-644-8*   *MSRP $25.45*

QTY

The Rosicrucian Cosmo-Conception Mystic Christianity by *Max Heindel*   ISBN: *1-59462-188-8*   **$38.95**
The Rosicrucian Cosmo-conception is not dogmatic, neither does it appeal to any other authority than the reason of the student. It is: not controversial, but is: sent forth in the, hope that it may help to clear...
New Age/Religion Pages 646

Abandonment To Divine Providence by *Jean-Pierre de Caussade*   ISBN: *1-59462-228-0*   **$25.95**
"The Rev. Jean Pierre de Caussade was one of the most remarkable spiritual writers of the Society of Jesus in France in the 18th Century. His death took place at Toulouse in 1751. His works have gone through many editions and have been republished...
Inspirational Religion Pages 400

Mental Chemistry by *Charles Haanel*   ISBN: *1-59462-192-6*   **$23.95**
Mental Chemistry allows the change of material conditions by combining and appropriately utilizing the power of the mind. Much like applied chemistry creates something new and unique out of careful combinations of chemicals the mastery of mental chemistry...
New Age Pages 354

The Letters of Robert Browning and Elizabeth Barret Barrett 1845-1846 vol II   ISBN: *1-59462-193-4*   **$35.95**
by *Robert Browning* and *Elizabeth Barrett*
Biographies Pages 596

Gleanings In Genesis (volume I) by *Arthur W. Pink*   ISBN: *1-59462-130-6*   **$27.45**
Appropriately has Genesis been termed "the seed plot of the Bible" for in it we have, in germ form, almost all of the great doctrines which are afterwards fully developed in the books of Scripture which follow...
Religion/Inspirational Pages 420

The Master Key by *L. W. de Laurence*   ISBN: *1-59462-001-6*   **$30.95**
In no branch of human knowledge has there been a more lively increase of the spirit of research during the past few years than in the study of Psychology, Concentration and Mental Discipline. The requests for authentic lessons in Thought Control, Mental Discipline and...   New Age/Business Pages 422

The Lesser Key Of Solomon Goetia by *L. W. de Laurence*   ISBN: *1-59462-092-X*   **$9.95**
This translation of the first book of the "Lemegton" which is now for the first time made accessible to students of Talismanic Magic was done, after careful collation and edition, from numerous Ancient Manuscripts in Hebrew, Latin, and French...   New Age/Occult Pages 92

Rubaiyat Of Omar Khayyam by *Edward Fitzgerald*   ISBN: *1-59462-332-5*   **$13.95**
Edward Fitzgerald, whom the world has already learned, in spite of his own efforts to remain within the shadow of anonymity, to look upon as one of the rarest poets of the century, was born at Bredfield, in Suffolk, on the 31st of March, 1809. He was the third son of John Purcell...   Music Pages 172

Ancient Law by *Henry Maine*   ISBN: *1-59462-128-4*   **$29.95**
The chief object of the following pages is to indicate some of the earliest ideas of mankind, as they are reflected in Ancient Law, and to point out the relation of those ideas to modern thought.
Religion/History Pages 452

Far-Away Stories by *William J. Locke*   ISBN: *1-59462-129-2*   **$19.45**
"Good wine needs no bush, but a collection of mixed vintages does. And this book is just such a collection. Some of the stories I do not want to remain buried for ever in the museum files of dead magazine-numbers an author's not unpardonable vanity..."
Fiction Pages 272

Life of David Crockett by *David Crockett*   ISBN: *1-59462-250-7*   **$27.45**
"Colonel David Crockett was one of the most remarkable men of the times in which he lived. Born in humble life, but gifted with a strong will, an indomitable courage, and unremitting perseverance...
Biographies/New Age Pages 424

Lip-Reading by *Edward Nitchie*   ISBN: *1-59462-206-X*   **$25.95**
Edward B. Nitchie, founder of the New York School for the Hard of Hearing, now the Nitchie School of Lip-Reading, Inc, wrote "LIP-READING Principles and Practice". The development and perfecting of this meritorious work on lip-reading was an undertaking...   How-to Pages 400

A Handbook of Suggestive Therapeutics, Applied Hypnotism, Psychic Science   ISBN: *1-59462-214-0*   **$24.95**
by *Henry Munro*
Health/New Age/Health/Self-help Pages 376

A Doll's House: and Two Other Plays by *Henrik Ibsen*   ISBN: *1-59462-112-8*   **$19.95**
Henrik Ibsen created this classic when in revolutionary 1848 Rome. Introducing some striking concepts in playwriting for the realist genre, this play has been studied the world over.
Fiction/Classics/Plays 308

The Light of Asia by *sir Edwin Arnold*   ISBN: *1-59462-204-3*   **$13.95**
In this poetic masterpiece, Edwin Arnold describes the life and teachings of Buddha. The man who was to become known as Buddha to the world was born as Prince Gautama of India but he rejected the worldly riches and abandoned the reigns of power when...   Religion/History/Biographies Pages 170

The Complete Works of Guy de Maupassant by *Guy de Maupassant*   ISBN: *1-59462-157-8*   **$16.95**
"For days and days, nights and nights, I had dreamed of that first kiss which was to consecrate our engagement, and I knew not on what spot I should put my lips..."
Fiction Classics Pages 240

The Art of Cross-Examination by *Francis L. Wellman*   ISBN: *1-59462-309-0*   **$26.95**
Written by a renowned trial lawyer, Wellman imparts his experience and uses case studies to explain how to use psychology to extract desired information through questioning.
How-to/Science/Reference Pages 408

Answered or Unanswered? by *Louisa Vaughan*   ISBN: *1-59462-248-5*   **$10.95**
Miracles of Faith in China
Religion Pages 112

The Edinburgh Lectures on Mental Science (1909) by *Thomas*   ISBN: *1-59462-008-3*   **$11.95**
This book contains the substance of a course of lectures recently given by the writer in the Queen Street Hall, Edinburgh. Its purpose is to indicate the Natural Principles governing the relation between Mental Action and Material Conditions...   New Age/Psychology Pages 148

Ayesha by *H. Rider Haggard*   ISBN: *1-59462-301-5*   **$24.95**
Verily and indeed it is the unexpected that happens! Probably if there was one person upon the earth from whom the Editor of this, and of a certain previous history, did not expect to hear again...
Classics Pages 380

Ayala's Angel by *Anthony Trollope*   ISBN: *1-59462-352-X*   **$29.95**
The two girls were both pretty, but Lucy who was twenty-one who supposed to be simple and comparatively unattractive, whereas Ayala was credited, as her Bombwhat romantic name might show, with poetic charm and a taste for romance. Ayala when her father died was nineteen...   Fiction Pages 484

The American Commonwealth by *James Bryce*   ISBN: *1-59462-286-8*   **$34.45**
An interpretation of American democratic political theory. It examines political mechanics and society from the perspective of Scotsman James Bryce
Politics Pages 572

Stories of the Pilgrims by *Margaret P. Pumphrey*   ISBN: *1-59462-116-0*   **$17.95**
This book explores pilgrims religious oppression in England as well as their escape to Holland and eventual crossing to America on the Mayflower, and their early days in New England...
History Pages 268

www.bookjungle.com *email: sales@bookjungle.com fax: 630-214-0564 mail: Book Jungle PO Box 2226 Champaign, IL 61825*

QTY

The Fasting Cure *by Sinclair Upton*   ISBN: *1-59462-222-1*   **$13.95**
In the Cosmopolitan Magazine for May, 1910, and in the Contemporary Review (London) for April, 1910, I published an article dealing with my experiences in fasting. I have written a great many magazine articles, but never one which attracted so much attention... New Age/Self Help/Health Pages 164

Hebrew Astrology *by Sepharial*   ISBN: *1-59462-308-2*   **$13.45**
In these days of advanced thinking it is a matter of common observation that we have left many of the old landmarks behind and that we are now pressing forward to greater heights and to a wider horizon than that which represented the mind-content of our progenitors... Astrology Pages 144

Thought Vibration or The Law of Attraction in the Thought World   ISBN: *1-59462-127-6*   **$12.95**
by William Walker Atkinson   *Psychology/Religion Pages 144*

Optimism *by Helen Keller*   ISBN: *1-59462-108-X*   **$15.95**
Helen Keller was blind, deaf, and mute since 19 months old, yet famously learned how to overcome these handicaps, communicate with the world, and spread her lectures promoting optimism. An inspiring read for everyone... Biographies/Inspirational Pages 84

Sara Crewe *by Frances Burnett*   ISBN: *1-59462-360-0*   **$9.45**
In the first place, Miss Minchin lived in London. Her home was a large, dull, tall one, in a large, dull square, where all the houses were alike, and all the sparrows were alike, and where all the door-knockers made the same heavy sound... Childrens/Classic Pages 88

The Autobiography of Benjamin Franklin *by Benjamin Franklin*   ISBN: *1-59462-135-7*   **$24.95**
The Autobiography of Benjamin Franklin has probably been more extensively read than any other American historical work, and no other book of its kind has had such ups and downs of fortune. Franklin lived for many years in England, where he was agent... Biographies/History Pages 332

Name	
Email	
Telephone	
Address	
City, State ZIP	

☐ **Credit Card**   ☐ **Check / Money Order**

Credit Card Number	
Expiration Date	
Signature	

Please Mail to: Book Jungle
                              PO Box 2226
                              Champaign, IL 61825
or Fax to: 630-214-0564

ORDERING INFORMATION

web: *www.bookjungle.com*
email: *sales@bookjungle.com*
fax: *630-214-0564*
mail: *Book Jungle PO Box 2226 Champaign, IL 61825*
or PayPal *to sales@bookjungle.com*

Please contact us for bulk discounts

DIRECT-ORDER TERMS

**20% Discount if You Order
Two or More Books**
Free Domestic Shipping!
Accepted: Master Card, Visa,
Discover, American Express